DOCTOR WHO

DYING IN THE SUN

JON DE BURGH MILLER

BBC

Published by BBC Worldwide Ltd,
Woodlands, 80 Wood Lane
London W12 0TT

First published 2001

ISBN 0 563 53840 6

Typeset in Garamond by Keystroke,
Jacaranda Lodge, Wolverhampton
Printed and bound in Great Britain by Mackays of Chatham
Cover printed by Belmont Press Ltd, Northampton

Trailer

It was the City of Angels, and the angels were screaming. Rain, lightning, thunder and wind swept through the valley with such power and such ferocity that those caught in the storm felt as if nature itself was in pain.

On a night like this the streets were deserted. Due to the poor drainage in the valley this sort of weather caused roads to become rivers and cheap houses to flood. These storms didn't hit that often, but when they did… 'We do things big in LA,' someone once said, and even the weather had a tendency to adopt that attitude. During storms like this, you stayed inside and prayed. But tonight, the storm was the last thing on eighteen-year-old Hannah Wyatt's mind. Tonight, someone else could do the praying.

As she ran blindly through the storm the rain blended in with the tears on Hannah's cheeks. She splashed through the puddles sending water cascading upwards and slid all over the street, several times almost tripping in the deep rivers that were spreading across the roads. But she didn't care about the rain. Her clothes and shoes were ruined, but she didn't care about them either. She just had to get away.

At last Hannah got to the end of the street and saw a bench overshadowed by a store canopy. She glanced at the road, at the pools of rain spilling over the kerbs, getting deeper and deeper by the second, and realised that she would be too wet to keep running if she didn't find some shelter. She'd stay here until the morning, until the rain cleared. As long as she was far away from Raymond, she'd be OK.

Sitting down on the soaked bench, she tried to ignore the damp sensation that quickly began to settle into her clothes. She reached into her coat pocket and took out the photo of her and Raymond. Staring at the grinning faces, she realised that it was two months since the picture had been taken. So much had changed since then.

She angrily tore the already soggy photo in two and threw the pieces to the ground. Letting out a long, resigned breath, she put her head in her hands. This was the first time she had been able to sit down since she'd run from Raymond. The first time she had been able to stop and think about what had happened to her. The enormity of her pain hit her like a punch in the stomach.

Five minutes of crying later, Hannah noticed the man in black.

'Pretty wet tonight, huh?' he said, smiling from beneath his panama.

Hannah glanced up at the stranger, making no attempt to hide her curiosity. He was a tall and slender man who held an umbrella steadfastly upwards as if in a gesture of defiance to the tempest above. Most of the details of his features were hidden in the shadows, but she noticed that he had smooth, young-looking skin marked by a small scar across his left cheek.

As if sensing her interest, the man walked over and sat down next to her on the bench. He looked up at the rampaging sky and smiled, revealing a row of sparkling white teeth with a single gold one at the front. The rest of the world was disturbed, but this stranger looked at peace. His features were clearer now, and he smiled at her in a way that she found reassuring. His eyes glowed with compassion and Hannah felt as if he could help ease her pain.

'Don't be afraid,' the man said, 'It will be OK.'

And she believed him.

After a few moments of silence, he spoke again. 'Do you want to talk about it?'

Hannah shook her head. No one wanted to talk about things like this. But she found she talked anyway. Over the next thirty minutes she let it all out to the stranger. She told him how she had met Raymond one night when she was working as a receptionist at the Grand Vine Hotel. How they had got on as if they had known each other for years, and how she had learned that he was not the humble salesman she thought he was, but was actually a movie producer sounding out the hotel for use in his next picture. Hannah told the stranger how Raymond had promised to make her famous, how he had told her that he believed she had everything he was looking for in a lead actress. He had told her everything she wanted to hear, and she had fallen for every word. She had fallen for him, and she had given him everything he wanted from her in return.

For three months their affair had lasted, until this evening, the day before filming was due to begin on the picture. This afternoon, the men from the studio had come in to prepare the hotel and all the production staff had been assigned their rooms. Wary that there was still no sign of a contract, Hannah had marched into Raymond's room demanding to know what was going on. She had found him in the arms of Linda Howard, Hollywood's latest hot property, straight from Broadway.

'Did I forget to mention?' Raymond had said. 'We've changed our minds about the casting. Linda has the role now.'

Hannah had thrown a fit at this news, of course, but Raymond had just laughed. 'Sorry baby, these things happen you know.'

'I'm sorry,' the stranger apologised, as Hannah's attention snapped back to the present. She still could not believe how much she had told this man. 'I'm sorry I can't do more than just listen.'

'He was going to make me famous, you know?' Hannah cried. 'He promised me! But he betrayed me.'

'Here,' the man said, handing her a blue handkerchief. 'Dry those tears.'

Hannah chuckled, surprised that she could find anything humorous at this moment. 'In this weather,' she mocked, 'what would be the point?'

The man smiled, again, and for a brief moment he had a look on his face that reminded Hannah of how her father used to look when he tucked her in at night, all those years ago.

'I'm so confused,' she confessed. 'I don't know what to do.'

The man paused, clearly trying to decide whether or not to say the words forming in his mouth.

'Do you trust me?' he asked her.

A peculiar request from a stranger, but one that Hannah found scarily easy to answer. 'A little,' she replied. 'I mean, yes, I suppose so.'

'Then let me show you something.'

He reached inside his coat and produced a small hip flask. He unscrewed the cap from the top of the flask and turned it upside down to use it as a cup. He turned away and Hannah heard the sound of the liquid trickling into the cup. He turned back to Hannah and placed the cup in her hands. She was surprised to find it was warm. Not hot, just pleasantly warm. Hannah brought the cup closer, thinking it must be soup or coffee or some other comfort drink, then gasped when she saw its contents. It was filled with a bright, golden liquid that sparkled like nothing Hannah had ever seen before. The glow from the drink illuminated her arms and chest. Sparkling orange dust swirled in the steam that rose from the liquid. It was the most beautiful thing she had ever seen.

'What is it?' she asked.

The man raised his hand in a gesture that told Hannah to drink from the cup.

'What is it?' she asked again, but she didn't need an answer. This was hope. Whatever was contained in this cup, the man was offering her something magical, something appealing. Something a million times better than Raymond's shitty film deal.

Hannah raised the cup to her lips, never for a moment questioning the wisdom of taking a drink from a complete stranger.

The warm liquid didn't taste of anything, but as she drank it a pleasant heat spread inside her and she felt a tingling sensation, like tiny sparks of static electricity, dancing down her throat. The moment she swallowed the liquid she became stronger, more confident, and the thought of Raymond and his whore grew further and further from her mind.

She turned to look at the stranger, marvelling at the effect his gift had had on her.

'Oh my… it's amazing! It's wonderful!'

'It likes you,' the man said. 'I can tell. You've acquired a taste for each other very quickly indeed.'

Hannah didn't quite understand what he was saying, so was content just to sit and listen to his words.

'You see Hannah, you don't need to sleep with producers, or take your clothes off for magazines, to be famous. All you need is glamour, poise and perfection. You have all that, you just don't know it. I can help you find those things inside yourself, you know.'

Hannah felt tears welling in her eyes once more, except this time they were tears of joy. 'I know, I know,' she told the man. 'Help me. Show me how.'

'Just drink the rest of that,' he said, pointing to the cup. 'Absorb it into yourself. Accept it, and agree to follow how it makes you feel, what it makes you want to do. Very soon, with very little effort, you'll be loved and wanted the world over. You'll be famous.'

Hannah finished the drink, wiped her mouth, then handed the cup back to the stranger.

'Very soon,' he promised, 'you'll be a star.'

First Reel

Chapter One

The colour red dominated the décor of the Sunrise Villa bar. Red velvet covered its seats, red silk curtains shielded its clientele from the outside world and deep-red European wine flowed freely in the glasses on many of the bar's tables. Given the colour scheme, Robert Chate felt it was a definite irony that this place was used as a meeting point for those groups most concerned with the growing problem of the Red Menace in the city of Los Angeles. The Sunrise Villa was a safe house for American values, for people who knew whom they could trust and for the security and prosperity that were the right of every American, but which the subversives sought so hard to remove.

Chate was here for other reasons tonight though, but the old man pestering him to make a contribution to the ADA just couldn't seem to get this through his booze-addled head.

'Come on, kid' the man ranted, 'you probably have a young family, yeah? Wife and baby maybe? Think about them. Surely for their sake you want to see the pinkos out as much as anyone?'

'I have no wife,' Chate snapped. 'No children. No family. I'm twenty-nine and all alone, but doing absolutely fine, thank you for asking. Now if you'll leave me in peace I just want some time to myself and a quiet drink. Good day to you, sir.'

The man shook his head, realising that Chate was a lost cause. 'You wanna watch that attitude of yours, kid. It's people like you the Reds go for. People who won't see the nightmare that's coming before it's too late. This city will go up in smoke soon, and you won't have done jack to help.' With these words of condemnation, he sidled off to harass a bourbon-sipping couple in a corner.

Chate darted into the bathroom, then splashed some water on to his face and into his dark-blond hair. He glanced in the mirror to see if he looked as tired as he felt and saw the well-padded form of Martin Revere, one of LA's most successful racketeers, standing behind him.

'I saw you annoying the locals again, Robert.'

'You're late,' was all Chate could think of to say.

'And you were getting worried,' Revere said, before leading Chate back into the bar area. 'How thoughtful.'

He took a sip from a glass of vodka and lit a cigarette. 'Where is it then?'

Chate took a quick look around to make sure no one was looking, then reached into his jacket and took out a weighty Manila envelope. Revere snatched it from Chate's hands, tore off the top and peered cautiously at its contents. 'Nine hundred, yeah?'

'Course.'

'I want you to take some stuff round to Sarah Freeman tomorrow – she's put in for a big load and she's keeping low. Rumour has it she split on some movie and broke her contract without making repayments. She don't get out much, and don't want attention, so if you're lucky you'll be able to shift me a grand for next time.' Chate could tell from the sneer in Revere's voice that he clearly wasn't happy with the return his peddler had been providing recently.

'You know you've gotta shift more, Robert,' he went on, as if reading Chate's mind. 'I'll give you as much as you can take, but if you don't go out and shift it, I don't get my money, savvy?'

'I don't know,' sighed Chate. 'I try but...' This was it, the moment he had been waiting for. 'Listen Martin, there's something I want to tell you.'

'Yeah?' Revere said, examining his vodka glass for grease smudges.

'It's just that... I want out.' There. Said it.

Maybe Chate was expecting an angry response. Maybe he was expecting an upset response. He wasn't expecting Revere to burst out laughing.

'You want out? You, Robert Chate, want out? What is this - a wind-up?'

'I'm serious -'

'I don't give a monkey's crap if you're serious, you're not going anywhere, pipe that?'

If it had been anyone else, Chate would have launched a hefty punch straight for the guy's jaw, but not with Revere. Out on the streets, out on his turf where he sold dope to businessmen, movie stars and gangsters, Chate had a reputation as a real no-nonsense guy. Eighteen months back a pimp named Barnet had tried to swindle him by siphoning off 10 per cent of a shipment, replacing that 10 per cent with garden soil, then returning it to Chate and demanding a refund because the stuff was impure. Barnet had been found face down in the gutter, choking on his own vomit after having his stomach beaten in with a baseball bat. He lived, but he never snitched Chate to the cops, or ever asked for a refund again. Chate enjoyed his notoriety. He enjoyed the feeling that people were always cautious with, and sometimes scared of, him. He was the cop's son turned bad, the jailbird who'd been paroled on a technicality. No one messed with his shit.

But at the end of the day none of this mattered because, as much as he was in control of 'his shit', it all belonged to Revere.

'You're such an ungrateful turd,' Revere muttered. 'After all I've done for you...'

'Yeah, Martin, I know the routine. I had nothing when I came out of the Big Q. You gave me a job, a car, clothes, an apartment... And I'm grateful, you know, but it's been two years now.'

'And?'

'And things are different. You know at first it was fun - the money, the danger, the biggest goddamn single-finger salute to Charlie a guy could give - but now...'

Chate reached into his pocket, pulled out a newspaper cutting and handed it to Revere. 'Natasha Silver, a young actress at United.'

Revere skimmed over the article, reading bits of it out loud. 'Found dead in her apartment, heroin abuse blamed.'

'H abuse my skinny ass,' Chate said. 'I sold her that stuff, there wasn't enough to kill a mouse. There was something screwy with that batch. I don't know what the hell your suppliers are doing but –'

'Hey!' snapped Revere. 'Shut the hell up. The junkies know the risks. If they don't take the stuff properly –'

'I don't care!' shouted Chate, before ducking sheepishly into his seat as he realised all eyes in the bar had turned on him. When everyone had lost interest and resumed their conversations Chate continued, only this time in a whisper.

'I don't care, you know. People are dying now. Dying because of me. I'll scare them, I'll take their sugar and I'll beat the crap out of them if they screw me, but I won't kill in cold blood. I just don't do that stuff. People who don't deserve it are dying, and I want out.'

Revere stared into space, not saying a word. After almost a minute of uncomfortable silence he scraped the legs of his stool away from the bar, stood up and motioned to the back room. Chate followed as he marched away, and soon they were in the darkened, private area of the bar where the more secretive dealings took place.

'Sit down,' Revere said, an order, not an offer. Chate did so, and prayed that he wasn't about to get his brains spread out all over the walls for the world to see.

'There's no way in hell you're getting out for free,' Revere said, bringing Chate's world down about his ears. Another long pause, followed by a single word that brought a ray of hope into the weary peddler's life. 'But.'

Another pause.

'But what?'

'But I might, just might, be persuaded to make a deal with you, if you were prepared to fully co-operate.'

Chate felt his stomach roll. He had seen Revere pull this kind of thing before, and it wasn't pretty. The man loved to play with people, and was probably trying to play Chate for everything he had before the two of them parted company.

'Go on,' Chate said.

'Wait here,' Revere said, before disappearing back into the front area of the bar. He returned less than a minute later clutching a copy of the *LA Times*. He retook his seat and slapped the paper on the table. Chate saw the date: 12 October 1947.

'You seen today's news?' Revere asked as he began to flick through the pages. Eventually he found what he was looking for, flipped the newspaper round so that Chate could read it, then pointed to the appropriate article.

The headline read COLEMAN TO STAGE COMEBACK? and was accompanied by a stock press photograph that Chate was very familiar with. It showed his idol, movie starlet Maria Coleman, at the December 1945 opening of *Cowgirls Abroad*, the picture that destroyed her career. Chate scanned the article – there was nothing he hadn't heard already, but it was still great news anyway. Maria had barely worked at all since that picture, but now, two years later, she had returned and had been re-signed to Star Light Pictures, the newest studio on the block. In less than three years Star Light had grown so big that some were claiming that by 1950 it would be as powerful as Warner Brothers. The public seemed to love Star Light movies, mainly due to shrewd marketing decisions such as picking up cheap, out-of-date but not forgotten stars for a new batch of pictures. Soon Maria's career would be back on track, and Chate couldn't wait to see the results.

'Looks like your bitch is coming back, eh?' chuckled Revere.

'Don't call her that,' Chate snapped. 'Her name's Maria.'

'Yeah, whatever. Now here's the juice. We all know how big a crush you have on her. Which is why I thought you'd be perfect for a little job I need you to do.'

Chate raised an eyebrow, and knew he wasn't going to like what Revere had to say.

'I understand your needs, you know. I can appreciate that you want out of our agreement, and I'm nothing if not a reasonable man.' Others might disagree, thought Chate.

'So here's the deal. Your bitch Maria is pretty well known for throwing some damn big parties, and she's less known for her damn big dope habit.'

'Yeah, so? She's a movie star, that's kinda what they do.'

'But not when they don't even have a damn career any more. And not throwing it around to that extent. She funded all that stuff through a friend of mine, and now he wants repayment.'

This sounded ominous. 'How much does she owe?' Chate asked.

'490 large. Plus interest... round it up to half a mill.'

Chate felt ill. He was pretty sure Maria didn't have that kind of money. Her fall from grace had been well publicised, and it was no secret that she was in financial trouble, though Chate had had no idea she was that badly off.

'And so,' Revere continued, 'all I want you to do is to get the mazuma from her. Simple. Do that for me, come back with the full half mill, and I'll release you from your side of the deal. Do this for me and you'll get your wish. You'll get your freedom.'

Bastard, thought Chate. Revere clearly had no intention of letting him out of their deal, and knew full well that he would never go along with a plan to ruin one of the few people he truly admired and respected in this town. If Chate ever asked for his freedom again, Revere would remind him that he had turned down the opportunity last time.

Chate sighed. 'I don't get it, Mart. This just doesn't feel right. I'm no bagman. Why can't your "friend" collect the money himself?'

'Maria's gone missing. Even Star Light have only been dealing with her through an independent mailbox and occasional phone calls. She's gone underground, or changed her name or something. Thing is, we just can't find her. You're probably her biggest fan, Rob –'

'Well, I wouldn't go that far –'

'Come on, you know more about her than anyone. Using you is the easiest, quickest and cheapest way of finding the bitch 'cause we know you'll find her fast. We reckon that if anyone can talk her round to coughing up what she owes my pal it's you.'

'She doesn't know me though. We've never met. I'm just a fan. And she can't afford it anyway, you've read the papers.'

Revere paused, and a look of mock disappointment crossed his face. 'Not everything you read in the papers is true, Robby. Besides, I knew you couldn't do it, but you can't say I didn't offer you the chance.' Revere took another long drag from his cigarette. 'Now, about other matters –'

'I'll do it.'

'I'm sorry?'

'I said I'll do it. I'll find Maria, I'll get your friend's money out of her.'

Revere shook his head, clearly puzzled yet impressed by Chate's bravado. Another pause, then he let out the long, heavy breath he had been holding. He shook his head, then held out his hand to Chate. 'Good. Does this mean we have a deal?'

Chate gripped Revere's hand and forced a smile. 'I think so.' The two men released their handshake and Revere stood up to leave. He looked away, then looked back, a broad smile sweeping across his weathered face.

'Oh yeah, Robby, one last thing I forgot to mention. If you can't get the money out of her...'

'Then I ain't going nowhere, yeah?'

'Not quite. If you don't get the money, you've got to rub her out.'

'What? You've got to be kidding? Didn't you hear anything I said?'

Revere put on a false face of hurt. 'Relax. I'm sure you'll get the money, but if not... well, it's her life or your freedom. I'll be in touch in a week, that should be enough time for you.' He reached for his cigarettes and lit one before marching out of the room. 'See you soon, Robby.'

Chate heard his low chuckle drift back through the closing door. With a sigh he headed for the bar.

After staying in the Sunrise Villa for another hour, Chate finally found the will to leave and head home. He hurried through the pouring rain until he got to the spot where his '46 Buick was parked. As he sat down inside and slammed the door shut, his head fell on to the steering wheel. He hadn't been this mixed up in a long time. He needed to be free more than anything, needed to get away from this life, but the only way to do so would be to destroy the life of a wonderful person. And that was just the kind of thing he was trying to escape from.

Chate heard the rain thundering down on the roof of the car and felt tears begin to drift down his cheeks. He reached over to the glove box, opened it and took out a crumpled photograph. The picture was of Maria at the height of her fame: a publicity shot from *A Piece of Sunset*. It had been sent to Chate by her fan club in response to the numerous letters he had written. The corner of the picture was covered in a little black scribble. Writing from a perfect hand.

'To Robert,' Chate read out loud, 'With love, Maria Coleman.'

Chapter Two

From the top floor of a restaurant on Hollywood Boulevard, a young woman named Polly stared through a window at the neon signs and car headlights on the street below as they flickered on. It would soon be night, when the city really came alive.

'Can I get you another drink?' asked the man Polly was having dinner with.

'Thank you, Leon,' she said, returning her attention to the meal.

Polly knew she should be getting back to see Ben soon. He'd returned to the hotel early, exhausted from a hectic morning of sightseeing. Polly had stayed on for a while, wanting to be a tourist for a few more hours. It was a decision she was glad she had made, as she had met Leon and subsequently been invited out for a meal. Leon was a producer for MGA Studios, one of the biggest studios in Hollywood. Polly found him intriguing, and terribly, terribly fascinating.

Every day Leon met some of the most famous people on the planet, yet barely seemed to care because he was so used to it. He seemed almost as intrigued by Polly as she was by him. Maybe he just found her British accent curious.

'You know, I have to admit I have reasons other than just being sociable for asking you to dinner,' Leon confessed.

'Oh? And what might they be?'

'I'm on the lookout for new talent at the moment, Polly. To be honest with you, my studio needs some new faces. Has anyone ever told you that you have star quality? 'Cause you do, and I think you'd make a wonderful actress.'

Polly couldn't quite believe what she was hearing. 'Me? An actress? Do you really think so?'

Leon nodded. 'Oh undoubtedly. I've been looking all over this town for someone like you. You could be a real star, you know.'

Polly felt herself blushing. 'That's very kind of you to say so, even though I'm sure you're just being polite.'

'Not at all,' Leon insisted. 'I'm serious. I've got a few starring roles coming up in really big movies. We're casting right now and I'd love you to audition with my studio. I really think you could go far, Polly.'

Polly had always wondered what it would feel like to be famous. The fans, the lights, the money… She had always secretly dreamt of something like that happening to her. And now Leon wanted her to audition for a movie? The prospect was ridiculous, but at the same time strangely compelling. It was only a bit of fun, after all, even if nothing came of it. It was something to do, at least.

'All right,' she announced. 'Count me in.'

Leon beamed. 'Wonderful. After the meal we'll head back to my place and we can conduct the audition later tonight.'

'Tonight?' Polly said. 'Isn't it a bit late now?'

Leon's warm hand touched Polly's leg and slowly began to stroke it.

'Almost all auditions in this town happen at night,' he whispered.

As his hand moved further up her leg Polly realised what was going on, shoved her chair back and stood up.

'What on Earth do you think you are doing?' she barked.

'I can give you everything in the world, Polly. All I ask is a little appreciation in return.'

'Why, you pig!' Polly exclaimed. 'You're certainly not going to get that sort of appreciation from me!'

Leon stood up suddenly, reached over the table and grabbed her arms. 'Careful how you talk to me, Polly. You need me if you're going to get anywhere.'

Polly slipped out of his grasp. 'I very much doubt that,' she said, fuming. 'Goodbye, Leon. Thank you for the meal.'

She wrapped her coat around her shoulders and marched out of the restaurant. She glanced back and saw Leon sitting down at the table again, smiling. He didn't even care. She wondered how many women he wined and dined and took advantage of. How many of them really did become movie stars?

'Isn't there anyone nice in this town?' she despaired to the maitre d' on her way out.

The maitre'd shrugged his shoulders and smiled. 'Welcome to Hollywood, lady. Welcome to Hollywood.'

Ben Jackson stared out of his hotel-room window and marvelled at the endless stream of traffic that filled the Los Angeles freeways at dusk. An infinitely long snake of cars trawled their way through the mountains, thousands of eager passengers desperate to get to somewhere different. Somewhere better. Despite only being in his mid-twenties, Ben's time as a merchant seaman meant he had already seen much of the world, but since he'd left that life behind to start travelling with the Doctor he'd found that everything he saw took on a new meaning. It was like he was looking at the whole world for the first time.

The rattle of keys in the door disturbed his concentration. The door opened and a scruffy little man marched in, placed a shopping bag on a table and smiled. 'Hello, Ben,' the Doctor said, reaching inside his tatty black jacket for a handkerchief which he then used to mop his brow. 'How was your day?'

Ben shook his head. 'Where have you been, Doctor? We haven't seen you for twenty-four hours. You could have phoned.'

'Ah, I'm sorry,' the Doctor apologised, as he began to unpack the shopping, spreading out various snack foods and bits of fruit into neatly arranged groups. 'I was somewhat delayed.'

'Did you meet your friend?'

The Doctor stopped his unpacking, looked up at Ben and was silent for a few moments. He walked over to the window Ben had been looking out of, stared at the view for a few seconds, then drew the curtains shut.

'Harold's dead,' the Doctor said softly. 'Murdered late yesterday evening.'

'Murdered? Doctor, I'm sorry.' Ben was unsure what to say. 'Were you close?'

The Doctor turned and looked him in the eye. 'Not really, I suppose. Old friends, but not close. It's so very sad though.'

Ben nodded. 'Yeah, of course. So who killed him?'

'The police don't know yet. They have some leads, but they still need to speak to a few witnesses.'

'So is that where you've been then? Helping the cops?'

The Doctor shook his head and began to pace up and down the room. 'I've been gathering my thoughts, so I haven't had time to go to the police yet.' He looked at his wrist, even though he wasn't wearing a watch. 'I think it's about time I did, though. What are your plans?'

'Not sure,' said Ben. 'I spent today sightseeing with Polly. She's gone for dinner with some bloke we met down by the Chinese Theater. I thought I'd just come back, put my feet up and bunk down here for a bit. I tell you, it's knackering work being a tourist.'

'Very wise, get some rest,' the Doctor said before turning to walk towards the door.

'You going now, Doctor? But you've only just got back!'

The Doctor nodded. 'I just wanted to bring you a bite to eat and to let you know that there was no need to report me as a missing person. I want to see the police now, as time is of the essence. The sooner this murder is solved the better.'

Ben tried to remember if he'd ever seen the Doctor sit still for five minutes.

'All right then,' he said, giving his friend a little wave. 'Have fun, and let's hope the police catch that murderer, eh?'

'They're the Los Angeles Police Department,' the Doctor said with a knowing smile.

Life is an unpredictable bastard, thought Detective William Fletcher as he stared at the corpse in front of him. One day multimillionaire movie producer Harold Reitman had been on the cover of the *LA Herald-Express* promoting his latest flick, the next he was lying face up on a table in the police morgue, nothing but a pale, comatose marshmallow.

'Now that's what I call a gut,' he smirked, prodding the body's stomach. The chilled white flesh rippled as he did so and a gush of not quite clotted blood spilled from the side of the man where the bullet had decided to make its exit.

The surgeon chuckled. 'Well, you must be the only thirty-five-year-old cop who doesn't have one. A couple more years and those doughnuts will catch up with you, I swear. Besides, you'd be a lard boy like him if you had the dough he had. You should see some of the stuff this guy ate. Some weird foreign rubbish, I'm tellin' you.'

'Anything else? Was he gowed-up?'

The surgeon shook his head. 'A day isn't really long enough for us to be sure, but preliminary tests aren't showing anything like that. Just food.'

'But nothing for the narco boys to get their greasy palms into? Well, that's something at least.'

Fletcher crouched down and stared at the exit wound. 'Can I see where the bullet went in?'

The surgeon lifted the body on to its side (which took a considerable effort from the little man) then pointed out the wound to Fletcher – as if a huge hole along the corpse's spine, black with clotted blood, wasn't obvious enough.

Fletcher poked his finger into the wound and noticed the patches of burnt flesh surrounding it. 'Point-blank, huh? Whoever knocked him off must have been able to get pretty close.'

'H'm... it's possible I suppose,' the surgeon conceded. 'I guess you never really know who your friends are.'

'Poor sucker,' Fletcher said, well aware that he was coming across as being apathetic about the whole case.

'Yeah well, that Reitman was a tough one. You know it wasn't the bullet that finally killed him?'

'What? His chest's half ripped apart, for Chrissakes!'

'I know, but he still managed to put up some kind of fight. It seems our killer had to push him into the swimming pool to finish him off. This man drowned, Detective.'

There was a knock at the door, and Fletcher turned to see the scarlet-cheeked floozy known as Lindsey McEllen. 'Sorry to interrupt, Fletch,' the secretary said in a long Southern drawl, 'but they need you down in interrogation. They've found that guy you were looking for – the booze hound seen hanging around the Reitman house. Well, actually, he found us. Just walked into the clubhouse, would you believe it. I guess he wants to confess or something. He seemed quite keen to talk to you.'

'The mood I'm in, darling, nobody wants to talk to me.' Fletcher sighed and looked at his watch. 'I'll be down in a minute, right after we've finished sorting out Harry's COD.'

Fletcher marched into the sparsely decorated area of the station that had been set aside as an interview room, and slammed the door shut. Inside he found a short man wearing a tatty shirt and garish checked pants, sitting back in the interviewer's chair with his feet on the desk. He clearly just had an unusual dress sense rather than being a drunken street bum, though the rounded mop of dark hair on his head would seem to indicate that he hadn't been near a barber's in a while.

The man smiled as he noticed Fletcher. 'Aah! Detective!' he said in a pronounced English accent. 'So good of you to see me!' He leapt up and held his hand out for Fletcher to shake.

'Actually,' Fletcher said with a heavy sigh, 'I thought it was you who was supposed to see me, not the other way round.'

'Well, Detective, I'm afraid I never was one for formalities. So have we established a cause of death yet?'

Fletcher was astounded by the stranger's audacity. When several witnesses mentioned a suspicious-looking man hanging around Reitman's estate, he had assumed that even if they found the guy he would be overly defensive about the situation. He hadn't seen this much enthusiasm in a suspect since the Dalia questionings.

'Quiet,' he barked, gesturing for the man to sit back down. He reached for an admin pad, ripped off a form, then handed it to the man along with an old pen he found in his breast pocket.

The stranger looked at the form as if he had never seen a piece of bureaucracy in his life, paused, then scribbled down his details in an almost illegible scrawl.

'There you go,' he said proudly, like a kid at a science fair.

Fletcher took the form, glanced over it then put it to one side.

'Right then, Doctor –'

'Just call me Doctor, nothing else. The Doctor, if you like.'

Fletcher was too tired to argue.

'Whatever. Now let's cut to the chase. Harold Reitman was murdered by someone close to him, and the only people we've found who appear to have seen something suspicious all put the finger on you as that something.'

'Oh yes, I'm sure they would have done. It wasn't me though, of course.'

OK, at least Fletcher knew he wasn't dealing with a confession case, although this made the question of the Doctor's motives for turning himself in far more intriguing.

'So spill, Doctor. Where were you last night if you weren't at Harold Reitman's?'

The Doctor shook his head. 'You don't understand, Detective. I *was* at Harold Reitman's. I was there for the whole thing.'

Fletcher sat down in the chair that faced the Doctor across the interview table and reached inside his jacket for his cigarettes. He pulled one out, lit it, then continued the questions. 'So what were you doing there?'

'I've known Harold for some years now,' the Doctor said, an undercurrent of sadness permeating his voice. 'We met when he visited England back in the twenties. I haven't been to America in some time, and found myself here unexpectedly. I decided to take the opportunity to get in touch with Harold, to see how he was doing. My friends Ben and Polly wanted to see California, so I brought them along. I didn't think things would turn out so tragically.'

'So you show up on the same night that Mr Reitman gets himself killed. Quite a coincidence.'

The Doctor stared out of a window, apparently lost in thought. 'Yes, indeed it is. I still can't believe it.'

Fletcher didn't know what to make of this guy. He just didn't get the message that the detective was trying to pin the murder on him. Innocent or guilty, by now any normal human being would have been worried that they might end up accused of the crime. But not this Doctor. He just didn't care.

'So did you see what happened? Can you tell me who *did* kill Reitman if it wasn't you?'

The man looked down, and Fletcher noticed for the first time a vulnerability in his confident exterior.

'No, Detective, I'm afraid not. I had arranged to be there for dinner at half past eight, but as I arrived earlier than planned I decided to take a look around the grounds of his estate. I heard shouting coming from inside the house, but assumed it was just a domestic argument between Reitman and his servants. As the house guest, I didn't feel it was my place to intrude. Five minutes later I went round to the back of the house, to the swimming pool, and there he was. Poor Harold, face down in the water, dead.'

'So you heard voices, but you didn't see anyone?'

The Doctor shook his head. 'When I tried the house there was no one there. Or at least they weren't answering the door. Someone must have alerted the police before I got there, as they arrived barely moments after I found the body.'

'And you just left, without waiting to talk to the cops?'

'I was busy,' the Doctor said with a hurt look on his face.

Fletcher decided to give him the benefit of the doubt about his tardiness to come forward.

'Do you think you could identify the voices you heard?'

'No, they were too muffled to make out. I think one was male, though that could have been Harold of course.'

Fletcher nodded. 'Of course.'

An uncomfortable silence followed, shattered by a vicious knocking at the door.

Fletcher sighed. 'Come in!'

It was Lindsey, again.

'Can I see you for a minute, Detective?' she drawled.

Fletcher got up and walked out of the interview room, closing the door behind him.

'Message from Captain Wallis. He's matched the roscoe from the Reitman place to a set of prints,' Lindsey told him, a smile plastered firmly across her face. 'I think the captain's having a bit of a hard time dealing with the news.'

'Why?' Fletcher asked. 'Who do they match to?'

Lindsey smiled. 'Only Robert Chate, would you believe.'

'Well well,' Fletcher said. 'Who'd have thought it, after all these years.'

He pointed to the interview room. 'Even if our guy in there isn't the killer, he might have seen something. Let me grill him for a few more minutes then tell the boys I'll be with them shortly.'

The secretary flashed him a toothy grin before marching down the corridor. Fletcher returned to the interview room, slamming the door behind him.

He sat down and stared at the Doctor, who was sitting patiently at the interview table.

He tried to read the strange man's face for signs of guilt, or signs of hiding something, or anything that would hint at information worth beating out of him, but the Doctor's face was expressionless – in many ways innocent.

'Tell me, Doctor,' Fletcher asked, 'you heard of a greaser named Robert Chate?'

The Doctor didn't even twitch. 'I don't think I've ever met him,' he said. 'Is he a friend of yours?'

Fletcher chuckled. 'Robert Chate's a friend of everyone in the LAPD, Doctor.'

'Oh? Do tell?'

Something in the Doctor's eyes told the dectective that giving out information would not do any harm, and might lead to the suspect revealing a little bit more about himself than he had done previously. Fletcher decided it was a risk worth taking.

'Chate's a deadbeat, a dropout. He did time for dope peddling a while back but was paroled early. We know he's involved in some pretty seedy dealings, but we've never been able to pin anything on him.'

'Until now?'

Fletcher was silent.

'You've clearly got some evidence against this Chate fellow in this case or you wouldn't be asking me if I know him. Alas, you seem to know much more about him than I do. I must say you seem rather pleased that his name has cropped up.'

Fletcher coughed and stubbed his cigarette out in an ashtray next to the Doctor's hands. The interview rooms were supposed to be soundproof. Surely there was no way the Doctor could have heard the conversation he'd had with Lindsey?

'Maybe, Doc, maybe. You know why Chate going down makes us all laugh, don't you? His father is Captain Charles Wallis, the high pillow round here. They don't speak, of course. Estranged or whatever. It's embarrassing for my boss, you know? The police captain with the jailbird son... sure makes us laugh.'

Fletcher scraped his chair away from the table and stood up. 'Now I've got to go and deal with some other business, so stay here until I get back...' He dropped the pleasant tone from his voice and put on his severe face. 'I haven't finished with you yet.'

'Oh indeed,' said the Doctor, 'but I was wondering if perhaps I might come with you? You are going to find this Chate chap, aren't you? I want to solve this murder as much as you do, and maybe if you share the information you have on the case, let me speak to this fellow... Well, they do say that two heads are better than one.'

Fletcher shook his head. 'If you want to speak to Chate, you can do so after the arrest.'

The Doctor's face fell. 'I'm not in town for very long and I do rather want to get this nasty business over with as quickly as possible. Please, Detective. Let me come along.'

Fletcher paused, trying to decide how much slack to give the Doctor, then realised that he ought to be as co-operative as possible. He didn't have anything to hold the man on, but he still wanted answers out of him. It went completely against orthodox procedure, but they did say the LAPD were only taught the rules so they could break them.

'Fine. Chate's a familiar face and if he's in town we'll find him in no time. I'll put out an alert to everyone in the area to look for him, let Wallis know what we're up to and if all goes to plan we'll head him off and bag him before sunrise. Be in the parking lot in ten minutes, Doctor. It's going to be one hell of a night.'

Chapter Three

The unobtrusive sound of a violin playing a romantic melody filled the air of the Silent Gold restaurant. Candlelight flickering off the walls illuminated the happy faces of couples having dinner and gave a warm glow to what was one of Beverly Hills' most up-and-coming eating establishments.

Robert Chate was bored before the waiter had even taken his order. As much as Revere had tried to train him into the world of high-class restaurants, he had never quite fitted in. The tuxedo was always too tight, and the bow tie was never quite straight. It was all a sham, really. Just like Revere himself. All Revere's wealth and all his influence came from other people. Stolen from other people. The man himself had done very little to earn it: instead he used proxies like Chate to gather his spoils.

Chate looked up to see Julie return from the rest room. She was a pro-skirt from Fourth, but the rumour going round was that she knew where to find Maria. She had refused to talk without payment, so Chate had decided to treat her to a meal (and a bottle of wine or two) to try to loosen her lips.

'There you go,' Julie said, handing a napkin to Chate. He looked down to see that she had scribbled an address on it in eyeliner. 'You'll find what you're looking for there.'

She gave him an expectant look. 'And my payment?'

Chate shook his head and sighed. He reached into his pocket and handed the woman a handful of bank notes.

Julie counted the money and smiled. 'That will do.' Chate wondered whether she'd be going straight to one of his rivals after the meal to spend her earnings.

Leaning back in his chair, he stared at the address on the

napkin and smiled. If this turned out to be a solid lead, then this might have been one of the most useful dinner dates of his life.

The Silent Gold was a classy place and almost everyone dressed up before visiting it, so when a group of heavy-coated men barged straight past the maitre d' without waiting to be seated it was obvious something was wrong.

'Over there,' Chate heard a fellow customer say to the men.

It took him a moment to realise what was going on, but by the time he had it was too late. He stood up as an athletically built man with closely cropped dark brown hair flashed a badge in front of his eyes.

'Stand still!' the man barked. They were undercover cops, and he was the person they were here to see.

'Glad to see our sources are as reliable as ever,' the cop said, a grin on his face. 'Robert Chate, I'm Detective Fletcher, LAPD. You're under arrest for the murder of Harold Reitman. Resist arrest and things won't be pretty.'

Murder? Chate wondered what the hell was going on. 'Did you say... murder? What? I haven't killed anyone!

'What's going on?' Julie asked.

Just when things couldn't get any worse for Chate, one of the men at the back of the group stepped forward and lifted his hat, revealing a weary lined face.

'Hello, Robert. How are you?'

Chate stared into the eyes of the man he hated more than anyone else on the planet. The man who had left him to rot in jail, led him to believe he was an unwanted, unloved failure. Charles Wallis. The man who had adopted Chate after his real parents had died in a gas explosion. The man who had taken the young boy in like a lost dog, then tossed him aside after marrying a woman with no interest in his excess baggage. Wallis's wife's views had soon become her husband's, and it wasn't long before they both decided the responsibility of raising a child was too much to bear, forcing Chate to leave home and sever contact with them.

'Haven't you retired yet?' Chate growled.

Wallis smiled. 'You have been a bad boy, son. Killing poor Mr Reitman like that.'

'What?' Chate yelled. 'I didn't kill anyone!'

'You know Harold Reitman,' Wallis sneered, 'don't you, Robert?'

Harold Reitman. A hophead movie producer and a major client of Revere's. Chate had been involved in several dealings with the man, but they had never been close.

Chate had been near the Reitman household last night. He had got very, very drunk in Old Joe's then staggered through Beverly, searching for a cab to take him home. He recalled seeing lights on in the Reitman place, had peered through the fence to see if he could spot anyone famous, but was sure that was all. After that... Oh shit. He realised that he couldn't remember a damn thing about the rest of the night. Surely he couldn't have killed someone? Even when that drunk he'd never go that far. But the police must have found something that pointed to him. What evidence could they have?

Stupid and suicidal as it was, Chate's emotions got the better of him and he ran. Seeing that the entrance was blocked by hostile parties, he dodged out of the way of the cops then ran towards the back of the restaurant.

'Get him!' Wallis yelled.

Chate rounded a corner and hurried through a door that led to the kitchen. A door on the other side of the room had the words FIRE EXIT emblazoned over its top in large red letters. In a corner of the kitchen a chef was busy preparing food, and when he saw Chate he began to gibber angrily in Spanish.

Ignoring the man, Chate tried the fire exit but the door just wouldn't open. It was a sign of the times when even fire exits had to be locked.

He moved to the door he had come through and listened. The footsteps of the police were getting nearer. He knew he had nowhere to run. He reached into his jacket and pulled out his gun. There was one last thing to try.

'Freeze!' he shouted, pointing the gun at the chef. The man raised his hands in the air and pleaded with Chate not to kill him. He began to tell Chate about his wife and kids, or some other heart-wrenching story.

Chate ran behind the chef and held the gun to his head. This guy could be his ticket out of here. Hopefully the police wouldn't be stupid enough to kill an innocent person.

After several seconds the cops burst through the door and pointed their guns in Chate's direction.

'Let me go or this guy's on the night rattler,' Chate shouted. He didn't mean a word of it, but prayed the bluff would be enough to fool the cops into not shooting him. He couldn't bear the thought of dying in agony on the restaurant floor. Part of him was too scared to move, but the rest of him knew he had to fight his fear. He had to find a way to survive.

'Let him *go*, Robert,' Wallis said, emerging from the shadows of the corridor outside the kitchen. 'He hasn't done anything, he's innocent.'

'I won't shoot him if you let *me* go,' Chate shouted. '*I* haven't done anything! I didn't kill anyone!'

Wallis smiled. 'Then put the gun away, kid. Let's deal with this calmly.'

Chate caught the scared-witless expression on the chef's face in a reflective surface, and realised that holding the poor guy at gunpoint whilst proclaiming he wasn't a killer probably wasn't the best way to convince the police of his innocence.

He was about to give up when a new voice started to speak.

'I believe you.'

Chate thought it was one of the cops until the man stepped forward from behind the other officers. Dressed in a dishevelled suit with a shirt that was about three sizes too big for him, was a small, dark-haired man.

'Who's this?' Chate yelled at the other cops.

'My name's the Doctor,' the man said in an English accent. 'Mr Chate, I promise I'm here to help.'

'Fletcher!' Wallis called. 'Get that deadbeat out of here!'

'Come on, Doctor,' said Fletcher, his gun still pointed at Chate. 'Leave this to us. Unless you want to be arrested too.'

'Listen to me, Mr Chate,' the Doctor continued, ignoring the internecine arguing. 'Robert... no one will harm you. They just want to ask you a few questions, that's all.'

The weariness on the man's face and the compassion in his eyes indicated that he was totally genuine.

A brief moment of silence followed, during which Chate could hear nothing except his rapidly beating heart and heavy breathing.

'Come with us,' the Doctor said finally. 'Everything will be all right, I'm sure. We know you didn't kill anyone, so you have nothing to fear. Let the man go, Robert. Let the man go.'

'I told you to get back!' Wallis shouted at the Doctor. He made a hand gesture towards one of his men, who stepped forward and pulled the Doctor away from the front of the group.

The cops' concentration had been momentarily broken by the Doctor and Chate decided to make the most of the opportunity. He threw the chef to the floor, away from the path of his gun, then fired two shots at the kitchen lights which smashed into a hundred pieces, plunging the room into darkness. Chate raced past the cops out into the main part of the restaurant, firing a few more shots behind him. A barrage of gunfire erupted as the police emerged from the darkened kitchen to pursue their prey, spraying bullets across the restaurant in a desperate bid to halt the suspect's escape.

Gunshots filled the air and Chate's world became a blur. He fired back in the direction of the police, feeling a burning pain rip into the back of his shoulder as he ran. He'd been hit, but he had to keep on moving. He looked round and saw bodies falling, heard people screaming. Police, customers and restaurant staff all panicking in the chaos. Yet still he ran, never looking back.

He ran round the restaurant until he got to the exit. Another cop was guarding the door, gun raised.

The cop seemed to be about to fire when he suddenly screamed and fell to the floor, clutching his eyes.

Chate turned round to see a bright, white light spilling from the body of someone who'd been wounded where there should have been blood. It wasn't one of the police, it was a customer. It was as if the sun itself flowed through the body, a dazzling, golden molten liquid that spilled out on to the restaurant floor, almost blinding in its brightness.

Chate didn't know what was going on, and he didn't want to stay around to find out. With difficulty, he managed to look away from the astounding spectacle and fled out of the restaurant, straight past the dazzled cop and out into the cold, rain-soaked night.

As he ran, trying desperately to ignore the pain in his shoulder, he glanced back at the restaurant and saw figures moving about inside, panicking as they tried to deal with the devastation and chaos. At that moment, Robert Chate knew his life had been changed for ever. He had to escape from this world of nightmares. He had to get away.

The next day, the LA Times *would report the news of the incident at the Silent Gold restaurant and would call it one of the biggest police blunders of 1947. Three members of the LAPD suffered gunshot wounds. One customer was killed in the carnage and several more were severely injured including, it later transpired, Caleb Rochefort, one of Hollywood's brightest up-and-coming stars, who had been enjoying an incognito meal with his latest bride. Those wounded in the shooting were rushed to Queen of Angels Hospital, where a barrage of journalists heard a statement from the district attorney on the night's events. He told them how a mad gunman had held up the restaurant, how the police had been called and had moved in, and how the man had gone on a shooting rampage before being shot himself by Detective William Fletcher. The shooter was dead, and the case was now closed. The incident was a great tragedy, however you looked at it, but thanks to the power of journalism those members of the LAPD who had been involved could sleep soundly knowing that the public would never know the truth about what had occurred.*

Chapter Four

Chate had been running for over fifteen minutes. Running through the floods, the wind, the traffic and the neon-lit streets. By 8.25 p.m. he had slowed his run to a walk, knowing that the cops couldn't be on his trail any more and that if he didn't slow down he'd soon collapse. His shoulder still hurt where he'd been shot, but the bullet had only grazed him so he'd been able to rip off a section of his undershirt and use it to bind the wound. He would have to seek medical attention soon, but he knew he'd be OK for a while and felt relief that he hadn't been more severely injured.

He thanked the God he didn't believe in that he'd been targeted during this kind of weather, as on a day when the roads were clear and visibility was good he wouldn't have stood a chance.

Chate wiped the rain from his eyes and began to get his bearings. He hadn't been concentrating too hard on where he was going, simply heading east and figuring that the closer he could get to downtown, the closer he could get to obscurity. Without a car he hadn't been getting anywhere fast. He needed a break. Needed time to catch his breath and decide where to go next.

Turning a corner, he found himself on the palm-tree-lined sidewalk outside the Pantages movie theatre.

He looked up at the powerful spotlights shining into the thick city air, and at the clean white pillars of the faux-Roman façade that covered the front of the theatre. Was he far enough away from the cops to hide out here? Could he risk it?

The rain continued to beat down, and Chate hoped that the weather would slow down the police searching for him. He smiled, then planted fifty cents on the ticket counter, startling a clerk who had been too engrossed in a pulp romance novel to notice the arrival of yet another rain-soaked customer.

'When's the next performance?' he asked, trying hard not to look over his shoulder as he spoke.

'Main feature starts in ten,' the girl said with a smile. 'It's *Magic Town*, the new James Stewart picture.'

Chate sighed. 'I've already seen that.'

The girl shrugged. 'Nothing I can do about that I'm afraid.'

'I know,' Chate said. 'Anyway, I don't really care what's on, I just need to get out of this rain, so I think I'll see it again anyway.'

The girl forced a grin, took his money, handed him his ticket and change, then wished him a nice day.

Chate sat down inside the auditorium as the movie began. He removed his jacket, easing the pressure on his shoulder, and for the first time since running from the restaurant was able to relax. The womb-like darkness that surrounded him was comforting and made him feel safe and secure. In here, no one could see him, no one cared about what he'd done. Everyone was here for one reason only, to escape to another world. As the film began he found it difficult to concentrate on what was going on, but it didn't matter. He loved going to the movies more than anything else, because in here, in the strange, erratic darkness of the movie theatre, nothing in the outside world mattered.

The only illumination was the flickering light reflecting off the screen, bouncing across faces and seats and popcorn sellers and the writhing, classical architecture that had been placed in the building to give it a feeling of history. It was in this state of near darkness that Chate was most content.

Images of dead bodies, small children and scarred policemen flashed through Chate's mind. A woman shouting in the film woke him from the dream, and he hoped he had not missed too much of the story.

He was using the film as a chance to relax, to catch his breath, to work out what to do next. Once it finished he would be thrown cruelly back into the real world. He knew the streets would be crawling with cops looking for him, and there was no point risking going back to his apartment. There was only one thing he could do. He would have to ask Revere for help.

The last thing he wanted to do was speak to his boss again before sorting out the Maria problem, but then this hadn't really been a day for getting what he wanted.

The whore in the restaurant had given him an address, but he was damned if he was going to give it to Revere and let him send his thugs over to ice Maria. No, he'd find her himself, but doing so was going to involve some pretty fast talking.

Frustration burned away in Chate's mind. Maybe he'd catch Revere in a good mood, maybe he could ask for more time to sort the situation out. Maybe Revere would kill him... Whatever happened, he knew his one great chance had been blown by someone framing him for a murder.

He couldn't help laughing at the tragedy of the situation. If he couldn't sort something out, he'd be condemned to a life as Revere's slave. Still, it was better than the gas chamber he might end up in if the cops pinned that murder on him, and you never know, maybe a lucky break could still present itself. Maybe a miracle could still happen.

The film soon ended and Chate crept out of the auditorium, half expecting a battalion of cops to be waiting for him, the ticket girl pointing a finger to say, 'He's the one'.

There was no one waiting. Maybe the cops had stopped the chase, maybe they had been delayed. At any rate, it looked like he wasn't dead quite yet.

He casually asked to use the theatre's telephone, made a call to Luis, Revere's message boy, and was told that a car would be on its way to pick him up in five minutes.

Chate waited just inside the lobby, hiding his face as best he could. At 11.19 p.m. one of Revere's trademark jet-black limos pulled up outside the theatre and Chate got in, taking care to avoid sitting too heavily on the upholstery in his still-damp clothes.

'It's only water,' Revere sneered from the seat next to him, smoking cigar burning away in one hand. 'I heard about what happened at the restaurant, Robby. They say you iced some producer. You didn't kill him, did you Robby?'

'No… No sir,' Chate stammered.

''Cause if I found out you did, killing on my patch, on my time… well, you know the rest.'

Chate nodded. 'It wasn't me, I swear. It's a frame job. Someone in the LAPD's idea, has to be. I don't know. I just need your help Martin. I know I wasn't supposed to see you yet but… things change, you know?'

Revere nodded, his face expressionless. 'I know,' he said.

Chate glanced out of the window. They were heading on to the highway. 'Aren't we going in the wrong direction for your place?'

'Relax, I don't think it's safe for you to stay around here tonight. We're going to my villa in Venice.' Revere pointed his thumb towards the limo driver. 'It's a little more private there, so we'll talk more once we arrive. For now, get some sleep. You look as if you need it.'

Chate agreed, muttered something about it having been a long day then closed his eyes, but he knew he wouldn't be getting any more sleep tonight.

It was almost 1.30 a.m. when they got to the villa, a modest affair facing right on to the beach, a nice distance away from all the shops and restaurants. Revere told the limo driver to return home and to expect a call from him tomorrow, asking to be picked up. They walked up to the house, past an old convertible that Chate assumed was part of Revere's half-baked attempt at being seen as an everyday Joe, even though chauffeur-driven limos were his preferred mode of transport most of the time.

Inside, the house had been painted a distasteful green while antique furniture appeared to have been randomly scattered around the living room. Chate guessed his boss didn't go a bundle on aesthetics.

Revere sat down in a large, comfortable-looking leather chair and beckoned for Chate to sit on the sofa next to it. A few moments of silence passed, during which Chate could feel the distant thunder of Revere's wrath getting closer.

'So,' Revere eventually said, 'first thing on the agenda. You got the jack from Maria yet?'

Chate paused, took a deep breath, then began his apology. 'I haven't found her. I've got a couple of leads, but with this murder business... I haven't been able to finish the job. Just give me a few more days. Please.'

'I'm sorry, Robby,' Revere said, shaking his head mournfully, 'I know I said I'd give you more time but... well, if you haven't even found her by now... Come on kid, you're screwed, you know that. I trust you when you tell me you didn't kill that guy, but the police won't and you can't afford to get caught. By tomorrow every cop in the county will be on the lookout for Robby Chate. You can't go anywhere, you can't see anyone, you can't do anything. I'm all you've got, Robby. Remember that.'

'I know,' said Chate, conceding reluctantly. He laughed at the futility of his situation. Not only would he have to forget his dreams of freedom, but he knew that Revere's goons would be out to find Maria and he was unable to do anything to stop them.

'So,' he said, trying to regain his composure, 'I guess we can forget the last few days and get back to business, huh?'

Revere's face was stony, unreadable. He stood up, walked over to an old drinks cabinet and poured himself a whisky. 'This is very hard for me, Robby,' he said solemnly.

'Hard for you? Why is it hard for you? I'm the one the hat squad's chasing all over –'

'Close your head,' Revere snapped. 'Let me finish.'

Chate was silent.

'I'm all you've got, which is why this is going to be very clean.'

'Clean? What do you mean, "clean"?'

Revere reached into a drawer on the side of the drinks cabinet. 'You're a liability, Robby. You're not the man you used to be. You want out, we'll let you out. Permanently.'

Revere pulled his hand out of the drawer, revealing it to be holding a .45.

Chate's recurring nightmare flashed through his mind. Seeing himself dying young, dying in agony. Dying before his time, before he had been able to accomplish anything in his life. There was no way he was going to let Revere make his fear a reality.

He ducked down behind a table as Revere fired a silencer-muffled bullet from the gun. He slammed his body into a wheeled-chair that went spiralling backwards, forcing the gangster to jump out of the way. Then he reached down, picked up a glass decanter and threw it at Revere. He heard a crash as the decanter skimmed the side of the man's head and collided with a wall. Revere hadn't been injured, but Chate had bought a valuable couple of seconds. He ran over and kicked Revere hard between the legs then grabbed his gun arm, forcing it away.

'Drop the gun!' he barked. Revere did so, and Chate caught it in his right hand. The gangster lunged towards Chate, throwing his weight into the lighter man, knocking him to the ground. He tried to prise the gun from Chate's fingers, then another shot was fired.

Revere collapsed on top of Chate, motionless.

Chate threw the body off and stared at the hole in Revere's neck and at the pool of blood and brains dribbling their way out of the remains of Revere's skull and spreading thinly across the walls and carpet.

He stood for several moments looking at the body, trying to take in what he had just done. Had he intended to kill Revere, or was he just defending himself in a kill or be killed situation? Killing another human being was against everything Chate believed in, and he didn't remember intentionally pulling the trigger. But in the heat of the moment maybe his subconscious had taken over?

He leapt away from the body, took off his jacket and trousers and ran into the hall to look for the bathroom. He soon found it and washed the blood off his hands, then found some antiseptic and a bandage and dealt properly with his shoulder wound.

This had been, without a doubt, the worst day of his life. He guessed he should feel glad that Revere was gone, but he didn't. The man was a bastard, an evil, evil bastard, but over the years he'd been the closest thing Chate had to family. But there would be time to grieve later. Revere's associates would come looking for him sooner or later, and this time the evidence for Chate being the murderer was much stronger than anything the LAPD had cooked up. He walked back into the living room, wiping his forehead with a towel.

Chate took another look at the body. If it wasn't for the huge hole in his head, Revere could have been sleeping. He looked almost peaceful. Perhaps he truly was.

Revere had tried to kill him, but why? If Chate was kept in a safe house, away from the cops, then he couldn't be - what was it Revere had called him? - a liability.

The sun wouldn't be up for a few hours yet, and Chate knew he had time to sort something out. It shouldn't be too difficult to make it look like a suicide. But first...

He carefully reached over the body and (being careful to keep his hands wrapped in the towel so as not to leave prints) searched the pockets of Revere's jacket and trousers for anything helpful. He soon found a scrap of headed notepaper from Boulevard Heights, an estate everyone knew was controlled by an up-and-coming racketeer named Cohen. A note was scrawled on the paper in extravagant handwriting. 'Ice Chate. See to it within 24 hrs, or we'll see to you.' The note was signed with an illegible signature. Chate shoved the note back into the pocket.

Revere's associates will soon put the blame on me for his death. The LAPD already think I killed that other guy. I can't go back home, can't go anywhere where I might be recognised. They won't rest until they have me in custody, or in the morgue. Everyone wants to see Robert Chate dead.

Chate stared at Revere's body and tried to resist his revulsion as an idea started to build in his head.

The room was a blood-soaked mess. It would be a while before anyone would be able to work out exactly what had gone on that night. After shoving the towel in the wound to block the blood flow, Chate wrapped Revere's body in a large refuse sack he found in the villa's kitchen, then dragged it out on to the driveway. He had found a bunch of keys in Revere's pocket, and was relieved that one of them fitted in the convertible's ignition slot. He opened the car's trunk and bundled the body into it – no easy task given Revere's weight and the pain in Chate's shoulder.

Chate went over the parts of the villa he'd touched and wiped them with a handkerchief, doing his best to remove any fingerprints he might have left, then walked out of the villa and locked the door with Revere's keys. He got into the car and pulled away, pleased that there seemed to be very little traffic on the roads at this time of night. As he made his way back to the city, he did his best not to break the speed limit despite the racing beat of his heart urging him to go faster. He had to appear calm, cool and collected. He knew he couldn't do anything that might attract attention.

At 4.35 a.m. Chate pulled the car into a side road off the street where his apartment – a simple but spacious affair on the top floor of a three-storey former hotel – was located.

From the corner of the street he could see that there were two cops standing on the porch in front of the building, and across the street from them another cop, obviously the backup, was dozing in his car. Chate guessed there would be at least one more, so he knew he'd have to make sure he didn't make too much noise.

He reached into the glove box of the car, took out the gangster's silenced .45 and checked it was loaded. He drove the car up to the front of the building to attract the cops' attention, stopped the engine, then got out and marched up to the front door so casually that he could have been delivering newspapers.

'Hey,' one of the cops shouted, 'stop right there.'

Chate smiled, raised his gun and brought it crashing down on the cop's skull. The other man shouted something as his partner collapsed, so Chate reached over and smashed the gun over his head too. Caught unawares, both cops lay groaning on the ground. Chate kicked them into unconsciousness before they could reach for their firearms, took their weapons, then ran back to the car.

He opened the trunk, threw the cops' guns inside, then pulled out the black bag that contained Revere's corpse and began to drag it across the street. He hoped the bag wouldn't split - the last thing he wanted was a blood trail - but luckily it remained intact. Only the best quality for Martin Revere. Chate glanced across the street to see if he'd attracted the backup cop's attention but the shape in the shadows was of someone asleep. No give-away cigarette light. Backups were usually assigned to fat bastards, so it was highly likely that at this time of the morning he'd be out cold. Chate was glad about the silencer on Revere's gun as without it the cop would almost certainly have been woken by the shots.

He wasn't surprised to find that the lock on the front door of the building had already been kicked open, and after dragging the body up three flights of stairs - something that felt like it took hours - he finally managed to get the stiff into his apartment. He pushed the body inside and closed the door behind him. He reached for his gun, expecting to find a cop waiting for him, but there was no one around. He laughed at the LAPD's overconfidence, and guessed that somebody would be severely reprimanded for this little oversight.

The first thing Chate noticed was that the place had been completely ransacked. Drawers were open, their contents spilled out across the floor, furniture was overturned, even the contents of his liquor cabinet appeared to have been drunk.

He knew he didn't have much time before the cops outside regained consciousness. He ran into his bedroom, pulled a small travel case down from above his wardrobe and stuffed it with a few essential items of clothing. He went to his coat cupboard and took out a trilby which he placed neatly on his head before returning to the hallway. He dragged Revere's body into the bathroom, ripped off the refuse bag surrounding it then threw the stiff into the bathtub, retching once more at its gruesome appearance. Resisting the urge to throw up, he took Revere's gun out of his jacket, placed it against the corpse and shot a bullet through its eyeballs. The bathroom wall needed a new coat of paint anyway.

Chate took one last look around, picked up his travel case and went into the kitchen where he turned the gas taps on the cooker to their highest settings. He hurried to the other end of the apartment, pulled a candle out of a cupboard and lit it with a cigarette lighter, knowing that it would take a while for the gas to reach the flame. He left the apartment, closed the door behind him then moved as fast as he could down the stairs and out into the street, pleased to see that the cops were only just starting to regain consciousness.

As he walked down the street Chate was almost thrown off his feet as the deafening noise of an explosion ripped through his eardrums. He could feel the heat from the blast and hear the crackling noise of his apartment burning behind him, but he didn't look back once. He smiled as he realised that his mad plan might have succeeded. The cops would report Chate breaking into his flat, a body would be found charred beyond recognition in the debris, and it would take a few days at least for them to realise that the corpse was anyone else apart from the intruder. Time in which to build a new life and get the hell away from here.

Chate walked to Revere's car then took the picture of Maria Coleman from inside his jacket pocket. He lifted his fingers up to his lips, kissed them, and placed them on the photograph. He then reached into the pocket again and took out the piece of paper on which the prostitute had scribbled the address. He knew he only had one possible ally in the world. Someone who had been the object of his desire for many years, someone who had never let him down.

Chapter Five

'Move out of the way, people,' screamed a white-coated orderly as he raced down the corridor of the hospital with the gurneys that carried those most severely wounded in the Silent Gold gunfight. 'Let these people through!' he shouted, as hospital visitors, wandering patients and uninvited press photographers jumped out of the way. Directly behind the orderly the Doctor, Ben and Polly followed, desperately trying to keep up with him.

Suddenly a dark shadow crossed their paths as a large security guard stepped out to block their way. 'Excuse me, sir,' he said, pointing at the Doctor, 'no members of the public are allowed here. If you'll kindly move to the waiting room, someone will be with you shortly.'

'But you don't understand,' the Doctor pleaded, pointing down the corridor at the disappearing gurneys. 'I'm related to one of the injured.'

The security guard was having none of it. 'As I said, go to the waiting room and someone will come to talk to you soon. They'll let you know what's happening.'

The Doctor looked as if he was about to argue, but obviously realised this was a lost cause, so instead he turned round and walked away, his face like a sulky toddler's. 'Come on Polly, Ben,' he said. 'We'll have to do as the man says.'

Ben didn't care what they did. He had been about to get some sleep when the Doctor had sent an urgent message to the hotel insisting that he and Polly get to the hospital as quickly as they could. At first Ben thought the Doctor had been injured, but now realised that he just wanted them around to show off the exciting night he had been through. Ben's night had been peaceful, Polly's had been relaxing. The Doctor had got himself mixed up in a multiple shooting. Typical. It was almost 2 a.m. and Ben just wanted to go to bed.

'How long do we have to stay here, Doctor,' he complained as they made their way into the waiting room and found some seats. 'I'm knackered! Can't we just deal with all this in the morning?'

The Doctor seemed to contemplate this for a couple of seconds, then shook his head. 'No... no, I don't think so. I'm finding all this rather fascinating, and I don't think the events of tonight have played out fully yet. You can go back if you like, but I think you'll be glad if you stay.'

Their attention was distracted as a tall man in a heavy black trench coat marched into the room. He took his hat off, revealing a balding head with deep-set features and a small but very visible knife scar along his left cheek.

'Which of you guys is the Doctor?' the man asked in a voice that had only a light American accent.

The Doctor seemed to snap out of a daydream, leapt to his feet then reached his arm out to shake the stranger's hand. 'Why, that would be me,' he said, rather pleased with himself. 'It's a pleasure to meet you. And you are...'

The man shook the Doctor's hand tightly, smiled, released his grip then cleared his throat before speaking. 'My name's Leonard De Sande. I take it you don't follow the motion picture industry, Doctor?'

'I've been out of touch for a while,' the Doctor admitted. 'I tend to stick to books for entertainment, I'm afraid. Far more me.'

De Sande nodded, understanding but not sympathising. 'Then it's not surprising you don't know my work.'

'You some bigwig film star?' asked Ben.

'You know these guys, Doctor?' De Sande asked.

The Doctor nodded and De Sande turned to Ben, chuckling. 'My British friend, I'm a director currently working for Star Light Pictures. You must have seen my past work. *The Cold Blooded*? *The Sword of Damocles*?'

'I've seen *The Sword of Damocles*,' said Polly. 'It's an old film about a woman who leaves her cheating husband and gets together with a millionaire. My mother loves that film.'

'I'm sure,' said De Sande. 'Everyone does. Sounds like she's got good taste, your mom.'

'Mr De Sande,' said the Doctor, 'may I ask how we can help you? You did, I assume, come here for reasons other than the pleasure of our company.'

'Of course,' nodded De Sande. 'I just wanted to thank you for what you did at the restaurant. I heard a reporter talking to the chef there and he claimed you saved his life, made the hatchet man run, stopped him killing more people.'

The Doctor shook his head. 'Well, it didn't happen quite like that, I'm afraid.'

'Well, according to the chef you were quite the hero. I can see the modesty in your eyes. If you hadn't intervened, even more people would have been killed by that maniac. Apparently you seemed to be quite persuasive with the guy. I was wondering, did you know him before tonight? Have you any idea what his motive was for what he did?'

The Doctor shook his head. 'I've never met him before in my life.'

De Sande shrugged his shoulders. 'Oh well. I thought maybe you could shed light on the matter. One of my people was injured and if he was an intentional target then it's in the interests of my security that I know all I can.'

'I'm sorry I can't help you more,' the Doctor apologised. 'Besides, it was the police who did most of the killing.' His voice was deadly serious. 'Even if they were only trying to stop the suspect.'

De Sande's expression was one of mock shock. 'You don't want to go saying things like that around here, Doctor. Believe me. Not if you value your freedom.'

'I tried to stop them,' the Doctor said, his eyes reddening slightly, 'but the sound of the guns firing was too loud. They couldn't hear me.'

'Well, thank you for whatever you did, Doctor. Caleb is very important to me, and I can't imagine how we'd cope if we lost him.'

'Caleb?'

De Sande looked puzzled. 'Caleb Rochefort, of course. Didn't you see? He was one of those wounded!'

'His name rings a bell...' Ben said.

De Sande seemed stunned by their words. 'Rings a bell? Caleb Rochefort is one of the most famous and acclaimed young actors in Hollywood!'

'Oh, right,' said the Doctor. 'I wasn't aware of that. How is the poor chap?'

'He's doing pretty well,' De Sande said. 'The bullet that hit him didn't do too much damage, so hopefully he'll be fine with a few days' rest. Word on the street is that if you hadn't convinced the shooter to run he'd have killed every last man in the place. Caleb would be dead by now. He's worth millions to me - he's the star of my new picture and he's contracted for a couple of years down the track. I need him alive for a while yet. You know, I really can't believe you haven't heard of him.'

The Doctor looked uncomfortable. 'Well as I said, I haven't been in town recently and I don't go to the cinema.'

De Sande looked bemused and more than a little suspicious. 'Don't? You mean you *never* see any movies?'

The Doctor shook his head. 'I haven't found much to attract my attention in recent times, really. They do say that the cinema's not what it used to be.'

De Sande looked away, a disbelieving smile on his face. Then he looked back at the Doctor and his eyes betrayed an idea taking shape. He put a finger up to his lips, deep in thought.

'I wonder...' he said. 'Do you know, Doctor, you could be just the sort of person I'm looking for.'

'Oh?'

'It's not long until my new picture is released, and I need to be sure it will... appeal... to all audiences. Everyone in this town loves the movies, so I fear many of my test... invitees, will be biased in my favour. But you... if a sceptic like you enjoys my film, then I'll know I've succeeded.

'I'd hate for you to be disappointed,' the Doctor said, 'but I fear I'm rather difficult to impress.'

De Sande paused for a while. 'I shouldn't be doing this, but I never could resist a challenge.' He reached into the pocket of his coat and took out an envelope which he handed to the Doctor.

'There, take it. It's an invitation to a private party at my place tomorrow night. I'll be screening the picture there. I'm not a betting man, Doctor, but if I were I'd wager half my Star Light shares that you'll change your tune.'

'It's very nice of you to invite me,' the Doctor said, 'but I don't know if I want to attend alone. Would it be OK to bring Ben and Polly along too?'

De Sande paused, unsure of himself, then sighed and smiled. 'Sure. Why not?'

'Thank you,' the Doctor said. 'Most kind.'

De Sande took a small notepad and pencil from his breast pocket and looked expectantly at Ben and Polly. 'May I have your names, so I can put you on the list?'

They told him and he scribbled their names down. 'The Doctor's invitation has all the details on it,' he explained. 'Now if you'll excuse me, I have to be getting off. Hopefully I'll see you tomorrow.'

He doffed his hat, then turned and slowly walked away down the echoing hospital corridor.

After Chate had escaped from the Silent Gold, Detective Fletcher had dispatched several units to pursue him, but the events at the restaurant had left the force in disarray and none had been successful. Fletcher had stayed to speak to witnesses at the Silent Gold and the woman Chate had been having dinner with gave him the address of a bar Chate was supposedly heading to. Fletcher had gone to the bar and searched it but there was no sign of the suspect there. So he had given up the search and decided to come to the hospital.

'I'm sorry, Detective,' said a young nurse, pointing disgustedly to Fletcher's cigarette, 'there's no smoking allowed in this part of the hospital.'

Fletcher shrugged his shoulders, got up from the conference-room seat he'd been slumped in for the last twenty minutes, then threw his cigarette to the ground and trampled it under his shoe. He'd been waiting long enough. Ostensibly, he had come here to note the details of the wounded, for taking witness statements once they recovered. He had an ulterior motive for visiting the hospital, however. He wanted to keep tabs on the Doctor. There was something not quite right about the guy's manner, something that was out of place - disturbing - though Fletcher couldn't put his finger on exactly what it was. All he knew was his instinct was screaming at him that he shouldn't be too hasty in exonerating the Doctor of the Reitman killing - and he couldn't stop himself from listening to his instincts, even if they occasionally proved to be wrong. Twice in the last year he had been pulled up for arresting a 'dead cert' who had been easily cleared, and he was damned if that was going to happen again. He had something to prove, and if the Doctor turned out to be guilty after all it would be quite a coup.

Fletcher's lack of promotion frustrated him. He wanted to be somebody, wanted to stand out from the other cops. Pinning a previously cleared suspect would certainly help him realise that goal. If there was the slightest chance the Doctor was hiding something, then he'd find out what it was and expose it.

He marched down the hospital corridor and walked into the emergency room waiting area. The first thing he saw was the Doctor chatting happily to a patient.

'Come here,' Fletcher ordered, grabbing the back of the Doctor's coat and pulling him up.

'Excuse me!' shouted the Doctor. 'There's no need for that kind of attitude.' He wriggled away from Fletcher's grasp and straightened out his jacket. Fletcher didn't think there was much point in doing this, considering that the jacket had been completely crumpled before he'd even touched the Doctor, but it seemed to make the little man a bit happier.

'In there,' Fletcher said, pointing to an examination room. He flashed his LAPD badge at a nurse who was busy preparing injections in the room and the man left hurriedly, asking him not to be too long. Fletcher ushered the Doctor into the room and closed the door behind him.

'What is this about?' the Doctor asked, clearly annoyed. 'Haven't you caused enough trouble for one night, Detective?'

Fletcher chose to ignore the barbed comment.

'I'll get straight to the point. Despite the events of tonight, and however you've managed to fudge away the evidence, I still think you murdered Reitman, or at least were more involved than you're letting on, and I'm going to make sure I prove it.'

'I can assure you, Detective, I most certainly did *not* kill Harold. A suspect was apprehended and subsequently went on the run, yet you still think I had something to do with it? Why is that, Detective? Why won't you leave me alone to be the simple tourist that I am?'

Fletcher shrugged. 'To be honest, I'm not sure. Los Angeles may be famous for harbouring its fair share of... how can I put it... "different" people, but I've never met anyone like you. To put it bluntly, I don't know if you're stupid or intelligent, but either way you creep me out. I reckon you're hiding something and I'm gunning for you. Ask Bobby Ardiles, ask Sam Rook. I sent both of them down with barely a shred of evidence. Both confessed, eventually, and you will too.'

The Doctor sighed. 'Is that a threat, Detective? How very tiresome.'

'It's whatever you want it to be, Doctor. I'll find out the truth behind the murder, so you'd better watch your back. I certainly will be.'

Fletcher decided that leaving the Doctor to stew on that thought would be more productive than an immediate attempt to beat a confession out of him, so he walked out of the room and left the hospital as quickly as he could. He needed to get home, to sleep. If the next day of the investigation was anywhere near as eventful as this one had been he'd need all the rest he could get.

'Wakey wakey,' said a familiar voice, snapping Ben out of his dozing.

'What time is it?' he asked the Doctor, staring around the waiting room to get his bearings.

'Almost four o'clock. I think we all need to get back to the hotel and get some proper sleep. Polly's just ordered a taxi. It should be here in a few minutes.'

'Well, that was a bloody waste of time,' Ben complained, letting out a large yawn.

'I can't help it if you don't take an interest,' the Doctor said defensively. 'I just thought you'd see a side of this city the guide-books never tell you about.'

Ben shrugged. 'Yeah, I suppose. And we did get those party tickets.'

They marched across the waiting room and met a smiling Polly, who looked very chirpy considering how long they'd all been awake.

'The taxi should be here in about ten minutes,' she told them. 'Everything OK, Doctor?'

The Doctor smiled. 'Yes. All the patients are stable, and I've had a very interesting conversation with one of my friends from the police force.'

Ben walked ahead of the others, looking forward to getting into the fresh air again. He turned round to see that there was no sign of the Doctor. 'Oh, what is it now?' he sighed. 'Where is he?'

Polly smiled, clearly sympathetic to his exasperation. 'He said he'll meet us outside. I think he's forgotten something.'

'Bloody typical,' Ben exclaimed. 'Wait here Pol, I'm going to fetch him. You know what he's like, we'll probably never find him again if he gets distracted.'

He retraced his steps back along the corridor and soon found the Doctor crouching behind a pillar. He was spying on a man who Ben recognised from their conversation earlier that night as being Mr De Sande. De Sande seemed to be having a heated conversation with a silver-haired man in a heavy trench coat who had a definite air of officialdom about him.

'There you are!' Ben said, tapping his friend on the shoulder.

'Shhhh!' chastised the Doctor, waving at Ben to get into the hiding position he himself was in. He turned to Ben and began to whisper. 'I'm trying to listen. That man there is a rather high-ranking policeman. He seems on very friendly terms with Mr De Sande, don't you think?'

Ben shrugged. 'Maybe they're old pals. You know... bigwig director like that, probably always dealing with the cops.'

'Maybe,' the Doctor said, but he didn't seem convinced. 'Look at what they're wearing. Do you see anything strange?'

Ben looked hard but couldn't spot anything out of the ordinary.

'Look at their lapels,' said the Doctor.

'Oh yeah,' said Ben, noticing that both men were wearing a small dark purple rose in their lapels. 'Maybe it's the fashion?'

'Or a signal,' the Doctor said with a slight smile, pleased at his powers of observation.

He suddenly flattened himself against the pillar, and pulled Ben back to do the same. The two men had finished their conversation and were walking away in different directions. De Sande passed the Doctor's hiding place, but didn't notice the eavesdroppers.

Once he was out of sight, the Doctor relaxed and moved out into the corridor.

'Yes, there's something going on here, I'm sure. Those roses must be a signal, but a signal for what?' He rolled his eyes skyward in thought and began tapping his chin. 'Do you know what, Ben, I think I'm going to enjoy that party tomorrow!'

Chapter Six

Bathed in ripples of moonlight reflected off the crashing ocean waves, Sunset Mansion stood like a lonely watchman looking out over Marina Del Ray. As the limousine carrying the Doctor, Ben and Polly drove along the narrow road leading to the house, the driver explained that the building dated from the turn of the century. Leonard De Sande had purchased it in order to thoroughly renovate the place and had turned it into a luxury mansion.

After sleeping in until late, the Doctor and his friends had spent a few hours seeing one or two tourist attractions before preparing for the party, and at seven o'clock the car had arrived at their hotel to pick them up.

As the limo drove through the heavy iron gates in front of the building and up the long gravel driveway, Ben noticed that the mansion was surrounded by beautifully landscaped gardens. They seemed out of place when juxtaposed against the almost sinister architecture of the house itself, which reminded him of something out of a Dracula film.

The limo driver stopped the car and the passengers got out to find themselves being welcomed by De Sande's butler. He escorted them through to an elaborately decorated entrance hall, where a large number of well-dressed people were exchanging gossip and small talk whilst drinking glasses of champagne and picking at bits of smoked salmon from plates being circulated by several waitresses.

'What do you reckon to this then, Doctor?' Ben said. 'Bit posh, isn't it?'

The Doctor smiled as a waitress handed him a glass of champagne. 'It is indeed,' he replied, passing the glass to Polly. 'I think Mr De Sande just wants to make sure we get the right impression of him. The hospitality here certainly seems very friendly.'

Ben looked around at the various other party guests, but saw no one he recognised or who looked remotely interesting.

'I do hope you're enjoying yourselves!' a voice boomed. It was De Sande.

'Yeah,' Ben said, turning to face the man. 'Amazing place you've got here. Surprised someone as flush as you wants to mix with the likes of us.'

De Sande looked hurt. 'I've had to work hard for my wealth, you know. I'm from a very poor background originally. My brother was even sent to prison because he had to steal to feed his family. No, I've seen hardship, and now that I've achieved success I don't think there's any harm in enjoying it, do you?'

Ben shrugged. 'I suppose not.'

De Sande turned to the Doctor, who was busy examining a shelled prawn as if he'd never seen one in his life. 'So good of you to accept my invitation, Doctor. I do hope you and your friends enjoy the evening.'

'Why, thank you,' the Doctor said, 'I'm looking forward to seeing what you have in store for us.'

The smile on De Sande's lips was conspiratorial. 'And I'm sure you'll change your tune about what movies can be like. Now if you'll excuse me...'

He scuttled over to a table of food and picked up a fork which he tapped several times on the base of his champagne glass, attracting everyone's attention. 'Ladies and gentlemen,' he announced loudly, 'if you'd like to make your way through to the screening room, tonight's presentation will begin very shortly. If you could all sign the nondisclosure forms my staff have prepared, on your way in, I'd be pretty grateful. It's just a formality but, hey, I don't have to tell you people that you can never be too careful in this town.' A ripple of polite laughter spread through the crowd.

* * *

The screening room had been converted from an old dining hall into a cinema complete with screen, aisles and seats. At the front a podium had been erected, behind which stood De Sande, ready to introduce his film once everyone was seated.

'And now,' the director announced, a wide grin smeared across his face, 'may I present my proudest work yet. I don't want to say anything about it now, I just want you to watch, enjoy and hopefully take away with you this evening something that you will always remember.'

The lights dimmed and the noise of a whirring projector could be heard from the back of the auditorium.

'Ladies and gentlemen,' De Sande said, 'my new picture.' He paused for dramatic effect. '*Dying*...' Another pause. '...*in the Sun*!'

The film began with an aerial view of a city street and at first appeared unremarkable, but as the plot unfolded the audience found themselves more and more involved in the action. It was a story about a man who saw monsters. At first only out of the corner of his eye, and eventually face to face, he saw terrifying beasts killing innocent people, yet he was the only one who could see them and no one would believe him when he told them about the creatures. The film explored the man's torment, his quest to find out whether he was insane or not.

As Ben watched it he found himself carried away to another world. The film contained incredible effects, unlike anything he'd ever seen before, and his concentration was only broken by the occasional sound of sobbing from other audience members. He couldn't believe the way the film was engaging with his emotions, was affecting him. This truly was a masterpiece.

Towards the end of the film the man finally confronted one of the monsters, facing demons in reality and in his soul. He ended his relationship with his girlfriend in a tearful but peaceful farewell, then ran away down a city street, chased by a terrifying demon that seemed to fly not only after the protagonist but also out towards the audience, making everyone gasp. 'Araka na kana arakah!' the demon cried. Ben had never seen a three-dimensional effect quite like it. As the man ran he looked back at the demon, every so often raising an eyebrow and muttering a witty one-liner. At one point a cop tried to stop his progress but he punched him in the face, knocking him out of the way. After he had finally defeated the monster, the city scene melted away to reveal that the man was actually in a Dantean vision of hell. Not just a studio set but a place unlike anywhere on Earth, filled with volcanoes, torture racks and demons. As he moved through hell, with no memory of his former life, the man discovered that he was a murderer who had killed a string of victims - the ones he had seen the monsters kill earlier in the film. The film's message was clear: that the only true monsters are the ones that come from within. After the man had finally returned from hell to begin a new life in Los Angeles, the image on the screen faded until the screening room was immersed in complete darkness.

Darkness. Nothingness. A chance to pause for breath, to gradually wake up from the perfect dream.

And then the film stopped, the lights went on and De Sande returned to the podium to a din of rapturous applause.

'Thank you, thank you,' he said. 'Now if you'd like to make your way through to the reception room there's plenty of food and wine for everyone, and I'll be happy to answer any questions you may have.'

Ben was still startled by the experience of watching the film, but soon gathered his composure enough to stand up. He looked down at the Doctor who was staring intently at the cinema screen, deep in thought.

'Come on, Doctor,' Ben said, tugging at his friend's sleeve. 'You heard the man. He'll be outside if you've got any questions.'

The Doctor looked up at him and smiled, breaking out of his trance. 'Questions? Jolly good, jolly good. Yes, I've got questions. I just hope Mr De Sande will be able to answer them!'

Back in the reception area the guests were excitedly discussing the film.

'That truly was amazing,' Polly said. 'I've never felt anything like that in my life. Such an emotional rollercoaster. Do you know, I think that could possibly be the best film I've ever seen?'

The Doctor seemed intrigued. 'You liked it that much?'

'Of course. I've never felt so... so alive. I could almost feel the story reaching inside me. It was a wonderful, emotional experience. Mr De Sande is so clever.'

'He is indeed,' said one of the party guests, butting into the conversation. 'I felt as if it was portraying the world I was born to live in. At first it was like looking into hell itself, but then the world changed and it was like I was looking into heaven.'

'I know what you mean,' Ben agreed. 'It just felt so strange, like the characters were speaking to me personally, not just to the audience. I felt like I was connected with the film somehow. Pretty amazing stuff, I reckon.'

'Do you know, I really can't see it,' said the Doctor. 'Everyone's saying the same thing. How they felt a link with the picture, how the characters were speaking to them. To me it seemed rather mediocre.'

The party guest looked at the Doctor like he was a madman. 'Are you sure you saw the same film I did, buddy?' Clearly bemused by the Doctor's criticisms, the man disappeared to hobnob with some other guests, leaving the Doctor alone with Ben and Polly.

'You must admit your reaction's a bit different from everyone else's,' Ben pointed out. 'Did you really think it was mediocre? Come on, Doctor, that was incredible. Besides, what about the effects? You've got to admit they're pretty impressive. I've never seen anything like them before.'

'Ah,' said the Doctor, picking up a sandwich from a table, 'the effects were indeed very interesting and very spectacular. I didn't think that sort of thing was possible yet.'

He looked around the room thoughtfully. 'Yes, I definitely want a word or two with our friend Mr De Sande.'

He shuffled to the front of the large crowd that had gathered around De Sande and Ben and Polly followed. The buzz of excited chatter that filled the room showed that everyone at the party was extremely excited by the film they had just seen.

A large man barged through the crowd and handed De Sande a drink. 'I tell you,' he bellowed, 'Paramount's pants are going to be mighty stained when this one comes out.'

'Did you see the camerawork?' a bespectacled man said. 'I could have sworn we were looking out of a window.'

'Please, my friends,' De Sande said, trying to calm things down. 'I'm grateful for your flattery, but I'm finding this all rather embarrassing. While I believe this is my best film yet, I don't know if I deserve this kind of praise.'

'Of course you do!' the large man said. 'Star Light's looking for investors right? I think you've found one tonight, my old friend!'

De Sande nodded. 'That's very kind of you, Alex.'

While the Doctor seemed enthralled by all the displays of sycophancy, Ben and Polly were rapidly tiring of the situation. As the discussion turned to money, another chaotic scramble for De Sande's attention began, and Ben realised there would be little point in hanging around in the crowd.

'Come on,' he said, hooking his arm round one of Polly's, 'let's get some food. You all right for drink?'

'I'm fine, thanks,' Polly said, 'though there were times in there when I wondered whether I'd had a tad too much already!'

'Yeah,' Ben agreed, watching the crowd around De Sande out of the corner of his eye. 'I know what you mean.' He reached down to a plate of food on a nearby table. 'Fancy a sandwich?'

'No thanks,' Polly said politely. 'I'm not really hungry.'

'Yeah, but let's enjoy it, eh? One night living the life of Riley never hurt anyone, and if some rich American wants to splash out his cash on us then that's fine by me!'

They clinked glasses and grinned at each other. 'Come on,' Polly said, 'we'd better go and rescue the Doctor.'

'Or rescue the others from him,' Ben added with mock disdain. 'I'm just off to the boys' room, see you in a mo.'

Polly marched over to the Doctor, who was engaged in a futile attempt to extract the secrets of the film from De Sande.

'Oh, do tell me,' he was saying. 'I'm something of a scientist, you know. I'm very curious to know how you created those three-dimensional effects. They truly were stunning.'

'Doctor, Doctor,' De Sande said, shaking his head. 'A magician never reveals his secrets. You know I can't tell you anything.'

He reached down to a nearby table and picked up a brochure which he handed to the Doctor. 'Take this, Doctor. It's a little piece of promotional material I had put together for the film. It should tell you some of what you want to know.'

'I don't want to read about the film,' the Doctor said dismissively. 'I want to hear the details from the man behind the camera... your good self.'

'I'm sorry, Doctor,' De Sande said, 'but I'm revealing nothing. Sure, ask me about the story, about the actors, about whatever you like, but I'm not revealing anything about the technical process. Just assume it's Hollywood magic and leave it at that.'

He walked away. The Doctor made a move to follow him but Polly held him back.

'Don't worry, Doctor,' she said, guiding her friend away from the crowd. 'I'm sure you'll learn all the tricks of the trade one of these days.'

As he left the bathroom Ben was about to return to the party when his attention was distracted by a distant, echoing noise on the edge of his perception. At first he thought someone must have left a window open and that he'd been hearing the wind. When he heard the sound again he realised that it came from the end of the corridor he stood in, a long, wood-panelled affair like something out of a Victorian library which ran deep into the house. He proceeded down the corridor and as he did so he heard the noise again, much louder this time. It was as if someone was trying to shout angrily yet was only able to whisper. He couldn't make out the words - he didn't think they were English and they were muffled by what he could only call distortion, a sound like a poorly received radio signal. He had heard that kind of thing while on assignment in the

Pacific, and wondered whether someone in De Sande's house was a bit of an amateur radio buff. The sound seemed to be coming from the end of the corridor, where he noticed a strange, green-gold light creeping through a crack in a slightly open door.

'Hello,' he muttered to himself, 'what's this all about?'

He reached the door and pushed it open. The noise stopped. The light disappeared. He reached for a light switch, flicked it on and saw that he was in an old storeroom with bundles of movie memorabilia strewn about the place.

thud

This must be where De Sande kept all the trinkets he'd picked up in his years as a film-maker.

thud

Ben was sure he'd heard something. A large antique-looking cupboard stood at the back of the room, the only piece of furniture.

He walked up to it and listened. He could definitely hear *something*.

One. Two. Three. He pulled open the cupboard door, but there was barely enough light to see anything so it took a couple of moments for his eyes to adjust.

When they did he wished they hadn't, as the sight that greeted him made him feel nauseous. On the floor of the cupboard were two pale white figures which were clearly human corpses. Their flesh was pale and wrinkling, but the bodies hadn't begun to decompose yet so they must have died relatively recently. Ben turned away and wanted to be sick, but after taking a few deep breaths he managed to regain his composure. He reached down to see if there was anything in the jacket one of them wore that would reveal where the bodies had come from or who they were.

Suddenly an arm flew up and grabbed his face. As he looked down at the corpse, Ben was sure its expressionless face was laughing at him. He felt the cold flesh grip at his features and pulled away quickly, shocked and startled. By the time he looked back the body was dormant again. He turned and ran out of the room.

It took him ten minutes to find the Doctor and another five to prise him away from the conversation he was having with someone who claimed to be one of the investors in De Sande's film. The Doctor seemed incredulous at Ben's claims but came along with him anyway, like a parent checking under a child's bed for monsters. By this time Ben had recovered from the sickening contents of the cupboard, but nevertheless made sure the Doctor went into the room first.

'My my, what a treasure trove,' the Doctor commented, looking around at the memorabilia.

'You just wait until you see what's in there!' Ben said, pointing to the cupboard. 'You'll have a bleeding heart attack, you will.'

'I'm sure there's a perfectly rational explanation for this,' the Doctor said. 'De Sande seems a very amiable fellow. I doubt he'd be hiding dead bodies in his house!'

He opened the cupboard door. Ben tried to peer over his shoulder but in the dim light could barely see anything.

'Now this *is* interesting,' the Doctor said.

'Do you see them?' Ben asked.

The Doctor turned round and smiled. 'Look around us, Ben. This room is full of collectables and film props from a hundred motion pictures. De Sande is a keen film fan as well as a director, you know.'

'So?'

'So...' The Doctor reached inside and hauled up the body inside the cupboard. In the light it was clearly made of plastic, and wasn't even that convincing. 'It's a prop from an old zombie film, I shouldn't wonder,' the Doctor said.

Ben took a good look at the body. 'But it grabbed me, Doctor, I swear it!'

The Doctor tapped the side of the body's head. 'It rattles! See, mechanical. You probably activated it accidentally.'

Ben felt embarrassed and ridiculous because of his mistake, but was still unnerved.

As they left the room he remembered one detail he had forgotten.

'Doctor, there was only one prop there, but I'm sure I saw two.'

The Doctor laughed. 'Didn't you see? The back of that cupboard was a mirror!'

As they made their way back towards the party Ben whispered in the Doctor's ear.

'Don't tell Polly about this, yeah?'

The Doctor smiled and nodded. 'Understood, Ben, understood. Now listen, you're clearly bored by this party, aren't you?'

'Well I wouldn't say that, Doctor.'

'It's all right, I'm not too enthralled with the company either. I think we'll say our goodbyes in a few minutes, but first I was wondering if you might do me a favour.'

The Doctor's voice dropped to a whisper. 'There's definitely more to this film than meets the eye. I'm curious to find out what, but it's clear Mr De Sande isn't giving up any secrets. Polly and I will distract the others.' He pointed in the direction of the screening room. 'See if you can "borrow" anything useful from in there, can you?'

'All right, Doctor,' Ben said, getting the gist of what his friend was implying.

Ben sneaked into the screening room and saw a couple of De Sande's servants busy buffing the seats and tidying things up after the night's performance. Even now the lighting was not particularly bright, so they didn't see him. He looked towards the back of the room and saw a small ladder leading up to the projection room. Moving as quickly but as silently as he could, he hitched himself up the ladder and snuck into the room.

'Can I help you?' asked a chirpy-looking dark-skinned teenager who was busy putting reels of film back in their canisters.

'Er, hello there,' Ben said, thinking on his feet. 'I just wanted to say congratulations on today's performance.'

'Oh thanks,' the boy said, 'but I just load the film reels into the projector. It's Mr De Sande you want to be thanking. He's a genius, probably the greatest film-maker in the world. Hang on a minute... What are you doing here? No one's allowed up here unless they're authorised members of Mr De Sande's staff.'

Ben looked around the room and saw rows and rows of film reels of varying sizes. He knew the Doctor would love him to 'borrow' a reel of *Dying in the Sun*, but it was clear that most of the film canisters were just too big for him to spirit one away. In the corner of the room were some much smaller canisters though, one of which could easily fit into his pocket. 'This is quite a collection you've got here,' he said, moving towards them. 'Are these all De Sande's pictures?'

'Please, sir,' the boy said, wringing his hands with agitation, 'if anyone finds you here I'll be in big trouble.'

Ben glanced down at the small canisters and saw that they contained extracts from different films. One of them was labelled 'Dying - rough cut'. Even if it didn't turn out to be very useful, this was the best he could hope for.

He picked up a different canister, being careful to choose one that didn't seem to be connected to *Dying in the Sun*.

'Yeah, quite a collection.'

'Please, put that down!' said the projectionist. As he did so Ben dropped the canister on the floor.

'Careful!' the boy shouted, kneeling down to pick it up. While he was doing this Ben took advantage of his distraction to slip the *Dying in the Sun* reel into his jacket pocket.

'I'm sorry,' he apologised as the boy inspected the canister for signs of damage. 'I'm just a bit of a film buff, you know. I find places like this... well, interesting.'

The boy appeared to react slightly. Ben had obviously struck a chord with him.

'Anyway,' Ben continued, putting on a disappointed act, 'I wouldn't want you to get in trouble, so I'll be off now. Goodbye.'

'Goodnight, sir,' the projectionist said as Ben climbed down the ladder and returned to the party.

Ben found a very bored-looking Doctor sulking in a corner. Polly seemed to be trying to cheer him up.

'What's up with him?' Ben asked.

'Oh, Mr De Sande won't let him in on any of his secrets, that's all,' Polly told him.

'Come on, Doctor,' Ben said. 'You heard what he said. He's like a magician. You can understand why he doesn't want the world to know how he does it.'

'That's just the point,' the Doctor said. 'What is it that the world needs to know about Mr De Sande?'

'Here,' Ben said, tapping his jacket pocket. 'I've got something that should cheer you up.'

The Doctor smiled. 'Best not show me here, eh?' He turned to Polly, and pointed at the exit through which people were gradually slipping away from the party. 'I think it's time we made a move, don't you think so, Polly?' She put her arm round the Doctor and they began to walk towards the door.

As Ben's feet started to crunch on the gravel just outside the house he felt a large hand clamp down on his shoulder. He turned round to see a burly security guard standing behind him.

'Excuse me, sir, we have to conduct a quick security check on all our guests. I'm sure you can understand.'

'What?' said Ben, panicking as he thought of the film reel in his pocket. 'You must be joking, right?'

'No, it's perfectly sensible,' said the Doctor, moving between Ben and the security guard. He threw his hands up into the air. 'I promise I haven't taken anything away with me other than a bit of a light head!'

The security guard didn't seem convinced and quickly searched the Doctor's pockets.

'You're clean,' he said. He pointed to Ben. 'Now you.'

'What?' Ben looked at the Doctor for support. 'I'm not being searched by that gorilla!'

The Doctor scuttled round behind Ben and tapped him on the back, pushing him towards the guard. 'Now don't be a silly, it won't hurt.'

Ben reluctantly lifted his hands and let the man search him. He expected all hell to break loose when the guard found the film but the guard didn't even seem to notice it.

'You're clean too,' the guard said, disappointment clear in his voice. He proceeded to search Polly but, when he couldn't find anything suspicious on her either, resignedly wished the group a nice day and told them to walk to the end of the driveway where a car would pick them up to take them home.

'Here, what was that all about?' Ben asked once they were out of earshot of the guard. 'Where's that film I nicked?'

The Doctor grinned and tapped his own jacket pocket. 'Sleight of hand, Ben, sleight of hand.'

As they passed through the gates at the entrance to the house they saw a fleet of cars waiting. Other party guests were getting into them and driving away.

'Polly!' hissed a voice.

The voice belonged to a tall man in a long dark coat who was pressing himself against the stone wall that shielded the house from everyday view. Although he was technically outside the gates to De Sande's estate, it appeared that he didn't want to attract too much attention from the security guards.

He looked around furtively, then moved closer.His face was briefly illuminated in the moonlight.

Polly gasped, though Ben couldn't understand why. There was nothing interesting or shocking about the man's appearance, he just looked like another middle-aged Hollywood businessman. The stranger smiled at Polly. 'How are you?'

'I'm fine,' Polly snapped. 'What do you want?'

'Hello,' the Doctor said to the man. 'I'm the Doctor.'

The man nodded, then tipped his hat. 'Polly told me about you. I'm Leon Zane, MGA Studios.'

'MGA Studios?' said Ben. 'The movie studio?'

Zane nodded. 'That's the one.'

'What on Earth are you doing here?' Polly asked. Ben wondered where she knew the man from. She certainly seemed to have very little time for him. 'Are you following me?'

Zane let out a bellowing laugh. 'You ain't that important, sister. One of our rivals is releasing a movie soon, and it's being screened tonight. No, I just came along to see what people thought of the flick... ask them on their way out, that sort of thing. Get some feedback so we know what we're in for. No one's saying much, though, and I keep getting dirty looks from those security guards. I was about to head off when I saw you and your friends.' Zane looked around furtively, clearly not too comfortable with speaking out in the open within earshot of the security guards. 'Listen, can the three of you come to my car for a minute? I wouldn't mind asking you a few questions and I don't like the idea of eavesdroppers around here.'

The Doctor appeared to be weighing up the wisdom of going with a complete stranger, but his curiosity soon got the better of him. 'Oh why not,' he said, rubbing his hands together. 'If you're a friend of Polly's... Come along, Ben.'

Zane's car, a luxurious white stretch limo, was parked in a side road well away from De Sande's estate. Once everyone was seated inside it Zane reached into his coat pocket and produced a business card which he handed to the Doctor.

'My contact details are on there if you ever need to talk,' he explained.

'If you're so fussed about that film,' Ben said, 'why couldn't you just ask De Sande for an invitation?'

'Something tells me De Sande isn't keen on letting his rivals see the film too early,' the Doctor said. 'Is that right?'

'Indeed,' Zane confirmed. 'No one at MGA has been able to get near it. Before tonight the security around the film was plugged tighter than Howard Hughes' wallet. But we've heard rumours. Rumours that it'll sweep the Oscars, rumours that it's using a whole new world of effects and technology. But until tonight no one apart from the guys who made the flick, De Sande's inner circle, have seen it. That's a dangerous situation to be in. Everyone hates Star Light. They've been going less than a decade yet they're already biting at the heels of the giants. They're young punks that don't respect us, and they deserve to be taken down. I'll be honest with you, Doctor, I can think of a large amount of people that would pay dearly to see Star Light fall. They're a threat to our business, our heritage and everything we believe in. Subversive communist propaganda from punks who think they can take on the industry and win.'

'And can they?' the Doctor asked.

Zane shook his head. 'You tell me. That's the worry, though, isn't it? All Star Light's ever produced are stupid low-budget pictures and a few big sellers, but we've always seen them as being something of a passing fad. The rumours coming out about this new picture, though... It's one week away from the public premiere, and we must have the chance to prepare an announcement to coincide with its release. We must show that MGA is just as advanced and clever as our rivals. We need to know if that film really is so special that we ought to be getting worried about it.'

'Oh, it's special all right,' Ben said. 'Once it's released no one will want to see anything else, I reckon.'

Zane looked worried. 'That seems to concur with the rumours we've heard.'

'But what does that have to do with us?' the Doctor wondered.

Zane's brow was furrowed, his eyes piercing. 'I'm concerned, Doctor, and more than a little suspicious. Polly told me all about you on our last meeting. You're new in town, here to see friends more than motion picture sights, yet you're on extremely good terms with De Sande - even getting invited to his preview party. I just want to know what your angle is. You three really work for Star Light, don't you? If you are new here, then why are you really in town? When I saw you coming out of De Sande's just now... it all clicked. Polly wasn't a tourist, but a disgruntled Star Light employee.'

The Doctor chuckled. 'You really don't understand, do you? Polly doesn't work for Star Light! None of us do! De Sande just wanted to use us as test subjects to see how the film played to a sceptical audience. That's the only reason he invited us to the screening.'

Zane reached into a compartment underneath one of the seats and retrieved a large envelope which he handed to the Doctor.

The Doctor opened the envelope, took a look inside, then handed it straight back to Zane. 'It doesn't matter how much you try to pay me, I can't lie about who I am.'

Zane was clearly shocked by this reaction. 'Did you see how much was there? That's a serious amount of green, and we're prepared to pay large amounts of it for the dirt on De Sande's picture. The money there is just a starter. We're prepared to double whatever he's paying you, more if necessary, if you switch over to our company. Polly's told me that you're something of a technical genius. If it's people like you that helped De Sande's picture become a reality, then we want people like you working on our next pictures too.'

The Doctor started to get agitated. 'I don't want your money.'

Zane shook his head. 'Doctor, everyone in this town is for sale. We both know that.'

The Doctor turned away, annoyed at Zane's insistence. 'Didn't you hear me?' he grumbled. 'I don't work for De Sande. None of us do.'

'So who do you work for?'

Ben reached over and prodded Zane in the chest. 'Listen, mate, the Doctor's told you all he knows, all right? We were only invited to see what the general public would think of it. It's a good flick but... well, you'll just have to wait till it comes out to watch it.'

Zane stared at Ben, then back at the Doctor. 'If that's true... well just think about what I've said, OK? If you do know anything about the film...'

'Come on,' Ben sighed, 'let's get out of here.'

Ben, the Doctor and Polly got out of the car. It seemed Polly couldn't get out fast enough. Ben wondered what had caused her to seem so rattled, but decided that now was not the time to press for answers. Just as they were about to walk away Zane called them back.

'Oh, Doctor?' he said. 'You should know that people like me

run this town, mister. You have my card. If you change your mind you can contact me on that number any time. And if you don't... Well, let's just say you should watch your back, if you know what I mean.'

'Thank you, Mr Zane, but I've already been given that advice once this week.'

Zane sneered at the Doctor. 'Well, maybe you should think about taking it.'

'So what do we do now?' Polly asked as she sat in the back of one of De Sande's courtesy limos with Ben and the Doctor, on their way back to the hotel.

'I'm not quite sure,' said the Doctor as he flicked through the information brochure De Sande had given him. 'Now this is interesting. This brochure consistently praises the picture yet reveals absolutely nothing about it. Nothing.'

'You're being a serious boffin about this, aren't you?' Polly said. 'Why are you getting so hung up about a simple film?'

'Because I believe that this is far more than just a simple film,' the Doctor explained. 'You saw the reaction it caused and De Sande's reluctance to provide any information only makes me more sure. There's something not quite right about that film, and I'm determined to find out what it is.'

'So what did you find out at the party?' Ben asked.

'Not much, alas. No one seems to know the full picture, so to speak. It's as if everyone involved in the production was told only what they needed to know to do their job, and that includes the contents of the script, who was working on the film and how the effects were done. No one was able to tell me anything that could explain how it was made, apart from information that could apply to a thousand other films.'

'Oh well,' said Polly, trying to cheer the Doctor up, 'you'll just have to find some people who *can* tell you more.'

Chapter Seven

Back in the hotel room, the Doctor had set up a crude home-projector system that he'd rented from a photography shop. He had found loading the smaller than normal reel into the projector an awkward process, but eventually this had been done and he told Ben and Polly to sit down in front of a collapsible screen he had erected against one of the walls. Once everything was ready he dimmed the lights and switched on the projector.

The image of Caleb Rochefort dressed in a torn and tattered suit appeared on the screen, an image that Ben recognised from the screening at De Sande's. Finally they had the chance to view the reel he had stolen from the party, and at last they knew that it definitely was from *Dying in the Sun*.

The action continued, and Caleb ran down a city street chased by a monster that was obviously just a man in a costume. As he ran the movie's hero looked back at the demon, every so often raising an eyebrow and muttering a witty one-liner. After the monster's defeat the city scene changed to a sequence set in hell, where the hero wandered through what was obviously just a set in a studio with some painted rocks strewn around, watched by agitated-looking actors in monster costumes.

'I'm sure it was better last time,' Ben said. 'I mean, it's still good, but... you know. It's not the same, is it?'

'Maybe the excitement of being at the screening just made the experience more fun before?' Polly suggested. 'You know, crowd hysteria or whatever it's called.'

'I don't think so,' chipped in the Doctor. 'This seems to be an early cut of the film as there don't seem to be any spectacular effects whatsoever. This really is quite peculiar. Treating film is such a laborious and expensive process... almost all special effects are created live on set. The technology film-makers use just isn't advanced enough to do anything else. Yet this... it's like a rough cut of a film waiting for the effects to be added in post-production.'

'Maybe this is a rehearsal film or something?' Ben wondered.

The Doctor didn't seem convinced. 'A first draft, you mean? Edited together as if it was a final version? Such things have been known, I suppose. Live-action versions of the Disney animated features were filmed to provide a guide for the animators drawing the cartoons, but I've never heard of that sort of thing being done when the end result is also live action. It's just too expensive to film rehearsals such as this. Anyway, the acting in both versions we've seen appears to be identical. The set may look bad, but at least it's elaborate. No, this is definitely part of the same footage we saw before. But what else did we see that we're not seeing now - that's what I want to know!'

'They must have found a way to alter it,' Ben suggested. 'Maybe De Sande's got some technical bods to invent a new editing machine or something.'

'Possibly,' the Doctor said, 'but very unlikely. Technically, this is a completely different film. Whilst we've all seen it, and recognise it, it's just not having any kind of emotional impact, at least not as much as it did last time.'

'Mind you, we're not exactly concentrating,' Ben reminded him.

'It doesn't matter!' said the Doctor, walking the fine line between being annoyed and excited. 'When watching the film originally, it had an effect because it felt as though *you* were connected to the film. You said as much at the time. Never mind concentration, even the most casual of glances at the screen will tell you that this film is not having the same effect!'

As if incensed by the Doctor's words, the film stopped as the reel finished.

'Well, that was a bit of an anticlimax,' Ben moaned.

'Oh, I don't think so,' said the Doctor. 'That reel proves something strange is going on. If it's the initial film before effects have been added... No, it can't be. This is 1947 - you just *can't* change a film in postproduction like that.'

'Well, De Sande's people obviously can,' said Polly. 'He did say he had the best in the business working for him.'

The Doctor rubbed his hands together, a plan clearly forming in his mind. 'He did indeed. I'd rather like to meet some of them, I think. I'll be very interested to hear what they have to say about the film.'

'But why, Doctor?' Ben wondered. 'Why bother?'

The Doctor smiled. 'Because none of us have ever seen anything like *Dying in the Sun* before, and I'm curious. There's something strange going on, I'm sure of it. I just need to put my finger on what it is.'

'But where do we start?' asked Ben, rapidly becoming exhausted by the Doctor's enthusiasm for his quest. 'We don't have any names, remember?'

'Since when has that stopped us?' the Doctor grinned. 'Ben, can you go out and pick up some newspapers, magazines or books - anything that may contain information or gossip about *Dying in the Sun*'s cast and crew. Polly, you and I will talk to the one name we do have. The one person we know worked on the film and who we haven't spoken to yet.' He held up the reel of film. 'What's more, we have a very good excuse indeed to pay him a visit.'

'We're here to see Caleb Rochefort,' the Doctor told the hospital receptionist.

'Not unless you're on the list,' the receptionist said, without even bothering to pretend to check her files for the patient's name.

'I'm the Doctor.'

The woman laughed. 'And I'm the receptionist.'

'Just check Mr Rochefort's guest list, will you?'

The receptionist did so, and a look of surprise flashed across her face as she saw there was indeed someone listed as 'The Doctor'.

'Just go through,' she told him. 'His brother is with him at the moment, so you've chosen a convenient time to visit.'

As the Doctor and Polly walked up to the private room where Caleb was being cared for they saw a short, youthful-looking man leaving the room.

'Hello,' said the Doctor.

The man stopped in his tracks and turned to look at the stranger. 'Hello?'

'You must be Caleb's brother. How is the poor chap doing?'

'Amazingly well,' said the man. 'And you are?'

'Just a friend. When you say amazingly well...'

The brother shrugged. 'Well, he just looks so good. He's always been short, weak and scrawny. Never had much of a presence before.'

'What?' Polly said, incredulous. 'I've seen several of his films. If that's not presence, I don't know what is.'

The brother laughed. 'That's effects, make-up, stuntmen and a sprinkle of Hollywood magic. They make him look like a big tough guy who gets all the girls, but in real life... Well, that's not quite the way things are.'

'Oh really?' the Doctor said. 'Go on.'

'How long have you known my brother?'

'Not long.'

'Then you probably won't have known him long enough to notice the change. The speed with which he's built himself up is astounding. His ego's always been pretty big, but recently he's also started to live up physically to his movie image. He's bigger than he was before, so I guess he must be spending time in the gym. He's much more confident, his skin's better... I tell you, the change in him over the last few months has been amazing. It's so sad he's been injured like this.'

'It's always sad when guns are involved,' the Doctor said mournfully.

'Yeah well, thank the Lord Almighty he seems to be making a speedy recovery and still looks great. I dunno, I'm from Tennessee so I guess this town can change people like that. I just thank my stars that Caleb's changed for the better.' He glanced down at his watch. 'Anyway, nice to meet you.' He tipped his hat. 'Have a nice day.'

The Doctor said goodbye, gave Polly a look that said he'd found the conversation intriguing, then turned the handle on the door to Caleb's room and marched in.

'Doctor!' Caleb said as his visitors arrived. 'How great to see you.' Polly found his voice alluring. It was booming, confident and contrasted strangely with the injured actor who was sitting up in his hospital bed reading a magazine. 'I never got to thank you properly for helping stop that lunatic. You might have saved my life, you know!'

'My involvement seems to have been somewhat exaggerated,' the Doctor said modestly, 'but I'm glad you're feeling a bit better.' He moved over to Caleb's bedside. 'You've certainly made a miraculous recovery so far.' He didn't sound as though he was trying to hide the suspicion in his voice.

Caleb laughed and whispered conspiratorially to him. 'One of the great things about being famous in this town is that people fall over themselves to help you. I've had the best doctors in the state looking after me.' He reached over to a frosted-glass fruit bowl on his bedside table and winced as he stretched his wound.

'That said,' he pointed out, clutching his bandaged stomach, 'it will be a while before I'm 100 per cent again!'

'Well, I hope you get well soon,' the Doctor said.

'You know, it's very kind of you guys to visit me,' Caleb said. He looked over at Polly, who was admiring the lack of taste evident in the hospital furniture that lined the room. 'What's your name, hon? I take it you want an autograph?'

On any other occasion, Polly would have been irked at the cheek of a statement like that, but the twinkle in Caleb's eyes as he said it meant that she couldn't help smiling at the actor's sense of humour.

'This is Polly,' the Doctor said. 'She's a big fan.'

The joviality displayed on the Doctor's face disappeared as his expression became far more serious. 'Now Mr Rochefort, I'm afraid I have a confession to make.'

'Oh?' Caleb said, one eyebrow raised.

'I'm afraid I did have another reason for visiting you besides meeting a celebrity. I was privileged enough to watch your new film the other night.'

The smile disappeared from Caleb's face.

'I didn't know De Sande had let anyone see it yet,' he said, clearly surprised.

'Oh, we've seen it all right!' said Polly. 'The Doctor wasn't that keen but I thought it was marvellous.' She found her attention trapped in the glare of Caleb's gorgeous, deep blue eyes. 'You were marvellous.'

Caleb smiled. 'Well, yeah, that's what they all say.' He turned to the Doctor. 'So why didn't you like the movie?'

'Oh, it was enjoyable enough,' said the Doctor. 'It just didn't seem to move me as much as it did the rest of the audience. Maybe I just wasn't in the mood for a film that night.'

'Well, I'm sorry to hear that. So what has your visit got to do with the picture?'

The Doctor started shuffling around the room, idly looking up and down the walls. 'Oh, this and that really. I was fascinated by the technical aspects of it more than anything else. I just wanted to ask you what it was like to be around such fantastical effects.'

Caleb frowned. 'I wasn't around them much, to be honest. De Sande wanted to shoot the film in two layers, one over the other. Our part was just done in the studio, with very few effects on the sound stage. Double exposure or something, he called it. It was a way of putting effects on the film without creating them on the set.'

'So none of the effects were created live during filming?' said the Doctor.

Caleb shook his head. 'Not really. To be honest though, they might have been when I wasn't there. I wasn't on set every day, and even when I was I barely spoke to De Sande.'

'But he was the director,' said Polly. 'Surely you'd be speaking to him all the time?'

Caleb shook his head. 'De Sande isn't an actors' director. He didn't seem to have any time for getting the best performances. "Just read your lines and get the hell home," he once said. Rumour has it that he's like that because he thinks a nervous actor, scared witless of drying or fluffing, gives off an unintentional vibe of tension and paranoia that ends up in his pictures free of charge. Sometimes though, on the really minor scenes that just didn't matter on a plot level, he'd spend hours, doing hundreds of takes until he got the performances he wanted. Strange guy, but damn, damn talented.'

'Tell me, did Mr De Sande do anything else during the filming, or ask anyone else to do anything, that you found a bit unusual?'

'Nope. I mean he always had his bodyguards around, which I thought mighty pretentious, but apart from that he seemed on the level, even if his methods were somewhat... unorthodox.'

'Bodyguards?' the Doctor said, intrigued.

'Sorry, that's our nickname for the guys he called the Quality Observation Group. They never used to leave his side. Two or three men, tall and thin, real pale-looking skin. They sure ain't from California, you know. They never said a word, never left De Sande's side and I never once saw any of them smile. De Sande used to say he had arranged for them to watch over his shoulder and suggest any problems that might come up as filming occurred. That's his secret to never going over budget, apparently. I thought that was a bit over the top, to be honest with you Doctor, considering we were only making a crappy B, but hey, they pays the wages, so who am I to argue?'

Polly felt like she could sit and listen to Caleb for hours. Even laid up in bed, still suffering from his gunshot wound, he had such charisma, such confidence. She was not remotely surprised that he had become such a celebrity.

Caleb closed his eyes and paused for several seconds, as if he'd heard something. He nodded then opened his eyes, coughed and clutched his chest, clearly in some pain but doing his best to hide it.

'I'm sorry,' he said. 'I'm not totally myself today.'

'Don't worry,' said the Doctor. 'You've been most helpful. I must say the more and more I hear about the making of this film the more intriguing it becomes.'

Caleb looked curiously at the Doctor, then started coughing.

'Are you all right?' the Doctor asked. 'You look rather off colour.'

Caleb shook his head. 'To be honest I'm not feeling that great. Do you think... do you think you could fetch the nurse?'

'Of course,' the Doctor said, nodding his head before scuttling out of the room.

'I must say I've never met a movie star before,' Polly said to Caleb as they waited for the Doctor to return.

'Do you have an autograph book, Polly?' Caleb wheezed.

He remembered her name. Just when she thought he couldn't get any nicer.

Polly was aware of Caleb's expectant look and realised that she hadn't answered his question. 'I'm afraid I don't.'

Caleb smiled and reached into one of the drawers beside his bed. He took out a pad of paper and showed it to Polly. 'Hospital notepaper. That way you'll never forget today.'

'Oh, I could never forget meeting you,' Polly said, not particularly intending to say that out loud.

Caleb signed the paper, handed it to her, then whispered in her ear. 'Tell me, Polly, have you ever wanted to be a star yourself?'

Polly could feel her cheeks flushing. How could he tell?

Caleb nodded enthusiastically. 'Of course. You have star quality, you know. You could do great things in the movies, someone as beautiful as you.'

Stop yourself, Polly thought. He's playing with you, toying with you. It's Leon Zane all over again. Don't listen to him. 'Do you really mean it?' she asked.

'Caleb nodded. 'Of course. And before you ask, I'm not trying to get in bed with you. I'm happily attached, thanks. No, all I want is to see that potential in your eyes realised. When I get out of here... I know people, I can get you a part. In a few months you'll be the next Joan Crawford.'

Polly felt her pulse begin to race with excitement at what Caleb suggested. This was it, a real chance to be a movie star. Unlike with Zane and his empty promises she knew she could trust Caleb. Knew that he was being totally genuine, totally honest. Leon Zane had lit the touchpaper that had made her start to think about stardom. Zane had promptly snuffed it out, but now... she could feel Caleb igniting it once more. After talking to him, after seeing how great he was with people, how witty, how charming... she knew that she wanted to be famous more than anything.

'So what do I have to do?' she asked.

'Just trust me,' Caleb said. He pointed to a chest of drawers on the other side of the room. 'Go over to that thing and open the second drawer down, will you?'

Polly walked across the room, opened the drawer and gasped as she saw a small pistol lying in the middle of some freshly laundered shirts.

'Relax,' Caleb said with a chuckle. 'I keep it close to me at all times. My father gave it to me before he died. It's kind of a sentimental token but it also keeps me safe in case of loonies and overeager fans, know what I'm saying? You can never be too safe, don't you think? Go on, pick it up. Isn't she a beauty?'

Polly lifted the gun and turned it over in her hands, feeling the cold metal against her skin.

'I need you to do something for me, Polly. Just one thing, and then I can help make sure that your dreams will all come true.'

Polly looked up at Caleb, then back down at the gun. Part of her didn't want to hear what he was going to ask.

'I need you to use that gun, Polly. I need you to kill the Doctor.'

Polly looked into Caleb's eyes, and could see that he was deadly serious. She could see that his words made sense, but she couldn't understand why she felt that way.

Why?' was the only thing she could think of to say.

Caleb smiled, and pointed to his chest. 'Look inside yourself. I think you know why. You've seen my latest film, haven't you Polly?'

She nodded. 'It's wonderful.'

'Then you understand. It has to reach the widest audience possible. It wouldn't be fair otherwise. If the Doctor starts asking awkward questions... he's interfering in affairs that are not his concern. His actions could lead to much pain and suffering.'

Polly was confused, but could see in Caleb's eyes that he told the truth. As he had suggested she searched inside herself, and all she could feel was the joy, the heartache, the comfort and the peace that she had felt when watching *Dying in the Sun*. The Doctor didn't like the film. He didn't get the film. And Polly knew that if he had his way he would not be happy until the film was banned. That he could deny so many people such amazing experiences... She felt tears of anger swelling in her eyes, and realised that Caleb was absolutely right.

'Do that Polly,' Caleb pleaded. 'And ignore everything I say from now on. I will try to stop you, but I won't mean it.

Polly's concentration was disturbed by the noise of the door handle clicking.

'Sorry we took so long,' the Doctor said as he walked in accompanied by a nurse. 'They're very busy today...'

He stopped as he noticed Polly, standing to his side, aiming the gun directly at his head.

'Oh, my God!' the nurse gasped.

'Polly?' the Doctor said, confusion in his voice. 'Polly, what are you doing?'

'Doctor, help me!' Caleb screamed, his acting talents in full force. 'She's gone mad! She keeps threatening to shoot someone!'

I'm sorry, Doctor,' Polly said. 'You have to die. It's for the greater good. Millions will find happiness through your sacrifice.'

The Doctor glanced at Caleb, then back at Polly. 'Wait,' he said. 'What's going on? It doesn't have to be like this! Every life matters, you know that, you've always believed that. Killing for the greater good can never be an option. Look after the pennies and the pounds look after themselves.'

Polly gripped the gun tightly. 'Doctor...'

'Come on, Polly, this won't help.'

'Polly!' Caleb shouted across the room. 'Don't shoot!'

'I'm sorry, Doctor,' Polly told her friend as she felt the damp of the tears on her cheeks.

She looked at the Doctor, then at Caleb, then back to the Doctor. She knew what she had to do. She pulled the trigger.

Second Reel

Chapter Eight

Although located on the outskirts of Hollywood, the Moon Beam Bar was such a run-down establishment that no one would ever think to look for a movie star there. As Chate looked around it, he felt it didn't seem the sort of place where someone like Maria would be found. Perhaps that was the point.

It was mid-afternoon and there were few customers. Chate walked up to the barman and asked him if he'd seen Maria. Looking disturbed at the question, the barman denied all knowledge of the woman, then retreated through a door into the back of the establishment. Chate sat patiently and waited. Four minutes later, a woman walked out of the door and glided round to the front of the bar where she took a seat next to him.

'How can I help you?' she asked. Chate, as starstruck as a person could be, barely heard what she said.

'Maria...' he stammered. 'Maria.'

The woman chuckled, a beautiful, high-pitched nightingale's song of a chuckle. 'That's my name. I must say, I'm surprised you found me. Only a few close friends know I'm staying here, and even when they let it slip I make sure the guys here don't tell.'

Chate plucked up the courage to close his gawping mouth and say something useful. 'Thanks for seeing me then.'

Maria smiled. 'That's OK. I'm feeling quite good today, and when my friend described you, you didn't sound like anyone I'm trying to avoid.'

'So what are you doing here?' Chate wondered.

Maria shrugged. 'To tell the truth, I'm getting a bit bored. We're not shooting for a few days so I'm kind of in retreat, you might say. I come to this bar during the day to be at peace.'

Chate tried his best to listen to what she was saying, but he was too enraptured to concentrate properly. All the pain he was going through, all the sadness of his life crumbling around him, had all been brushed away by this one meeting. Maria Coleman was everything he had ever imagined her to be. Long blonde hair cascaded down the back of a golden dress, large blue eyes and a perfectly made-up face smiled at him like an angel. And what's more, she was just as nice and polite as she had seemed in all her letters and all the interviews he had read. The perfect fantasy made real.

'I need your help,' he said finally, sensing that if he didn't pull himself together he could risk his idol losing her patience. 'I'm a former associate of Martin Revere. I'm sure you've heard of him.'

Maria's face paled, the smile fell from it. 'He's linked to Milchan, the guy who's trying to extort half a million from me. I heard rumours that Milchan was calling in favours to try to get his payments.' She gestured around the bar. 'Why do you think I'm hiding away in this part of town in the first place?'

She took Chate's hand, her touch warm and sensuous, instantly removing all the tension from his body. 'S'funny,' she said. 'I can usually tell a lot about people by looking into their eyes. Yours show you to be a good person, a kind person, yet you're here from Revere? Maybe I'm losing my touch.'

'Revere's dead,' Chate explained. 'I used to work for him, but I'm here for my own reasons. Before he took the night train he put a price on me, as have the LAPD. They've all ribbed me up for a crime I didn't commit. Please, I need a place to hide, just for a short while.'

'How do I know that this isn't some kind of set-up? That you're not really one of Milchan's goons?'

Chate shrugged. 'I don't know, but please, trust me. I need your help. I've got nowhere else to go.'

'Why me though?' Maria asked. 'Surely there are plenty of other places you can go?'

'You're the only person I feel I can trust. I've followed your career for years, read every interview. You're the only person I give a damn about.' He reached into his jacket and produced the signed photograph he carried with him at all times. 'You sent me this.'

Maria looked at the photograph and smiled. 'So I did. You're very sweet, Robert. But I have to be careful, I can't afford not to be. Star Light keeps me safe during the day, but when I'm not working Milchan could catch up with me at any time.'

'Believe me,' Chate pleaded. 'I'm as fearful as you are. We're two of a kind. Both on the run from a world that won't leave us in peace.'

Maria's suspicion appeared to be beginning to crumble. 'I'm pretty good at reading people, and your eyes don't seem to be lying.'

A bubbling sea of excitement was growing inside Chate.

'I'm sorry if I'm embarrassing you,' he said. 'It's just that it's not often I meet someone I've thought so much about during my life yet never even met.'

'That's OK,' said Maria, taking his hand in hers. She was clearly warming to him, though an undercurrent of fear was pervasive in her eyes. 'It's very sweet of you. I can understand what you're going through – I was a big fan of a couple of stars myself once upon a time. Besides, I like the attention. Now that I'm supposed to be making a big comeback, I guess I'll have to get used to it again.'

'I was so pleased to hear about that. You deserve top billing on all the best pictures. I can't believe the studios have been such bastards.'

Maria shrugged. 'I'm really not worried by it, it's all in the past now. Do you know what's it's like to lose all your privacy? To wake up in the mornings and think "My God, I'm Maria Coleman the movie star!". At least my career nose-dive gave me some peace. Some freedom.'

For a moment, a very short moment, Chate thought he could see sadness in her eyes, like she'd caught a fleeting glimpse of a past that was too painful to bear.

'Anyway,' Maria continued, 'I'm with Star Light now, and they've been so supportive it's wonderful. At last I'm back on track, doing what I want to do with people who understand me.'

'I'm glad to hear it,' Chate said, moving his head to get a better view of Maria's eyes. He was relieved to see that, this time, when he stared into the deep blue pools of enchantment the sadness had gone. Indeed, Maria's eyes looked bright and happy, almost sparkling.

A pause. A pleasant silence, not an uncomfortable one. But still Chate was unsure what to say next.

'So how did it happen?' he asked. 'How did you start working for Star Light?'

'You sound like a journalist, Mr Chate.'

'Maria, I make the headlines, I don't write them.' Moments ago he had been scared stiff about meeting his idol, but the effect her personality had on him was so relaxing that as every second passed he became more and more at ease with her. More and more of his true self was starting to seep through his defences.

Maria waved to the barman, who had returned from the back room, and ordered Chate and herself a drink. She took a sip, then began her tale. 'I came to Star Light quite by chance. I was visiting an old friend on the set of Leonard De Sande's new picture, and I was introduced to a few guys in charge of things at the studio. We got on well, and when they started talking about their plans to revitalise the place I saw a golden opportunity to get involved. They were all over me, and before I knew it I was choosing which movies to star in.'

Chate was impressed with Maria's guile. 'Was it really that simple?'

'Pretty much, though at first when I suggested we work together they threw me some pretty lame ideas that put me right off them.'

'What made you change your mind?'

Maria smiled, her beautiful white teeth glinting in the light. 'I'll show you,' she said, standing up and dragging Chate by his arm. 'Follow me.'

She pulled him into a small cloakroom behind the bar, and reached inside a fur coat that could only belong to a film star.

She pulled out a small black box and held it up to the light. 'To try to convince me they were genuinely interested, the boys at Star Light gave me this. Soon, I understood what they were trying to do, and suddenly realised that they were prepared to give me everything I've ever wanted. I signed up straight away after that.'

Chate had trouble understanding what Maria meant. 'How can a stupid little box like that make you change your mind about their terms?'

Maria's eyes showed pity. 'This box is more than it appears. It's turned my life around. It told them that I wasn't some desperate actress to throw back on to the streets. It told them the best way to move my career forward.'

'What do you mean, "it told them"?'.

'Here,' Maria said, handing Chate the box. 'Open it and you'll see, you'll understand.'

Chate was starting to get scared. Curiosity led him on, so he ignored the protests in his mind and opened the box.

As he did so a dazzling, sparkling gold light reached out and bathed the room in a warm glow. The box was only warm to touch, though its inside glowed white-hot. He almost dropped it at the sight, almost blinded by what he saw.

Robert.

A voice which wasn't his, yet came from inside his head.

Robert. Be at ease. You're safe with us.

And he knew he was. Staring into the golden, magical light, Chate felt nothing but serenity. Whatever he was looking at knew him, loved him. He felt enriched, like someone understood him, and he knew just why the box had made Maria realise that it held the potential for her to be truly appreciated. She had been empowered by the strength the box gave her, and no doubt those at the studio had used its influence to craft their plans for her return to the screen.

Chate shielded his eyes and tried to look at the contents of the box, but the light emanating from it meant that any kind of identification was impossible. He was about to reach inside the box when Maria snatched it from him and snapped it shut. Darkness returned, or at least that's how normal daylight seemed after the marvel they'd just experienced.

'Do you see what I mean?' Maria asked. 'There's magic inside that box, and it speaks to us. Did it speak to you, Robert?'

Chate nodded, stunned by what he had just witnessed. 'I heard it, like it was inside my head. What is it?'

Maria shook her head. 'I'm not sure exactly. Just think of it as magic and don't worry about it. It focuses the mind, gets rid of the garbage and provides clarity and inspiration. It releases all the trapped potential you'd otherwise never be able to realise. And it's the most beautiful thing in the world. Have you ever seen anything quite as wonderful before?'

Chate thought back to the restaurant, thought back to the first time he saw the light when it had spilled out of the wounded man's body. Whatever this substance was, its popularity appeared to be growing. He wondered whether to tell Maria that he had seen this kind of thing before, but decided against it. All he wanted was her happiness, and he could tell that she wanted him to be impressed.

'No,' he said, smiling. 'I've never seen anything like it.'

Maria picked her coat off its hanger, threw it over her shoulders and thrust the box back into her pocket. She turned away from Chate and walked out of the cloakroom.

'Wait!' Chate beckoned. 'Where are you going?'

Maria stopped and turned. 'I'm going back to my safe house to fetch something.' A broad smile flashed on her face before she delivered the killer line. 'So are you coming back with me or aren't you?'

Chate grinned and hurried after her, knowing that this was his lucky day.

Chapter Nine

In Caleb Rochefort's private hospital room Polly dropped the smoking gun and stared at the body.

'What have I done?' she whimpered, seeing blood dripping from the blackened bullet wound in the victim's chest and forming a pool on the floor.

The Doctor ran over to her, took the gun from her hands, then placed it inside his jacket. Polly hurried over to Caleb and took hold of one of his hands. Tears began to roll down her cheeks. 'Come on,' she cried. 'Don't die!'

'I'll get help,' the nurse shouted, running out of the room.

Caleb opened his eyes. 'Araka na kana arakah!' he cried. His screams were impossible to understand, but the anger and fire in his eyes told Polly that the dying man was stunned by what had happened and furious at her for shooting him.

And she knew she had heard the screams somewhere before.

Caleb stared up at Polly, into her soul, and suddenly everything that had appealed to her about him disappeared. The anger in his face was replaced with sadness. His charm, his charisma, the intense feeling that he was right about everything... all that was gone. Caleb let out one final cry, then fell silent.

The Doctor moved over to join Polly at the bedside and felt Caleb's pulse. 'He's dead.' Concern filled his face as he stared at the wound in Caleb's chest. 'My goodness, this is interesting.' He put his hands on the wound and lifted them, revealing palms that were not only soaked in blood but also in a strange, glowing substance that had an aura so bright Polly had to shield her eyes from the glare.

'What is it?' she asked.

The Doctor was engrossed in his study of the corpse. 'This is Caleb's blood. Whatever is making this... this spectacle, it runs throughout his body.' He poked his fingers around the wound and a spurt of golden blood dripped out. 'It appears that Caleb is not quite the human being we thought he was.'

'What do you mean, not a human being?' asked Polly, trying to comprehend the Doctor's implications. 'Are you saying Caleb's an alien?'

The Doctor rolled his eyes upwards, thinking things over, then put a finger to his lips. 'I don't know,' he said, as if working through a thousand different ideas in his mind as he spoke. 'I don't think he's an alien, at least, not quite.' He glanced down at Caleb's body and an expression of surprise crossed his face. 'Look at this!'

Polly saw the sparkling blood swirling round the edges of the wound, pulling and stretching sections of flesh, gradually trying to seal it. Caleb's body appeared to be healing itself, but there was no sign of him coming back to life.

It seemed that the wound could close any minute, sealing the strange blood inside it. The Doctor clearly realised this because he reached into his jacket, produced a small jam jar and held it to Caleb's wound, letting a small sample of blood seep in. 'I think a few scientific tests might be in order,' he said, sealing the lid on the jar and putting it back in his pocket.

Before the wound could close the impressive sight of the body healing itself slowed, then stopped, and the light died away, leaving a still half-open wound which was much less evident than it had been but was still clearly fatal. Even the dead man's unusual biology hadn't been able to save his life.

The door to the room suddenly flew open and three members of the hospital staff burst in. 'We heard a gunshot,' one of them said. 'Is everyone... Oh, no.' He and his colleagues looked with expressions of pure horror at the blood-soaked corpse in front of them.

'I'll call his family,' the Doctor announced then ran from the room, grabbing Polly's arm as he did so to make sure she came with him.

'Hey you!' Polly heard a doctor shout as they hurried out. 'Come back here.'

'Don't worry!' the Doctor called back. 'We won't be long!'

'That won't work, Doctor,' Polly exclaimed. 'They'll know he's been shot... I'm going to get the blame for killing Caleb.'

The Doctor shook his head and tapped his jacket pocket. 'I've got the gun and the bullet wound has almost healed up, so the only evidence will be the nurse's testimony and from the witnesses who heard the shot. I don't think that's enough for a convincing case, especially when he will appear to have died from his restaurant wounds rupturing.'

They made their way out of the hospital as quickly as they could, sneaking past reception and leaving through a side entrance to attract as little attention as possible.

'It wasn't your fault,' the Doctor reassured Polly once they were clear of the hospital. 'Caleb must have been exerting some kind of mind control on you. The way the real Polly snapped awake the moment you fired the gun shows that. You must have been able to summon up the strength to turn the gun away from me, despite what he was telling you. He still made you pull the trigger, though. You could say he was a victim of his own success.'

Chapter Ten

The lavishly decorated bar of the Regent Hotel was usually fairly empty, but as night settled in it began to fill up. By the time Polly got down there it was bustling with businessmen, tourists and all the other guests who made the building come alive. The atmosphere in the bar was relaxing. It was a place where you could get away from it all without ever feeling lonely.

'A Flaming Hero, please,' she said. 'And no ice.'

The barman smiled and reached for a whisky bottle. 'Charged to room 208, yeah?'

Polly nodded, trying to raise a smile. She'd been here for just over half an hour now, but was already on her third cocktail.

'Easy, duchess,' said a familiar voice. 'You'll be on the floor if you're not careful.'

Polly turned to see Ben's smiling face, and gestured for him to sit on the stool next to her.

'Sorry,' she said. 'I just wanted a drink or two. It's been a rough day.'

Ben looked at her understandingly, paused for a while, then reached over and asked the barman for a pink gin. He tipped the barman, then took Polly's hand and squeezed it gently. 'Are you OK?' he asked.

'Is it that obvious?'

Ben pointed towards her drink. 'It's that important, obviously. The Doctor told me what happened. It wasn't your fault, you know.'

Silence. A moment or two to think things over. And then: 'I killed someone, Ben.'

More silence. 'No you didn't. The Doctor told me what happened. That bloke Caleb killed himself. He was just using you.

It doesn't matter whose hands were actually on the trigger, he still pulled it.'

Polly took a sip from her drink. 'I know,' she said finally. 'But that doesn't make it any easier.'

'I know it's hard, but you know what they say – time heals.'

'I'm sure it does, but that won't stop me from feeling terrible today.'

Ben pointed to her drink. 'Neither will that, you know.'

Polly managed a slight laugh. 'You can talk.'

Ben smiled, compassionately. 'I'm a sailor. I'm allowed'

'I keep seeing him when I close my eyes, you know? I've never killed anyone, always abhorred the idea, yet tonight someone is in the morgue because of me.'

Ben looked as if he was struggling to find comforting words. 'But he was an alien or something. He tried to kill the Doctor and messed with your mind, don't forget that.'

Polly thought back to how Caleb had managed to reach inside her, thought about the vulnerability she had felt, thought about her helplessness to resist as Caleb twisted her thoughts to fit his will.

'I hate him, Ben. I'm not mourning him at all. I'd barely met the man, yet I killed him. I'm upset because I killed. For the first time in *my* life I ended another. But I'm not sorry he's dead. What he did to me... I'm not sorry.'

Ben reached over and gave her a hug. She realised she was crying into his shoulder. 'I'm not a killer,' she sobbed. 'I'm not.'

'I know,' Ben reassured her. 'It'll be OK. Just let it all out. Don't bottle it up. You'll be OK.'

Polly broke their embrace and stood up, draining the rest of her drink.

'Never again,' she said. 'Never again will anyone control me like that. I'm me, and I'm not a killer, I'm not a slave, I'm not an adoring fan. I'm not what Caleb tried to make me.'

As she walked out of the bar, she prayed that she wasn't.

Back on the second floor of the hotel the Doctor was sitting cross-legged in the middle of his room, flicking eagerly through the pile of gossip magazines Ben had managed to purchase and using a magnifying glass to get a more detailed look at some of the photos in them. Issues of *Stars*, *Confidential*, *Whisper* and *Hollywood*. littered the floor, along with a stack of recent newspapers.

'How's it going, Doctor?' Polly asked.

The Doctor looked up from his reading.'Oh, not that good, not that bad. There must be some clues somewhere in these, I'm sure.'

'Those rags are riddled with info on all the celebs,' Ben pointed out.

'And that's exactly why the answers must be here,' the Doctor said.'I just need to put all the pieces together in order to work out what's going on.'

Ben walked over to the sink at the side of the room, poured Polly a glass of water, then made sure she was sitting comfortably on the sofa. The Doctor appeared to be unaware of any distress in his friend, so Polly guessed that either her crying hadn't affected her make-up, or that the Doctor was simply too absorbed in his work to notice.

'First, we have a man murdered,' the Doctor announced, as if he was the detective addressing the suspects at the end of an Agatha Christie novel.'Now, while Harold's death is indeed tragic, that sort of thing is unfortunately not out of the ordinary in these parts.'

'Yeah, but it's not every day a tourist gets accused of being the killer,' Ben reminded him.

'Of course, but I was soon exonerated once the so-called real killer was found. Let's think this through. The man the police call the murderer is someone they've been wanting to pin a crime on for a long time. And then we come to the hospital, to Caleb Rochefort's blood.'

'Please,' Polly said.'Don't mention that.'

The Doctor turned to her. 'I'm sorry. I think uncovering whatever Caleb was is the key to all these mysteries, though.'

'So you think he's an alien?' Ben asked, trying to catch up with events.

The Doctor was noncommittal. 'I'm not sure, Ben. I'm hopeful we'll find out soon enough, though. And then we have *Dying in the Sun*, the film that has intrigued us all. A film that Caleb starred in. Is the connection a coincidence, I wonder?'

'But what can we do now?' Ben asked. 'We can't find out any more from De Sande, and we've exhausted pretty much all our leads, haven't we?'

'I have to get to the bottom of how *Dying in the Sun* really affects the people who watch it,' the Doctor announced. 'I have to learn what those behind it are really planning. Nothing feels right about this. It's far more than just an impressive film, I'm sure of it. If only I could prove my suspicions. Caleb may or may not have been an alien, but there's certainly some kind of supernatural presence at work here, something that ties everything together. If only we could figure out what it is.'

Ben walked over to the pile of magazines and began to ruffle through them. 'These should be useful, Doctor. There's tons on the actors from *Dying in the Sun*. Interviews, scandalous gossip from anonymous sources and, what's more, according to the people I was speaking to down by the cinemas all of the cast members' careers were pretty much dead until recently.'

'Really?' said the Doctor. 'Yet now these periodicals seem to be full of them. There's a centre spread on Mr Rochefort in one, a page of rumours about De Sande's love life in another, and an article on a former waitress called Hannah Wyatt, which mentions nothing about the film apart from her being given a small role in it at the last minute. None of the journalists writing in these publications seem to know anything about *Dying in the Sun*, but they're obsessed with the actors in it.'

'Maybe De Sande's people are just good at promotion?' Polly suggested.

'I'm sure they are, Polly, but I don't think that's the reason behind the sudden surge of interest in the actors.'

'Look at this picture of Caleb,' Polly said, holding up a photo-spread for the Doctor and Ben to see it. 'He looks wonderful here... so tall, so muscular. Just how he looked before I shot him.'

'Oh Pol,' Ben said, snatching the magazine away from his friend. 'Stop reading that, you'll only be torturing yourself.'

'Let me see that,' said the Doctor, taking the magazine from Ben's hands. 'She's right, you know.' He lifted the magnifying glass to the magazine. 'In this photograph Caleb looks exactly as he wanted people to think he looked. While I must admit this picture is clearly him, he looked somewhat different in the hospital. I've a strong suspicion this picture does not portray the true Mr Rochefort accurately.'

'He looked just like that before I shot him,' said Polly. 'At least I thought he did. After though... When he died, whatever ability he had to make us see him as more than he was fell away. His true self, the man behind the star, was revealed.'

'Which leads to an obvious conclusion,' the Doctor said, his voice rising. 'Caleb had some kind of ability that made him appear more impressive than he was. Indeed it seems he was even able to fool the camera. The popularity of, and interest in, the cast of *Dying in the Sun*, seemingly appearing out of nowhere, could mean that the other actors in the film also possess this ability.'

Ben was finding the Doctor's theory hard to believe. He'd seen the film, seen the cast. They weren't aliens, they were human beings.

'So what do you think we should do now, then?' Polly asked.

'Well, tomorrow I'm going to see if I can force De Sande to reveal what's going on, but first I'd like to find out who really killed Harold. Somehow the two mysteries are connected, I'm sure of it. The gunfight at the restaurant involved a member of the *Dying in the Sun* cast and a wanted suspect for the murder. Reitman worked as a producer for Star Light Pictures, the same studio that made the film, and died just over a week before it will be released.'

'Come on, Doctor,' said Polly, incredulous. 'That's a bit of a tenuous link, isn't it?'

The Doctor smiled. 'We'll see, Polly. We'll see.'

In the reception area of Star Light Pictures the Doctor, Ben and Polly stood talking to a middle-aged woman who had, until four days ago, been Harold Reitman's personal assistant.

'Ruth,' the Doctor said, shaking her hand. 'How good of you to see me. I just wanted to pop by and express my grief. I know you two had worked together for many years.'

'Since the Depression,' the woman confirmed.

'I'm sorry,' Polly said.

It's so sad,' the Doctor said. 'Why on Earth would anyone want to kill Harold?'

The woman shook her head. 'I've no idea. I don't think there was anyone Harold met who didn't think the world of him.'

'I don't suppose you have his family details do you, so we can send our condolences?'

Ruth looked at the Doctor with a puzzled expression. 'He never told you about that, huh? No, Harold has no contact with what's left of his family.'

'So what will happen to his estate now?' Ben wondered.

'I think he said it's all going to FOCAL. I sort of assumed you were from them, actually. Either them or Nathanson.'

'Nathanson?' the Doctor asked.

'Nathanson and Wolper, Harold's lawyers.'

The Doctor shook his head. 'No, we're not from them. What about this FOCAL? What's that?'

The woman looked irked. 'Nothing. It doesn't matter. Just a charity.'

'What sort of charity?'

'Doctor,' the woman pleaded, 'I really don't know much. Harold was always quite secretive about it. From what I gathered it's a fund-raising organisation of some sort. Harold used to be a very active member. I think it's a charity for actors and other workers in the industry who are going through hard times. I don't know anything else about it, though.'

The Doctor smiled. 'He always was a very generous man.'

The woman reached into a drawer and took out a small business card. 'FOCAL are organising the funeral too. Here's their address if you want to send flowers or anything.'

'Flowers?' the Doctor said, staring intently at the card. He handed it to Ben and pointed to a small illustration, a silhouette of a rose. 'Yes, flowers. I'm sure they'd appreciate that.'

The office of Nathanson and Wolper reminded Polly of a library. The musty smell of old wood and documents permeated the place and several rows of desks were neatly arranged in the middle of the room. Behind these sat various people making phone calls and inspecting legal documents.

'Do you think this will work?' Polly whispered.

The Doctor grinned. 'If Harold wasn't in touch with his family, then I doubt he'd have told his lawyers much about them. At least we'll know if there was anyone else who stood to benefit from Harold's death.'

'It can't hurt to try anyway,' Ben pointed out.

The secretary at the desk closest to the front of the office hung up the phone she'd been chattering into and looked up expectantly at the visitors. 'Can I help you?' she asked.

'Hello,' the Doctor said. 'We're related to Harold Reitman and we were wondering if we could talk to someone dealing with his estate.'

The secretary nodded and called to a bespectacled potbellied man who was poring over a newspaper at the back of the room.

The man scuttled across and peered over his glasses at the Doctor. 'Richard Nathanson,' he said. 'What can I do for you?'

The Doctor smiled. 'I'm the Doctor, and these are Polly and Ben. We're members of Harold Reitman's family and we were wondering if he had left anything to us in his will? I can't help thinking that if there was something it would ease our pain at this sad time.'

'I'm sorry, Doctor,' Nathanson said, 'he didn't leave any of you anything.'

'Nothing?'

The lawyer shook his head. 'I'm sorry.'

'But that can't be!' Polly said. 'Surely he must have done?' She slouched down in a chair, put her head in her hands and started to sob. 'Oh, Uncle Harold, what have they done?'

'It's hard, I know,' Nathanson said, 'but I'm afraid that's the way it is. He never mentioned you to me, I must say.'

'Mr Nathanson, are you sure about this?' the Doctor asked. 'I don't suppose we could take a look at the will, to see for ourselves that you're not mistaken?'

Nathanson shrugged. 'I'm sorry, Doctor. That will is confidential.'

'Oh go on,' the Doctor pleaded. 'Look at poor Polly.'

Polly looked up, her eyes red. 'Someone changed it, they must have done. Harold would never have done that.'

Nathanson shook his head and sighed. 'I suppose it won't do too much harm.' He lowered his voice. 'Just don't tell anyone I showed it to you.' He stood up and walked over to a filing cabinet, opened it, sifted through a row of folders then retrieved a document which he placed in front of the Doctor.

'Let me see,' Polly said, looking over the Doctor's shoulder.

'I'm afraid he's right, Polly,' the Doctor said, inspecting the will. 'It's all been left to the Friends of the Community of Los Angeles.' He looked up at Nathanson and smiled. 'Ah, of course. FOCAL must be a nickname.'

He flicked through the will to the last page, smiled then handed it back to Nathanson. 'Thank you,' he said. 'You've been most helpful. I'm sorry for taking up your time.'

Nathanson shrugged. 'Death is never pleasant, Doctor. It's a very tense time for the family. Mr Reitman paid us to administer his estate and part of that included making sure the relatives are informed. Just don't go spreading it around that I showed you that will. I've done you a massive favour, you know.'

The Doctor nodded and began to walk out of the office.

'Thank you very much.'

'Did you see that?' he asked once he and his companions were out of earshot and on their way back to the car. 'At the bottom of the will was a signature. A signature from an independent witness, the only person other than the lawyer who could know the contents of the will. A signature belonging to a "C. Wallis".'

Chapter Eleven

The house, in a quiet part of the San Fernando valley, was a small one-storey building covered in greying white paint that had peeled off the timber walls revealing a layer of mould underneath. Mosquitoes hovered around the overgrown garden, and a sign saying NO TRESPASSERS had long been trampled into the browny-green undergrowth.

'Here we are then,' said Maria, as she slid her key into the door.

Chate shook his head in disbelief as he stepped over the threshold. He'd seen Maria's old house on Wilshire, or at least seen photos of it. The giant stone walls surrounding the building meant it was very difficult for the public to get a good view of the place - an enormous mansion guarded by a gang of very unfriendly bulldogs. This house, this out-of-town shack, was about as far removed from that one as Chate could imagine. He just couldn't connect his image of Maria Coleman, glamorous multimillionairess, with this dive.

They walked into the house and Maria flicked on the lights, filling the room with a warm yellow glow.

'Do you live here?' was all Chate could think of to say as he stared at the fading paintwork and dust-covered antique furniture.

'For now,' Maria told him, her voice slightly tinged with sadness. She sat down in a large armchair and gestured for Chate to sit as well. 'I wasn't joking about being on the nut you know.'

Chate knew she was bankrupt, but he just couldn't imagine her living this kind of life. She was a movie star, she was meant to be a movie star for the rest of her life. It just wasn't right that she should spend her life as an everyday citizen.

'So how long have you been here?' he asked.

'About six months now. I've lived in three places over the last two years, each less glamorous than the last. I had to get away, you know? I had to leave LA, leave the people, leave my failed career.'

'Leave your debts?' Chate blurted it out before he could stop himself.

'Possibly,' Maria said, glaring at him. 'Anyway, I've purposely been lying low. I'm surprised you found me.'

Chate smiled. 'It took a bit of work. So why don't you move out? Now that you're back in business, so to speak.'

Maria shrugged. 'This place used to belong to my grandparents, you know. I inherited it when they died, but never had any use for it until now. I don't know, I kind of like it here I guess. I'd had enough of Hollywood, and this place just seems to suit me. At least until the hype for my new pictures starts to build, then I'll no doubt be forced back to the city by my job and will soon forget this rural idyll.' She let out a light chuckle. 'Excuse me,' she said before standing up and disappearing into a side room that looked like a kitchen.

Chate glanced around, admiring the furniture. His attention was caught by a few tiny plastic bags on a desk at the side of the room. Bags of white powder, sitting next to a couple of medical syringes.

Before he could worry about what he'd seen, Maria returned from the kitchen carrying two glasses that brimmed with dark red wine.

'Here,' she said, handing one to Chate. 'A toast to our new friendship.'

Chate raised his glass. 'To our new friendship. And to your future success.'

Tasting the wine, he was surprised to find that it was quite bitter. He associated everything about Maria with being sweet, and had even expected her wine to be the same.

'So about that box,' Chate said, finally deciding to broach the subject. 'Have you decided to ask the Star Light people what it is?'

Maria looked at him as if he'd asked the most ridiculous question possible. 'Why would I? When I connect with them, I know all I need to know. There's no point in trying to find out anything else when you have total knowledge.'

'Them?'

'Them. It. The magic, the fairies. Whatever the hell it is that makes that box such a wonderful thing to own. And there's more, you know.' Once again, Maria stood up. This time she beckoned for Chate to follow her into the kitchen.

She reached into a cupboard and pulled out a large clay jar. She unscrewed the lid, and handed the jar to Chate. 'Be careful,' she said, 'I'd hate for you to drop that.'

Chate looked inside the jar and saw a swirling pool of light, like white-hot volcanic lava, swimming and sloshing around inside it. Was this the same stuff that had been in the box or was it more than that? Specks of gold jumped up in the air from time to time, and Chate was sure he could hear the liquid crackling.

'Look closer,' Maria said. 'You'll see what I mean. What I showed you earlier was just a talisman, a confidence-booster. This is the real stuff, this is the natural form of the raw material the box was coated with.'

Chate was barely aware of Maria's words: they were only drifting around the edges of his consciousness.

'Drink it,' she said. 'Go on.'

He did, and felt a warming and empowering sensation like nothing he'd ever felt before. He could feel an abundance of energy flowing through his body as the liquid went deeper into his system. He could feel the weight of all his problems just drifting away.

'Careful,' Maria said.

Chate took one last sip, then placed the jar back down on the table. He could feel the liquid darting around his body nipping and tucking all the problems and nags, warming the places where he was cold and soothing the anger in his soul. He felt like he had a new sense of purpose. He could taste the feeling of heading for a new destiny.

He had a vision of Revere's villa. Of the body lying on the floor. He laughed as he realised that he'd won. Today the world thought he was dead. Tomorrow they'd check the dental records and realise he hadn't died in the fire, sure, but for today he was free and, more than that, he was complete. He knew now that it didn't matter if Reitman's death, Revere's death or any other crime was pinned on him. He was beyond that, he was better than that. He could bend anyone to believe what he wanted them to. The golden liquid made him feel untouchable. It made him feel alive. It made him feel invincible, like he could live for ever. One simple drink, one moment in time when he could have been doing a million and one other things, and his life had completely turned around.

'I think I love you,' he told Maria, without even thinking about it.

Maria smiled, and moved closer to him. Chate reached out and put his arms around her. They kissed for a few moments, then Maria separated their embrace. Chate pulled her closer to him, then felt her gently pushing him away. 'Later,' she said softly. 'I think you ought to see the effect my gift has on the public at large. See how much they love you.'

'I don't understand,' Chate said, wondering what Maria was implying.

'Let's go to Star Light,' she suggested. 'You can meet some of my friends. Then tomorrow we'll go back to the Moon Beam, have a few drinks, and plan the future.'

'You like that bar, huh?'

Maria nodded. 'They love me at that place, and I'm sure they'll soon love you just as much.'

Chate grinned. 'Sounds like fun.'

'So is that OK then?' Maria asked, pointing to the jar. 'You're going to help me and my friends to help others discover the light we've found?'

Chate nodded. 'Oh God, yes. We'll work together, you and me. We'll spread the word, we'll make millions happy. We'll be worshipped, loved and adored for all time.'

Maria grinned. 'Do you know what, Robert?' She paused, then reached down, picked up the jar and began to walk towards the door. 'I think I love you too.'

Robert Chate knew then that this was the happiest moment of his life.

Chapter Twelve

The bad weather that had plagued the city had finally ceased and golden-yellow sunlight blazed through the window of Captain Charles Wallis's office. The light reflected off the brown oak panelling and exposed for all to see the dust particles that filled the air.

From a comfortable chair in front of Wallis's desk Ben sat watching the grizzled policeman, who shielded his eyes as he looked out on the busy street five storeys below.

Wallis took a sip of his coffee and smiled.

'This is the best bit of my job, you know,' he told Ben and the Doctor. 'That time when I can just look out across the city and know that I'm the one in charge. All the criminals, all the fraudsters, all the Communists... Slowly but surely they're all being rounded up. Somewhere in this city, my boys are making a difference.'

'Yes,' the Doctor said quietly. 'But are your boys making a good difference or a bad difference? Is justice really being served, or are innocent people getting harmed?'

'We're the LAPD, Doctor. We protect the innocent.'

The Doctor smiled. 'Do you know, Captain, I'm so pleased to hear that, because that's exactly what I wanted to talk to you about.'

'Yeah, well, it had better be good, because I only have a few spare minutes, and after the way you interfered in the operation at Silent Gold I really should have you locked up, you know?'

'Hey,' Ben said, his first words since sitting down, 'that's not fair. If it wasn't for the Doctor, loads more people might have been injured.'

The Doctor shot Ben a look that told him to be quiet.

Wallis sighed. 'Spill then, and quick.'

'I've come here about a film,' the Doctor announced. 'A film I believe you might have heard of.'

Wallis turned away from the Doctor and returned to his window-gazing. 'I don't go to the movies. Waste of time, waste of money.'

'Well, putting aside your personal prejudices, there's one film you really should be looking into. It's a film that I suspect could be part of a conspiracy to exert mind control over the people of this city. You must force the production company to submit all their documents for inspection. We have to be sure that there's nothing untoward about the film. If possible, I think it would be wise to contact the MPPDA and ask them to halt the film's distribution until we're sure that its safe.'

Wallis's face was a picture of bemusement. When the Doctor had said his piece, the policeman could no longer withhold his emotion and burst out laughing. 'Come on, Doctor!' he said. 'Mind control? I think you've perhaps been to the movies one too many times!'

'Oi,' Ben snapped. 'Hear him out.'

'I like you,' Wallis said, with a hint of intentional menace. 'You seem sane enough. Not like your wacko little friend here.'

Although Ben was annoyed by Wallis's smugness and criticisms, he could tell that the Doctor wanted him to keep quiet so that he could try his own methods to get his way with Wallis.

'Captain,' the Doctor began, 'I think you should start by investigating the actions of the film's director, Leonard De Sande.'

Wallis put his head in his hands. 'Why me? Please God, why me?'

'I suppose you're just one of the lucky ones.' The Doctor seemed oblivious to Wallis's mockery. 'What I've told you is pretty shocking, isn't it? So will you help me? Will you try to expose the film's true purpose?'

Wallis's face fell blank, amusement draining from it. After

several seconds of silence he spoke. 'No.'

'No.' No questions. No arguing. Wallis's face said it all.

'What do you mean "no"? Lives are at stake here!'

'Doctor, don't.'

'It's all right, Ben, I'll handle this.' The Doctor looked away, took a deep breath, then looked up at Wallis. 'Why won't you help me?' he asked, like a child asking its parents why the pet hamster won't wake up from its nap.

Wallis stood up and leant over his desk, his imposing height casting a long shadow over the Doctor and Ben. 'I don't believe you. It's a film, for God's sake. A piece of trash. The whole damn industry turns people into zombies every day, so why should I care about this one?'

Wallis pointed out of his office window. 'Doctor, out there hundreds of crimes are being committed every day. Crimes against people, not art. Dealing with those is what I'm paid to do, and you can either leave my office now or you can jump straight out of that window and get a real close-up look for yourself at what life on the streets is like.'

'Captain,' the Doctor said, raising his voice, 'I don't think you quite understand the severity of the situation!'

'No, Doctor, you're the one who doesn't understand! I can't go up to the DA and ask him to put an injunction on a film just because some guy claims it's going to brainwash the city. It's ludicrous, and you don't have a shred of evidence to convince me otherwise. Besides, this is Hollywood. The studios and the city have... an agreement. Off the record, they're not quite as subject to the same laws as the rest of us. They're powerful, you know. They're everything here, and they can do what the hell they like, whatever the LAPD think. And do you know what? That little system works quite well.'

'But -'

'No buts, Doctor. You come back here when you can prove in court that the movie should be banned, not before. Now do I have to call someone to escort you out of here, or what?'

'No, no,' the Doctor said with a sigh. 'That won't be necessary.'

He paused. 'Before I go, there is one other thing I want to ask you. Until the other day, I was a major suspect in the murder of Harold Reitman.'

Wallis turned away suddenly, placing one of his hands on the window as if he was unsure of his balance. 'They found the killer. You were cleared of suspicion.'

The Doctor nodded in agreement. 'Oh yes, of course, Captain Wallis. But you saw me without an appointment, you didn't even ask me about the murder once, yet the evidence against Mr Chate was very thin indeed.'

Wallis walked up to the Doctor and pulled him out of his chair by his jacket. 'Meaning what?' he growled.

The Doctor's voice was calm, collected. He wasn't intimidated in the slightest. 'Meaning that I don't think Chate was the killer at all. And I think you know that.'

Wallis was silent.

'I'm right, aren't I?'

Wallis let the Doctor go, and raised his hands in the air. 'You want to talk about Chate?' he sneered. 'Let's talk about Chate. Robert Chate died the other night in his apartment. He blew himself up. Suicide! One final, oh so typical act of cowardice. Why would he kill himself if he didn't murder Reitman? And if it wasn't Robert, then who the hell do you think was the killer?'

'Ah well,' said the Doctor, clearly troubled by Wallis's news, 'that remains to be seen. Tell me, Captain, did you love your son?'

Wallis's face was reddening.

'He was *not* my son!'

The Doctor smiled. 'Well, of course he was adopted, but then there's nothing wrong with that. It's the emotional connection between parent and child that matters, surely, not the biological connection?'

'After the tragic fire that killed Chate's parents I took him in because I felt pity for the child. My first marriage had just ended and I wanted a chance to do right by someone. Never once did I receive any thanks for my favours. I gave that kid everything, risked my career to look after him, and he did nothing but throw it back into my face - nothing but leave my care for a world of crime, a world far more suited to an abomination like him than that of the good American citizen I hoped I could bring him up to be. I gave that boy everything and he betrayed me. When I finally found happiness with my second wife he left me and refused to stay in touch. That's when he turned to narcotics instead of college, that's when I knew there was no longer any "emotional connection" between us.'

'But you've been keeping an eye on him all this time, haven't you? I can see it in your eyes. You're concerned. There's a part of you that still cares about him. A part of you that is grieving over his death.'

Wallis shook his head. 'You're wrong. He betrayed me. I don't care if he's dead, he would have gone to the gas chamber for what he did. I hated him, he hated me. We were both more than happy with things being left that way.'

'I believe you framed your son.'

Wallis was fuming. 'You're tooting the wrong ringer, Doctor. Why the hell would I do that?'

Ben sighed. The last thing he needed was another of the Doctor's smug summations.

'For one simple reason,' the Doctor began. 'I saw Chate's reaction at the Silent Gold. He didn't strike me as a murderer. I saw the fear in his eyes as people fell wounded all around him. I've seen the convenience with which he has been blamed and the case has been closed. It smells of scapegoating, and let's face it, who better to choose for that? We've all heard the stories, how your men snigger at you behind your back, how they laugh at the cop who turned his son into a criminal. You can't deny that if you pin a case on Chate that gets him life imprisonment, if not the death penalty, then you'll at last get the respect you deserve from the rest of the force.'

'How dare you?' Wallis shouted. 'Get out of my office before I have you arrested for trespassing.'

The Doctor straightened his jacket, clearly affronted. 'Come along, Ben,' he said indignantly. 'I think we know when we're not wanted.'

They walked out of Wallis's office, and Ben slammed the door hard behind them.

At the end of the corridor outside the office was a flight of iron stairs leading down to the rest of the bustling police station. As the Doctor and Ben began to walk down them a burly man with a disgruntled look on his face barged his way past them, clearly unhappy about something.

'Detective Fletcher!' the Doctor called cheerily to the man. 'Hello! Remember me?'

The man turned and glared at the Doctor. 'What the hell are you doing here?'

'Ah, I was just learning one or two things about how your fine force operates. I'm on my way out now, though, but perhaps we should meet up for a bite to eat some time?'

Fletcher glared at the Doctor, then stormed down the corridor and barged straight into Wallis's office.

'Come on, Doctor,' said Ben, shaking his head as they continued to walk down the stairs. 'Some people just don't like small talk.'

Uninvited, Fletcher marched straight into Wallis's office. He was angry and he wanted to make a point. He found Wallis rummaging around in a cupboard at the back of the room. The light bulb inside it must have been on as the interior of the cupboard glowed brightly despite the room being filled with daylight.

'Sir,' Fletcher said, in a tone that was nowhere near as aggressive as he had intended it to be.

Wallis slammed the cupboard doors shut. He spun round and glared at Fletcher.

'Detective,' Wallis reprimanded. 'Don't you know to knock?'

Fletcher had planned to give him a piece of his mind. He wanted to tell him he was too angry to knock, that Wallis didn't deserve the respect that knocking on his door would show him, but as he stared into his boss's steely black eyes he felt his spine crumbling away as the old fear of damaging his career filled his mind once again.

'Sorry, sir, I did but you mustn't have heard it.' Cowardice. Pure cowardice.

Wallis seemed to accept the explanation and smiled. 'So what can I do for you on this fine day?'

'What do you think?' Fletcher said. He reached into a pocket in his trench coat, retrieved a piece of LAPD-headed notepaper and slammed it down on Wallis's desk. 'This, of course. Traffic duty? What the hell? Do I look like a goddamn traffic cop? I'm a better detective than anyone in the bureau. You can't do this.'

Wallis moved closer to Fletcher and prodded him hard in the chest. 'William, my friend, you have an attitude problem.'

'An attitude… Sir, this is extremely unorthodox. How can you –'

'How could you lose a suspect who was surrounded by five armed cops? How could you spend all night looking for him, then let him be found dead in his own apartment? An apartment your men were supposed to be guarding!'

'It wasn't my fault,' Fletcher insisted. 'You know that.'

Wallis paused, then walked over to the window and closed the blinds, reducing the light level in the room.

'For every police error,' Wallis lectured, 'for every public outcry, someone has to pay. Suspending you from the bureau will show the public that the LAPD isn't beyond accountability. Your reassignment is only temporary. Once the papers have forgotten the story – four weeks, at the most – you can return to your current position.'

Fletcher was silent as what Wallis was asking of him sunk in.

'You want me to take the fall.'

Wallis still stood facing the window and Fletcher was unable to read his face.

'Damn right you're taking it, and you deserve everything you get. The way you handled the Chate pursuit was abysmal. Never in all my years on the job have I seen such a bungled effort.'

Fletcher looked down at Wallis's desk and saw a pile of

stationery, along with a letter-opener in the shape of a sharp-looking dagger. On its hilt a rose had been engraved. He reached over and picked up the letter-opener, then started to turn it over in his hands.

'That's not fair,' he argued, 'and you know it. I followed procedure to the letter. I did everything in my power to find him. I'll make sure my men know they messed up.' He slipped the letter opener into his pocket, forgetting that it wasn't his to take, stood up and placed his hands firmly on the desk. 'But please, let me stay. Don't send me down.'

Wallis turned round and Fletcher could have sworn he saw his boss's eyes moistening slightly. 'I feel that perhaps you've become too confident,' the captain explained. 'When we get confident, we get sloppy. You've been through some rough patches, but you've been getting some good results and I think they're making you sit back, making you lose the alertness that made you a detective in the first place. I think you need some time on the street to get your head together. Some time to yourself. Do you have a family, Detective? Go on vacation, take the girlfriend on vacation. You do have a girlfriend, I take it?'

'Until recently,' Fletcher growled. 'And a one-year-old son. Both living with her mother in Monterey.'

'You have a son? Well, maybe you should go and visit him, let him know you care.'

Fletcher took a deep breath, and began to work out what this was really about.

'I didn't kill your son,' he said quietly. 'He killed himself.'

Wallis sat down at his desk. 'Go now, and flip the "Do Not Disturb" sign on the door round on your way out, will you?'

Fletcher thought about arguing more, thought about trying to make Wallis understand the unfairness of the situation, but the severity in his boss's eyes told him there was nothing he could say to change his mind.

'Oh, Detective,' Wallis said as Fletcher walked out of the room. He paused, then shook his head. 'I have no son.'

Chapter Thirteen

Fletcher checked the number of the hotel room. 208, this was it. He rapped hard on the door, unused to knocking on doors rather than breaking them down.

A pretty young blonde opened the door and looked at him expectantly. 'Can I help you?' she asked.

Fletcher barged straight past her, ignoring her protests, and marched into the room where the Doctor and the other English guy were sitting at a table drinking coffee.

The Doctor looked towards Fletcher and his eyes lit up.

'Good evening, Detective Fletcher!' he said, with surprise in his voice. 'How wonderful to see you! I really didn't think you'd take me up on my offer. I don't think we're quite ready to go out for dinner yet, though.'

Fletcher shrugged. What the hell was he talking about? Whatever... he'd learned by now to ignore most of what the Doctor said. The man was a nut, but unfortunately he just couldn't seem to avoid running into him. 'I have some things to ask you,' he told the Doctor. 'Some things I want to talk to you about.'

'Not Harold's murder again?'

Fletcher shook his head. 'No, not the murder. I don't give a damn about that any more. They won't let me touch the case, so I'll be damned if I'll work on it for free.'

'But I thought you were the officer in charge of the investigation?'

Fletcher shook his head. 'Not now. I've just been kicked out of the detective bureau for losing Chate, something that I attribute fairly and squarely to your interference.'

'I tried to help,' the Doctor said, unrepentant. 'I doubt he'd have let you take him even if I'd said nothing.'

'Well, I don't agree with you,' Fletcher sneered, 'but, like I said, I don't give a damn. I just want to know what the hell you were doing talking to my boss. A civilian like you, especially a vacationer, has no business being in his office. What the hell did he want with you?'

'Oh well,' the Doctor said, wringing his hands and glancing skyward, 'this and that really. It was more me wanting to see him, to be honest. The subjects we discussed really wouldn't interest you, I'm sure.'

Fletcher glanced over at the Doctor's two friends. 'Is there somewhere we can talk in private?'

The Doctor shook his head. 'What you can say to me, you can say to Polly and Ben. They won't tell a soul, I promise you.'

Fletcher was unsure about how much trust to put in these strangers, but he felt so tired and miserable that a large part of him just didn't care. The key thing was that the Doctor spilled the beans on what was going on.

'So do continue,' the Doctor urged. 'Tell us what it is that's troubling you.'

Fletcher reached into a pocket, took out his cigarettes and lit one. 'It's Wallis. He's not right, you know? Putting me, his most trusted officer, in charge of goddamn traffic? I know he's upset by his son's death and all, but... well, between you and me, I don't think that's the root of the problem.'

'Oh?' The Doctor's interest seemed to have been piqued by Fletcher's last statement. 'Tell me more.'

Fletcher shrugged. 'Recently, he's been acting a little weird. Arriving late for meetings when in twenty-five years he's never been late, ordering exhaustive investigations into really minor crimes. It's as if his mind's been on something else. And do you know what the weirdest thing is? All the time I've known him Wallis has been one of the most miserable bastards on the force, but in the last few months he's been damn happy the whole time.

'Maybe he's fallen in love?' the girl called Polly suggested.

Fletcher burst out laughing. 'You've got to be kidding. Not the captain. He's married, adulterated and bigamised his way through enough women in the past, and never have any of them made him smile.'

'That's lovely to know,' the Doctor's friend Ben said, 'and I'm very pleased for the fella, but what's this got to do with the Doctor?'

'Ah, well, that's the question, isn't it? I saw you two coming out of Wallis's office this afternoon. I don't trust the Doctor one bit, and it's only since he showed up that Wallis started getting weird enough to transfer me. Coincidence? Probably, but I just had to know, just had to check what was going on.' Fletcher moved closer to Ben, lowering his voice to lend an air of intimidation to his words. 'I think I ought to warn you, I'm pretty sure your friend has got himself involved in a little conspiracy. Wallis is up to something, and it's pretty obvious that the Doctor is too.'

'Oh, don't mind me,' the Doctor said, looking around the room distractedly, 'I'm always up to something.'

'But what the hell were you up to in Wallis's office?'

The Doctor sighed melodramatically and rolled his eyes upwards. 'Oh, if you must know... Would you care to enlighten the detective, Ben?'

The Doctor's friend grinned. 'You know that murder, the Doctor's mate who snuffed it? Well, we went to see Wallis to find out how the investigation was going. Apparently they're closing the case. They know who the killer is, and he's died in some fire. They claim they've worked out the motive, too.'

'I know all this,' Fletcher said, exasperated. 'Until this afternoon I was the guy in charge of the case. Chate was a hitman for some two-bit Bugsy Siegel wannabe. Reitman owed the guy several K, wouldn't pay up, so Chate was asked to deal with him. Is that what Wallis told you too?'

'So tell me, Detective,' the Doctor piped up. 'What do you think of that as an explanation?'

Fletcher took one last long draw from his cigarette then threw it to the floor and trampled it into the hotel carpet. 'I don't know. I guess it's vaguely plausible, but I think if Chate was a hitman he'd have been a bit more professional than to leave his prints around.'

'And then go swanning off to a very public restaurant rather than lying low,' Polly pointed out.

'Yeah,' Fletcher nodded, 'but he was meeting someone.'

The Doctor looked intrigued. 'I'm sorry?'

'Some broad I spoke to after the shooting. She had only just met Chate that night and didn't know anything about Reitman, but he did tell her he was planning to meet some friends at a dive called the Moon Beam Bar.'

'I wonder,' the Doctor said, 'whether Chate had reasons other than socialising to go to that bar. Considering that he may have witnessed the murder the night before, or at least seen something, or may even have some involvement, there's a slight chance that his business in the bar might be connected to it. It's a tenuous lead, but one I really think we should explore.'

'I was with the unit that checked the bar for Chate,' Fletcher said. 'I went there before I came to the hospital. No one there had ever heard of him.'

'Still, I wouldn't mind making my own inquiries. No offence intended, Detective, but people sometimes reveal slightly more to fellow customers than they might to a policeman.'

Fletcher looked concerned. 'You know it was Wallis who found the item that linked Reitman to Chate? And it was Wallis who conducted the forensic test against the prints? If they were switched, then Wallis would have to be responsible.'

'Exactly,' the Doctor said with a smile. 'I'm sure Wallis framed Chate.'

Fletcher shook his head. 'I don't care a jack how much he hates him, surely he wouldn't have hauled his own kid up on a gas-chamber beef?'

'I'm sure most people wouldn't,' the Doctor said, 'but Wallis is definitely hiding something and, while he certainly seems to have been affected by Chate's death, I can't help thinking that his reactions aren't quite right for someone who is supposed to be in mourning.'

'But different people deal with death in different ways,' Polly said. 'Maybe he's just regretting not spending more time with his son.'

The Doctor looked thoughtful. 'Maybe, but something about all this doesn't feel right.'

'This better not be true,' Fletcher said angrily. 'If I've been fired for losing a guy who isn't even the goddamn murderer, by the goddamn guy who set him up... Doctor, you'd better pray that you're wrong or I'm going to be one nasty bastard.'

'There's more, you know,' sighed Ben. 'And you won't like it.'

Fletcher slumped down on a chair and put his head in his hands. 'Go on,' he said. 'Hit me.'

'Have you ever heard of an organisation called FOCAL?' asked the Doctor.

Fletcher shook his head. 'Nope. Should I have done?'

'I'm not sure. FOCAL is the group that's inheriting all the money from Mr Reitman's death, and I have reason to believe that Captain Wallis may be a member of that group. Tell me, Detective, have you ever wondered why he wears that purple flower in his lapel?'

'Fashion, Doctor. Why else?'

'I suspect it's a FOCAL symbol. That's why it has to be a sign, a message to other members. You see, I don't think FOCAL is just a charity. It's almost impossible to locate it in telephone directories, and no one has heard of it. Even its address is only a post office box. Yes, I think the charity angle is a front, and in reality FOCAL is a secret society responsible for arranging Reitman's death in order to secure his fortune.

'Indeed, I've also learnt another very interesting piece of information. According to Reitman's lawyer, the only person other than him who was privy to the contents of Reitman's will before he died was a member of the general public who witnessed the signing of the will. A Mr C. Wallis.'

Fletcher let out a deep breath. 'So you're saying Wallis killed Reitman?'

The Doctor nodded.

'I need a drink,' Fletcher sighed.

'Pretty explosive stuff, don't you think?' the Doctor said with a grin.

'He's dead.'

Fletcher got up, looked around the room for alcohol of some kind, then realised there wasn't any in the place and began to head towards the door.

'He's damn well tried to screw my career, and he's the killer?' Fletcher could feel his heart pumping faster, the beating of Wallis's death drums. 'He'll pay for this,' he growled. 'He'll pay.'

The Doctor stood up and started wringing his hands. 'Now, Detective, don't do anything rash. I know you're angry, but there is a better way to get back at him than using physical violence.'

He reached for a newspaper and held it up, pointing to a small subheading on the front page that read MYSTERY MOVIE UNVEILED SOON.

'This film,' the Doctor said, 'is the twine that binds everything together. I observed the director of the picture, another advocate of rose-based fashion, speaking to Captain Wallis on the night of the restaurant shootings. I've been conducting an investigation into this film and I'm being drawn towards some disturbing conclusions, although as yet I have no evidence. I mentioned the film to Wallis today to see how he reacted, and I'm now more convinced than ever that he's up to his neck in this business. The film, Wallis, the Reitman murder. They're all connected, and I believe the final step to solving this puzzle is to solve the mystery behind the film. Help me with my investigations, Detective. Work with me, not against me. I've a strong suspicion that you'll come across more than enough material to get back at Captain Wallis and regain your old posting.'

Maybe it was his tiredness, maybe it was just his curiosity, but for some reason Fletcher agreed with the Doctor's plan. Dealing with Wallis could wait.

'Go on then,' he said with a sigh. 'How can I help?'

The Doctor shuffled over to a coffee table in the corner of the room and picked up a round silver disc that Fletcher soon realised was a film canister.

'I've obtained this,' the Doctor said. 'It's an extract of the film, or at least a partial extract. It's nothing special, but nevertheless I think there's more to it than is at first apparent. I need access to some equipment. Powerful microscopes, that sort of thing.'

'What makes you think I can get hold of those?'

The Doctor grinned. 'You're a policeman, aren't you? I'm sure you can take Ben and myself on a tour of your forensic labs. They should have everything I need down there.'

'I don't know,' Fletcher said, not at all happy about the Doctor's idea. 'I could be in major-league trouble if we get caught.'

The Doctor clapped his hands together excitedly. 'Then we'll just have to not get caught, won't we!'

'Shall I come?' Polly asked.

The Doctor shook his head. 'It's too dangerous, Polly. If we get caught in those labs there could be all sorts of trouble. You'd better stay here I think.'

Polly seemed to grudgingly accept the Doctor's words.

The Doctor tapped his wrist. 'Now come along, Detective. Time is short, let's get to those labs.'

'What? Tonight?'

The Doctor nodded enthusiastically. 'What else did you think we were going to do? Go to the pictures?'

When the Doctor, Ben and Fletcher had left for the forensic labs, Polly wondered if the Doctor really expected her to wait in all night while they were off having fun. If so, he was mistaken. After making sure she looked good enough to go out on the town, she scoured the newspaper for an article about the Silent Gold shootings that gave the address of the bar Chate had allegedly been heading to. Having left a note for the Doctor and Ben explaining where she had gone, she took a cab to the bar. By the time she got there sky was black. The street lighting in the area was extremely poor which made her feel rather exposed and nervous. The outside of the bar looked rather tatty and she hoped that the inside would be classier. She could hear laughter coming from within.

Polly took a deep breath, barged past a bored-looking bouncer and found herself in an unremarkable room crowded with people sipping drinks, playing cards and listening to old blues records that played lazily in the background. She noticed a few men glancing at her and smiling lecherously as she walked past – perhaps she'd put on a little too much make-up – but none of them seemed intimidating. From the look of the people she'd seen, she'd be safe here.

'Rum and Coke please,' she said to the barman. The man poured her a drink and she perched on a stool in front of him. 'Busy night tonight,' she commented, but he wasn't interested in small talk. He smiled at her, then moved on to serve the next customer. When he had done so, Polly gestured and managed to attract his attention.

'I was wondering something.' She rummaged in her handbag for the picture of Chate she'd found in a newspaper, then held it up and cleared her throat. She had always wanted to say this. 'Have you seen this man?'

The barman grinned and nodded his head. 'Yeah, course I have. Saw him today, in fact.'

Polly was sure he had made a mistake. How could he have seen Chate today? 'Blond hair, about six foot, late twenties?'

'Yeah,' said the barman. 'That's the one.'

Polly shook her head. 'But you can't have seen him today. He's dead.'

The barman burst out laughing. 'Oh is he now? Well, he's certainly been ordering a lot of drinks for a dead guy.' He leant across the bar and stared across the room. 'Nope, he looks very much alive to me.'

'What do you mean?' Polly asked, turning to follow his gaze. And there he was, exactly as the Doctor had described him. Robert Chate. Alive and well.

'Thank you,' Polly told the barman. 'You've been a great help.'

She walked over to a booth at the back of the bar where a stylish-looking couple were sitting next to each other, laughing and chatting as they drank. As she got to her table she saw the couple up close and was amazed by the sheer glamour they seemed to posses. The man had perfect blond hair, impenetrable brown eyes and perfect skin, toned cheekbones and an immaculate smile. The woman could have been his female counterpart, though in her case her hair flowed gracefully over her shoulders and her eyes were an icy blue. The couple looked awe-inspiring. They looked like movie stars.

'Excuse me,' Polly said nervously, unsure why she was so worried about how they'd react. 'Are you Robert Chate?'

A wide grin crept across the man's face. 'Isn't he supposed to be dead?'

Polly nodded. 'I thought so but… you're him, aren't you?' The photo she had seen had been of a man with a paler and more heavily scarred face, but despite this he was definitely the same person.

The man smiled. 'If you can keep it under your hat, then, yeah. I guess I am.'

'But aren't you supposed to be dead?'

'Listen sweetheart, I'm not the same guy I was, and a gorgeous thing like you shouldn't believe everything you read in the papers.'

Polly felt ridiculous and embarrassed, but at the same time she found the man's words calming. He had a voice like silk and everything he said, every body gesture, just seemed to relax her.

'So what's your name?' the woman sitting next to Chate asked.

'Polly. Pleased to meet you…'

'Maria.'

'Pleased to meet you, Maria.'

Chate looked at Polly with an expression of surprise. 'You don't recognise Maria? Maria Coleman?'

Polly shook her head. 'Should I?'

A bemused Chate let out a small chuckle. 'She's a movie star. The best there is. Do you like movies, Polly?'

At last. Now the conversation was turning in the direction Polly had hoped it would. If they could talk about movies, then maybe Chate could reveal if he knew anything about *Dying in the Sun*.

'I love movies,' she said. 'Although I haven't seen any for a while. I've been out of town, you see.'

'Not everyone's heard of me anyway, darling,' Maria told Chate. She looked up at Polly. 'He's so lovely. Sticks up for me about the smallest things.'

Polly felt her heart sink. This Maria woman was clearly more than friends with Chate.

'So what can we do for you?' Chate asked.

Polly barely heard what he had said. She just knew that every word washed over her and made her feel at ease. And then she remembered what this reminded her of.

In her mind's eye she saw herself pointing the gun at the Doctor, felt her finger being forced to tighten against the trigger, remembered the total trust she had felt in Caleb Rochefort. A feeling she was getting again now.

Her heart began to race. This was it. Her chance for redemption. Whatever had seemed strange about Caleb seemed to be present in these two. This was her chance to find out what these people really were, to give the Doctor the evidence against the film that he needed. If she could only resist their influence, though. You have to be strong, Polly, she told herself. You have to be strong.

'I want to be in the movies,' was the first thing she could think of to say. 'Got any tips?'

Chate looked intrigued, and put his arm round Maria. They huddled down and whispered a few words to each other out of earshot of Polly.

The couple stood up, then Maria walked out of the booth and gently placed an arm on Polly's shoulder. 'You're very pretty,' she told her. 'Hollywood is crying out for pretty girls like you. You could easily be a star, you know.'

Polly's rainswept face was reflected in a window and as she caught a glimpse of it she wondered what planet this woman was from. Literally.

But then she saw something in Maria's expression that made her realise that the sentiments were totally genuine.

'We can make it happen, you know,' Chate said. 'Maria works for a... a studio, let's call it, and we know people who make stars out of ordinary girls every day. If you're really serious about wanting to be in the movies... You are serious aren't you?'

So many people in this town were telling Polly she should be famous. Surely that many people couldn't be wrong? She had visions of limousines, of signing autographs, of knowing that millions of fans would be appreciating her work. She had travelled more than anyone, and had enough experience to draw on to know that she would make an amazing actress. She just knew.

'Yes,' Polly said with determination. 'I'm definitely serious.'

'Then come with us now,' Chate said gently. 'We'll show you what we're talking about.'

Part of Polly was wary. Part of her knew that if she wasn't careful she'd end up losing control to Chate in the same way she had to Caleb. But she had been caught off-guard before. This time she was prepared. This time she could shield herself against their influence. After all, they were so genuine, so honest. Caleb had wanted to make her kill the Doctor, but all Maria and Chate wanted to do was make her a star. She knew she had to trust them. If they tried to persuade her to do anything stupid she'd just leave, just walk away. Wouldn't she?

Chate, Maria and Polly got up and walked over to the exit where Chate picked up a large brown fur coat, put it around Maria's shoulders, then put on his own jacket. Polly suddenly realised that she hadn't taken off her coat at all, and was surprised she hadn't felt too hot.

They walked out into the warm night and Maria led them to a large car that was waiting across the street. She unlocked it, got into the driver's seat, flicked on the reading light, then gestured for Polly to sit in the passenger seat. Chate got in the back, and once they were all inside he and Maria fell silent for a few moments.

'So where are we going then?' Polly asked.

'Back to mine,' Maria said. 'We all need to get some rest. I've got some errands to run tomorrow, and then in a day or two I'll take you to meet the director. You'll want to take time to make sure you look your best for that.'

'Who's the director?'

'He's the guy ultimately responsible for introducing America to the wonders we'll show you,' Chate explained. 'He's organising a campaign to distribute it to as many people as possible. He's a philanthropist of the highest order. His vision of peace and prosperity for this city... it's unbelievable. A place where there's no crime, where everyone is worshipped as stars. We have some things to discuss with him, but I'm sure he'd love to meet you.' He smiled. 'But first we want to show you something.'

'It's OK,' Maria said. 'You'll like this.'

'Reach into the glove box,' Chate said. 'Take out what you find.'

Polly did so, and found a small clay jar that weighed more than it looked like it should.

'What's this?' she asked.

'Inside that jar,' began Chate, 'is the key to being a celebrity. It's not who you know, it's what you know. And this is what you should know if you're going to be famous.'

'Go on,' Maria urged. 'Open it.'

Polly pressed the lid off the jar and a dazzling light spilled out. The jar contained a bright liquid that popped and crackled as if it had an electrical current running through it. Sparks in a rainbow of metallic colours swirled energetically around. Looking into the liquid was like looking into paradise. It reminded Polly of something. Of the hospital, when she had seen Caleb's blood. That hadn't looked as dazzling as this liquid, but the bright glow, the entrancing illumination that was both painful to look at and impossible to look away from, was the same.

'Is this… is this blood?' Polly asked.

Chate shook his head. 'It's not blood. It's a marvellous substance that will do you no harm. Medical science in years to come will marvel at what it will do for mankind. Drinking that has completely changed my life, it completely changed Maria's life. It heals your ailments, gives you confidence in your own looks and abilities. Without even thinking about it you'll be able to tailor your body scent to attract anyone you want, and repel anyone you don't. In short, it gives you everything you need to be appreciated. Everything you need to be a star.'

For years Polly had hoped to one day find a place where she belonged, to find a life away from the mundane, but in all her travels she'd never found anywhere. Until now. The truth of her situation hit her like a crashing wave. She had been looking for a place to fit in, and that's where she had been going wrong. She could fit in anywhere, as long as people were made to treat her how she should be treated. Looking at Chate and Maria, she knew they had everything she wanted for herself. Their charisma, their attraction… they were pure stars, and oozed pure happiness. Polly knew that if she followed their advice she would soon be on magazine covers, dazzling millions in cinemas across the world… knowing that her true destiny had been realised.

'Drink,' Chate urged.

Cautiously at first, and then hungrily as she realised how good it tasted, Polly drank from the jar. She expected the liquid to tingle in her mouth, but instead the experience was like drinking warm honey. As it slipped down her throat she felt its heat begin to radiate through her body, relaxing her. Whatever it was made of, Chate was right. It was a miracle cure. Every care, every itch, every cough; all ailments and worries just slipped away. Polly couldn't stop herself from smiling. She handed the jar to Chate then reached into her handbag, took out a vanity mirror and looked at her reflection. As she stared, her features began to change. Very subtly, very slowly, but they were definitely changing. Her white skin was getting browner, smoother. The bags under her eyes were sliding into nothingness, and she could almost feel her hair getting stronger and more radiant. For over a minute she watched her reflection, until she couldn't stop herself from bursting out laughing. Chate and Maria had been right. This truly was a miracle. In no time at all she had gone from being everyday Polly to looking like a million dollars.

She looked up at her new friends. 'Thank you,' was all she could think of to say.

'It's a pleasure,' said Chate. 'You deserve it.' And Polly knew that she did.

Chapter Fourteen

It was almost midnight by the time the Doctor, Ben and Fletcher got to the LAPD forensics lab, a sparse-looking room with whitewashed walls that were dotted with various memos in illegible scrawls. Its centre was dominated by several rows of plastic-coated examination benches. Spotlights, microscopes and other analysing equipment were arranged neatly on the benches and rows of cardboard boxes were stacked along the sides of the room. The place just oozed science, a field Fletcher had never felt particularly comfortable near.

The cop had managed to wave himself, the Doctor and Ben through security by explaining that he needed the two strangers to accompany him to identify a body, and had managed to get inside the lab and lock the door. The Doctor was carrying a small sports bag which had got him one or two suspicious looks from security, but no one had bothered to question him about it. It seemed that no one here was in the mood for a row with Fletcher. For such a thug, he obviously had a considerable amount of influence in the place.

'OK,' Fletcher said, checking his watch. 'You've got one hour, then they'll start to get suspicious.'

'Wonderful,' the Doctor said, rubbing his hands together as he looked around the room. 'I think this place has everything I need.'

He walked over to a metal table lined with several microscopes and beckoned for Ben and Fletcher to join him.

He reached into the sports bag and took out the film canister, which he placed on the table next to a microscope. He then lifted off the canister's lid and, being careful not to let the whole reel fall out, unwound a small section of the film and positioned it under the microscope's lens.

'So what is it you're looking for?' Fletcher asked.

'Well, it's rather complicated,' the Doctor said, 'but I'm starting to suspect that something about the actual film stock itself is peculiar, and this is the best way to find out what's going on.' He looked through the microscope. 'Ah, interesting.'

'What is it, Doctor?' Ben asked. 'What do you see?'

'Well, nothing at the moment,' the Doctor admitted. 'Just a frame of exposed film emulsion. I wonder...'

He lifted his head, reached around to the base of the microscope and flicked a switch. A small lamp on the front of the instrument came on, illuminating the film the Doctor was studying. At first Ben thought the film was reflecting the light from the lamp, but then he realised that the bright gold glow was emanating from the film itself.

The Doctor bent down to look. 'My, my, this is interesting.' He turned the dial on the side of the microscope. 'When I decrease the magnification to the extent where I can see the picture on the frame, I see Mr Rochefort's character standing in a street. If I zoom in a little bit closer I can see the expression on his face moving, adjusting. And if I increase the magnification even more...' The Doctor stood up and gestured for Ben to take a look through the microscope. He did so, and was amazed by what he saw.

He found he could see into the chemical structure of the film. The layers of emulsion, dust, fingerprint grease and celluloid should have been motionless, but instead they were frantically swirling about in a whirlwind of chaos. As if conducting an animalistic mating ritual, fire-coloured sparks in a multitude of different sizes were dancing in patterns that seemed almost co-ordinated. Tiny golden globules, like the tops of jellyfish, glowed and shimmered. It was as if the very atoms of the film were alive. Perhaps they were.

'What's it doing?' Ben asked. 'I'm no expert, but surely it shouldn't be wriggling like that.'

'No Ben,' the Doctor said. 'It shouldn't. If you look closely you'll see that the film is indeed just a piece of celluloid with exposing emulsion on top, but another layer of chemical has been pasted on top of that, and that's what you're seeing move.'

Ben stared through the microscope's lens at the dazzling light-show and found that just watching the patterns and absorbing the colours was one of the most relaxing experiences he'd ever known. He felt in harmony with what he was seeing and felt his cares slipping away. He tried to increase the magnification, tried to see deeper and deeper into the chemical structure of the film, but found that the microscope was already on it's maximum setting. He looked at the sparks, at the flickers, at the glowing perfection of the sight, and realised that this sort of thing was not meant to be seen by human eyes.

'It's beautiful,' he heard himself saying. The spectacle was so perfect, so enthralling, that he felt saddened that humanity would never be able to achieve such a marvellous state of existence. He thought of the suffering, the injustice and the nightmares around the world, and felt ashamed of being human. All humanity did was cause pain, yet the sight he was witnessing now caused nothing but joy. He felt at ease, and knew that he wanted to be a part of what he was seeing.

'Let me see that,' Fletcher's voice said on the edge of Ben's consciousness.

'Come on, Ben,' the Doctor said. 'Let the detective take a look.'

Ben shook his head and continued to watch. Suddenly he was pulled away from the microscope and the white blandness of the forensics lab smashed back into his frame of vision like a colliding train.

'Oi!' he shouted angrily. 'What did you go and do that for?'

'What do you mean Ben?' the Doctor asked. You got a good look, didn't you?'

Ben shook his head, the memory of what he had seen starting to fade. 'I did, but... I could watch for ever, you know? Let me look again. Magic, that's the only way I can describe it. Magic.'

Fletcher barged his way over to the table. He slumped on to a stool and stared into the microscope. 'My God,' he said. 'What the hell is that?'

'What you're seeing,' the Doctor said, his voice grave, 'appears to be a life form of some sort. Tiny gelatinous creatures which clearly have a life of their own... unlike anything else I've seen before. In short, that film is alive.'

Fletcher began to laugh. 'Alive? Come on, Doctor. How can film be alive?'

'The actual film isn't,' the Doctor explained, 'but this life form certainly appears to be. It has entwined itself with the film, embedded itself into its chemical structure. It's as if the creatures are clinging on to the very fabric of the film and moulding the appearance of the image in the frames as they see fit.'

'You mean the creatures are intelligent?' Ben wondered.

'Either that, or they're being controlled somehow. Maybe our reel is just as much a final cut as the one we saw at De Sande's, and it's these creatures that make it never the same film twice.'

'I...' The Doctor and Ben waited for Fletcher to finish his sentence, but the words never came.

'Interesting, eh, Detective?' the Doctor said as he pulled him away from the microscope. Fletcher looked startled, bewildered. It was as if he was in a trance.

'Incredible,' was all he could say. 'When I... when I saw that, it was like... Everything I've ever wanted, all the power, all the control, everything. It all felt not just within my grasp but... I can't really explain it.'

'Let me try,' said the Doctor. 'When you look through that all your dreams are suddenly tangible. Everything you've ever wanted or hoped for seems to be present in that film and you get an overwhelming sense that this is the key to unleashing your potential, to fulfilling your destiny.'

Fletcher nodded. 'That's it. That's it exactly. Let me look at it again.'

He bent down to look through the microscope but the Doctor pulled him away before he could. 'I don't think that's a very good idea, do you? Whatever those creatures are, they want you to look. They're manipulating human emotions, driving you to support them in the belief that they are supporting you.

'I looked through that lens and saw perfection.' Fletcher was staring into space, almost in a trance. 'How can I look at the world in the same way again?'

'That's only what the film wants you to think,' the Doctor reassured him. 'You'll get over it in time, no doubt, but it shows how powerful this thing is. If the police won't ban the film we need to find some other way of stopping its release. There's no doubt there's some form of life on that film that's capable of advanced psychic control. Whatever its purpose, we can't allow it to manipulate humanity like this.'

'But Doctor,' Ben said. 'What if humanity wants to be manipulated? Maybe these creatures will make life better for everyone.'

The Doctor shook his head. 'Ben, in my experience open benevolence rarely occurs without some kind of hidden agenda. I wonder...'

He removed the film from under the microscope, wound it back into its reel and placed the lid back on the canister. After replacing the reel in his bag, he reached into his jacket pocket and took out a small glass vial. He looked around the lab for a cotton swab, found one, then unscrewed the vial lid and used the swab to dab some of the vial's contents on to a glass slide which he placed under the microscope lens.

He looked through the microscope, muttering to himself as he adjusted the magnification settings. 'Excellent,' he said, clearly very pleased with himself. 'Exactly as I suspected.'

He stood up and clasped his hands together, a thoughtful expression on his face. 'This is the first time I've had the chance to examine the blood sample I took from Mr Rochefort. That blood, too, appears to contain a life form almost identical in appearance to the ones we've just seen when we analysed the film frame. Whatever these creatures are they're part of the film, or at least this version of it, and they were part of Mr Rochefort's biology. All that remains to find out now is what these creatures are, who placed them in the film and why. How, and why, did they alter Rochefort's blood? Was he always like that and, if so, what was he? So many questions, but where to begin?'

'I say we go and find De Sande,' Ben suggested. 'Let's have words, give him a piece of our mind and tell him what we know. He's the one behind all this. He's the one who'll know the truth.'

'No,' said the Doctor. 'Not yet. I'd quite like to see how things play out for a while. No one knows how much we've discovered. Let's play our cards close to our chest and not reveal our true hand until later in the game.'

'I think I'm going home,' Fletcher whispered. Ben wasn't used to hearing him speak with no aggressive undercurrent. 'I need a lie-down.'

The Doctor looked concerned. 'I think you're right. That film's affected you more than you realise.' He turned to Ben. 'How are you feeling?'

Ben gestured to Fletcher. 'Fair enough, I suppose. Is it OK if I take one last look at the film before we go?'

The Doctor shook his head and zipped up the sports bag. 'No, I don't think that would be very wise, do you? I don't think either of you looked at it long enough for it to have any lasting effect, but who knows what kind of hypnosis or brainwashing long-term exposure could cause. No, this film is staying in the bag. Whatever's going on, I can sense that it's evil.' His voice dropped to a cold whisper. 'And evil must be fought.'

Chapter Fifteen

It was early morning, and a thin mist was in the air around Victory Van Owen Park. The Doctor and Ben sat on a bench at the edge of the park, watching the city slowly come to life. The traffic was getting heavier, lights were flickering on in houses as the world began to wake up and the distant noise of car radios started to drift through the air.

It was a peaceful time, although it still seemed chaotic and unfriendly compared to the joy Ben had felt while looking at the film last night.

'Danish pastry?' offered the Doctor. 'They're very good, although I don't think they're made in Denmark.'

Ben smiled and took one of the pastries from the packet. 'So how long do we have to sit here then?'

Another enigmatic grin spread across the Doctor's face. 'Oh, not long now, I would have thought. If Detective Fletcher wasn't mistaken about Wallis's daily routine, that is.'

After their visit to the labs, the detective had returned home to freshen up and get some sleep. He had told the Doctor he'd be in touch soon, but the Doctor had advised him to leave matters for the moment.

'Best to keep him clear for a while,' the Doctor had said. 'It's for his own safety.'

Ben glanced at his watch. Almost seven o'clock. 'I'm worried about Polly. She didn't go back to the hotel last night.'

The Doctor looked down at the large purple rose on his jacket lapel and sniffed it, then adjusted its petals. Ben had told him that it was out of place, that it looked like it should squirt water and made him look like even more of a clown than he usually did, but he hadn't listened. Not feeling remotely self-conscious, he'd told Ben that he needed to make sure people would see it, so Ben had let the subject drop.

The Doctor shoved the pastry packet into a nearby rubbish bin then brushed the crumbs off the front of his jacket. 'Oh, I shouldn't worry about her,' he said, waving his hand dismissively. 'She did leave a note, and she's certainly a resourceful girl. No doubt she made some friends in the bar or something. I'm sure she can look after herself, so we'll wait until tomorrow before sending out a search party, yes?'

Ben nodded in agreement, but in his heart he was still concerned for Polly's safety.

After several minutes, he spotted a figure emerging from the morning mist. A tall man marched decisively along the path that bisected the park, shoulders hunched and his right hand holding a long lead on the end of which was a small chihuahua. As the man got closer the Doctor stood up and began to walk towards him. Ben hurried to catch up with his friend and saw a look of total pain on the man's face.

'Good morning, Captain Wallis!' the Doctor said. 'What a surprise to see you here!'

'Doctor,' Wallis said, tipping his hat. He continued down the path without stopping, and the Doctor began to walk with him. Ben stayed a few paces behind them, listening to their conversation but not wanting to get involved.

'I was wondering,' the Doctor said, 'if you could answer a couple of questions that have occurred to me over the last day or two.'

Wallis's despairing face showed that he was clearly not in the mood for dealing with the Doctor. 'If you need to speak to me make an appointment with my secretary.'

The Doctor moved in front of Wallis so that he was walking backwards and facing him.

Ben noticed the policeman's angry expression suddenly fall away to be replaced with a look of confusion as he saw the rose in the Doctor's lapel.

The Doctor smiled and sniffed the flower's aroma. 'Lovely

things, roses. Don't you agree?' He spun round so that he was walking forward again, and returned to his position by Wallis's side.

'You're not part of the group,' Wallis said after a long pause, as if he had been considering his words carefully.

'No, but I'm doing my best. You see, Captain, we're both rather keen to join FOCAL ourselves and were hoping you might be able to arrange membership for us.'

'Don't be ridiculous. Now just go away, will you?' Wallis's voice rose slightly as his anger with the Doctor increased. 'We don't want you as a member.' His chihuahua barked as if in agreement and Ben noticed it growling at him, showing a disgusting row of biscuit-crumb-filled teeth.

'Are you sure?' the Doctor said. 'You see, I've learnt rather a lot about the organisation, hence my desire to join. More than is good for me, I shouldn't wonder.'

Heavy creases settled across Wallis's forehead as he squinted at the Doctor. 'What are you talking about?' he asked.

'Oh, I don't know,' the Doctor said loudly, spinning slightly as he walked like a child splashing through puddles. 'How about the Reitman murder? You know, the one that left your organisation rather better off than it had been before.'

'You don't still think Robert was innocent, do you?' Wallis said, fuming. 'Whether you like it or not, he's the goddamn killer. If you think he killed Reitman to help FOCAL... I can assure you there's no way he would have been allowed anywhere near the organisation while I walk this Earth. Now, Doctor, I've had enough of your ridiculous theories. Please, just leave me alone and let me walk my dog in peace!'

The Doctor shook his head. 'Actually, I don't think I will. At least not until you become more helpful.'

Wallis scowled. 'Do you want me to arrest you for harassing a police officer?'

'Oh no,' the Doctor said, as if refusing the last of the roast potatoes, 'that won't be necessary. All I want is for you to let Ben and myself join FOCAL.'

The expression on Wallis's face was priceless. 'You've no evidence of any wrongdoing, and even if you had you can't blackmail us into letting you join. '

The Doctor's face was an expression of hurt. 'I'm just trying to suggest ways in which our membership might be mutually beneficial. I've been doing my research and I think it sounds a fine organisation. If you really did have nothing to do with the murder, then you won't have anything to hide.'

'Leave me alone.'

'No.'

A stalemate silence. And then: 'OK, Doctor,' Wallis said with a heavy sigh. 'I'll tell you what, I'm meeting with my associates from the organisation this evening. I'll bring the subject up with the others and we'll see what they say. However, I'll only do this on one condition.'

The Doctor's interest was piqued. 'Oh?'

'That if your membership is turned down you make a promise never to come within fifty feet of me ever again.'

The Doctor smiled. 'If that's what it takes, Captain, then you have my word.'

Chapter Sixteen

Dusk was setting in as the Doctor and Ben sat in the Doctor's rental car, parked a few doors away, and on the other side of the street, from Wallis's house.

'Is he ever going to leave?' Ben sighed. They'd been watching the house for two hours since Wallis had returned from work and the cop still hadn't emerged. 'We could be looking for Polly, you know.'

'She's probably gone back to the hotel by now. Besides, I've left a message. She'll know what we're up to. I've asked Fletcher to keep an eye out for her, too. Don't worry, I'm sure she'll be fine.'

Ben was about to argue when he heard the sound of a door slamming. He looked across the road to see Wallis leaving his house and marching down the driveway towards his car.

The Doctor and Ben instinctively ducked to make sure he couldn't see them then, as Wallis's car pulled away, the Doctor started his own vehicle and began a cautious pursuit.

'Keep your eyes open, Ben,' he said. 'We mustn't lose him, but we can't get too close in case he sees us and realises he's being followed.'

Wallis's journey through the Californian countryside seemed to take for ever. After they'd been travelling for over an hour Ben started to get restless.

'Are you sure this is right?' he wondered. 'Why hold a meeting so far away? Maybe the FOCAL thing's been cancelled, maybe he's made other plans.'

'Maybe,' said the Doctor, 'but I think it's more that they're trying to keep the meeting as secret as possible. We'll see, anyway.'

Eventually Wallis drove up a long path leading to a magnificent castle surrounded by palatial gardens, fountains and wildlife, then stopped his car.

'What is this place?' Ben wondered as the Doctor parked some distance back from Wallis, making sure they were safely concealed by the darkness.

The Doctor and Ben followed the policeman as he got out of his car and walked through an imposing archway at the front of the castle. They found themselves inside a luxuriously decorated entrance hall. The walls were made from stone in various pastel colours and were covered in elaborate classically styled marble and corniced architecture tinted with gold. Around the edges of the hall was a collection of statues, paintings and art treasures. Whoever owned this place certainly had a great deal of money.

They tried to keep back to conceal their presence, and followed Wallis as he walked through a side door off the hall that led to a large auditorium which looked as though it might once have been a theatre. Where there would have been seats there were now just deep-pile red carpets on which stood a crowd of people, presumably other members of FOCAL, enjoying food and drink from the tables scattered around the edges of the room. It looked as though there were about a hundred men and women, of various ages though Ben seemed to be one of the youngest among them. He and the Doctor tried to keep to the sides of the auditorium, staying in the shadows to make sure they weren't conspicuous.

'Well, well,' whispered the Doctor as he looked around, clearly impressed. 'Some of the most influential people in the motion picture industry are here it seems.'

'We'll stick out even more then,' Ben grumbled.

They walked towards one corner of the auditorium where a cluster of people appeared to be congregating. In the centre of the crowd stood Leonard De Sande, cigar in one hand and champagne glass in another.

'What's he doing here?' Ben wondered.

The Doctor cleared his throat then, much to the consternation of those around De Sande, pushed his way to the middle of the crowd and marched straight up to the director.

'Mr De Sande!' the Doctor exclaimed, a broad grin on his face. 'Surprise!'

De Sande's face whitened and he looked at him with an accusing stare. 'Doctor?' he said. 'What the hell are you doing here? Security!'

'That won't be necessary,' the Doctor reassured him. 'I'm not here to cause trouble. We just want to join FOCAL, that's all. Surely Captain Wallis told you we'd been asking to join?'

De Sande shook his head. 'He didn't say a word. I didn't think you two got on.'

The Doctor smiled. 'Well, perhaps that's why he didn't mention it.'

A puzzled smile crossed De Sande's face. 'I wish I could believe you, Doctor.'

'De Sande,' the Doctor insisted, 'you made the film, you know of its power better than anyone. Please, we've seen the film. We can see how important it is, how it's going to lead to the start of something rather special indeed. All we want is to be a part of that. To be a part of the future.'

Having temporarily excused himself from the Doctor's company, De Sande hurried over to a corner of the auditorium where Wallis stood speaking to one of the other guests.

'Charles,' De Sande said. 'Have you seen who's here?'

Wallis shook his head. 'Evening, Leonard. Who are you talking about?'

De Sande pointed to the centre of the auditorium where the Doctor and Ben were waiting. 'There. They claim you said you'd look into letting them join.'

'My God,' Wallis said, his face white. 'I'll kill them.'

'Relax,' said De Sande, trying to reassure his friend. 'Best to have them where we can keep an eye on them, eh? If they want to be Initiates, let them. Once they're partnered with the creatures we'll have full control over them. We'll be able to keep track of them at all times, making sure they do nothing to jeopardise the plan.'

Wallis shook his head. 'I don't like this idea, Leonard. I really don't like it.'

De Sande smiled. 'Relax. It'll be fine.'

Wallis shook his head again and stormed off. 'I need to phone the station to check on things. I'll speak to you later.'

'Where did De Sande go?' Ben wondered, looking around the auditorium.

'I'm here,' De Sande said, tapping Ben on the shoulder. He turned to the Doctor and a resigned smile crossed his face. 'I've made a decision. While turning up here unannounced is not exactly approved of, you're here now and there's very little we can do about it. So I've decided we might as well let you join. You have a keen mind. Maybe you could be benefit from our teachings.'

The Doctor smiled. 'Thank you, Mr De Sande. I'm sure we will gain a great deal from being members.' He pointed to a group of robed figures near De Sande. 'So tell me, who are your friends?'

'FOCAL is a charitable organisation,' the director explained, 'but it's also a religious one. While not a religion in ourselves, we have certain beliefs about the universe, about the way life works, and about how we should live, and these honourable people have dedicated their lives to making sure we stick to the rules we've made for ourselves.'

'Well, I'm very pleased to meet you,' the Doctor said to De Sande's friends. They nodded their hood-concealed heads before stepping back into the shadows of the room.

De Sande smiled. 'Now, before we begin the Initiation I must introduce you to Brother Reinert. He's a great teacher and will explain more about our beliefs and answer any questions you may have on our faith. We have a small group of monks from various orders working in the castle. Between them they formed our belief system and are living here until our work is complete. FOCAL was created from a collusion of minds, monks and money, and without any of us trying we've reached a stage where we're almost ready to stop hiding... to end our secrecy. The monks are helping us prepare for that day, as you'll see shortly.'

De Sande led the Doctor and Ben over to one wall of the auditorium where gold-framed paintings in a long line were being observed by various members of the crowd. He walked up to a short old man with a shaved crop of white hair and a long, sloping face who was standing peacefully in front of one of the paintings, a flickering candle held in front of his flowing red robes.

'Brother Reinert?' De Sande said gently. 'I'd like you to meet the Doctor and Ben. They're going to be initiated tonight.'

The old man turned to the Doctor and smiled. 'I can see,' he said. 'I can see all sorts of turmoil and torment within your eyes.' He raised a hand so that its palm was facing towards the Doctor. 'Be at peace,' he whispered. 'You're amongst friends now.'

'Why thank you,' the Doctor said in a bemused tone. 'It's a pleasure to meet you too.'

'Brother Reinert is our spiritual leader,' De Sande explained. 'He'll try to encourage you to stick to a very defined system of morals and values. I suppose you could say it's less of a religion and more the promotion of a guideline which, if followed, will lead an individual to enjoy a more satisfying life. FOCAL started out in the 1890s as an organisation dedicated to raising money for the less privileged, and it is that spirit, along with the other beliefs of our founders, that Brother Reinert makes sure we never forget. These beliefs are what makes FOCAL what it is, and I hope that once you learn more about them you two will find it easy to adopt our ways for yourselves.'

'We have some time before the ceremony,' Brother Reinert said. 'Would you two like a quick tour of the castle?' He glanced over to De Sande, who nodded his head in endorsement.

'That sounds wonderful,' the Doctor said. 'Thank you.'

Reinert looked up at the painting, placed the candle he was holding in front of it, then bowed his head in prayer before marching towards a door at the side of the auditorium. 'Come along then,' he called back. 'We haven't got all night.'

The door had led to a small library, and at the end of that Ben had expected to find a chapel, or a museum, or something else consistent with what they had seen so far.

Instead they came to a vast cavern carved out of rock. Stalactites pointed precariously at them and the sound of distant rainwater echoed around the cave. The door from the library led on to a dangerous flight of stone steps that appeared to have been carved out of the rock. An unsafe-looking metal handrail was all that prevented anyone who slipped on the steps from meeting an early grave at the bottom of the cavern.

'After you,' the Doctor said politely to Reinert, gesturing for the old man to step forward. Reinert did so, then reached for one of the fire torches on the wall of the cavern.

'That's a bit OTT isn't it?' Ben said. 'I'm sure De Sande will have a proper flashlight in there if you ask him nicely.'

Reinert put his index finger on his lip to quieten him. 'I take fire down here because everyone who has ever been down here has taken fire. It may give us light, but it also keeps us safe and keeps us warm. A flashlight would only give light.'

Fair enough, thought Ben.

Reinert slowly began to make his way down the stairs and the Doctor and Ben followed cautiously behind him.

Although it hadn't been visible from the top of the steps, as the party descended deeper into the cavern it became clear that the cave contained another chamber in its walls.

'In here,' Reinert said, leading them into the chamber. It had been carved out of the rock and exotic rugs were scattered across the floor to cover the cold stone underneath. The room was lined with more fantastic paintings and statues. De Sande's private collection, Ben assumed. They must have been a nightmare to move down here.

'All fakes,' the Doctor whispered, a conspiratorial smile on his face.

'Through here are the screening rooms,' Reinert said. 'They actually connect to a storage hut in the car park, and most of the people who visit access them through that rather than the more precarious route we just took. I prefer to go this way round, though, as we are not only shielded from the elements but also get the chance to gaze at the magnificent beauty of the inside of the hill this castle has been built on.'

'I hadn't heard of any castles in California,' sighed Ben.

Brother Reinert had a twinkle in his eye. 'We try not to publicise this place's existence too much. FOCAL values its privacy, and we have to respect Mr De Sande's wishes. If he hadn't stepped in a couple of years ago when we were going through some rather serious financial trouble I doubt we'd still be here today, so the very least we can do is respect his wishes. Mr De Sande and the other chosen leaders want FOCAL to step into the public limelight soon, to convert as many people as possible to the Way of Light.'

'Ah yes,' the Doctor said. 'The Way of Light. I must say I'm rather keen to learn more about that.'

'It's the path we try to encourage all our members to follow. We don't give our organisation a formal religious name beyond "the Friends", but we have given a name to our doctrine. Learn about the horror in the world, learn what causes it, then turn your back on those causes and light will fill your soul. That, Doctor, is the Way of Light. You really should try to follow it, you know. You can't imagine how it can enrich a life.'

'So it seems,' the Doctor said. 'You certainly have a lot of supporters.'

Brother Reinert walked over to a small wooden door, then took a large iron key from his robes and slid it into the keyhole. A lock clicked and the door creaked open. Reinert stepped through, the Doctor and Ben following.

The familiar juddering sound of a film projector filled the dark room. It was a tiny cinema with five rows of seats facing a small screen. In the seats sat a group of children, and enough light from the projector reflected off the screen on to their faces for Ben to see that most of them were watching the film with their mouths wide open, enchanted by the spectacle before them.

'What are they watching?' whispered the Doctor.

Brother Reinert pointed to the screen. A woman was running along a beach, images, apparently in her mind, flashing on to the screen. A recap of her life, passing before her eyes. An image of her stroking a pet Labrador, an image of her being beaten by a man with tears streaming down his face, an image of her swimming in bank notes. The final image appeared and it was of her standing helplessly as her belongings were repossessed. A newspaper headline, DEPRESSION HITS, was superimposed over the woman lying on her porch in tears, a knife hovering above her wrists. The film then cut back to her standing alone on the beach. She smiled, walked off into a sunset, then the credits rolled.

The lights in the room went up and a monk who had been chaperoning the children began telling them to behave as they stood up.

'What was that all about?' Ben asked, as the monk led the children out of the screening room.

'I believe it's about education,' the Doctor said.

Reinert looked impressed. 'Go on,' he said.

'Your beliefs are based around light, and around hope springing from sadness, are they not?'

Reinert nodded. 'Indeed. We believe that for every period of sadness the human soul endures it will eventually experience an equal amount of happiness. However, if a person brings that happiness on themselves, they will experience twice as much sadness. We believe death, destruction and pain are good things, for through them comes repentance, an understanding of oneself and a closeness to the Way of Light - a purity of soul that will let any person be freed from worry.'

'And this is what you're indoctrinating those kids with?' asked Ben.

'No,' said Reinert. 'We take the most gifted and mature children from local schools and screen films they might not otherwise have the opportunity to see. That picture you saw just then, about the woman who had everything, lost it, then realised she was happier than money had ever made her, was made by one of our members. It's a classic, and I guarantee every child in there came out of the experience richer. If it wasn't for us, all they would ever be shown would be *Bambi*. If they take a message from the film, then all the better, but we're mainly doing it just to give them something to think about.'

'But why?' the Doctor said. 'Why go to so much trouble?'

Brother Reinert looked confused, as if the Doctor had just asked a ridiculous question. 'Because we want people to find peace in themselves of course, we want them to find the Way of Light. We want to help them.'

'And you do so by spreading your message through movies,' the Doctor said, his index finger tapping his bottom lip. 'How interesting. I do hope we're not giving those children nightmares.'

Reinert began to lead the Doctor and Ben back the way they had come, up the long stone staircase that led back to the auditorium.

'Doctor,' Reinert said. 'The films may contain large amounts of terror and unpleasantness, but the end message is always positive and we would never show the children anything unsuitable. If any child is upset they are sent straight home. We care, and we're only trying to help, after all. If they're not enjoying the experience, there's really no point in us wasting our funds on them. No, everyone who comes here does so voluntarily, and most of the children appreciate the benefits they get from the experience.'

'I see,' the Doctor said. 'So, out of interest, would you let them watch *Dying in the Sun*?'

Reinert shook his head. 'No, that's different. A simple reel of film like most pictures our members make is fair enough, but Mr De Sande's latest opus... It's so realistic, so vivid. Such a perfect vehicle for our message that I don't think the children are quite ready for it.'

'Very wise,' said the Doctor. 'Though I hope they're not missing out. It's such a marvellous picture.'

Reinert smiled at the Doctor's words. 'Everyone here is very pleased with *Dying in the Sun*. It's been a most satisfactory project.'

'So it's basically a propaganda film for our organisation?' Ben asked

Reinert shook his head. 'I wouldn't say propaganda, just that it encourages the sort of approach to life that we endorse. If people follow the lifestyle encouraged by the film, their lives will no doubt be enriched beyond their imaginations. This film will improve more lives than any other motion picture in history, mark my words.'

The Doctor nodded. 'It works on so many levels, too. Technologically alone, it's something of a marvel. I don't suppose you know how they did some of those effects, do you?'

Reinert shook his head. 'I simply provided spiritual guidance to Paul Roth while he was writing the script, then gave my feedback on the finished film. I'm afraid religion, not technology, is my forte.'

'Well, that's everything I think,' he said as they reached the top of the stairs. 'If you have any more questions, feel free to ask.'

'Thank you,' the Doctor said, shaking Reinert's hand. 'It has been a most fascinating tour.'

He and Ben walked back into the main room.

'Excuse me,' the Doctor said to a bored-looking waiter who was standing in a corner holding a drinks tray. 'Have you seen Paul Roth around, perchance?'

The waiter nodded and pointed him in the direction of a scrawny little man with scruffy straw-coloured hair and tiny round glasses that perched precariously on the end of his long, beaky nose. The man was on his own and seemed to be scrutinising a pile of bread rolls on a table, trying to decide whether to take one or not. The Doctor hurried over to him and tapped him on the shoulder.

'Mr Roth?' he said as the man turned round. 'I'm sorry to interrupt, but I was wondering if I might have a few words. I'm the Doctor, I'm new here.'

At first Roth looked confused, and then a flash of recognition crossed his face and he smiled slightly. 'Oh yes, the Initiates. How are you finding things tonight?'

'Oh very good, very good. Tell me, is it true you're the writer of *Dying in the Sun*?'

Roth waved a hand in the Doctor's direction in a gesture of false modesty. 'I am, yes,' he said. 'Have you seen it yet?'

'I have. It's most impressive. Tell me, how did you come up with the idea for the film?'

Roth shrugged. 'It wasn't that complicated really. So much of the film is in the direction, so much was improvised. It's all down to Leonard really. I just provided a frame for him to work within. We had to have a story that promoted FOCAL, that would inspire others to go out and live a pure life dedicated to helping others through personal gain. The "man in hell" concept came to me quite easily, to be honest.'

The Doctor looked content with this answer. 'I see. So you're something of an expert on FOCAL's religious persuasions?'

Roth let out a high-pitched chuckle. 'Well, I hear as much as the rest of us do and follow Brother Reinert's instructions, but not as much as De Sande would like. Very few of us do. I mean, come on, let's face it... Knowing De Sande, knowing half the others here... it's all networking, isn't it? I'm quite prepared to change my religion if it means I skip a few rungs on the Hollywood ladder, if you know what I mean. I'm sure you've noticed that expertise in our religious beliefs is hardly a prerequisite for joining this lot.'

The Doctor let out a false laugh and jokingly nudged Roth in the ribs with his elbow. 'Indeed, Mr Roth. Indeed.'

Ben was about to ask the Doctor how much longer he was going to spend hobnobbing with the Hollywood brass when his attention was grabbed by the noise of raised voices coming from the back of the auditorium. He and the Doctor, and most of the other people in the room, turned to find out what was going on and saw Captain Wallis standing in front of De Sande waving a white piece of paper in the air.

'Excuse me,' the Doctor said to Roth, before scurrying off in De Sande's direction. Ben followed and soon they were within earshot of De Sande's ranting.

'How can he be alive?' the director yelled. 'What the hell has happened here?'

Wallis seemed to notice people looking at them and fell silent. De Sande turned to the crowd, took a deep breath, then straightened his tuxedo and stormed off towards the front of the room. A raised stage area contained a circular stone stage and a lectern. De Sande hurried behind the lectern, switched on the microphone and cleared his throat.

'Lights please,' he called. The moment he'd spoken the crowd silenced and the lights dimmed. A spotlight burst on to the stage, simultaneously illuminating De Sande's face and casting deep shadows across it. A brief silence, and then he began.

'My friends,' he said gravely. 'I'm afraid I have to interrupt the evening's festivities to bring you some terrible news that our friend in the LAPD has just brought to my attention. It is my sad duty to report a terrible incident, one that I'm sure will cause great sadness to all our members. We assumed he had gone on vacation, but today forensic scientists matched the dental records from a body found in a local arson attack to Martin Revere.' The crowd gasped and began to murmur among themselves.

De Sande continued his announcement. 'The full details of what occurred are still unclear, but it does seem as if he was murdered by the same person who killed Harold Reitman – a madman who was believed to have been killed in the arson attack until today's results proved that the body isn't his, that the killer is still very much alive and at large. This is a great tragedy, and one which we must not let get in the way of our work. Martin would want us to move on, to keep pursuing those goals that we all know are so important. But we must be wary. It seems that someone has a grudge against our organisation for some unfathomable reason, and thus it is imperative that we keep our guard up. Be strong and be brave. I have assurances from Captain Wallis that everything possible is being done to catch this madman before he hurts us any more. And now, let us mourn this sombre news and continue with the evening's discussions.' He glanced at his watch. 'The Initiation will take place in thirty minutes.'

He stepped down from the stage and the lighting in the auditorium returned to normal.

'Who's Revere?' the Doctor asked, sidling up to De Sande.

'Someone who should never have got involved with this bastard,' a voice said from the shadows. A glamorous girl with shoulder-length brown hair and a face made up so well that she glowed stepped into the light.

'Rachel!' De Sande said. 'What are you doing here?'

'Shut the hell up, Leonard. I heard what you just said. What are you trying to pull with all that poor Martin stuff? You don't give a damn that he's dead.'

'Rachel!' De Sande said in a patronising tone. 'You're upset. You shouldn't be here. Charles said you were told this morning about Martin's death. We thought you'd stay at home tonight.'

'You're a bastard, De Sande. Martin was a million times the man you are and he deserved better than to get caught up in your stupid little games. If he hadn't started running your little errands he'd never have got out of his depth with that punk Chate.'

'Rachel, I...'

'Yeah, that's right. I know all about your little deal with Martin.'

'What are you talking about?' sighed De Sande. 'I had no deal with Martin.'

'Oh yeah?' Rachel sneered. 'No deal saying that if he offs Chate you get Wallis to cut your brother free from the caboose. He told me all about it which means that in my book, as you were the one who sent Martin to find Chate, you were the one who killed him.'

'You're wrong, Rachel,' De Sande insisted.

The expression on Rachel's face was pure anger. 'Liar,' she muttered, before throwing her drink at De Sande and running out of the room.

Ben glanced at the wine-soaked De Sande and decided to go after the woman. He saw her darting up a flight of stairs and followed her into a plush boudoir where she collapsed on a large four-poster bed, crying into a pillow.

'Easy,' Ben said, cautiously sitting next to her on the bed. 'Don't cry, you'll be OK.'

Rachel looked up, confused. 'Who are you?' she asked.

'My name's Ben. I'm new here.'

A silence followed, one that Ben found strangely comfortable.

'So had you been married long?' he asked eventually.

Rachel shrugged. 'Three years, give or take.'

'And you loved him?'

She nodded. 'I guess so. As much as any couple in LA at least.'

'I'm sorry,' Ben said softly.

'It's not your fault,' Rachel said bitterly. 'It's the fault of Leonard De Sande. Him and that Wallis guy. They let Chate live to kill my Martin. They should have cut him down when they wanted to originally.'

'What do you mean?' asked Ben.

She waved an arm half-heartedly around the room. 'Me and Martin came here last week sometime. He left me in here to sleep but I weren't tired. I went downstairs and heard him, Leonard and that Wallis guy talking. They didn't see me, but I got the gist of what was going on.'

'Which was?'

'They were deciding whether to kill this Chate guy or not. They seemed mighty displeased with him. I think he'd seen something he shouldn't have.'

'What do you mean? What did he see?'

'I dunno.' Rachel pouted her bottom lip. 'They kept mentioning murder. I guess Wallis must have killed someone or something. The cop didn't want to kill Chate, but did say they should arrange to have Chate locked up. Set him up as a murderer, then lock him up and throw away the key. Wallis is close buddies with the DA, so he could stop Chate from getting the death penalty.'

'Bloody hell,' Ben said, 'the Doctor's going to love this.'

Rachel looked at Ben sternly. 'Be careful, yeah? I never liked De Sande, and now Martin's dead... I just wanted to confront him, to let him know that I was unhappy.'

Ben nodded. 'Don't worry, love, I can keep my trap shut.'

This made Rachel chuckle, and as she did so she took Ben's hand in hers and squeezed it. 'Look, you'd better get back to the party. I've said my piece now.'

Ben let go of her hand and stood up. 'Will you be OK?' he asked.

Rachel nodded. 'I'm fine, just give me a few minutes. I'm getting out of here before the ceremony. I can't stand this place any more. Martin used to bring me along for the socialising, but I'm not exactly on good terms with his friends. Anyway, it's been nice meeting you, Ben.'

Ben smiled. 'It's been nice to meet you too.'

Chapter Seventeen

Ben went back downstairs to the FOCAL gathering and found the Doctor talking to De Sande, who appeared to have changed into a different tuxedo from the one Rachel had thrown her drink over.

'Doctor,' Ben said, 'can I have a word?'

'Ah, Ben!' De Sande said. 'How is Mrs Revere?'

'She's fine,' Ben replied, trying to sound as friendly as possible.

'I'm sorry,' De Sande said. 'That woman is quite upset at the moment. Prone to rambling , I'm afraid.'

'Don't worry,' Ben said. 'She wasn't saying much at all when I saw her.'

De Sande appeared to relax. 'That's how it should be,' he said solemnly. 'She needs all the rest she can get.'

Ben nodded, and pulled the Doctor aside on the pretext of wanting to show him one of the paintings at the edge of the auditorium. He described what Rachel had told him, and the Doctor was clearly impressed with his friend's findings.

'There's only one thing to do now,' the Doctor said. 'Let's ask Wallis what really went on that night.'

'Doctor, are you sure that's wise? They're holding a ceremony or something in a minute. Shouldn't we wait until later, or until the morning?'

The Doctor looked unfazed. 'Oh no, no time like the present.'

He marched over to another corner of the auditorium where Wallis was sitting in front of a buffet table chatting to a group of businessmen, explaining the reasons for the recent drop in the city's crime rate.

The Doctor crept up close behind him.

'Hello, Captain Wallis,' he said in the policeman's ear. Wallis spun around, clasping his chest.

'Don't do that,' he said angrily. 'You scared the life out of me!'

'Oh, I'm sorry,' the Doctor said, pouring himself a glass of bright red punch. 'I hope there's still some left.'

Wallis looked uneasy. He'd blatantly been avoiding the Doctor all night. He stuttered, trying to find something to say that would disguise his clear dislike for the two newcomers. He waved away the men he was talking to, then led the Doctor aside. 'So tell me,' he asked. 'How are you finding FOCAL?'

The Doctor ignored Wallis's words. 'You must be relieved to learn your son is still alive, Captain.'

Wallis scowled. 'It's certainly unexpected.'

'Indeed,' agreed the Doctor, 'though I would expect you to be a little more pleased with the news.'

'As you know,' Wallis said, shrugging, 'I don't get on with that man, and I also don't think it's appropriate to go showing my emotions off in public.'

'Of course,' the Doctor said. 'I understand.' He looked down and began examining the food on the table intently, as if searching for a clue in the quiche. 'Ah,' he said finally, picking up a bread roll. 'Here we are.'

He began to munch noisily on the roll, swallowed a mouthful, then washed it down with a swig of punch.

'So go on, then,' Wallis said. 'How are you finding us?'

'Oh, it's a very interesting set-up you've got here. You all seem very friendly... I can't quite believe what Mr De Sande was saying, that the man who killed your friend holds a grudge against your organisation? Tell me, what exactly did he mean by that? You claim Chate's the killer. Do you really think your own son has a vendetta against your organisation? Or is it just you he dislikes?'

Wallis sighed, then shook his head. 'Who knows?'

'But aren't you eager to learn which it is?'

The policeman shrugged. 'Doctor, I'm just going to keep doing my job. It's all I can do if I want to stay safe. Getting too worried about my lunatic son will only end with me going down the same path. No, Doctor, there's one thing you learn when you serve the LAPD for twenty-five years, and that's to keep your head above water, stay away from places you really don't want to go to and to keep telling everyone else what they want to hear.'

'Oh really?' the Doctor said, smiling. 'And what is it that I want to hear?'

Wallis turned and stared up at a painting on a wall. 'I didn't kill Revere, if that's what you think.'

The Doctor peered round to look at the expression on his face. 'No, you didn't, did you?' he said, intrigued.

Smiling, the Doctor began to rub his hands together. He rolled his eyes skyward, clearly connecting the pieces of the puzzle in his mind. 'My, my, this is interesting. For all your bluster about Chate, for all your accusations, I don't think you ever believed he was the killer. But now... He's the only one who could have murdered Revere, and the very prospect of this has knocked your world out of balance. Everything you thought you knew was wrong, as they say.'

Wallis turned to face the Doctor and Ben, fire in his eyes, anger bubbling up through his voice. 'No,' he said quietly. 'Robert can't have been the killer.'

The Doctor nodded his head and backed away slightly. 'And that, Captain Wallis, is all I needed to hear.'

Wallis looked perplexed as the Doctor continued his explanation.

'You don't believe Chate could kill, thus you can't believe he killed Reitman, and my theory still stands. You did it, didn't you? You killed Harold?'

Wallis lashed out and grabbed the Doctor's coat, pulling the smaller man towards him. He threw out his fist, connecting it to the Doctor's face with an unpleasant crack. The Doctor sprawled to the floor, blood dripping from his nose.

'Oi!' Ben said, leaping to his friend's defence. He tried to punch Wallis himself, but the older man, more agile than his appearance implied, was too quick. He grabbed Ben's arm mid-punch and twisted it round in an old police hold.

'This is my fight,' he growled. 'I'm sure the Doctor can do without your help.'

Ben struggled to escape his grip but found his efforts were futile. Lack of blood numbed his arm, and when Wallis finally dropped him to the floor a few moments passed before the pain receded enough for him to be able to sit up. 'Now shut up and get ready,' the policeman said. Your Initiation is about to begin. Something tells me you'll be a bit less confrontational after that.'

Wallis walked off into the crowd, ignoring the startled onlookers who had noticed the brawl. The Doctor was sitting up, dabbing his nose with his handkerchief. 'Oh my,' he said. 'I seemed to hit a nerve there.'

'Come on, Doctor,' Ben said. 'Let's teach him a lesson. That was well out of order!'

The Doctor shook his head. 'No no, Ben. There's no need to make the situation any worse. I have all the proof I need of what happened to poor Harold.'

'You sure you're OK, Doctor?' Ben said as he stood up. 'That bloke packs quite a punch.'

'And I've got quite a thick skin.' The Doctor grinned. 'I'm fine. Come on, I think I want a few more words with our sponsor.'

At one end of the auditorium was a large stone podium with small holes into which a group of people dressed in the same type of robes as Brother Reinert were busy slotting candles.

De Sande's mighty form stood over the podium watching the careful operation, his eyes seemingly transfixed by the flames.

'Mr De Sande?' the Doctor said quietly as he moved to stand beside the director. 'I just wanted to say thank you for giving us the benefit of the doubt tonight. I had no idea our organisation made such a... "unique" contribution to the welfare of this city.'

A small smile crept across De Sande's face, revealing his famous golden front tooth. 'I'm very glad of that,' he said.

The Doctor paused, looking for the right words. When he spoke, his voice was a reverential whisper. 'I don't believe Robert Chate killed Harold Reitman.'

De Sande shook his head and sighed. 'Charles warned me you were rather obsessed with this subject. What the devil has he been feeding you this time?'

'I believe Mr Wallis knows his son didn't kill Harold. He knows this because *he* was the killer.'

De Sande's face was cold and expressionless, like a poker player keeping his cards close to his chest. 'You told the police you didn't see anything. What makes you think such things? Charles is one of my oldest friends. I know you two don't get on, but to accuse him of being a murderer? Come on, Doctor!' The director shook his head and took a deep breath. 'Anyway, whether Chate did or did not kill Reitman is irrelevant now. He's made his bed by killing Revere. The police want him for double homicide. He's dead even if he only goes down for one.'

'Do you really think he killed Revere?'

De Sande's voice contained little emotion. 'No one else could have. Martin's body was found in the wreckage of Chate's apartment, Chate was seen going in there, then no sign of Chate... He has to be the killer. Besides, he seems the sort who would be capable of that kind of thing. Yeah, he had a killing streak, all right. Ruthless, dangerous. You wouldn't want to cross him, you know? We should have dealt with him when we had the chance. We shouldn't have let him go like that.'

One of the robed men sidled up to De Sande and tugged on the sleeve of his tuxedo. 'We're ready,' the man rasped, his head bowed. 'It's time.'

All the holes in the podium were now filled with burning candles. The robed group stood back and the auditorium filled with silence.

De Sande moved to the front of the room and held his arms out as one of the monks draped a long red robe over him. A gong sounded and the lights dimmed the room so that only the podium was illuminated.

De Sande stepped forward into the spotlight and began his speech.

'It's been a poignant evening, so far,' he said, 'and now I'd like to invite you all to witness a modern miracle.'

The crowd bustled excitedly in agreement.

'And now, ladies and gentlemen, I'll hand you over to one of the representatives.' He turned to one of the cloaked figures standing in the shadows behind him. 'Sir?'

'Oh dear,' whispered the Doctor. 'I don't like the look of this at all.'

Slowly, the figure lifted its hood and dropped it back to reveal the face underneath. The face of death.

Pale white flesh, barely attached to the protruding bone, peeled off a skull with rotting eyeballs in its eye sockets. Clumps of dead hair sprouted from the top of the figure's decomposing head and the flesh around the mouth was shrivelled, wrinkled and decaying. Whatever this thing was, it wasn't human. It didn't seem alien, either. Ben could think of only one way to describe it. The thing was a corpse. A corpse that walked among men.

Third Reel

Chapter Eighteen

Their faces were made of wrinkled white flesh, their sunken eye sockets revealed rotting veined eyeballs, their facial muscles were altered by rigor mortis. They were dead. Yet they were alive.

The corpse in the middle of the group stepped forward on to the podium. Its walk reminded Ben of the skeletons in that *Jason and the Argonauts* film. It was like they weren't quite real, as if they had been animated frame by frame. The corpse's face was expressionless, as if it was in a trance.

The creature looked like it would fall over at any moment and crumble into a pile of dust, but it managed to keep its balance until it reached the microphone De Sande had been using.

'Friends,' it croaked in a slow, rasping voice. It made Ben think of a coma patent trying to speak for the first time in years, and he wondered whether the corpse's voice would get clearer once it got used to speaking again.

'We are at a junction,' it said. 'A nexus in our quest. The first stage of the plan has been successfully completed. You have all done well.'

The crowd started to murmur excitedly.

'There is still much to do,' the corpse continued. 'It is less than two days until *Dying in the Sun* is released across the country. In less than two days the clearest vision of our beliefs ever created will be released, bringing our way of life to more people than has ever been possible before. Once the film is in the public domain our plan will be complete, and the first stage of our work will be done. Be watchful, and be there to help those who begin to understand our way. A new era begins here.'

The corpse stepped back and the crowd applauded. Once the applause had died down, the lights went up and people began to chatter excitedly amongst themselves.

'What the hell is this all about?' Ben whispered to the Doctor. 'What was that thing?'

The Doctor's brow was furrowed. 'I'm not sure, Ben.'

'And now,' De Sande announced, 'will the Initiates please come forth.' He glanced down at the Doctor and Ben and beckoned for them to come forward.

The crowd cleared a space and a small group of people, presumably the other Initiates, stepped forward. Middle-aged men with potbellies, younger people not much older than Ben and a couple of heavily made-up women - the group was a mixed bunch, but all had a look of pure excitement on their faces.

The lights dimmed further, and the whirring noise of machinery could be heard. Suddenly the giant projector screen behind the podium leapt into life as the spinning star of the Star Light logo began to rotate gracefully on the screen.

'If I'd have known we were going to the pictures I'd have brought some popcorn,' Ben whispered.

The Doctor shushed him quiet as the film began. The canopy of a jungle, a camera flying down quickly to eye level and focusing on a man in a suit marching hurriedly through the undergrowth. The film was *Dying in the Sun*.

'I've seen this one,' Ben joked. 'I wonder what else is on?'

As the film continued the Doctor and Ben joined the Initiates, who were now standing in a horseshoe formation around the screen. Slowly, in harmony, everyone in the auditorium began to chant in a language Ben didn't recognise.

As he watched the film he became aware that it wasn't quite the same as the version he had seen before. As the creatures on the film worked their magic, blood flowed from wounded bodies stabbed by the hero, there were images of naked natives being slaughtered at the hands of a businessman from LA, the heroine was attacked and rescued in a heavy rainstorm that drenched everything in sight. The chaos and the nastiness of the film the Doctor and Ben had seen at De Sande's mansion had been turned up several notches. It was unpleasant, it was addictive, it was incredible.

The chant went on, and as he glanced around Ben realised that very few people were actually watching the film. It was as if they didn't even need to see it to absorb the emotions it generated within them. Like a besuited congregation they worshipped the flickering images on the screen, images that became more and more intense as the chanting continued, as if the film itself was feeding on the hysteria of the crowd. Perhaps it was.

A low rumbling sound began, emanating from the podium. The chanting silenced and the Initiates all stood back. Slowly, the rumbling turned into a scraping sound as the centre of the podium began to sink into the ground leaving a large hole in its centre.

A fast whooshing noise, then suddenly a rush of bright light burst from the hole. Somewhere in the room, though Ben could not quite work out where, a distant choral singing began.

A stone pillar rose up through the hole, slowly blocking out the rush of light. On top of the pillar was a glass vase that glowed brightly with a bubbling, fiery gold liquid. The pillar stopped moving, all noise died and the light dimmed, leaving only the glow from the liquid as illumination.

De Sande reached down and carefully picked up the vase, lifting it above his head where he held it for several moments. He then passed the liquid to the Initiate on his left and one by one the group began to drink from the vase. An unholy communion, if ever there was one.

As the vase was passed to a man facing towards Ben and the Doctor they saw what was happening in detail. Small lights danced around in the liquid like fireflies, and as people drank it you could almost see the brightness shining through the translucence of their skin as the liquid slipped down their throats. Ben got a sick feeling in his stomach as he realised what he was seeing. There were living things in the liquid and the Initiates were swallowing them live.

The vase was passed to Ben and he paused, looking to the Doctor for advice on how to proceed.

'Drink it,' De Sande whispered. 'Go on.'

Ben raised the vase to his lips, then shook his head and handed the vase to the next Initiate. 'I'm sorry,' he said, rushing from the podium. 'I can't.'

'Oh dear,' the Doctor said to De Sande. 'Let me see if he's OK.'

He walked over to the side of the room where Ben had collapsed into a chair.

'It's OK,' De Sande announced. 'Continue with the ceremony.'

Once the last Initiate had drunk from the vase, it was handed back to De Sande who replaced it on the podium. The podium receded into the ground, becoming the simple stone platform it had been before. The extract from *Dying in the Sun* disappeared from the cinema screen as the projector was switched off. De Sande stepped forward to the lectern.

'The ceremony is complete,' he announced. 'The Initiates have welcomed the Selyoids into their lives.' He turned to one of the Initiates. 'How does it feel?'

The Initiate looked bewildered, but her face was covered in a smile. 'It's beautiful,' she said, tears in her eyes. 'I finally realise what life is all about. Thank you.'

De Sande nodded and gestured to one of the monks to lead the Initiates away from the podium so that they could sit down and recover from their experience.

'She should not thank me,' De Sande told the crowd. 'She should thank the Selyoids.' There was a round of applause from the audience and he stepped down from the stage, then marched straight up to the chair where Ben was sitting. 'What's going on?' he asked. 'Are you OK?'

'What was that corpse thing?' Ben asked. 'It scared the willies out of me.'

'You shouldn't have been upset by it,' De Sande said, confused. 'The ceremonial atmosphere should have relaxed you enough for it not to have proved a problem. It seems I was mistaken, though. Perhaps I should have let you know what you were in for earlier.'

'Ben's just been feeling a bit under the weather,' the Doctor explained.

De Sande shrugged. 'Oh well. At least you participated in most of the ceremony. We can complete your Initiation in a few minutes once you've got yourself together.'

'Indeed,' the Doctor said. 'Tell me, are the corpses animatronic devices or genuine?'

'Genuine corpses, Doctor. John Does from the local morgue. One hundred per cent genuine walking dead. Nothing but the best for FOCAL, I assure you.'

'Glad to hear it,' Ben said sarcastically.

'They are dead bodies, but they are being animated by a highly intelligent life form unlike any ever documented by science. These creatures have a great capacity for intelligence, and while they are almost microscopic in size they can meld with a human host and experience life through their eyes and ears. If the creatures merge with a living being they are subject to the will of the person's mind, but if they adopt a stiff they can exert complete control on it. Doctor, the creatures controlling those cadavers are going to change the face of America for ever.'

'What are they?' Ben asked.

'I don't know exactly,' De Sande admitted, 'but you can rest assured they're totally benevolent. Science has no record of them, so they have no name. I call them Selyoids. It's kind of a joke.'

The Doctor sighed. 'But what *are* they?'

'They're perfect, Doctor. Every time I close my eyes I remember the first time I saw them.' De Sande's voice was quiet, almost a whisper. It was as if he was dreaming out loud, revelling in the perfection of the vision in his mind. It was as if he was on another plane of reality. 'It was when I was in Alaska filming for *The Cold Blooded*.'

* * *

Three years previously, Leonard De Sande stood in an ice cave near the airstrip and smiled. He'd found the perfect location to film the movie's finale, though getting a camera all the way in here would be difficult. Perhaps if he took some photographs the cave could be re-created back home.

He was about to leave the cave when something on the edge of his perception caught his eye. A flicker of colour, of gold. He turned to examine what he'd seen. Part of the ground was glowing. A mass of colour. Glowing like fire, alive, yet motionless. Tiny specks of glitter embedded in the ice. Magic made real.

Leonard took out his pick and began to chip away at the ice. Eventually he removed the layer covering the substance and saw that it was a pool of liquid warm enough to not freeze over, but not hot enough to melt the ice it had been trapped in.

Be at ease. You're safe.

'Curtis!' he called towards the cave entrance, beckoning for his cameraman to see the spectacle.'Curtis, come here, you have to see this!'.

Leonard stared at the substance and felt drawn to it. It was beautiful, an incredible sight. He reached out and, with caution, dabbed his finger into the liquid. He felt a warm tingling around his finger, like a minor static shock. Felt the liquid surround his finger, caressing it. He lifted the finger up and tasted the liquid, then felt all his troubles tumble away. At that moment he knew he had discovered his destiny.

Several hours later Leonard gathered the rest of his party around a campfire in the centre of their base camp.'My friends,' he told the rest of the film crew,'I've made an amazing discovery today.' He held up a cup and passed it around the group.'Inside this cup are living creatures, creatures that are trapped, unable to reach their true potential. They need our help, and are prepared to give us incredible gifts in return.'

'Leonard,' Curtis said, 'you're looking... different. What's happened? You look amazing.'

Leonard grinned. 'It's the creatures. They can help us in ways we could never imagine. Enhancing our personalities through changing our body gestures, our aromas, skin quality, posture... You name it, they can help. They'll make us perfect. They've made me perfect.'

'Natural cosmetic surgery, eh?' Curtis said. 'Impressive.'

Leonard continued. 'I believe that nature didn't intend them to stay trapped in the ice for ever. Nature has a purpose for these creatures, and that purpose is to help humanity better itself in exchange for experiencing the life they are denied. We must find a way to thaw them, to transport them back to California. I'm going to contact every scientist I know and see if we can find a way to help them achieve their destiny. We'll return home tomorrow. The future begins here.'

Leonard felt the creatures inside him warming, pleased at his words. 'Things are going to be very different from now on,' he announced. 'Oh yes, very different.'

'Eventually,' De Sande explained, his attention appearing to return to the present, 'the team of scientists I hired created a way for the creatures to be preserved that allows them to revitalise a human being at any time. The liquid the Initiates were drinking is composed of a raw concentration of living Selyoids working to enhance their partners. When you drink it you'll see what I mean. There really is no feeling quite like it.'

'And what do the Selyoids get in return for their favours?' the Doctor asked.

'Why, I would have thought that was obvious,' De Sande said. 'They get to see through our eyes. They're as intelligent, maybe more intelligent, than us yet they can do nothing in their natural environment. Nothing to see, nothing to do, no stimulation. They get bored. They want to see life through someone else's eyes.'

'Like when we go to watch a film,' Ben pointed out. 'They want to escape from their problems, escape from their normal existence. Only they don't just want that for a couple of hours, they want it for ever.'

'But why is seeing life through our eyes so important?' the Doctor asked.

'Because they'll be able to see what needs to be done to sort this country out,' a gruff voice said from behind him and Ben.

'Captain Wallis,' the Doctor said. 'How are you?'

'The Doctor was curious about the Selyoids' intentions, Charles,' De Sande said.

'You want to know what the Selyoids intend, huh? You want to know what they're going to do?' Wallis moved uncomfortably close to the Doctor and sneered. 'You'd be better asking what they won't do, the changes they'll make.'

'Go on,' said the Doctor.

'If I may?' chipped in De Sande. Wallis shrugged and De Sande continued. 'One of the major benefits of being partnered with the Selyoids is that the general public sees you as a celebrity. The creatures make anyone partnered with them so appealing, so charming, that you won't want to say a word against that person, steal from them or do any damn thing they might find unpleasant. You get enough people like this and, hey, you wake up one morning and there's no more crime. At the end of the day, the Selyoids have a lesson to teach humanity, Doctor. The FOCAL Way of Light *is* the way to happiness. People won't listen to religious wackos, they won't listen to people like Brother Reinert, but they'll listen to celebrities. They'll listen to the stars. No one will be forced to partner with the Selyoids, no one will be forced to follow the Way, but no one will need to be forced. They'll want to join through their own free will. The Selyoids will win the hearts and minds of the nation, will charm the pants off anyone remotely interested in Hollywood. We know it can work, we know it will be wonderful, which is why, one by one, we're introducing the stars to the Selyoids. One by one, we're making those already partnered with the Selyoids into stars. Slowly but surely our message will be spread, until the day when all America follows the Way of Light.'

Ben tried to take in everything that De Sande was saying. How far had the Selyoids got already? How many celebrities were working for them? How deep did this go? The Doctor's investigation had unveiled a conspiracy more frightening than he could ever have predicted.

'So,' the Doctor said, 'why are you involved in all this Selyoid business, Captain?'

'What's the biggest threat to world security today, Doctor?' Wallis asked. 'Go on, take a guess.'

The Doctor shrugged his shoulders. 'Not enough milk in the fridge?'

'Communism, Doctor. A single word that could destroy this country if we're not careful. That's why I support FOCAL, Doctor. The Selyoids create peace by making sure there's always someone better, someone more famous, more attractive. There's always a chain of command, of respect. And while that inequality is there Communism will flounder. The country will see the benefit of a hierarchy, and the reds will be driven out faster than a Bob Feller pitch.'

The Doctor looked grave. 'And would I be right in assuming that members of FOCAL get first pickings at the top positions in the new order?'

Wallis grinned. 'Doctor, thanks to myself, Mr De Sande and the rest of FOCAL, a country as screwed over as ours is going to be transformed into the most perfect nation on the planet. I'll go down in history as being the one who came up with the way to make this dream real. I'll be the man who rid California of Communism, and FOCAL will go down as the creator of world peace.'

'You'll be famous,' the Doctor said quietly.

'So will lots of people,' De Sande said. 'The Selyoids give everyone who agrees to absorb them a presence and a charisma that inspire awe in other people. Everyone will be treated with respect, everyone will be appreciated. In time, there will be peace.'

'But how are you going to tell people about the Selyoids?' asked the Doctor. 'Is it through the film?'

De Sande nodded. 'And more, as you'll soon see.'

As the director led them through to a small side room the Doctor whispered to Ben, 'I want to get a quick look at the projector, then we'll get out of here as fast as we can.'

'This is where we store the Selyoid essence,' De Sande announced as he lifted a cup of the liquid from a table in the middle of the room.

'Now drink,' he said, handing the cup to the Doctor.

The Doctor looked around and lifted the cup awkwardly to his lips. He let it drop to the ground and it smashed, its contents spilling all over the floor.

'Oh dear!' the Doctor said. 'I'm such a butterfingers!' He glanced around. 'I'll get a mop. Come on, Ben!'

He dragged Ben out of the room and began to run towards the podium end of the auditorium, where he ducked behind a curtain near the movie screen on which the *Dying in the Sun* extract had been shown during the ceremony.

Ben followed the Doctor behind the curtain and saw him looking inside a series of large wooden crates. 'They've already dismantled it,' the Doctor said, sifting through the projector components in the boxes.

'Doctor!' Ben heard De Sande call from the other side of the curtain. 'Where the hell did you go?'

'Come on, Doctor!' Ben said. 'He'll find us in a minute!'

'Now this is interesting,' the Doctor said, holding a small crystal-like device in his palm. 'I've been reading up on how projectors work and I'm sure they don't use anything like this.'

'Perhaps that's why the film doesn't always have the 3-D stuff?' Ben suggested, pointing to the device. 'Maybe only some projectors have that thing in them.'

The Doctor nodded. 'And if this is the key to making the film stand out, I think it could be the key to stopping it, too.' He slipped the device into his jacket pocket. 'De Sande shouldn't miss this. Come on, let's get out of here!'

They emerged from behind the curtain and slipped past the crowds in the auditorium.

'Hey,' De Sande called, spotting the Doctor. 'Where are you going?'

Ben and the Doctor ran out of the castle as other FOCAL members started to chase after them. They got to their car, jumped inside and the Doctor started it. As they sped away Ben glanced back and saw a crowd of FOCAL members shouting at them, but there didn't seem to be any cars following them.

'Oh dear,' the Doctor said, a cheeky smile on his face. 'De Sande won't be too pleased with me.'

By the time they got back to LA the sun was rising. Ben was struck by the ocean of a million colours that filled the sky as day broke. For the first time since seeing the living corpse, Ben relaxed. Daylight. He was safe.

Chapter Nineteen

Ben dreamt of monsters. Monsters, guns, dead bodies and movies coming to life. The scream of a maiden on a railway line became shriller and shriller until Ben realised it was the sound of his alarm clock going off. He snapped awake.

Yawning, he got out of bed. He checked the time - 10.30 a.m. - then drew the curtains and shielded his eyes from the glare of the LA morning sun. He was still pretty tired, but at least he'd had some sleep.

He walked into the bathroom, splashed some water on his face, then threw on some clothes. Before he left the hotel room he noticed a little paper note that had been slipped underneath the door. He picked it up and read it. The note was from the hotel reception. Two messages had been left for him. One from Polly and the other from Detective Fletcher who wanted to speak to the Doctor ASAP.

Ben walked out into the hotel corridor, where he came face to face with the Doctor who was chatting to a cleaning lady who stood behind a trolley full of soaps, shampoos and towels. He appeared to be inspecting the trolley's contents as if looking for the biggest slice of chocolate gâteau on a sweet trolley.

'Morning, Doctor,' Ben said.

'Isn't the service in this place wonderful?' the Doctor said with a smile.

'We try,' the cleaner said. She looked at her watch. 'Oh, goodness me, we've been talking for almost an hour. I really must get on. Lovely to meet you, Doctor.'

She waved, then began to push her trolley down the corridor.

'What's that all about?' Ben whispered.

'That, Ben,' the Doctor said, 'was a lady who's been working here for almost ten years. I had a long conversation with her about living in this city. The things that have gone on in this place... Anyway, how are you this morning?'

'I'm OK, Doctor. Listen, I've just got a message from Polly. She says she's safe and well but isn't coming back for a couple of days. She's got herself tickets to the premiere of *Dying in the Sun*, you know. Sounds like she's doing OK for herself, but I reckon we should go and fetch her. I'm worried, Doctor.'

The Doctor shook his head. 'I'm looking forward to finding out whether she's found Chate, but right now we've got more pressing things to worry about. She says she's safe so there's no cause for concern. I wouldn't mind going to that premiere myself. If we don't find her before then, at least we should be able to see her at that. I wonder how we can get tickets...'

'But what if this note isn't from her? What if she's in trouble and someone's trying to cover it up?'

'It's a worry,' the Doctor conceded, 'but we both know Polly can take care of herself. The moment we've finished the rest of our business we'll make an effort to catch up with her, I promise.'

Ben nodded. 'Yeah, hopefully it's genuine anyway. Oh yeah, Doctor. Almost forgot, there was another message. It's Fletcher. He's trying to get hold of you.'

'Oh dear,' the Doctor said, pouting his bottom lip. 'I wonder what the detective wants now?'

Several minutes later, Ben went down to the hotel lobby where he found the Doctor arguing on the phone.

'I'm sorry, Detective,' he was saying, 'I don't know anything about it.' A pause. 'I'll try, Detective. Keep in touch, won't you? Goodbye.'

The Doctor hung up the phone and stood up. 'There's been an explosion,' he told Ben. 'De Sande's mansion was severely damaged last night in a bomb blast. No one was injured but the film-production wing was almost destroyed. De Sande had been duplicating the prints of the film there for distribution. Apparently he had already shipped them out to a secret warehouse, but it seems that whoever planted the bomb was unaware of this and was attempting to destroy all the copies of *Dying in the Sun* before they could be sent to the cinemas.'

Ben tried to think whether he'd actually seen the Doctor to his room last night. 'It wasn't –'

'No, Ben, it wasn't me. But it seems we're not the only ones in this town who have concerns about the film. Somewhere we have an ally, and I have a strong suspicion about who it could be.

The midday sun bore down on the MGA studios and today the place was a hive of activity. A wide concrete road ran through the middle of the complex, lined at its edges by an endless stretch of palm trees. Stagehands, press reporters, actors, actresses and scriptwriters hurried through the lot, moving from building to building. The front of the grounds seemed to be composed of rows of offices, while towards the back towered the warehouse sound stages where the latest movies were being shot. In the centre of the complex a water tower was emblazoned with the MGA logo in bright red letters.

The chauffeur driving Ben and the Doctor to the studios pulled up outside the most impressive looking of the offices and stopped the car.

There you go,' he said. 'His office is just here.'

The Doctor and Ben got out and walked through a large glass revolving door.

As they entered the building they saw Leon Zane standing against the reception desk chatting to the girl behind it.

'Ah, Doctor!' he said as he saw the visitors. 'What an unexpected pleasure it was to receive your phone call.'

'Hello, Mr Zane,' the Doctor said.

Zane smiled. 'I knew you'd come round to my way of thinking eventually.' He gestured through a door. 'In my office?'

Ben and the Doctor walked into Zane's office and sat down.

The Doctor wasted no time in getting to the point.

'Mr Zane, I take it you've heard about the explosion at Leonard De Sande's mansion?'

Zane nodded. 'Indeed. I hear much of his duplication plant was destroyed, and the prints of his new film, no less.' He had a wicked glint in his eye. 'What a tragedy.'

'Mr Zane, I think you know who planted the bomb, or at least have an idea who is responsible.'

Zane shook his head. 'Listen, Doctor, Hollywood is one giant business, and the number one rule in business is that there are no rules. There's rumours flying around about Star Light's latest opus, rumours which have got every studio in town worried. The bomb could have been set up by anyone, so don't go accusing my company of anything, not without proof.'

'Yes, well,' the Doctor said, 'the thing is it made me realise there are other people out there who could prove useful allies in my attempts to block the film's release. So I want you to talk to everyone and ask them to leave the situation alone. I'm as intrigued by *Dying in the Sun* as you are, but I'm conducting my own investigation in my own time. I'd really appreciate it if you, and all the other studios expressing concern, would trust me to deal with the situation and not interfere. I appreciate the bomber's gesture, and want to stop this film as much as you do, but please, let me handle things my way. If we're too brutal, too exposed, then we risk ruining everything.

Zane's expression was serious. Although he hadn't admitted anything, it was clear he had assessed the Doctor well enough to know that there was no point in making a big show of protesting his innocence. 'You'll never find out anything about the film now, Doctor. All the prints have been destroyed.'

'That's what you think, mate,' Ben said.

'The prints were moved,' the Doctor told Zane. 'Just before the bomb exploded. They'd been making them more quickly than planned. There are far more copies of *Dying in the Sun* out there than you realise.'

Zane's face paled. He took a deep breath, then turned and

stared out of his office window. 'What can we do now?'

'Don't worry,' said the Doctor, trying to reassure him. 'I'm going to do everything in my power to stop this film from reaching the cinemas. I don't think your studio will be in much danger.'

'Do you really think you can succeed?'

The Doctor's face was grave. 'I must succeed.'

The Doctor's quest to stop the film being released began at the post office. Ninety-seven urgent telegrams were sent out to cinemas in the area, urging them not to accept prints of *Dying in the Sun*. The prints were faulty, the Doctor told them. The film reels they had were not the ones they should have.

Next, the Doctor returned to the hotel and spent several hours on the telephone to cinemas and distribution warehouses, desperately trying to convince them that they should do everything in their power to stop the general public from being exposed to *Dying in the Sun*. He was walking a fine line between convincing them of the film's danger and convincing them that he was a lunatic.

Problems with the prints, censorship issues, even claiming that the film contained subliminal messages planted by Communists... the Doctor tried everything to get his way. Most people laughed. Most said they'd look into it, in patronising voices that meant they wouldn't. One or two seemed genuinely concerned and promised to send the reels back to their source, but generally the Doctor had little luck. The movie had been sent to the cinemas. It was too late to stop the *Dying in the Sun* contagion. No matter how many prints were destroyed or stolen, other cinemas would still have theirs. The genie had been let out of its bottle.

The Doctor finally let the old lady who had been tapping her watch indignantly as he made his never-ending stream of calls use the phone, and he and Ben slouched down in two comfortable armchairs in the hotel lobby.

'Any joy then?' said a familiar voice. Zane had just walked in through the revolving doors. He sat down on a sofa next to the Doctor and Ben.

'We've tried everything,' Ben told him. 'Do you have any idea how ridiculous it sounds? "Stop the film, it's dangerous." I've never felt so embarrassed in all my life.'

'Embarrassment is a small price to pay for saving this city from Selyoid servitude,' the Doctor pointed out. 'We have to stop the film, but I don't know what else we can do.'

'You guys don't even work in the industry,' Zane said, 'so I don't see why you want to stop De Sande's picture, but you clearly need my help. Let's go down to Star Light's distribution office and work some magic. They're the only people who can stop this film, no questions asked.'

The Doctor sighed and stood up. 'It's our last chance. If they don't recall the film there's nothing we can do to stop it. Do we need an appointment to see whoever's in charge down there?'

'Most certainly,' Zane said.

The Doctor grinned and began to walk towards the revolving doors. 'In that case, let's go down there now,' he called back. 'We'll surprise them.'

Zane and Ben exchanged bemused glances before following the Doctor out of the hotel.

James Hensleigh, head of distribution at Star Light Pictures, took a long puff from his cigar and stared with beady eyes at the newcomers. 'So you want me to pull our greatest picture before anyone has had the chance to see it? Are you insane?'

Ben looked around the office. Sparse, with movie posters decorating the walls. This place was functional and efficient. To Ben's left sat Zane who was being very quiet, listening intently to the Doctor's pleas.

'There's more at stake here than your profit margins,' the Doctor insisted. 'This film is the most essential piece of propaganda in a plan to make Americans slaves to... outside influences.'

Hensleigh shrugged. 'I'm sorry, Doctor, it's perfectly legal. If you're that worried about subversive motion pictures then give HUAC a call and let them pay us a visit.'

'It's not as simple as that,' the Doctor said, clearly frustrated. 'If this film gets out it could have a disastrous effect on the health of the nation. It could turn America into a race of slaves.'

A shrill laugh from Hensleigh mixed with his cigar smoke and he started to cough. 'I'm sorry Doctor,' he said, once he'd recovered, 'I just don't see how it could. Do you want me to get security to escort you out of here?'

'Have you seen the film yet?' the Doctor asked.

Hensleigh shook his head. 'A few of my people have, but I'm waiting until this evening's premiere.'

'That will be too late,' the Doctor said agitatedly.

'I don't care,' Hensleigh said. 'Look, the prints are already in or on their way to theatres. There's nothing you can do to stop the film now.'

'Nothing except a direct order from you blocking its display,' the Doctor pointed out.

'And why would I want to do that?' Hensleigh asked.

The Doctor put his index finger to his lip, clearly thinking something through in his mind. 'You said you didn't want to see the film until the premiere, but am I right in thinking you could see it earlier if you wanted to?'

Hensleigh nodded. 'Of course. There are several prints of the movie downstairs.'

'Then I beg of you, please watch it as soon as you can. Watch it with an open mind and think about what I've told you. Look at what you see on screen and then think about your emotions, think about your feelings. Think whether the actual contents of the film should have made you feel that. Unnatural techniques are being used to, for lack of a better word, brainwash the public. Your life, the lives of everyone in this city, possibly everyone in the country, depend on this film being stopped.'

Hensleigh took a long deep breath and paused for a moment to consider. He glanced across at Ben and Zane as if trying to assess whether they genuinely believed the Doctor's wild claims, but seemed to find nothing in their eyes to help him. Eventually he lifted his hands and sat up. 'OK, Doctor.' He glanced down at his watch. 'I've got a couple of hours clear here. Let's head down to the screening room and take a look. You can point out what's amiss, and if I believe you I'll pull the film. How's that sound?'

The Doctor nodded his head. 'That would be ideal, thank you.'

The Doctor, Ben and Zane followed Hensleigh down several flights of steps to the screening room. It took ten minutes for the reels to be loaded into the projector, but at last the lights dimmed and once again the screen filled with the haunting images of the *Dying in the Sun* title sequence.

As the film played out the Doctor began to explain what the director was intending at each stage. He pointed out how De Sande filled frames where nothing happened with action, how the emotion of each scene was heightened. Watching the film for the first time since discovering the existence of the Selyoids, Ben began to forget once more why the Doctor wanted the film stopped. He felt wonderful and at peace, but had to keep telling himself that those feelings were only due to the Selyoids' influence on his mind, due to the subliminal messages they were sending out.

'There don't seem to be any of the three-dimensional effects I remember,' commented the Doctor.

'I think I can explain that,' Hensleigh said. 'The film uses some new technology that requires modifications to existing projectors for the full effect to be achieved. All of Star Light's theatres have been modified but the projectors in this screening room haven't been altered yet.'

Despite the lack of effects, watching the film still had as much impact on Ben as it had had on the previous occasions when he'd seen it. The Doctor had told him that the film changed according to the audience that was watching it, that the Selyoids had acute senses that could pick up on the mood of those in the room. Today they seemed to pick up on the hostility from the audience, and responded in kind. The lead character's break-up with his girlfriend involved them shouting and screaming at each other. As the man ran down the street he was confronted by a policeman and disembowelled him with a knife to get him out of the way.

The film finally finished, and the lights went up.

'As you can see,' the Doctor concluded, 'this film is a threat to everything your nation holds dear, and there's no way you can let it be unleashed on the general public.'

Hensleigh stood up and let out a hearty laugh. 'Doctor, you really are insane.'

'I'm ruined,' a quiet voice moaned.

'Are you all right, Mr Zane?' the Doctor asked.

Zane shook his head and buried it in his hands. 'That film... It's worse than I thought. My studio is ruined. We'll never be able to create anything with as much impact.'

'Not unless you too learn the secrets that make the film so different.'

Zane looked up, tears welling in his eyes. 'No, Doctor. What would be the point? That film is perfect, we could never equal it, and even if we could... why would we?'

'Money?' suggested Ben.

Zane let out a disdainful laugh. 'You saw that film. You must have felt the same way. Who cares about money now? There are just too many other more important things in life.'

'But don't you see!' said the Doctor, raising his voice. 'Don't you see how it has changed you, how you're not the same? Whatever good De Sande claims it's doing, it's changing people without their consent.'

'Doctor, please!' Hensleigh shouted. 'That's enough. That film is the finest motion picture I've ever seen and I'd never dream of stopping its release. As for changing peoples' emotions... Well, that's the power of a good story.'

The Doctor shook his head. 'No,' he pleaded. 'Don't you understand? There's more to it than that!'

'Doctor,' Ben said, trying to calm his friend down. 'Maybe they're right? Maybe the film will bring peace? Maybe the Selyoids' intentions are good?'

'Ben,' the Doctor said. 'Try to keep a clear head. I know the film has affected you too, but can't you see... it's just not right. We have to fight it!'

'Now leave,' Hensleigh ordered. 'Now.'

The Doctor sighed. 'I'm sorry, Mr Hensleigh. I don't mean to be a pain. Maybe I just need to watch the film in the right atmosphere.'

Hensleigh shrugged.

A plan seemed to be forming in the Doctor's mind. 'You wouldn't be able to get hold of tickets to the premiere would you?' he asked. 'I suppose they've all sold out by now?'

Hensleigh shook his head. 'De Sande's kept this film pretty secret, so there's still plenty of space. And yes, I can get tickets. I'm head of distribution, for Christ's sake!'

'I don't suppose you could get a couple of tickets for me, could you?' the Doctor asked. 'I think I will find the response there quite educational.'

A smile crept across Hensleigh's face and he led them back to his office. Once there, he hurried over to a filing cabinet, opened a drawer and took out three small pieces of cardboard. 'Here you go,' he said as he handed the tickets to the Doctor. 'I think it will be quite funny to see you amongst all that lot, actually. Watch it again, see how the audience love it, then try telling me I should stop it.'

The Doctor took the tickets from Hensleigh's grasp. 'Thank you. I won't waste any more of your time.'

Hensleigh gave an insincere wave as the Doctor, Ben and Zane walked out of his office, and called out after them. 'See you at the premiere, Doctor! Seven o'clock tonight, don't be late!'

'Oh I won't be,' said the Doctor gravely. 'I wouldn't miss it for the world.'

Chapter Twenty

Polly could scarcely believe the changes she'd experienced since meeting Chate and Maria. She'd spent yesterday getting used to the creatures that now lived inside her, adjusting to feeling like she was a star, and now this morning Maria had announced that she was taking Polly and Chate to meet the director. Polly wasn't at all surprised to learn that the director was none other than Leonard De Sande.

In daylight, his mansion looked far less intimidating and impressive than it had in the darkness when she had first visited the place. Nevertheless, it was still an incredible building, oozing wealth and prosperity. The American Dream made real. Except for one side of it, where the peace of the landscaped garden and polished clean brickwork had been shattered by the bomb blast.

Bright yellow police-cordon tape had been wrapped around the edge of the building, window frames, brick debris and shattered antiques lay scattered across the grass, and LAPD officers swarmed around the garden looking for clues. A makeshift tarpaulin had been placed over the blown-out area to keep the elements out, but the building still looked like something out of the Blitz.

'Who did this?' Polly asked.

'Someone pretty jerked with De Sande,' Chate said, adjusting his jet-black shades. Polly was ahead of Chate and Maria, who were bringing up the rear with their arms around each other, but as they neared the front door Chate tilted his eyebrows towards Polly in a gesture that told her to let him do the talking.

A young policeman in a sparkling blue uniform stood proudly in front of the door.

'Excuse me,' Chate said, about to push past the cop.

'I'm sorry, sir,' the young man said tilting his head regretfully, 'no unauthorised persons are allowed inside the building at this time.' He said his lines with a hint of a smile on his face, as if he'd been waiting all day to say this.

'You new to the force, kid?' Chate asked.

The policeman looked indignant. 'I'll have you know I've been in the LAPD three months now.'

Chate laughed. 'Not surprised you don't recognise me. I'm Captain Wallis's son, you know.'

The cop looked startled. '*The* Captain Wallis?'

Chate nodded. 'So don't give me any hassle, OK? I have an appointment with Mr De Sande, so if you'd kindly let me through I'd be most grateful.'

'Er, I'm not sure.' The cop looked worried, paused for a moment to consider what to do, then pushed the door - and fell in as it was opened from the inside.

'Sorry, officer,' said the familiar voice of De Sande, as the cop crashed to the floor. 'Are my friends being disrespectful?'

'Er, no, sir,' the cop said, getting up and adjusting his hat. 'I was just letting them through, sir.'

'Keep up the good work.' De Sande turned to the others and grinned. 'Maria, welcome. It's so good to see you. Sorry about the security, but after what's happened I can't be too careful.'

Polly, Maria and Chate stepped over the threshold, past the embarrassed policeman and into a hallway that looked even grander than Polly remembered it being.

'This way,' De Sande said, ushering them into an office, panelled in stained wood, that led away from the entrance hall.

A formal desk stood in one corner of the room, as did a sinister-looking figure draped in a hooded blue robe that covered its head. In the middle of the office was a coffee table, in front of which stood a cluster of comfortable armchairs. De Sande gestured for his visitors to sit down and, once they had done so, a waiter brought through jugs of orange juice and water to cool them down.

'Mr Chate, welcome,' De Sande said, pouring his visitors' drinks. He turned to Polly. 'Welcome to you too. Polly, isn't it? Yeah, I'd never forget a pretty girl like you.'

The man was quite a charmer, and his eyes glowed with a fire that made Polly feel appreciated. 'Thank you,' she said, taking a glass of water from him. She hoped she could keep her composure. They had business to discuss, after all.

You're someone special, Polly. Don't forget that.

Polly gasped.

'Relax,' De Sande said out loud. 'One of the benefits of bonding with the creatures is that they give us the ability to pick up on the feelings of others and communicate through pure emotion.'

'You'll soon get used to them,' Chate told Polly. 'You're already much happier than you were.'

Polly nodded. 'Of course. So how are we going to let everyone else in on the act?'

'Intriguing,' said De Sande, a wicked glint flashing in his glowing eyes. 'You're concerned about your friends. You haven't seen them for two days and you want them to feel the peace the Selyoids are giving you.'

Polly felt uncomfortable at the ease with which De Sande had plucked the thoughts from her head. 'How did you know?'

Relax. I won't read your mind. I just can't help picking up on strong emotions. Your mind is feeding the Selyoids and they need to communicate.

De Sande in his own words. In her mind. Polly felt incredibly happy as she realised what this new skill meant for the world. Through the creatures, De Sande could communicate directly with her and with her emotions - all people sharing with the Selyoids could. A wave of calm could sweep through everyone until all unhappiness disappeared.

'You have nothing to worry about as far as your friends are concerned,' De Sande said. 'It seems they aren't quite ready to join with us yet, but I've already shown them some of the marvels the Selyoids bring to our lives.'

'But they will join the sharing?'

De Sande nodded vigorously. 'Oh yes, almost everyone will. Once *Dying in the Sun* is revealed to the public we'll have our work cut out trying to satisfy all the people who decide to follow our way.'

Concern. Dying in the Sun. *The Doctor's fears. What's happened to the Doctor? Thinking back to watching the film. Joy. Happiness. Torment. Catharsis.*

'Polly?' De Sande said inquisitively. 'What's going on? Your mind's racing, I can hardly hear anything else.'

'You must learn to calm your thoughts,' Chate said. 'If you don't relax everyone in the room will hear what you're thinking.'

'I'm sorry,' Polly said. 'I'm not quite sure what I'm supposed to do.'

De Sande lifted his palms towards her and half-closed his eyes. Polly could almost see the healing energies he was concentrating on her.

'Just draw on the Selyoids within you,' he said calmly. 'Trust them to regulate your thoughts and trust that they'll look after you. They'll keep your secrets. They love you.'

Polly closed her eyes, felt the warm presence of the Selyoids in her bloodstream and found she was on another world.

The light was dying. Across the planet, darkness was closing in. Polly saw a giant column of light swirling around in the rainbow-coloured sky. The light swept down to the ground and reached out, touching her mind. It was a living being, a being made of light yet with form and shape. Fire, heat, energy. As it shimmered through her mind, Polly felt it singing to her. The creatures that made up the light called themselves the Children, and they just wanted to expose others to the beauty of their creativity. They described to Polly the epic tales and histories their civilisation had created. She saw the magnificent cathedrals, tombs and pictures made from photons and sunlight. She looked around and saw more of the creatures. One by one they were ceasing their dancing as the storm clouds above started to release the rain down on to their world. They were panicking. Polly could sense their fear. They were a civilisation of artists, of dreamers, of living stars. Each and every being on this planet burned brightly, a fire creature more beautiful than anything she had ever seen on Earth.

As the rain fell Polly felt their fear. They knew their time was at an end, they knew the future looked bleak, but they pinned all hope on the scientists. The outcasts who had begun to see life as more than an excuse for creativity. Those who had worked at breaking the Children down into a corporeal form, a primordial soup capable of giving them existence in a world that defied every law of physics they had ever known. A world far away that, according to information that had been gathered, would be equally receptive to the Children's artistic visions. It was a chance to survive, a chance to leave a legacy.

Polly found herself flying, lifted up into the sky by the other creatures. They were on their way now, they could feel each other breaking down, their physical nature changing, preparing them for the long journey away from home. They soon reached a lonely rock in space, a rock on a course for the hope planet. And as they settled in, as they fell to sleep, they watched the darkness completely envelop their planet; and the tears they cried, knowing that most of their people would be dead by now, flowed for many years.

Polly opened her eyes and smiled as the vision ended. She was back in De Sande's office, but now she knew more than ever before that she was doing the right thing. She felt the Selyoids inside her continuing to ease her tension. They told her to relax, told her that she was a part of something great. Told her that she was a star, that she was perfect. They were making things better.

She smiled. 'Thank you,' was all she could think to say. She looked up at the hooded figure behind De Sande. 'Mr De Sande, if I may ask, who is that?'

De Sande smiled. 'This is one of my associates, one of the creatures' representatives. The representatives stay close to me at all times, guarding me, making sure I have support if I encounter anyone who threatens our peace plan.'

He turned to Chate. 'So, Robert,' he said, as he poured himself another glass of orange juice. 'How are you finding things in our little group?'

It was Chate's turn to laugh. 'How do you think?' he said. 'It's amazing. I've never felt so good.'

'You know, we were worried about you for a while,' De Sande said. Polly didn't fail to notice the threatening undercurrent in his voice. 'We heard you'd died.'

Chate shrugged. 'I had. But I'm back now.'

De Sande chuckled politely. 'So I see. Back where we can keep an eye on you.'

Chate looked confused. 'I... I don't understand.'

'We know what happened to your former employer, Mr Chate.'

Chate tried to look calm but the look in his eyes betrayed a terrified panic. 'How... How do you know Revere?'

'Relax,' De Sande said. 'You're part of our group now. Our plan is still on course for success despite that little mistake. You've been absolved.'

'Thank you,' Chate said, though Polly could tell from the confused expression on his face that he wasn't quite sure why he had said this.

'It's nothing,' De Sande said. 'All we ask is that you remain loyal, that you let the Selyoids into your soul, that you try to understand the good we're doing here.'

'I understand,' Chate said. 'Don't worry.'

De Sande smiled. 'Good. I'm glad we've cleared that up.'

There was a knock on the door and De Sande excused himself. He opened the door to the butler, who whispered a short message in his ear.

Turning to face his guests, De Sande began to wring his hands. 'I'm terribly sorry, folks,' he said, 'but I've been called away to an urgent meeting. We'll continue our little chat later, but if you'd like to follow my butler he'll fix you up some rooms in the guest suite while you're staying.'

'Thank you,' Maria said. 'That's most kind of you.'

There was a twinkle in De Sande's eyes. 'It's my pleasure. After all, you are a star.'

Chapter Twenty-One

The noise. The lights. The flashes. The shouts. Everywhere Ben looked there was chaos. Fans leant over barricades, stretching out in the vague hope of touching the stars, and packs of photographers snapped hungrily at everyone who walked along the long red carpet leading to the entrance of the Chinese Theater, the venue that tonight was playing host to the grand premiere of *Dying in the Sun*.

The Doctor marched along the carpet, smiling at the crowds, totally in his element. Ben and Fletcher moped slowly behind him, both less than relaxed about the attention they were receiving.

The Doctor seemed to sense Ben's bemusement and flashed him a knowing look. 'Just smile for the cameras,' he muttered under his breath. 'You never know, we might be in the papers tomorrow.'

'Wallis will love it if *I'm* in the papers,' Fletcher said dryly.

Ben straightened his bow tie – there had been little time to get the fitting right when he had hired it – and marched into the cinema, trying his best to ignore the screaming crowds. He still felt uneasy about attending the event. The Doctor was insistent that they go, sure he'd learn something vital to his investigation, but Ben would rather have spent the time looking for Polly. He hoped she'd get in touch tomorrow.

The atmosphere inside the cinema was a little more relaxed. The lobby was decorated with artificial palm trees and jungle paraphernalia, and various props from the film were displayed around its edges.

Turning a corner, they reached a reception area away from the prying eyes of the general public where a large cluster of celebrities was gathered, making small talk and eating delicately prepared food from oversized plates.

Fletcher looked around and whistled. 'There sure are a lot of stars out tonight,' he said.

'Yeah,' Ben agreed, 'and we might as well make the most of it. It's not often you get to go to a big Hollywood premiere.'

Fletcher smiled. 'Indeed.' He looked across the room. 'Is that Gregory Peck I see over there? I've *got* to talk to him!'

He darted off into the crowd, leaving the Doctor and Ben alone.

'Chips and dips?' a waitress asked, offering them some snacks. Ben politely helped himself but the Doctor wasn't interested.

Ben stuffed a few corn chips into his mouth and looked around the reception area. He suddenly realised that he was somewhat out of his element here. It was all very well going out with the stars, but it was quite clear they would have no interest in talking to the likes of him. He'd even seen the film before, so there wasn't even that novelty to look forward to, although he did have a strong desire to see it again. He supposed that at the end of the day this sort of thing just wasn't his style.

'Now where's Mr De Sande?' the Doctor wondered. 'I wouldn't mind a few words with him tonight.'

Ben glanced around the room but there was no sign of the director. Suddenly his attention was caught by a gorgeous-looking blonde, standing tall and perfectly formed in one corner of the room, oozing with star quality and standing out a mile from the drab besuited individuals surrounding her.

'Polly!' Ben said excitedly, tugging at the Doctor's sleeves. 'Look Doctor, it's Polly!'

He scurried over to see his friend and gave her a big hug. 'How are you, duchess?' he asked. 'We wondered where you'd got to.'

Ben felt Polly resist slightly, felt her push him away.

'Hello, Ben,' she said softly, her voice confident and strong.

'You're looking amazing,' Ben told her. 'What have you done to yourself?'

Polly laughed. 'I've been given some very useful advice by my new friends.' She gestured to a smartly dressed couple standing next to her. Ben could tell from the way they stood, from the way they dominated the people around them, that they were movie stars. 'Ben,' Polly continued, 'I'd like you to meet my new friends, Maria Coleman and Robert Chate.'

Ben had to look twice at the man before the realisation of who he was sunk in. 'Robert Chate? The one the police were after? You're never him! You look... well, different from the picture in the newspaper!'

Chate laughed. 'Let's just say I've moved up in the world a little. But please, careful who you give my name to. I'm supposed to be dead, you see.'

'Well, it's good to see you alive.' The Doctor had joined the group. 'Remember me?'

Chate nodded. 'Vaguely, but it all seems so long ago. Things have changed. I'm different now.'

'So why haven't you been in touch, Polly?' the Doctor asked.'

Polly sighed. 'Doctor, look at me. I'm a star now. A literal overnight success.'

Ben was puzzled by Polly's words. 'A star for what? What have you done?'

'You don't understand,' the woman next to Polly said. 'It's not about what you've done, it's about who you are. Look at Polly. Isn't she amazing?'

'And amazing people,' Polly said cockily, 'don't need to keep civilians informed of their movements.'

'Civilians?' Ben couldn't believe what he was hearing.

'We were just worried about you, that's all,' the Doctor said.

'Well, you shouldn't be. In the last forty-eight hours my life has changed for the better in a way I could never have dreamt of before.'

'Calm down,' Ben said. 'You've only met some celebs, that's all. Now come on, the Doctor and I have made some discoveries we want to show you.'

Polly laughed. 'Do you really think I care about your silly little investigation?'

'What's going on?' Ben said, trying to figure out why she was acting so strangely. 'Talk to me, Pol!'

'If you want me to talk to you,' Polly sneered, 'then you should become a star yourself. To be honest, there's nothing the likes of you can say that I want to hear right now. When *you're* famous, when *you're* loved as much as I am... then maybe we'll have a few words.'

'There is a way,' the woman next to her chipped in. 'You too could become a star, if you let us guide you in the same way we have Polly.'

'Shut up!' Ben snapped at her. He turned back to Polly. 'What the hell's going on?'

She seemed ruffled by Ben's outburst. 'Listen,' she said curtly. 'I'm more important than you now, I'm better than you. I haven't got time for you.'

'I'm not having this,' Ben said, fuming. 'If you want to be a stuck-up little tart then fine, but don't expect me to be there for you on the way down.'

'Polly,' the Doctor said. 'What's the matter? This isn't like you.'

'And how do you know, Doctor?' Polly asked. 'Who are you to tell me what I'm like.'

A brief silence. 'I'm your friend.'

'No, you're not,' Polly said, shaking her head. 'You're just a scavenger, a hanger-on, desperately trying to grab some of my own fame, my own glory to reflect upon yourself.'

The Doctor turned to the other woman. 'This is your doing, isn't it?' he said. 'Your people have changed Polly, infected her with the same substance you infected the cast of *Dying in the Sun* with?'

The woman smiled. 'I don't know what you're talking about.'

'Oh, I think you do,' the Doctor insisted. 'Yes, I know what you're up to. I know that you're not completely human any more.'

The woman laughed and looked edgy. 'Robert,' she said out of the side of her mouth, 'shall we call security?'

'That won't be necessary,' the Doctor said.

The uncomfortable exchange was broken up as a man in a dark green coat barged between Maria and the Doctor. 'Excuse me, Miss Coleman,' he said, reaching out a hand for her to shake that she ignored. 'I'm with the *Herald*. Can I have a few words with you?'

Maria nodded. 'Of course,' she said, 'anything for the public.'

The reporter smiled and began scribbling in a notebook. 'So tell me,' he said, 'have you seen all the other De Sande pictures?'

'You're a reporter, are you?' the Doctor said, butting in before Maria had a chance to answer.

The man nodded, and glared at the Doctor. 'Excuse me, sir, I'm trying to conduct an interview here.'

'Yes, yes, yes,' the Doctor said, 'but you're asking the wrong questions.'

The reporter cocked an eyebrow. 'Oh, am I?'

The Doctor nodded. 'Why don't you ask how she's suddenly made such a comeback. How they're looking so good, how they're getting everyone to follow their whims without any difficulty.'

The reporter laughed. 'I can answer that one, Mister. It's because they're stars. That's what stars do.'

The Doctor began walking around in circles, his frustration evident. 'But you don't understand. They're not human. They're not like us!'

'Of course they're not!' the reporter said. 'They're motion picture idols! They're the top dogs in our magical little town.'

Ben realised that a small crowd had gathered around the Doctor.

'That's not what I meant,' the Doctor said. 'Those people are being controlled by creatures totally unlike the human race. Creatures more dangerous than anything previously known to man.

This was too much for the crowd around the Doctor, and simultaneously they erupted with laughter.

The reporter smiled and looked intrigued. His expression of

embarrassment suddenly turned to smugness, as if he'd just realised what was going on.

'I get it,' he said. 'You're the comedian.' He pointed to the Doctor's clothes. 'I should have guessed it from those threads.'

'I see you've met the Doctor,' a loud voice said. Ben turned to see De Sande, who hurried up and put his arm around the Doctor's shoulders. 'He's a joker, isn't he? Kept the crew entertained for days on the film set.'

The crowd surrounding them laughed and began to disperse.

De Sande took the Doctor to one side, and Ben sidled over to hear what was being said.

'I'm amazed you showed your face after your behaviour last night,' the director said. 'Where have you been all day? We've been looking all over the place for you.'

'Oh, I've been closer than you might think,' the Doctor said.

'You betrayed us, Doctor. We let you in, but you wouldn't let us in. I thought you'd seen the light. But now I see that's not true. Your continued interrogations here and at the meeting prove your insincerity.'

'It's too late, De Sande,' the Doctor said. 'I know what's going on now.'

De Sande chuckled. 'Why do you keep trying, Doctor? You know you can't succeed. The media won't listen to you, the distributors won't listen to you... There's nothing you can do, you know? Just give up, you can't do anything to stop us. It's too late.'

The Doctor turned away from him and hurried back to the crowd. 'Please,' he urged them, 'you have to listen to me.'

The crowd burst out laughing once more and his face fell. He knew he was beaten. Embarrassed and dejected, he scowled and hurried towards the men's room.

'And now,' De Sande announced loudly, rubbing his hands with glee, 'if you'd like to take your seats, the movie is about to begin.'

The crowd began to buzz excitedly and everyone made their way through the large double doors that led to the auditorium. Ben watched Polly as she moved with them. She'd been so rude, so hurtful. She wasn't the Polly he knew, and he hoped that if the Doctor was right, and if Chate and that woman had done something to Polly to change her, it was something that could be reversed.

He wondered whether he should talk to her again, try to get her to change her mood, but he knew this was not the time or the place. He had been embarrassed enough by the reaction the Doctor had received just now. How red would he go if he confronted Polly about her change of mood?

He thought better of the idea and instead headed towards the men's room. The Doctor would take humiliation in his stride, but even so he could probably do with a friend right now.

Chapter Twenty-Two

Ben followed the Doctor into the rest room.

'Are you OK?' he asked him.

The Doctor began running a basin of water and splashed some of it on to his face. He reached his hand out and Ben passed him a towel.

'There,' the Doctor said, mopping himself dry, 'I'm quite all right now. The attitude of some people though... It really is quite amazing.'

'That's what being a multimillionaire does to you, I guess,' Ben said with a shrug.

'Yes, well, I think I've had quite enough of this little party. Are you sure you don't want to stay a while longer?'

Ben thought about Polly. She seemed happy but even so... 'Actually,' he said, 'I might stay on for a while, just to make sure Polly's new friends are treating her right. Maybe I can try to have another word with her.'

'Yes,' nodded the Doctor. 'It might be wise to keep an eye on things. But whatever you do, don't drink anything and try to ignore the celebrities.'

'Got you, Doctor,' Ben said with a smile. 'Don't worry. The last thing I want to do is be brainwashed by glow-worms.'

His words were interrupted by a distant rattling noise, like metal on metal, coming from somewhere in the room.

He made his way past the toilet cubicles and saw that the duct of a metal ventilation fan had come loose. Swinging on its hinges, it kept crashing into the wall.

'What is it?' the Doctor asked.

'Nothing,' Ben said. At that moment the lighting in the room flickered and the buzzing sound of an electrical discharge could briefly be heard. Ben was about to ask the Doctor if he could smell burning when the room was plunged into darkness, the lack of windows preventing any light getting in.

'Oh my,' the Doctor said. 'The power seems to have blacked out. I do hope the whole cinema hasn't been affected. Now carefully, use the walls as a guide, and feel your way along them. We should find the door easily enough.'

Ben reached out for the wall and felt a heavy blow knock his arm down. 'What the...!'

Something charged towards him, hitting him in the stomach. His breath knocked out of him, he fell to the floor.

A terrible animalistic cry filled the room and in the shadows Ben could make out few details of his attacker. Its growl seemed to mix a low, bear-like rumbling with the shrill scream of an animal in jeopardy, but judging from its size and the terrible bonfire-like smell it was giving off this thing wasn't human.

'Doctor!' Ben tried to shout, but it was too late.

He heard the Doctor gasp, heard the thud as the creature smashed into his friend.

'Ben!' the Doctor called. 'Are you all right?'

'Fine,' Ben gasped, pulling himself up. Something sharp suddenly smashed into his face, sending him reeling back to the floor. He felt a wet and painful sensation and he realised he was bleeding.

There was a deafening screech from the creature.

'Where... the key...' it growled, clearly enough for Ben to understand the words even if they couldn't quite be counted as speech.

'What?' the Doctor said, coughing. A series of smacking and slicing noises followed. 'I don't know what you mean,' Ben heard the Doctor shout. 'I don't know anything about a key!'

Ben tried to get to his feet and almost stumbled as he did so. He ran blindly forward to where he thought the creature would be and collided into it. Its skin was soft but leathery, and it was so bulky that Ben felt as if he had just run into a concrete wall. He catapulted across the room and felt the edge of the basin unit stab into his spine. He flinched and steadied himself against the unit.

From somewhere on the edge of his perception he heard a creaking noise. Suddenly light shone through the doorway into the room.

'What the hell?' a gruff voice said. There was a clicking sound as a switch was flicked and the room was illuminated once more.

Ben looked over and saw the creature for the first time. With rows of glistening teeth and bulging red, lizard-like eyes, the thing was a terrifying monster.

Ben's attention was snapped away from it by the cracks of three gunshots being fired in succession. He looked up to see Detective Fletcher standing open-mouthed at the door to the rest room, one hand hovering near the light switch and the other on his gun.

Growling, the creature lurched forward but another shot from Fletcher sent it flying back. Ignoring the Doctor and Ben, it ran to the back of the room, bouncing off the walls as it did so and covering its eyes, blinded by the light. Its screams continued, but it was clear that this time they were less like war cries and more like screams of agony.

The creature ran to the open ventilation duct. It leapt up but failed to reach it and landed in a crumpled heap on the floor.

With one final defiant growl, it stopped moving and began to melt away, its skin peeling as if on fire. In a matter of seconds, it had faded away. The only evidence that it had ever existed was the damage to the rest room.

Fletcher was breathing heavily, trying to take in what he had seen.

Ben looked over at the Doctor who, apart from a couple of cuts, looked like he hadn't been seriously injured.

The Doctor stood up and dusted himself down.

'It's all right, Detective,' he said, getting his breath back. 'It's gone now.'

Fletcher was breathing heavily, shaking his head, his eyes wide with bewilderment. 'What... What was it?'

'A bloody nightmare,' Ben said, checking the mirror. His nose was bleeding, but there wasn't too much damage.

'Well, at least we've had an eventful night,' the Doctor concluded. Ben marvelled at the way he appeared to be able to take anything in his stride.

The Doctor turned to Fletcher. 'Tell me, Detective, why aren't you watching the film with the others?'

'I damn well hate the movies,' Fletcher murmured. 'I only came for the party.'

'Doctor,' Ben said, trying to come to terms with what he'd just seen, 'that monster, what was it? Doctor, what the hell's going on?'

'Hell indeed,' the Doctor said sombrely. 'Whatever it was, it wanted something from me.'

'But what was it?' whispered Fletcher.

Ben was trying to place the extraordinary sensation of *dé-jà vu* he'd felt when he had seen the monster in the light. 'I've seen it somewhere before,' he said.

The Doctor appeared to think for a moment, then smiled and nodded his head. 'Indeed you have, Ben. That creature was one of the demons that attacked the main character in a certain film you and I have seen a couple of times recently.'

'*Dying in the Sun*?' Fletcher asked.

The Doctor nodded. 'If that thing was real, then it's no surprise the film's effects were so good.'

'What do you mean?' Ben asked. 'You mean the film shows those creatures in the flesh?'

'Oh no,' the Doctor said. 'I think the film *is* those creatures in the flesh!'

Chapter Twenty-Three

The premiere was over and Hollywood was bubbling with excitement. The crowd at the screening had never seen anything like it. Journalists and celebrities were entranced by De Sande's masterpiece and word spread rapidly around town that this movie was something pretty special.

The Doctor, Ben and Fletcher had made sure they'd left before they got caught in the crowds, and soon they were back at the hotel.

'Thanks for the lift,' Ben said as he got out of Fletcher's car.

'This better be worth it,' Fletcher said, ambling into the Doctor's room. 'If that monster was anything to go by, then...'

'What are we going to do about Polly?' Ben asked.

The Doctor looked at Ben with compassion. 'Try not to worry. We'll do all we can. I've a suspicion we won't be able to avoid running into her tomorrow. We'll get some sleep, then do all we can to find her and work out why she's acting so strangely.'

He clapped his hands and glanced around the room, then smiled as he worked out what he wanted to do next.

He picked up the device he'd obtained during the FOCAL meeting and placed it on a table. 'In all yesterday's madness I never got a chance to examine this properly,' he explained.

The object appeared to be made of glass, or perhaps finely cut crystal. It reminded Ben of an elaborate Christmas decoration, with points sticking out and swirling around a central column. The thing seemed vaguely star shaped, and glistened spectacularly as mirrored surfaces bounced light off each other. Ben reached down and picked the object up. As he did so, pieces of it clashed together making an almost choral chiming sound.

He held the glass object up to the light. 'So that Christmas decoration's supposed to be the key to stopping the film?'

'I certainly hope so,' said the Doctor.

'Is that what the creature was after then? You reckon De Sande sent it to get back this knick-knack you stole?'

The Doctor smiled.

Ben winced as the object caught a ray of sunlight through the window and amplified it, dazzling him. He almost dropped the object but, just in time, managed to keep hold of it.

'Here you go,' he said, handing it back to the Doctor. 'You want to see what that thing does to the light. It's lethal, I tell you.'

The Doctor held the object up and turned it around, studying it. 'I wonder how this thing would react when placed in close proximity to the film?'

He pointed to the safe in the corner of the room. 'Ben, get the film reel out of there would you? You know the combination.'

Ben hurried over to the safe, unlocked it and took out the reel.

'What's that?' Fletcher asked.

'Oh, you'll see,' the Doctor said, a broad smile on his face.

After ten minutes he had set up the projector, which he hadn't yet returned to the hire shop. He closed the curtains, loaded the stolen film reel into the projector then switched it on. Several seconds into the reel the monster appeared. Ben found the sight disturbing. On the surface level, it was clearly a man in a rubber costume. While it was recognisably meant to be the same as the thing that had attacked them at the premiere, it clearly wasn't real. But, despite its appearance, Ben found that just looking at it gave rise to the same emotions that he had felt during the attack.

The logical side of his mind could see that the thing was fake, just a costume, but the irrational side screamed that it was real, that he was in danger from the monster. Ben could feel its breath on him, could sense the fear the characters in the film felt as the creature attacked them. Logic told him not to worry, that it was just the Selyoids changing the film's appearance, triggering his senses to manipulate his emotions, but his body couldn't help reacting as it was expected to react, and he found the experience of watching the film as uncomfortable as it had been before.

'Quite frightening, eh?' the Doctor said. 'Before, the reel seemed to have no emotional impact at all, but now we know more about the film... it's feeding off our emotions, changing as it reacts to our thoughts.'

'I don't get frightened,' Fletcher said. 'But I know what I saw with my own eyes. Whatever that animal is...' He stopped talking as a woman was sliced in two by the creature's claws. 'Was that... was that real?'

'I don't think so,' the Doctor said. 'You can't tell the colour of blood in black and white.'

'But I saw that creature in real life, Doctor,' Fletcher said. 'That murder... that looked pretty real to me. If this turns out to be a snuff movie... that De Sande's gonna be in a whole ton of trouble.'

'No, I don't think the monster's real,' the Doctor said, 'but that doesn't mean it can't appear real. The thing we saw was a real-life interpretation of the image on screen. Somehow what's on there has been brought to life out here.'

He held the glass object up in the projection beam. 'I wonder...' he said. A patch of the screen warped slightly as the light from the projector was disrupted by the device.

The Doctor stood up, walked to the projector and placed the object on the table immediately in front of its lens. 'This round piece on the end of the device,' he commented. 'It's exactly the same size as a standard projector lens. The people De Sande hired to create this thing must have been master craftsmen.'

As the light began to pass through the object it glowed and sparkled as the hundreds of tiny mirrors inside it bounced the light waves around, finally throwing them back on to the screen. The device seemed to switch on, as if powered by electricity, and Ben was sure he could hear a slight humming noise.

'It's intriguing, isn't it?' said the Doctor. 'But not as intriguing as what's happening on screen, I feel.'

Ben turned and saw what the Doctor meant. The reel had reached the point where one of the lead characters was meandering through a crowded city street. He seemed more on edge than he had the last time Ben had watched the reel, looking back over his shoulder and checking the time on his watch more often.

As the sequence continued the street appeared to collapse. At first the change was so slow that it was barely perceptible, but slowly the buildings in the background of the scene began to peel away like onions, shedding one layer of reality at a time. The walls peeled away to reveal floors of people working in offices, and then those people were peeled away to reveal a swirling mass of nothingness, as if the entire city was melting out of existence.

The film had been silent up until this point, but a distant noise of shouting and distorted cries was now audible. Eventually, the entire scene was replaced by a chaotic mix of dark colours, speckled with the occasional appearance of characters from the film. The colours coalesced, forming images of stalactites, flames and pillars of smoke. An image of a corridor was forming, a corridor in a cavern, along the walls of which hundreds of people were chained, all being tortured with a variety of gruesome-looking devices.

The walls of hell rippled and the stone became sandbags, the tortured souls became First World War soldiers scrambling through the trenches on their way to their deaths. The soldiers' faces fell away, their flesh melting as the effects of a nuclear bomb hit them.

Pictures of children, the real victims of war, flashed across the scene. Innocent lives left blinded, mutilated and cancered by a war over before they were old enough to talk. Slowly the images mutated again, this time back into the monsters that had originally attacked the characters in the film. This time the monsters weren't men in suits. This time they really were real. Ben tried to look away but couldn't. He saw the monsters staring directly at him, beckoning him to join them. One of the creatures reached out beyond the confines of the screen, its talons grasping for him. The others started to follow it, bone fragments shattering to the floor as wings sprouted from their backs. They screamed and flapped their wings, propelling themselves away from hell and towards their captive audience.

'Incredible,' Ben heard the Doctor say. 'I think I understand now. By Jove, I can see what's going on!"

Before he could say any more one of the creatures let out a scream that shook the room like a minor earthquake. It lurched forward, its wings making a heavy swooshing sound as they sliced through the air. Ben cowered away, covering his eyes as it bared its teeth, saliva dripping off several rows of razor-sharp fangs. The creature circled around the room, seemingly unbothered that it was supposed to be a fictional character, supposed to stay on the screen. Another scream and it moved in for the kill, flying straight towards the Doctor.

Fourth Reel

Chapter Twenty-Four

Ben could hear screams, could smell sulphur, but he could see little in the darkness except a terrifying shape flying straight towards the Doctor. No, not towards him. It had flown straight through him. And then the room filled with light, and Ben heard the sound of the whimpering scream as the creature faded away until it had disappeared completely.

'Doctor,' Fletcher said loudly. 'I've made a decision. This is all beyond me, so I give in. I'll help you, OK? Just let me know how to stop that thing. I'd hate to end my days as demon dinner.'

'I suspected that those projections can only take on a physical presence with enough supportive energy from the audience,' the Doctor explained. 'If we don't believe they're real, if we don't believe they can hurt us, then they're helpless, nothing but advanced projections of light. At the end of the day, all this is about light. Everyone at FOCAL is obsessed with it, with good reason. It's the one thing that makes going to the cinema possible. The projector has to have a bright light, but the rest of us *can't* have light if anyone is to see what's being shown on the screen. Without darkness, with too much light, we can't see the projected images any more and the Selyoids have no way to influence us. No way to create their illusions. Once I'd turned on the light we couldn't see what was on screen any more. When we couldn't see them, we couldn't fear them, and when we couldn't fear them they couldn't feed.'

He walked over to the projector and switched it off. 'Light will find a way.'

He reached down for the glass device and picked it up. 'Ow!' he said, almost dropping it. 'It's hot!'

'Hot?' Ben said. 'How can a piece of tat like that get hot?'

'It's clearly generating heat somehow. If it's powered that would explain why it appears to glow so unnaturally. Maybe it creates a thermal field that alters the room temperature enough to create the ideal environment for the creatures to come to life in? I believe that this device concentrates light and heat on to the film in such a way that it transforms the creatures embedded in the film, giving them life, giving them the freedom to move around in a form other than a dried-out chemical. You saw the way that monster glowed... I'm starting to think that what we saw was our minds' interpretations of the Selyoids' natural form. We saw them shift through several different interpretations. For some reason they've been trapped on the film, but that device... It has the power to give them life, to give them form away from the film. Normally we just see the impression of the creatures on the screen, but with this device they can reflect off the screen into reality. And that's how De Sande's effects are so special.'

'But what about that thing from the premiere?' Ben asked. 'There wasn't any device there... There wasn't even a projector.'

The Doctor looked puzzled. 'Indeed, that is a mystery. It certainly looked the same as the other creatures and it was almost as vulnerable as them to bright light that wasn't coming from itself or the projector. Maybe it was a more evolved being than the others. Maybe the creatures are finding a way to leave the confines of the film without needing projectors and strange glass devices. In that case...'

'In that case we're all on the night train,' Fletcher sighed. 'The last thing we need is a horde of those monsters overrunning the city.'

'But it's OK, isn't it?' Ben said. 'They'd all die the moment the sun comes up.'

The Doctor shook his head. 'They've found a way to leave the confines of the film... Who's to say they won't find a way to become immune to other sources of light?'

He reached down towards the projector and removed the glass device. He held it up to the light, turning it round to examine it. 'This object...' he said. 'This gives the Selyoids life. Without it they're nothing but projections on a screen. De Sande wanted it back. I wonder how many he has?'

The Doctor walked over to window and opened the blinds, then checked his watch. 'It's midnight,' he said in a serious tone. 'A new day begins here. The day when we find out just how terrifying the impact of the Selyoids will be on these people. The day we try one last gambit to stop the madness.' He turned and looked Ben in the eye. 'This morning *Dying in the Sun* will be released in cinemas. I hope with all my soul that we live to see tomorrow.'

'What about Polly?' Ben asked. 'You saw how she was last night. We have to find her today and work out what's up with her.'

'Don't worry,' the Doctor consoled him. 'We'll find her, and find out what's going on. We'll find her.'

It was almost eleven o'clock in the morning and the streets were jammed with cars. Angry commuters beeped their horns and shouted at each other whilst traffic cops desperately tried to keep order in the mounting tension.

The Doctor's rental car was moving at a crawl.

'We'll never get there at this rate,' Ben said. He rolled down the window and poked his head outside the vehicle. 'Oi!' he shouted. 'Come on! This isn't a car park you know!'

'I don't get it,' Fletcher said. 'I've never seen so many cars round here. Where the hell are people going?'

The Doctor pulled in to the side of the road and turned off the engine. 'At this rate we'd be quicker walking,' he said.

They got out of the car and the Doctor hurried up to a traffic cop who was frantically trying to direct vehicles away from each other.

'Excuse me, officer,' the Doctor said, 'is the road ahead closed? Why is there such a delay?'

The cop turned to the Doctor and shrugged. 'It's the movie theatres on Hollywood Boulevard. The queues are stretching back miles. Everyone in town's trying to get there.'

The Doctor turned back to Ben and Fletcher. 'Right then,' he said, rubbing his hands together. 'Let's see what all the fuss is about, shall we?

They hurried down towards Hollywood Boulevard, past the endless line of gridlocked traffic. The sun was beating down on the cars, making the passengers hotter and more flustered.

After fifteen minutes they reached the stretch of the boulevard where the cinemas were. Outside each one a long queue of people trailed along the pavement, and as they walked past Ben heard various arguments and shouting matches coming from the crowds.

The Doctor walked up to tall, blond-haired and extremely bored-looking girl who was standing on her own in one of the queues. 'Excuse me,' he said, 'could you tell me what everyone's waiting for?'

The girl shot him an indifferent look. 'Don't you know?' she said. 'It's that film everyone's been talking about. The one about death under the sun, or something.'

'But why?' the Doctor asked. 'It's only just been released. Why is everyone so keen to see it now? The cinemas won't have been open very long, surely?'

The girl shrugged. 'I was just driving along, saw some posters for it and thought, why not? It'll get me out of the heat, at least.'

The Doctor thanked her for her time and began to walk away, muttering to himself as if he was working on a particularly complicated calculation.

'Come on,' he said, 'let's see what the cinema staff think of all this.'

He began to walk faster, Fletcher and Ben hurrying to catch up with him. There must have been thousands of people queuing up, far more than could fit in to all the screenings at all the cinemas that day, but this didn't seem to put the public off. The crowd seemed edgy and nervous but all were quite patient.

They were prepared to stand around just in case extra screenings were announced, just in case some of the people in front of them decided not to bother with the wait.

As he walked along the boulevard with the Doctor and Fletcher Ben noticed that several people were giving him evil looks, as if to chastise him for pushing into their queues. He wondered why the crowds assumed he was there to see the film. On any normal day hundreds of people walked down this street without giving the slightest thought to the cinemas. Why should today be any different?

'I've seen the film,' Ben called out for a joke. 'It's not very good, promise!'

'Liar!' a tearful woman shouted angrily as if Ben had kidnapped her child. 'I saw it earlier and it's wonderful. The best film ever!'

'Did you see that?' said the Doctor as they walked on. 'Can *Dying in the Sun* really be affecting people that badly? When we saw it at De Sande's the hysteria in the room seemed to bounce off everyone watching it. I wonder if the effect is amplified when the film is viewed in a forum with hundreds of people.'

'Amplified?' Fletcher said. 'You mean the more people that watch it, the stronger the effects, and the more they want to go and see it again?'

The Doctor nodded. 'Like an exponential addiction racing through the city. A few days of screenings and the entire city will be affected, will be slaves to the Selyoid whim. If humanity is to retain its freedom we have to stop it happening.'

He barged forward through a queue, pushing his way towards the box-office booth.

'Excuse me!' he called to the waiting cinema-goers.

'Excuse yourself,' a voice said.

'Get in line like the rest of us!' another shouted.

The Doctor seemed unfazed by their remarks and soon reached the box office. The sales window was closed and a sign plastered across it said THIS WEEK ONLY: DYING IN THE SUN: FREE PREVIEWS.

'Get in line!' a tall, hardened-looking man shouted, grabbing the Doctor by the collar of his jacket. He threw the Doctor aside and Ben ran up to help his friend.

The Doctor brushed himself off and eyed the tall man with suspicion. 'I don't think they're going to let us through, somehow.'

The noise of shouting could be heard from the front of the queue, as people became more and more desperate to see the film. A commissionaire was trying to keep everyone back, telling them they still had a while to wait before the next available screening. 'You're not the only ones who've got complaints about today,' he shouted.

A barrage of excited laughs and screams came from somewhere to the side of the cinema. Ben turned and saw a crowd of people emerging from an exit. Judging by the excited buzz coming from them, they were the ones who'd just seen the film.

'I wanna go again!' Ben heard one girl say.

'Oh, yeah, but look at the line,' another said.

'Do I care? I just wanna see it again.'

'Well come on then, let's get in line now!'

Ben shook his head in amazement. Couldn't these people see what was happening? Couldn't they see that they were becoming addicted to *Dying in the Sun*? For the first time the enormity of what was going on hit him. It was the process of seeing the film with so many others, the buzz people got from the hysteria of watching it - that's what people craved. Ben remembered how he had felt when he had watched the film at De Sande's, and thought how terrifying yet amazing it would feel if those feelings were multiplied by several times. You'd never want to leave, and it was clear that this lot certainly didn't.

A bulky individual who had just left the film barged through the crowd and, out of the blue, threw a punch at another customer that sent him flying to the floor.

'What the hell are you doing?' a woman next to the injured man said.

'I must see that film again,' the bulky man said. 'You don't understand. I have to see it now!'

'No, you damn well don't,' said another man. He threw a punch right under the bulky man's chin, then threw another one that sent his opponent flying backwards, knocking over several customers like bowling pins.

'Oh dear,' the Doctor said as the fighting began to ripple through the crowd. 'I think we'd better get away from here.'

Fletcher nodded and reached into his jacket. He took out his gun and fired a shot into the air. The crowd dispersed slightly, leaving enough space for him, the Doctor and Ben to get out on to the street.

'Let's get to my car,' Fletcher said as they paused to catch their breaths. 'I'll radio for backup.'

The Doctor shook his head. 'Just remember that somewhere in that crowd Selyoid partners are generating waves of emotion that are driving people into the cinema, driving them to hear the Selyoid message, to have their minds converted to the Selyoid cause. It doesn't matter how many police come down here, they're also human beings, susceptible to the same sounds, smells and influences that everyone else is. All that will happen is that they'll get involved in the fighting too, only they'll have more guns.'

'So what do we do then?'

Ben noticed that the queue didn't stretch anywhere near as far as it had minutes before. 'Where did everyone go?' he asked.

'Down there,' said Fletcher, pointing along the street to where a large number of people were getting into their cars.

'Well, come on then,' the Doctor said, running in the direction of the crowd.

They soon caught up with the men and women who looked panicked as they started to drive their cars away as fast as they could, past the gridlock of traffic coming in the other direction.

'Where are they going?' asked the Doctor. 'Why don't they want to see the film any more?'

'I think I can answer that,' Fletcher said, pointing to the side of the street.

Ben looked up and saw a giant billboard. A standard poster for *Dying in the Sun* was plastered across one half, with the title in giant red letters and a painting of Caleb Rochefort staggering through a jungle, but on the other half was a picture of the hills over Hollywood showing the HOLLYWOODLAND sign. Looking at the picture made Ben uneasy. There was something not quite right about it. Something unreal.

It reminded him of being in a dream state. How you can read a book or see some writing on a sign, and even though you can't read in your sleep, can only see shapes, you somehow just know what the writing says. You can read by simply looking at the text, rather than actually reading the individual letters. That was how he felt now. The logical side of his mind told him that what he saw as a billboard was in reality a blank, a large stretch of dark violet. The irrational, emotional side could see that the space was a photograph - no, not a photograph, a real image like a window on whatever it wanted to show.

Ben realised why it looked so vague. The image was being projected on to the billboard, and that could mean only one thing. The Selyoids were using it to direct people through it, and this explained why the image he saw seemed so real. They were telling his mind that he was seeing reality. And he knew what he had to do.

'How interesting,' the Doctor said. 'A still-frame projector nudging the general public's behaviour.'

'Can you see it, Doctor?' Ben asked.

'I can see how people are reacting to it. I wonder if it's giving everyone the same message? What is it telling you? Where is everyone going?'

'See the film...' Fletcher said. 'It's saying, see the film and then get out, get away from here. It's not safe, we need to see the film and then go.'

'Go where?' the Doctor said, hands tight to his chest, keenly awaiting the answer.

'Away from here,' he growled, 'up into the hills.'

Chapter Twenty-Five

The chauffeur taking Chate, Polly and Maria to their destination finally drove up to the enormous warehouse known as the Star Light Hangar. The building looked intimidating, silhouetted against the orange dusk sky, a giant monument to Star Light's dominance of the town.

On the way to the hangar Maria had explained a little about its history. While the studio's main complex was in Culver City, Star Light had bought this warehouse overlooking Burbank airport for the purposes of accommodating overflow productions, for providing extra office space and to store the numerous private planes owned by the company's executives.

The building faced directly on to one of the airport's runways, so was the perfect place to welcome visitors of importance who had recently flown in. Flying in over the HOLLYWOODLAND sign always made a good impression on sponsors.

A row of security guards stood in front of the warehouse while hundreds of people swarmed around it, trying to get a look inside, peering through windows and pleading with the guards to let them into the building. They could sense what was inside it, sense that the ones in charge of changing their lives were here, that the quickest way to bond with the new presence was in this building.

The chauffeur pulled the limo up to the side of the hangar and stopped the engine. A member of the crowd saw the car and pointed. Gradually, the rest of the mass of people began to look at it and soon they all began to make their way towards the vehicle.

Polly, Chate and Maria got out of the car and made their way towards the building.

Before they could get to the entrance door the crowd of people reached them and started grabbing their clothes. Polly felt a tug at her shirt.

'Oh, my God!' a woman said. 'It's Maria Coleman herself! You must be her co-stars!'

The crowd began to babble excitedly. 'Maria! I love your pictures!' one man said.

'I can't believe you guys are here,' said another.

'Can I have your autograph?' A teenaged girl asked, thrusting a pen and autograph book into Polly's face. Polly scribbled her signature and pushed her way through the crowd.

As the people mobbed them, Polly felt a strange tingling sensation inside. She felt the creatures she had bonded with relaxing her, releasing chemicals into her skin that made her more appealing, more attractive and more confident. As she looked at the fans she felt loved, felt they all believed she was better than other people. There was no doubt about it, she had star quality and these people worshipped her for it.

'Excuse me,' Chate said loudly. 'Can you give us some space here, please?'

The crowd obligingly moved away, still chattering excitedly at the sight of the three newcomers.

'Go inside quickly,' one of the security guards at the door called to Maria. 'These your friends, yeah?'

Maria nodded then ducked under the barrier. Polly and Chate followed behind as the guards moved in to stop the crowd from doing the same. Maria directed her companions through a small door and closed it behind them.

Polly was impressed with the scale of the hangar. The roof seemed incredibly high from inside the building and bright spotlights attached to the ceiling swept beams of light across the interior, giving it a spooky feeling. Large windows at the top of the building let what remained of the daylight stream in, and film memorabilia were displayed along the walls. The whole front of the building was a giant open space containing several small aeroplanes that were being busily serviced by engineers and technicians. Behind the plane area was a row of smart-looking office huts and, when they got to them, Maria ushered her friends into a large double-storey one that stood at the front of the others.Roman-style pillars decorated its front and gold paint lined the frosted-glass windows.

Inside, the office had been painted a pleasant mint green and was brightly lit with filtered bulbs that gave it a relaxing ambience. Luxurious furniture was scattered through the room, and at one end Leonard De Sande sat behind a large, wooden desk, puffing slowly on a cigar and looking extremely smug and content.

His eyes lit up as he saw he had visitors. He snuffed his cigar out in an ashtray, pushed his chair back and stood up.

'Hi guys!' he said, striding over to the front of the office. 'Polly!' he said with a wide grin across his face. 'Dear Polly.'

He took her hand and gave it a gentlemanly kiss. 'It's so wonderful that we still have your support. You can't imagine what wonderful surprises I've got in store for us all tonight.'

'I'm looking forward to it,' Polly said. 'This really is a fabulous place you've got here.'

De Sande smiled. 'Well, we try.'

He looked at Chate and shook his hand. 'Hope you got some sleep, my friend.' Finally, he turned to Maria and opened his arms towards her. They hugged for a few seconds, then De Sande separated their embrace. Both of them looked slightly uncomfortable, slightly awkward. There was a strange tension in the air, and Polly felt the Selyoid essence inside her become agitated. Strong feelings of confusion were coming from somewhere in the room, and Polly couldn't help picking up on them.

Maria and De Sande looked awkwardly at each other, then suddenly De Sande pulled the actress towards him. Maria wrapped her arms around him and they began a warm, passionate kiss that seemed to last for ever.

Polly glanced across at Chate. His breathing looked heavy and his eyes were red, showing a tempest of confusion and jealousy.

She cleared her throat politely as De Sande and Maria disentangled themselves.

'Maria,' De Sande said softly, cocking an eyebrow. 'That was quite a kiss.'

Maria smiled. 'You've kissed me many times,' she said affectionately.

De Sande's face hardened. 'But you've never actually *wanted* me to do it before,' he reminded her.

The meaning of De Sande's words was just beginning to sink into Polly's mind when Chate exploded.

'You goddamned animal!' he shouted at De Sande. He ran over and grabbed the director by the neck. 'I'll kill you, you bastard!'

Polly ducked out of the way as De Sande struggled to escape from Chate's grip.

'Robert!' Maria screamed, desperately trying to pull him back. 'It's OK!' she screamed. 'It's OK! I realise the truth now! I realise that I love him!'

'Security!' De Sande gasped as the air drained from his lungs, 'Security!'

Chate's hands were clenched too tightly round De Sande's neck for the man's cries to be loud enough for the guards to hear them.

Chate looked at Maria, his eyes red with anger. 'What have you done?' he cried.

Maria clawed at him with her nails, doing her best to wrench him away from De Sande. 'Let him go!'

Polly felt helpless watching the struggle so she ran to the entrance to the office and called for the security guards.

She returned in time to see Chate tighten his grip on De Sande before throwing him to the floor. The director began gasping for air, desperate to get his breath back. Polly ran over to his desk and picked up a glass of water.

'Are you OK?' she asked as she sat De Sande up and handed him the drink. She looked up at Chate. 'Look what you've done!' she scolded.

A couple of no-nonsense security guards came into the room.

'Get him,' De Sande wheezed, clutching his neck. The guards ran over to Chate and grabbed his arms, twisting them round and holding them tightly behind his back.

'I thought you loved me,' Chate growled angrily at Maria, tears flowing down his cheeks. 'I thought we had something special.'

She turned away from him, unable to look him in the eyes. 'I didn't want to hurt you,' she said, 'but we had to be sure of your loyalty. We had to make sure you'd stick with us. We wanted you to be part of us, so you could experience the joy of the Selyoids. We sensed your potential, sensed how much you cared about me, and we knew you should join with us.'

Chate looked shattered. 'You've been playing with me. Toying with my emotions.'

Polly was stunned by what she was hearing. Chate had seemed so confident, so secure... such a star. And all the time he was being tricked. She wondered whether he was the only one who had been manipulated.

'You made me think you had feelings for me,' Chate shouted at Maria. 'Yet all the time...'

'All the time it was just one big illusion,' De Sande said. 'One trick of the light.'

Chate glared at De Sande. 'Why?' he said angrily.

'Because you saw something you shouldn't have,' De Sande said, his voice still croaky but quickly recovering. 'You know who killed Harold Reitman.'

Chate looked confused, his face red with a rage of conflicting emotions. 'No,' he said. 'I don't...'

'Oh, you do,' De Sande said with machiavellian delight. 'You may not remember now, you may have blocked it out, but if you think hard enough... I'm sure you'll recall seeing your father take an innocent man's life.'

'No,' Chate said. 'He thought I was the killer. It can't be him.'

'Wanna bet?' De Sande chuckled. 'He framed you, Robert. He ribbed up his own son to save his skinny ass.'

'But why?' Chate cried. 'Why me?'

'Your father is known as a very public advocate of an organisation we both belong to called FOCAL. He was seen killing Reitman, and if that got out... Well, let's just say our organisation can't afford that kind of negative publicity at the moment. One of our most noted members a murderer?'

'If I did see it, then why didn't you kill me?'

De Sande cocked his head. 'What makes you think we didn't want to? Your father wanted a deal, tried to save your life. You should be grateful, you know.'

'But why? I wouldn't have done the same.'

De Sande shrugged. 'He's getting old. Maybe he's starting to repent his sins, maybe it's the Selyoids making him see things differently. Or maybe, despite everything, he's just still your damn father. He arranged to have you framed to save your life. Knew there would be no questions asked. The LAPD really hate you, did you know that? Wallis knew he could have words with the DA to get you a gas-chamber bounce. Any testimony you gave against him could be ignored. So we let him go ahead.'

The guards were still holding Chate tightly, but he had collapsed in their grip, sobbing uncontrollably. 'If I'd known... I'd have told them every damn thing.' He opened his eyes and looked across the room, the fire burning in his soul. 'He hurt me. He hurt me more than anyone, more than...' He looked over at Maria and shook his head, the will to live barely there.

'I knew you wouldn't care,' De Sande said, walking over to his desk, 'and I know that Wallis is starting to trip up. He's not as friendly with the DA as he thinks. If it went wrong, if you spilled the beans and FOCAL was linked... Well, we knew that you were still a liability, so I asked a friend of mine to fill you with daylight.'

Chate looked up and his mouth fell open. 'My God... Revere? You're the one who sent Revere after me?'

De Sande put his hand into a drawer inside his desk and when he took it out was clutching a chunky-looking pistol. He aimed the gun at Chate.

'No!' Polly heard herself saying. De Sande threw her a look

that told her to relax, to keep quiet. She felt the Selyoids inside her release soothing chemicals into her bloodstream, felt them pick up on De Sande's mood. The Selyoids told her that this was necessary, that she should watch, listen and learn.

'Don't shoot me!' Chate sobbed, staring down the barrel of the gun. 'Please don't shoot me! I don't want to die! I don't want to die!'

De Sande shrugged. 'Neither did Martin.'

'It was an accident,' Chate mumbled.

'I know you, Robert, remember. The Selyoids inside you betray your feelings. You wanted him dead. It was all you prayed about every night. We can see it in your mind, we can feel it from your soul.'

'No,' Chate said, 'I used to think it, but I never meant it... You're getting the signals confused, seeing the outside not the inside. I never meant to hurt him, he was trying to kill me!'

'We panicked when we felt Martin's death,' Maria said solemnly. 'When we knew you were on the loose. You don't know how pleased Leonard was when he realised who I'd met. The poor dear had been looking everywhere for you. The moment we knew you were still alive we needed to find you, we needed to stop you from talking. And then you walked into that bar, and through the Selyoid essence in me Leonard recognised who you were, knew we had to get you to join us.'

'But why not kill me?'

'Because you killed my best friend,' De Sande said. 'I wanted to see you suffer, but the Selyoids wanted to use you as an example, to give you the opportunity for redemption. They wanted you to know the glory of being one with them.'

'When I first met you,' Maria explained, 'you had nothing to live for. No life, no friends, no home... Nothing. To kill you then... well what pain would you feel? How much would it hurt?'

'Whereas now,' De Sande said, 'thanks to the Selyoids, you have everything. You've got star quality, people love you. How much more painful will death be?'

Uncontrollably, and bizarrely, Chate burst out laughing. 'You're so wrong,' he said. 'I never wanted to die. Never.'

'Well, it's immaterial now,' De Sande said, clicking the safety catch on the gun. He rubbed his neck with his free hand. 'You've proved that you're too dangerous.' He suddenly looked puzzled, then a broad grin swept across his face. 'Oh dear,' he said insincerely, 'it seems my associates don't like the way this conversation is going.'

He walked over to his desk, put the gun down and picked up a large clay jar. 'Let him go, please,' he said calmly, looking up at the guards.

They did so, and Chate fell to the floor. His eyes widened, almost bursting out of their sockets, and he clasped his neck as if he was having trouble breathing. De Sande walked over to the younger man, grabbed his head and forced his face against the jar's opening. There was a disgusting retching noise as Chate threw up, and Polly could see a bright glow beginning to emanate from the jar. It was the Selyoid essence, getting out of Chate's body as quickly as it could.

When Chate had finished, De Sande let him fall to the floor, replaced the jar on his desk and sealed it with a lid. He picked up his gun once more.

'How does it feel,' he said, 'to be lonely? How does it feel to be inferior? No more Selyoids, no more belonging... no more friends. You're nothing now, nothing.'

Chate was sobbing uncontrollably. 'I was a star,' he cried. 'I was everything.'

'Not any more you're not,' De Sande said, pointing the gun at Chate. 'Now, where were we?'

Polly could feel the tension, feel the joy in De Sande's heart, feel Maria's relief that she was soon to be rid of her annoying fan.

And most curiously of all, she could feel pain. The pain that the Selyoids were experiencing. She realised they were mourning the loss of Chate from their essence, were trying to regroup and pull together to get over the loss of strength.

Looking at Chate, a pathetic, snivelling wretch, Polly wondered just how perfect the Selyoid society would be. Maria had told her that she'd be a star, and so far she'd been treated just like that, but at what cost? She'd become an overnight success, one of the Chosen, one of the select few elevated to stardom by the Selyoids' gifts. But people were suffering. She looked at Chate, at the expression on his face. Had she really become so dispassionate? Was it all worth it? Who else would the Selyoids hurt?

She thought back to the premiere, to her argument with Ben. She thought about what she had said to the Doctor. The Selyoids gave her a family, gave her stardom, gave her happiness and security. They gave her everything she wanted, but what had they taken from her in return? Why be loved if you're incapable of loving back? She had lost her friends, and it was her own fault.

Caleb Rochefort flashed through her mind. He'd been one with the Selyoids, like she was now. He hadn't been strong enough to fight the influence of the Selyoids within him and they'd made her kill him. Polly looked at De Sande and realised that he genuinely wanted to kill Chate. The expression on his face showed pure delight in his actions. Polly had seen the final, mournful expression on Caleb's face. She realised now what his expression had meant: that in his dying seconds the star had regretted his pact with the creatures.

Polly saw Maria walk over to De Sande and kiss him, one final piece of salt to rub in Chate's wounds before they shot him.

Someone had already died because of Polly. She couldn't let that happen again.

Polly walked over to De Sande, her soul screaming at her to stop. She felt the Selyoids burning inside her, trying to reassert their control, trying to alter her hormones to make her feel better. She hesitated and almost stopped but knew she had to fight the creatures, had to ignore their words of comfort. Getting closer, the Selyoids screaming... The whole sequence of events took seconds, but felt like hours. She neared De Sande and as she did so he looked up, the Selyoids within him triggering a reaction, picking up on the panic emanating from her. He turned his gun away from Chate, and she seized the moment, sending her fist crashing down on his arm. The gun went spinning to the floor. Polly dived down and picked it up.

The security guards leapt for her, but she managed to flip herself round and point the gun at them before they could touch her. They froze, slowly lifting their hands into the air.

'Move!' Polly shouted, gesturing for De Sande and Maria to go and stand with the security guards. They did so and she slowly walked over to Chate, making sure not to take her eyes off the others. 'Get up,' she said sternly, trying to act calmly despite the raging emotions inside her.

Polly, stop this. Think how happy you are. You don't want to lose that, do you?

'Get out of my head!' she shouted to De Sande. 'Get out!'

She reached down and pulled Chate to his feet. 'Come on,' she said. 'You want to live don't you?'

Chate looked up and his eyes filled with relief. He had given up on life and yet now, out of the blue, a second chance had appeared. Polly put her arm around his shoulder, supporting him. 'Can you walk?' she asked. He nodded and they began to stagger out of the office, Polly keeping the gun trained on Maria and De Sande.

As they got to the doorway, Chate stopped and looked back at the others.

'Screw you,' he said quietly. 'I'm never going to die.'

He and Polly hurried out of the hanger as quickly as they could, Chate's strength quickly returning. They pushed their way through the crowd then moved into the undergrowth surrounding the airport before De Sande's security guards could be sent after them. The Selyoids in Polly continued to scream at her but she managed to silence them by looking at Chate, by seeing and thinking about the pain in his eyes. De Sande's men would be all over the area looking for them, and until the Selyoids decided to extricate themselves from her in the same way they had from Chate, she knew that De Sande would be able to locate her.

They had to get away and Polly knew where they had to go. They had to find the Doctor.

Chapter Twenty-Six

The seething mass of cars drove steadily along Western Canyon, blindly following the Selyoids' subliminal influence.

In one of the cars, the Doctor, Ben and Fletcher were frantically trying to get as far ahead of the traffic as they could. 'How much further?' Ben asked.

The Doctor pointed towards the hills in the distance. 'Not much. I think wherever we're heading is just up there.' He turned to look at the side of the road and pointed to a billboard advertising *Dying in the Sun*. Another proclamation of the movie's merits. Another vision of hope, of perfection.

'What do you see?' he asked Ben. 'What's the sign telling you?'

Ben looked at the billboard and realised that he really wanted to see the movie again. The poster made it look so good, so epic...

'I want to see *Dying in the Sun* again,' he said. 'But not as much as I want to follow everyone else.'

'But how would you feel if you hadn't seen the film before?' the Doctor wondered.

Ben shook his head. 'Oh, can you imagine? What a nightmare. I'd probably do anything to see it. Anything.'

'I haven't seen it,' said Fletcher, and suddenly Ben realised why the cop had seemed agitated. 'Maybe I should. It sounds so good.'

'No,' the Doctor insisted. 'Once you see the film you'll be as susceptible to the Selyoid influence as everyone else here. Stay with me, and try not to look at the billboards. You'll be fine.'

'I must see that picture,' Fletcher moaned. 'Maybe I can catch you up afterwards?'

'No,' insisted the Doctor. 'Don't you see what's happening? You're being influenced by the posters. They're telling everyone who hasn't seen the film to see it, and once they have the posters tell them to move along this road, to head for the hills. Notice how there's one of these billboards every three hundred yards? It's like they're navigation points, giving these people new instructions at every interval.'

They'd been driving for almost an hour when they finally reached the car park in Griffith Park where the pilgrimage of thousands had gathered. At the sides of the parking area, several large illuminated billboards displayed posters for *Dying in the Sun*. A large canvas marquee had been erected near the billboards and a long queue trailed from it.

'Come on,' the Doctor said to his friends, 'let's take a little detour.'

Ben and Fletcher followed as he ran around the edge of the car park, moving through the undergrowth until they got to a position behind the tent, away from the queue.

'Hey, Doctor,' Ben said, thumbing around the marquee, 'the entrance is on the other side.'

The Doctor grinned. 'Is it really? Well then, it's a good job I don't want to go inside yet, isn't it?'

Placing his hand on the side of the marquee, he felt along it until he found a join in the canvas sections.

'Do either of you have anything sharp enough to cut this?' he asked.

'Here,' Fletcher said, pulling a sharp letter opener in the shape of a dagger out of his pocket and handing it to the Doctor. 'I picked this up by accident from Captain Wallis's office. It should do the trick.'

The Doctor used the letter opener to slice a hole in the marquee's side. 'Now,' he said as he handed it back to Fletcher, 'let's see what's going on inside.' He knelt down and peered through the hole. 'Now this is interesting,' he said. 'Very interesting indeed.'

He stood up and gestured for Ben to take a look.

'I feel like a right old Peeping Tom,' Ben grumbled as he knelt down to peer through the canvas.

Inside the tent, he saw a crowd of people queuing up to a bright white podium similar to the one the ceremony with the corpses had been conducted on at the FOCAL meeting. Behind the podium was a large vat from which robed figures, who Ben assumed were Selyoid animated corpses, were scooping the golden Selyoid liquid into vials and offering these to each member of the public in turn. To the side of the crowd, on a raised platform, stood an audience of smartly dressed, good-looking men and women who seemed to have captivated the public with their charms. Everyone was looking and pointing at them. Ben realised these were the ones who didn't just believe in the Selyoids' way and follow their orders but had physically melded with the creatures and subsequently been given an irresistible quality that made everyone believe they were stars.

At the front of the platform stood De Sande, immaculately dressed as always, a self-satisfied grin across his face. His dream of Los Angeles succumbing to the will of the Selyoids was coming true. No wonder he was happy.

Ben fought the urge, tried to ignore what his brain was telling him. Go on, it said. Join the queue. You know you deserve to be celebrated.

'Are you all right, Ben?' the Doctor asked.

Ben blinked and stood up. 'They're all mad in there,' he said, ignoring his feelings.

'Yes, well,' the Doctor said, rubbing his hands together, 'what we need to do now is find a way to stop those people helping the Selyoids. Without De Sande and his friends, the Selyoids are helpless. They need human help to perpetuate their plan, and if we cut off that help...'

'Then we win,' said Fletcher.

'Come on,' said the Doctor. 'Let's see if we can stop those billboards displaying the Selyoid messages. If we can snap some people out of their delusions, maybe they'll help us.'

* * *

Inside the marquee De Sande sat in a chair on the edge of the celebrity-filled podium and took a well-deserved drag from his cigar. He looked out over the willing crowd, all nervously hoping to join with the Selyoids, to feel the joy the messages from the billboards promised them. After years of snubbing him, years of laughing at him, the people of Hollywood were now in the palm of his hand. This was power. This was justice.

He glanced at Maria who was standing up at the front of the podium, addressing the crowd. She was explaining the way forward to the general public. Explaining that a new celebrity order was coming.

A lucky few - De Sande estimated that about two hundred people were needed - would be Selyoid hosts, and everyone else would serve them. He realised he had to be careful not to spread the creatures out too thinly. Caleb had died because his dosage hadn't been strong enough. He hadn't been able to exert the power he should have done, but now De Sande knew better. From now on the people merging with the Selyoids would be stronger as they were drinking a liquid that contained a far stronger concentration of the creatures than previously.

Caleb and Martin had both been sharing themselves with the Selyoids, and both had been killed. De Sande had revelled in the joy of making their killers, Polly and Chate, into Selyoid servants. The ultimate revenge. Now though, against De Sande's wishes, the Selyoids had deserted Chate, and while they liked Polly too much to leave her it was clear she wasn't responding to their wishes as much as she should.

De Sande could deal with Chate once the Selyoid control of Los Angeles was firmly established. Once all the Selyoids were living as humans, living their lifestyle in human bodies, he could worry about locating the traitors. While the Selyoids remained in Polly she and Chate wouldn't be hard to find anyway.

Besides, did it really matter? He'd already humiliated Chate for what he did to Revere, and there were so many thousands of people all desperate to serve, to join with the Selyoids. If two helpless individuals rebelled... so what? But what if more decided the Selyoid way wasn't for them?

De Sande looked out over the crowd, at the smiles on their faces, and realised that no matter what happened these people, the people who'd seen *Dying in the Sun* in a crowd with hundreds of others, who'd been exposed to the right stimuli to become loyal servants of the Selyoids, would remain loyal for ever. Not because they were slaves, not because they feared the repercussions if they rebelled, but because these people loved the Selyoids, because these people wanted the celebrities to have a part in their lives. Everyone here knew what they were getting into, and everyone wanted it more than anything. If you weren't sharing your body with the Selyoids, you might as well be dead.

But still doubt raged in De Sande's mind. Every time he closed his eyes he saw Polly, saw her face as she ignored the screams inside her. The memory scared him.

Rapturous applause echoed through the tent as the crowd cheered Maria. They loved her. They adored her. She was everything they wanted, and everything they wanted to be. To see someone like Maria, who was now so in love with him, being treated in this way by so many people made De Sande feel amazing. Today, this was his town, and he was pleased.

He felt a wave of passion, of excitement, and he realised that though it mostly came from the people, it partly came from the Selyoid essence inside him, feeding off the crowd's energies and reflecting these back to the celebrities on the stage. The more people listened to the celebrities, the more they fell in love with them, and the more they'd listen to the Selyoids' message.

De Sande listened to the Selyoids inside him. They told him to be careful, told him not to get complacent, but he knew they were just being overcautious. At the end of the day, he was the one who had freed them from the ice, and he knew they were only trying to make sure nothing went wrong. They loved him unconditionally, and this knowledge had given him the security and confidence he needed to build FOCAL up over the last couple of years, to secure funding for *Dying in the Sun*, and to put into practice the ambitious plan now unfolding before his eyes.

He stood up and walked through to a closed-off reception area at the back of the marquee where FOCAL members were eating and drinking, taking a rest from the business of preaching to the fans.

He saw Wallis entertaining in one corner and made eye contact with him. The cop excused himself from his conversation.

'How's it going?' Wallis asked.

'Reasonably well. Apart from a little trouble earlier with your son, things seem to be going to plan.'

'I told you, we'll find him. He's with that English bitch. He won't get far.'

'Oh, Chate will get his just desserts,' said De Sande. 'I've no doubt about that.' His voice dropped to a whisper. 'What I'm worried about is how easily Polly managed to shake off the Selyoids' influence. They should be more powerful than that. The girl shouldn't have had so many doubts.'

Wallis looked concerned and put a finger to his lips, as if thinking. 'I wonder if the crowd need a little more convincing,' he suggested. 'Polly wasn't exposed to *Dying in the Sun* under optimum conditions and wasn't completely convinced that the Selyoids were the ones to follow.' He gestured in the direction of the crowd. 'Because there are so many willing people gathered in one place, the Selyoids' power over them is far stronger. Maybe if we do a little more convincing we can boost any stragglers.'

'But how? How can we prove that our way is right? How can we be sure that no one else will doubt the benefits they'll get from following us, that no one else will try to break away from our influence?'

Wallis smiled. 'Easy. We show them just how powerful the Selyoids are. We scare the general public out of their minds.'

'You have a plan?'

Wallis nodded. 'In operation as we speak. Within an hour you'll feel a whole lot better about everything, I promise.'

The Doctor, Ben and Fletcher reached the open space where the crowds were waiting just in time to see a fleet of police cars pulling up, sirens blaring. Ben ran towards the edge of the crowd and looked down the road leading up to the car park. A long chain of police cars was making its way along it, as if every unit in LA had decided to come to see what was going on.

Several cars drove up the paths leading away from the parking area, blocking all escape routes, while the rest surrounded the crowd.

The door of the lead car opened. A cop got out and started to shout through a megaphone. 'OK everyone. Can you leave this area immediately. I repeat, disperse from this area immediately.'

The doors to all the cars flew open, and like front-line soldiers an army of policemen rolled out and began running towards the crowd.

They began manhandling people in the crowd, grabbing them by their arms, trying to pull them away from the queue.

Fletcher turned to the Doctor and Ben. 'Stay here,' he said. 'I'm going to see what the hell my guys are up to.'

He ran into the crowd and Ben was about to follow him, but the Doctor put an arm across his friend's chest, telling him not to move. If they stayed on the edge of the car park they'd be safe.

Ben looked up at one of the giant billboards advertising *Dying in the Sun* and realised that the messages were getting stronger, getting harder and harder to resist. The crowd's activity seemed to show that they also felt this.

The police met with strong resistance from the crowd and the situation became more threatening. Several people decided they were being too obstructive and lashed out. At first the cops involved in the scuffles tried making arrests, tried cuffing the troublemakers, but soon too many people were leaping to the defence of those arrested. The arguments rapidly turned into fist fights, and in a short while a chaotic melee had broken out across the car park. A festival of punching, kicking and screaming ensued. Police fired guns into the air in a desperate attempt to stop the crowd. The crowd ignored the police, prepared to do anything to stop them blocking the way into the marquee.

Some of the police retreated, while some seemed to revel in the fighting.

Ben looked for Fletcher and saw him pummelling someone's face into the ground, relishing the chance to be involved in a purely physical brawl. Chaos broke out and the fighting developed into a full-scale riot. Bottles and other items of litter were thrown at the police and bodies fell to the ground as the cops fired shots in self-defence. Several people made a run for it, either fleeing down the road away from the hills or pushing through the crowd to see if they could get into the marquee.

Everyone seemed to be fighting everyone else. They didn't care who they attacked, they were just out for themselves. Everyone was trying to get to the front of the rabble that had moments ago been a queue, everyone was trying to become something greater than anyone else.

The police might have had guns, but the sheer force of numbers in the crowd meant they were being overpowered. Some of them retreated, some of them were trampled underfoot and kicked half to death.

'Fight them!' a loud voice said over the chaos. Ben looked over to see that a small group of suited people had emerged from the marquee. They were clutching microphones connected to giant amplifiers and speakers that were being hastily erected outside it. 'Don't let them stop you!' the celebrities shouted in unison. 'You deserve better. You *are* better.'

As the words of their idols sank in, the crowd appeared to surge, getting more and more violent and aggressive, deepening the blood bath.

'We must stop this!' said the Doctor, panic clear in his voice.

'But what can we do?' cried Ben. 'There's thousands of them!'

'I don't know,' the Doctor said, frustration dominating his voice. 'But we must do something!'

Chapter Twenty-Seven

Ben and the Doctor watched helplessly as the fighting continued.

A blinding flash of light filled the area, momentarily startling the fighting crowd as remote charges burnt out whatever was holding the illuminated film posters to the movie screens they'd been concealing. The screens lit up as projectors in front of them activated.

There were four screens around the area and Ben noticed a small cluster of De Sande's robed followers standing next to each one, operating the projectors.

At first the screens were filled with a montage of images from *Dying in the Sun* and the crowd made impressed noises. Ben realised that they were no longer screaming. Both the police and the people they were fighting were entranced by what they saw, captivated to the point where they forgot about the fight. This was the largest crowd ever assembled in front of a Selyoid projection, the highest concentration of willing minds ever gathered in one place. Ben just wanted to watch, felt himself being drawn in, felt himself wishing he could be part of the Selyoid experience.

The place was like a surreal drive-in theatre, with no cars and four screens. The moonlight shone down, rippling off people's faces, and the bright colours emanating from the screens appeared to dance around the crowd like tormenting spirits.

'May I have your attention please,' a deep voice boomed over the speakers - a voice amplified so strongly that it seemed that the hills themselves were talking. The voice didn't need the crowd's attention, of course. It already had it. 'Everyone, prepare to witness the true power of your new friends.'

With that the screens flickered, and in the moonlight the robed figures began busily adjusting the projectors.

For a second the screens went dark. Then, before anyone's concentration could be broken, they filled with bright white light.

Images of light and fire played across them, images that swirled and danced, black-and-white images that suddenly burst into colour, like in *The Wizard of Oz*. And then the bright mass of light advanced through another technological revolution. The fire and the light and the moonbeams on the screen seemed to take on a three-dimensional appearance.

A giant roar filled the skies like thunder from heaven. Suddenly the fire burst out of the screens, surging above the crowd.

The thousands of people gathered by the screens gasped as they craned their necks to see the battle going on above them, the heavens ablaze as the trails of fire from all four screens met above their heads - cinema projections made real.

'My word,' Ben heard the Doctor mutter. 'What have they done?'

The crowd watched with awe, captivated as the flames expanded, fireballs swirling in the sky like living objects, dancing around each other in a celestial ballet. Some people began to run away, screaming with panic at the amazing spectacle in the heavens above them.

Choral singing erupted from the speakers and soon half the crowd began to sing as well, the Selyoid spectacle pushing them to give their souls to the situation.

Those who weren't singing gasped as if watching an expensive fireworks display.

The fire in the sky began to spark, started to grow brighter, then separated out into beams of a thousand different colours. They became one giant entity, a lightball the size of several football pitches, which flew up into the night sky then came crashing down to earth, splitting off into several giant pieces.

Part of the crowd ducked, worried about being hit by the fire, while the rest stood motionless, rooted to the ground by terror.

As the pieces of the lightball reached the ground they seemed to solidify, gaining mass and losing their inconsistency. Gradually each of them formed a solid object like a huge block of burning magnesium.

One of the pieces landed between the point where the Doctor and Ben were standing and the rest of the crowd. The enormous mass of people began moving away from the light in unison, clearing a path in front of it. They could see it changing, forming a shape that consisted of two large pillars of light supporting a bulky weight. It seemed to be turning into a giant person.

No, Ben realised, as the light began to scream with a terrifying animalistic roar that shook the hills. It wasn't turning into a person.

'Oh, my God!' Ben heard one of the crowd scream. 'It's a monster!'

The light spread out forming a wide mass above the pillars, a mass that became chest-shaped, forming the upper body of a creature with hunched shoulders and giant drooping arms. At the top of the creature a lightball took on the shape of disproportionately large facial features.

The crowd's screaming grew even louder when they realised what they were seeing. The light had turned into a fifteen-storey-high gorilla. It began pummelling its chest and waving its arms around as if swatting at imaginary aeroplanes.

'What is that?' Ben asked.

'I'm not sure,' the Doctor said, putting his hands to his ears and shouting over the din. 'It's just a projection, but it's appearing as if it has a physical form, altering our perceptions so that we see it as more than just light.'

The gorilla took several steps, seemingly shaking the ground with its weight, and Ben instinctively ducked out of the way to avoid being trampled under its feet.

'So it can't hurt us then?'

The Doctor shook his head. 'I don't know for certain.' Then he pointed to the police, and to the crowd. Terror was clear on all their faces. 'But I know *they* can hurt us!' He gestured towards the bank of hills that surrounded the car park. 'Come on!' he shouted, grabbing Ben's arm.

They raced round the crowd and, as the gorilla's massive bulk moved out of his field of vision, Ben began to see the cinematic forms the other projections were taking on.

One of them had split up into an army of Roman soldiers, who filled the air with their battle cries as they bore down on the people below with swords held high and shields held tight.

As the Doctor and Ben ran they witnessed one marvel after another. They saw the police shooting at the monsters and bullets passing straight through the projections. They went through a pass and came face to face with a hundred giant horses, each five times as large as it should be, each mounted by a rider wearing the white hood and robes of a member of the Ku Klux Klan. The horses stampeded and Ben and the Doctor scrambled on to the undergrowth around the edges of the car park, desperately trying to escape the carnage.

Horrified, Ben watched as a giant dinosaur, moving in jerky stop-frame animation, crushed three police cars underfoot, while the Klansmen and the Roman legions fought it out with each other and with the LAPD. The dinosaur roared and the hills were filled with war cries from the battling factions. The cops were joining in the chaos, having clearly given up on trying to bring any logic to the situation. They fired wildly into the sky at the projections, which seemed to be targeting them directly and deliberately ignoring the general public. The Romans sliced down on them with their swords, the Klansmen tried to trample them with their horses. The police fired back in retaliation but their weapons were useless.

The scene was a nightmare, but Ben found he couldn't take his eyes off the spectacle. It was fascinating, enticing and absorbing. It was a scene greater than any that could ever be shown in a motion picture epic. It was the greatest movie of all time, taking place live in Los Angeles.

The crowds were screaming as they fought, panicked and confused by what was going on. Peoples' faces said it all. They wanted to run, wanted to get away, but while the Selyoids were projecting their messages to them they knew they had to stay, knew they had to be a part of the new era that was coming. Ben moved away from the undergrowth at the edge of the car park, wanting to get closer to the action.

'Where are you going?' the Doctor asked.

'I've got to be there,' Ben said. 'I've got to be a part of it.'

The Doctor grabbed him, pulled him back and looked him in the eye. 'No,' he said sternly. 'Ben, don't listen to them. Fight it. Stay with me!'

'But it's everywhere, Doctor. I can't think about anything else!'

'You must!' the Doctor urged. 'You must fight it!'

Ben nodded, then rubbed his eyes. He took a deep breath and tried to clear all thoughts of Selyoids from his mind. 'I'll try, Doctor.'

'Now,' the Doctor explained, 'we need to get to those projectors.'

He scuttled over to the nearest one and Ben followed him.

'Will you be able to switch it off?' Ben asked.

The Doctor shook his head and pointed to the small electricity generators at the side of the projector. 'There's no way we can get close enough to find the "off" switch.'

Ben waved his thumb in the direction of the robed figures guarding the projector. 'Not unless we get rid of that lot, eh?'

'There's too many of them,' the Doctor said. 'Besides, we don't know how strong they are.'

They ran towards the projector and Ben felt revulsion as he saw the decaying features of a rotting corpse beneath the robes of one of the figures.

The Doctor walked all round the projector, going as close to it as he could without getting a reaction from the corpses. 'Look at this,' he called from the other side of the mammoth object.

Ben ran round to its front to see what the Doctor was talking about and found he had to shield his eyes. The glow from the projector was so bright, sparkling... no, sparking. Tiny bits of light darted around its edges, as if the entire thing was live electrically.

'Careful, Doctor,' he said. 'It looks dangerous.'

The Doctor stared at the projector and reached up with his arm. He jumped and, for a fraction of a second, stopped part of the light beam hitting the screen. The projections rippled slightly, but the Selyoid influence was too strong, too powerful, for a simple light disruption to have any effect.

The corpses growled at him and he took several steps back to stop them coming any closer. 'Now this is interesting,' he said, pointing to the lens. 'Look at the front of the projector.'

Ben craned his neck to try to see what he was referring to. On a small ledge sticking out in front of the projector lens was a large crystal-like object. An object that looked very similar to the device the Doctor had stolen at the FOCAL meeting.

'That's it!' the Doctor said with excitement. 'They've managed to create more industrial versions of the filter that made the monster that attacked us come to life. They are what's causing those apparitions. If we remove them, then the apparitions should disappear.'

'We'll never be able to do that,' Ben said. He gestured to the corpses. 'There's too many of them. And they're only the ones guarding the projector.'

The expression on the Doctor's face became one of defeated resignation.

'Maybe we can convince everyone that the projections aren't real?' Ben suggested. He pointed towards the crowd. 'Fletcher's in there somewhere, maybe he can help to calm them?'

The Doctor sighed. He thought about this briefly, then smiled. 'We need a way to communicate with them...' He pointed to a steep path that ran up from the car park and along the edge of a steep precipice, a road several of the police cars had taken before the chaos began. 'This way,' he said. 'Hurry!'

They ran up the path and about halfway along it they encountered Captain Wallis. He was standing next to his car, watching the battle raging between the police and the projections.

'Where *is* Fletcher?' Ben wondered.

'I don't know,' said the Doctor. 'Perhaps you could look for him while I have a word with Captain Wallis.'

Ben nodded, rolled up his sleeves and ran back down to the crowd, ready to fight his way through it until he found Fletcher. Wounded bodies littered his path as he ran. He tried not to look, tried to avoid them, and hoped the detective wasn't among them.

Wallis watched the action below with satisfaction. He felt the Selyoids inside him buzzing with excitement, feeding off the crowd. This was a perfect moment that he knew he'd savour for the rest of his life. Then he sensed that the Selyoids were trying to tell him something. That there was still something not quite right. That a familiar presence was nearby.

Before he could listen to what the creatures had to say he felt a tap on his shoulder. He spun round to see a scruffy-looking man with a deadly serious look on his face.

'Stop this madness,' the Doctor ordered.

'What the hell are you doing here?'

'Look at that,' the Doctor said through gritted teeth, pointing to the chaos in front of them. 'Why are you letting your men be slaughtered? Why won't you stop this?'

Wallis turned round and smiled. 'It's a show of strength, Doctor. A display to convince the people down there that if they share in the Selyoid glory they'll be indestructible. They'll be so protected they won't need the LAPD.'

'And they won't need you,' the Doctor added.

Wallis laughed. 'No, but they'll get me. I'm one of the most important people in the Selyoid plan. I'm one of the Chosen...' He gestured to the city skyline. '... And a large part of this will soon be mine.'

'Just think about what's going on,' the Doctor pleaded. 'Look down there. Your men, your colleagues, are killing each other in their fear and confusion.' He pointed to the megaphone lying on the driver's seat inside Wallis's car. 'You can stop this now. End the bloodshed. Call off your men.'

Wallis shook his head. 'We must let this play out,' he insisted. 'The public have to see the true strength of the Selyoids, have to realise the possibilities the new world will bring them.'

'But your men will all be killed,' the Doctor shouted. 'Innocent lives lost!'

Wallis shrugged. 'Their sacrifice is a noble one. If you were one of the Chosen, you'd understand. But you didn't embrace our doctrine. The Selyoids are the only way to beat Communism. Unity with order and inequality, universal happiness but not at the expense of the rich, of the good Americans.'

The Doctor looked around edgily, then suddenly pointed upwards. 'Oh my, what's that!' he shouted. Wallis glanced up and the Doctor threw his body weight into him, keeping his own balance but sending the policeman flying to the floor. As Wallis lay there the Doctor pulled out the megaphone, flicked a switch to turn it on and began to shout. The sound of his voice filled the air. 'Stop shooting!' he called. 'Stop fighting! They're just projections, they won't hurt you if you don't fight. You're the LAPD. You don't need to fight. Stop, please!'

Wallis pulled himself together sufficiently to stand up, then reached for his gun. He held it in the air and fired a shot. The Doctor stopped shouting and turned round slowly. Wallis slammed the gun against his chest, pointing it directly at the man's heart. One shot and the guy wouldn't be annoying anyone else again.

He pulled the trigger, but just before he did so he felt himself being ripped away from the Doctor, saw the world spin round and felt his gun arm fly away from its target, the bullet ricocheting off the side of the car as it was fired. And then he saw who had pulled him from his prey. A face from the past. A face from the grave. His own son.

Chapter Twenty-Eight

'Hello, Dad,' Chate said as he launched a powerful uppercut that connected to Wallis's chin with a sickening crack. The policeman's head smashed against the metal of the car roof.

Chate stood back and Wallis collapsed to the ground.

Turning to Polly, who had climbed up with him to the vantage point, Chate pointed to the Doctor. 'Make sure he's OK.' She nodded.

The Doctor dusted himself down. 'I'm fine, thank you.'

Chate looked down to see his father reaching for the gun that he'd dropped. Chate darted swiftly over to it and kicked the weapon away from his father's grasp.

Wallis stood up. 'I should have let them kill you,' he growled.

Chate looked into his eyes, at the Selyoid fire that burned within soulless sockets, and smiled. 'They almost did, but I saw the light.'

'Stop this,' the Doctor shouted. At first Chate thought he was shouting at the warring police, but then he realised the Doctor's voice didn't have the distorted interference of the megaphone. He realised the Doctor was talking to him.

'No more violence,' the Doctor insisted. 'No more fighting.'

'I'm sorry,' Chate said as he wrestled his father to the ground, 'but this is personal.'

Wallis flung an arm up, making contact with Chate's face. Chate recoiled and the policeman used the moment to throw his son's weight away from him. Wallis scrabbled across the ground, across to the side of the path, next to the steep precipice. He looked around frantically for the gun, hoping it hadn't fallen over the edge, and was relieved to see it had been caught between two clumps of flowers. He grabbed it and swivelled around so that it was pointing directly at Chate's chest. The action froze, both parties breathing heavily, each trying to anticipate his opponent's next move.

Wallis stood up, his balance precarious. He clutched one hand to his bruised face, while the other held the gun.

Chate took a step forward.

'Don't move!' Wallis yelled.

'You wouldn't let De Sande kill me,' Chate said matter-of-factly. 'You won't kill me now.'

Wallis's eyes were filled with anger. He seemed to have an aura of hatred, but when it came down to it he didn't know if he could do it. And then his expression changed. He was listening. Chate recognised what that meant. Somehow Chate could feel the Selyoids inside Wallis telling him to kill his son.

The expression on the old man's face was confused, unsure. 'You should have died in that fire,' Wallis said angrily. 'That would have been a sweet irony. Your mother, your father, you... Three Chates, three arson victims.'

'Arson attack? My parents didn't die in an arson attack,' Chate said. 'That fire that killed them started by accident. That's what you've always told me.' Confusion filled his mind and his speech faltered. 'Unless you were lying, in which case... why would you...? Oh God. Oh God, no. You!'

Wallis laughed.

'You killed them!' Chate shouted. 'You killed them, didn't you?'

'Your father was blackmailing me,' Wallis sneered. 'I needed him out of the way.'

Chate looked away. 'No, it's not possible. It's not possible!'

He stared at Wallis's finger tightening on the gun's trigger, and wondered how the man could have kept such a terrible secret hidden for so many years.

Glancing out of the corner of his eye he saw the precipice, saw the sheer drop deep below.

'Why?' was all he could whimper.

'I'm... not sorry,' Wallis said, a tear rolling down his cheek. He fired the gun and Chate felt a burning bullet rip into his chest.

He collapsed to the ground and screamed in agony. He looked up and his eyes were blinded by a bright light. Amazingly, he was able to get up, was able to stagger towards Wallis. He looked down and saw that the bright light was surging from the wound in his chest. But how could it? The Selyoids had left him, hadn't they?

He saw Wallis screaming, cowering as the light blinded him. Saw his father shield his eyes and stagger back, back over the edge of the precipice.

Chate leapt forward and grabbed his father's arm. Wallis dangled precariously over the edge, desperately scrabbling at the earth to try to get a foothold, trying to get up. Gravity dragging him down.

Chate was in too much pain to lift his father up, but nevertheless he strained with all his strength to hold on to him. 'Climb up!' he urged. 'Climb up!'

He felt hands grab him from behind. Polly and the Doctor, doing their best to help pull the old man up. Their efforts were in vain. Gravity was too strong, Wallis was too heavy.

'I can't!' Wallis screamed, struggling violently, but the more he moved, the more Chate felt him slipping from his grasp.

His father's weight pulled Chate towards the edge, and he knew the laws of physics were against him. 'I can't hold on!' he cried.

He and Wallis made eye contact one more time, and in his father's eyes Chate saw the burning agony of the Selyoids inside him, desperately trying to change his physique, to make him stronger, but to no avail. But was there something else? Was that a hint of regret he could see?

He tried one more time to pull the old man up, but it was no use. His father slipped from his grasp and, with a final, mournful moan, crashed to the rocks far below.

Chate looked down into the darkness, tears in his eyes. No one could survive a fall like that, even someone sharing with the Selyoids.

He paused for several moments, trying to contemplate what had happened, then turned to face the Doctor and Polly.

'I *am* sorry,' he said quietly. 'I am.'

The police began to halt their attacks. Most of them did so through no choice of their own because they had run out of ammunition. But some stopped due to a genuine desire to test the truth of the Doctor's words or because they'd lost the will to fight. They stopped attacking the horses, the soldiers and the monsters. They let the projections wash over them, let the light clouds swirl around their vision. They stopped firing their guns, stopped beating the crowd and each other up and slowly, a little at a time, the violence stopped.

The battle between the various projections still raged overhead, but on the ground the two factions of humanity - the LAPD and the civilian humans - stood still, like shocked mourners at a funeral, barely saying a word.

Looking across at the dumbstruck masses Ben saw a bruised and battered Fletcher emerge from them, nursing a black eye.

'You OK, kid?' Fletcher asked as he hurried over to Ben, coughing dust out of his lungs.

Ben nodded, and pointed up the path that led along the precipice. 'Come on,' he said. 'Let's go and find the Doctor.'

Chate felt a warm hand clasp his shoulder. 'It's OK,' Polly said. 'You did your best.'

He turned over and winced as the pain in his chest hit him. He looked down and saw the bullet fly out, expelled by the Selyoids as they worked on sealing and repairing his wound.

'These Selyoids seem to be instinctive creatures,' the Doctor told him, 'and if you die, they die. It doesn't matter that the ones in Wallis wanted you dead, there were some in you that must have refused to leave, that were more than happy to stay a part of you.'

Chate smiled. 'I can hear them talking to me. They're scared, confused. Trying to regroup and repair themselves.'

'They're healing your injury, it seems. You should be fine soon.'

Chate shook his head. 'I won't heal for a while yet.'

The Doctor held his hand out and Chate grabbed it. As the Doctor pulled him up, Chate was surprised at the little man's strength.

'Your father wasn't himself at the end, remember,' the Doctor said. 'The Selyoids drove him over the edge.' He glanced over the side of the precipice. 'Sorry.'

He placed a comforting arm on Chate's shoulder. 'You can't blame yourself.'

Chate shrugged. 'Can't I? Could I have tried harder? Was there a part of me that wanted him to fall? A part of me that let him go? Did I do the right thing?'

The Doctor's face was deadly serious, cold. Behind his eyes, Chate could see a deeply tortured soul, could see that he was perhaps more familiar with this sort of situation than his normal joviality implied. 'Never ask that question,' said the Doctor. 'It never helps.'

'You're lucky some of the Selyoids didn't want to leave you,' said Polly. 'They didn't want to lose you. De Sande told us that the Selyoids love us... perhaps he's right.'

'I guess,' Chate said, clutching his wounded chest, 'they've achieved their goal. Through me they lived again... and now they don't want to leave.'

'What do you mean?' asked the Doctor.

Polly decided to continue the explanation. 'Doctor, no one else seems to have picked it up but there's something about the Selyoids... I keep getting visions, brief flashes of imagery, of the place where the Selyoids originate from.'

'Another planet?' suggested the Doctor.

Polly nodded. 'I think so. A planet where the Selyoids were magnificent beings of solid light, but beings that were too big for one planet, it seems.'

The Doctor nodded. 'Go on.'

'Once they arrived on Earth,' Polly continued, 'they realised that all they needed was to be found by a suitable life form. A life form that would bond with them and find a way to restore their race to its natural form. Someone like De Sande.'

'But why Earth?' the Doctor asked.

Polly shook her head. 'The Selyoids are beings of solid light and fire. They're living stars and humanity is obsessed with the stars. The Selyoids work with a life form, changing them, bringing joy to their lives. With our media, with our capacity to dream... where better to rebuild their civilisation than on Earth?'

'But this isn't their planet,' the Doctor insisted. 'This isn't their time. They should be living their own lives rather than just being an audience to ours.'

'Do you think the Selyoids like being trapped in film chemical?' Polly asked. 'Or in jars of liquid or human blood like some primordial soup? They want to return to their natural form, they want to regain the status their race once held. Through humanity they've found a way to do that. It will take a long time, many years and more resources than any one person could possibly hope to provide, but with the Selyoids living within some humans as a temporary measure and the rest of humanity devoting their lives to helping to restore them... With our help they'll live again, live in their natural form, without needing projectors or lenses or any more human help. They'll live again, on Earth.'

'No,' the Doctor said gravely. 'Humanity has a better destiny than to become the servants of the Selyoids. This is not their planet. Tell them that, Polly. Tell the creatures inside you. This is not their planet. This is *your* planet.'

'No,' Polly said. 'Everyone loves the Selyoids. Great things will come from them. It's the next stage in the world's existence.' She gestured to the crowds of people down below. 'Just ask any of them. All of them will gladly give their lives to the Selyoids. Not because they've been brainwashed, not because they'll be killed if they don't, but because they love the Selyoids, because they feel a happiness they never felt before.'

'But only because of the Selyoid propaganda,' the Doctor said desperately. 'The Selyoids know exactly what to say to win people's hearts and minds, exactly what to expose the humans to. They might as well be brainwashing them. At the end of the day humanity is still being manipulated. They're selling the Hollywood dream, but in reality it's nothing but a nightmare.'

'But you don't understand, Doctor,' Polly said. 'It's survival of the fittest. Every day thousands of people in this city spend money on things they don't need. Why? Because the media tells them to. They may be convinced they need things they don't, but they still only buy them because they want them. That's exactly what the Selyoids are doing. They have an idea to sell, and they use every way in their power to sell it. Is that so wrong?'

'But isn't there another way?' asked the Doctor.

'No,' Polly told him. 'De Sande's already poured millions into his research. His scientists thought they'd succeeded, thought they'd found a way to give the Selyoids life without projectors or screens or humans, but the prototype went disastrously wrong. It took on the literal form of the demon creature it had been displaying in the film, a terrifying demon that lacked all remembrance of its true self. But more disturbing than that, in the transition to a solid form the Selyoid lost all its intelligence, all its memories, all its spirit. It was a living nightmare, and for the Selyoid a living hell '

'This prototype. Was that the thing that attacked us at the premiere?'

Polly nodded. 'Barely capable of being anything else than a servant itself, and incapable of having any physical presence or power in bright light. The Selyoids would rather die than live such a pathetic existence.'

'Or at least,' the Doctor said, 'would rather enslave humanity.'

'They'd rather persuade humanity to aid them in their quest. They need all our resources, all our wealth... anything we can do to push their research forward, to find a way for them to be revitalised that won't destroy their minds. They need our help, Doctor. Can't you see that? They deserve our help.'

Chapter Twenty-Nine

'What the hell happened here?' Ben asked as he and Fletcher reached the high outcrop where the Doctor, Polly and Chate stood beside what looked like an abandoned police car.

'Captain Wallis,' the Doctor said, pointing at the ravine, 'had an unfortunate accident.'

'My God,' Fletcher said. 'We've lost a lot of good people today.'

'And we can't lose any more,' the Doctor said. 'I have to find De Sande. He's the only one that can stop this.' He turned to Polly. 'Where is he? Where can I find him?'

Polly looked as if she was scouring her mind for the information. 'I think... I think he's still in the marquee.'

The Doctor rubbed his hands together. 'Come on, then.' He pointed at Fletcher. 'Detective, I want you and Ben to come with me. Polly, you stay here.' He gestured to Wallis's car. 'You'll be safe and warm inside that. I'll come and find you shortly.'

'I don't think so, Doctor,' Polly said indignantly. 'I'm coming with you.'

'Polly,' the Doctor urged, 'you have to understand. You're still vulnerable, still very susceptible to the Selyoid influence. If you come too close to the nexus of things, come too close to De Sande... I fear they'll be able to fully reassert their control over you. Please stay here. It's for your own safety.

Polly looked as if she was about to argue, then shook her head and got into the car. 'Don't be long, Doctor,' she said.

'Just stay there, please.' The Doctor glanced up at Chate. 'You'll look after her?'

Chate nodded. 'If she looks after me.'

'Maybe I should stay with Polly?' Fletcher suggested.

'Oh no,' the Doctor said vehemently. 'I need you to come with me. I doubt we can win the day without your help.'

The detective smiled, surprised at the Doctor's confidence in him.

Since the dramatic Selyoid show of power had begun, the queue for the marquee had dissipated. Everyone was far more concerned with watching the spectacle being projected in the skies above Hollywood. Now, while the fighting had stopped, the film reels continued to play out and the Selyoids continued to feed their propaganda to the masses.

This distraction meant it was easy for the Doctor, Ben and Fletcher to slip inside the marquee. They hid behind a canvas partition and stared at the scene inside. A large congregation still sat listening to the celebrities but the crowd had dwindled, sensing that the real excitement was happening outside. The queue to take the Selyoid communion was still long, however, and De Sande's corpses continued to feed people with the glowing substance.

De Sande stood gleefully on the celebrity podium observing proceedings like a marshal preparing his troops. A small group of corpses stood close to him like bodyguards. Their hoods were pushed back, exposing their rotting flesh for all to see. It was as if De Sande had decided that the macabre sight would serve as yet another reminder to the humans that the Selyoids were more powerful than they were.

'What are those things?' Fletcher asked, pointing to the corpses.

'Temporary Selyoid hosts,' the Doctor explained. 'In humans the Selyoids can live again, can slowly change a human body into a form more suitable for accommodating them. They can't do that with dead cells, but can still use the bodies as vehicles to move around in, to see the world through. I imagine they're the ones controlling the other Selyoids.' He pointed to one particular corpse that was wearing a blue robe rather than a brown one. 'You see that one in blue? It seems to stay unusually close to De Sande. I think it's the one that controls the others. That's the leader, if you like. That thing oversees the Selyoid side of things, while De Sande oversees the human side. That corpse filters down orders to the other bodies, who instruct the rest of the Selyoids about how to act.'

'But why do they need to use living humans at all?' Ben asked.

'Probably because sharing in human life means everything to the Selyoids,' the Doctor suggested. 'The creatures in the dead bodies are the ones who don't want to take the risk of melding with a human who could reject them, and who are prepared to make the sacrifice of not merging with a living human. If we stop those monsters, the Selyoids' control over the humans should diminish.'

'But it's not control, is it?' Fletcher said. 'You saw how happy everyone is. How successful they are. Why shouldn't we all help the Selyoids? Why shouldn't we join with them?'

'Because it's not meant to be,' the Doctor said. 'It's wrong. Humanity is not a race of slaves.'

'Didn't you see that film out there?' Fletcher asked. 'Didn't you listen to anything Polly said? The Selyoids aren't making anyone slaves. In fact, they're freeing us from everything that makes our lives so goddamn pointless in the first place.'

'He's right, Doctor,' Ben said. 'The Selyoids are only trying to help.'

'No, Ben,' the Doctor said. 'Remember what I told you. See things logically. You don't want them, you don't want to be a part of them.'

Fletcher looked at the Doctor. 'When I was out there,' he said, gesturing away from the marquee, 'when I was out fighting and defending myself and in the middle of a whole damn sea of movies come to life, I felt the Selyoids calling to me. Felt them telling me that they were part of my future. That with them I could make the kind of difference I never could with the goddamn LAPD. They want me to be one of their Chosen, one of those Joes who gets to live with our new friends living and breathing inside of them, being part of them.'

'No,' the Doctor said. 'You don't want that. You don't want what they'll give you. They'll change you, alter you. You'll be mobbed, you'll be attacked. You'll feel like you're a star, but it will all be surface detail. You'll still be the same person, but you'll be trapped, muffled by a creature that will come to control your every action. The change might appear beneficial, but that's only on the surface. When you realise what it will do to you, how they'll corrupt you, how they'll change you... No, it's something you definitely don't want.'

'Who gives a damn? I'd be important...' Fletcher's eyes were glowing with passion. 'I'd be somebody. For the first time in my life I'd be somebody.'

The Doctor nodded. 'But not through your own doing. Not through your own achievements. You'd just be using the efforts of others and taking all the glory yourself.'

'Doctor,' Fletcher argued, 'it doesn't matter how I become famous. This is the city of casting couches, of corruption, of blackmail, scandal and vice. No one gets to the top unaided, but all I know is I deserve to get there. I was born to reach the top.'

The Doctor waved his hands. 'I don't have time to argue with you. Let's go and see Mr De Sande. I'll do the talking!' He looked up at Ben and pointed to Fletcher. 'Make sure he doesn't do anything stupid.'

Ben nodded, and the three of them marched through the centre of the marquee, up to the podium where De Sande and his corpses were standing and watching over the creation of their new world.

'Doctor!' De Sande said angrily as he saw the intruders approach. 'What the hell are you doing here?'

'Stop this nightmare now, De Sande,' the Doctor urged. 'People are dying out there!'

'But the Selyoids are living!' De Sande said gleefully. 'Soon they will all be housed in temporary hosts, and after that the rest of the population will devote their lives to finding a way to restore them to their true destiny. And as they do so I will lead them, as the most important, most respected, most loved person on this entire planet.'

The Doctor walked up to him. 'Stop this now!' he said forcefully.

As he got close to De Sande the corpses swarmed around him, stopping him from getting too close.

'You haven't seen what it's like yet,' the director said. He pointed to a table where a row of vials containing the Selyoid essence were sitting, waiting for willing humans to drink their contents. 'You haven't felt the joy, felt the pleasure, of being one of us... of being a star.'

Watching the fire in De Sande's eyes, Ben felt a strong desire to join him. He tried to remember everything the Doctor had said, tried to block the Selyoid attraction out, but it was incredibly difficult. This was pure happiness, pure perfection. But it was wrong. Ben knew that, and he had to fight it. He had to fight the signals, fight the messages the Selyoids were bombarding him with. He had to tell himself it was just propaganda. That nothing is as good as the movies make it appear to be.

He looked over to Fletcher and saw desperation burning in the cop's eyes. The poor guy hadn't even seen *Dying in the Sun*, but he had witnessed the spectacle projected outside the marquee — a series of images impressive enough to convince the public of the Selyoids' power as easily as the film could. Fletcher had been reasonably quiet since the fighting calmed, and Ben was starting to realise why. He'd seen something in the projections, felt a connection with the messages the Selyoids were sending out. An empathy.

Ben's train of thought was shattered as he saw Fletcher leap across towards the corpses.

'Oi!' Ben shouted, running after him.

He grabbed Fletcher and tried to pull him back, but the cop turned round and launched a heavy punch into his jaw that sent him crashing down to the ground. Ben saw Fletcher reach into his jacket and pull out the letter opener.

The detective grabbed the blue-robed corpse's face and slammed the letter opener into its decomposing skull.

'Stop him!' De Sande shrieked. The other corpses began to move in on Fletcher, who kicked and punched them away. The crowd surrounding the fight looked on in confusion, unsure whether to get involved, and so staying on the sidelines just to be on the safe side.

The corpse Fletcher had grabbed wriggled in his grasp, but the cop was too strong and it couldn't escape. He shoved the letter opener deeper into its skull and wrenched it apart as if it was a boiled egg. There was a flash of light and the Selyoid essence, golden ooze mixed with congealed blood, began to spill out of the shattered skull.

The other corpses shrieked and continued their attack, but half of them were little more than skeletons, rotting flesh falling off their bones as they moved, and they were unable to stop Fletcher who kicked them away like scavenging rats. He was far more interested in concentrating on the task ahead of him.

A wide smile crossed his face and he scooped the Selyoid essence out of the corpse's skull with his hands. He shovelled it in to his mouth and drank it, pools of glowing liquid spilling through his fingers. Ben had never seen anyone look so thirsty.

'Fletcher!' the Doctor shouted. 'Stop this now!'

Fletcher looked up and smiled, blobs of the liquid dribbling down his chin. He put his hands up and the corpse from which he'd stolen the Selyoids fell to the ground.

'I'm not Fletcher any more,' he said, his voice croaking. 'I'm one with the Selyoids. And I control hundreds of people!'

'You don't control them,' De Sande said angrily. 'You just direct them. Don't you understand? Why do you think the Selyoid leaders use dead bodies as their hosts? There's too much interference inside a living mind, too many other variables to worry about. They use dead people because that way the Selyoids can be in total control, and are free to communicate with any living person who shares in the Selyoid experience. You can't control them if you're alive, so give it up!'

'He's spilling the stuff!' Ben said.

'It doesn't matter,' the Doctor explained. 'Each Selyoid is self-regenerating, duplicated millions of times inside that liquid but comprised of one consciousness. Only some of each creature needs to be ingested for the individual Selyoid to live on.'

Fletcher grinned.

'Stop it!' De Sande screamed, insane with panic. 'You don't know what you're doing!

'Oh I know,' Fletcher smirked. 'You know full well that I'm right, that I'll become the supreme power behind these creatures. You're scared because you know I'm right, and you want to stop me.'

'No,' De Sande shouted. 'You're wrong. The Selyoid director will die inside you! In a living being it has no control, no power. Give it up, or I'll kill you.'

Fletcher started to gag as if the Selyoid he'd just swallowed was trying to escape from his system, but he kept his mouth tightly shut. His eyes were going red and his skin paled, but he held on to the Selyoid until it had no choice but to merge with him.

Ben wondered if the remaining corpses would try to attack Fletcher, but they just stood motionless as if waiting for orders.

'That's the Selyoid leader, isn't it?' the Doctor said. 'The creature inside Fletcher... It's the one that controls everything else, the top mind...' he looked at De Sande and raised an eyebrow. 'That's why they won't attack him. They don't want to injure their leader! The Selyoids in you and Fletcher... they're the ones in charge.' The Doctor's face lit up. 'Which means they're the ones who can stop this before it's too late!'

Fletcher's hands were clasped over his face as he tried desperately to hold the Selyoid director inside his body. De Sande ran up to him and tried to pull his hands away.

'Give it up!' De Sande screamed. 'You're killing it!'

'It's too late,' the Doctor said. 'The Selyoids' leader is dying. Their control is fading. You've lost, De Sande. You've lost!'

Chapter Thirty

Polly drove Wallis's car as fast as she could down Western Canyon. She didn't know where she was going, but knew she had to get away from De Sande's marquee, had to get away from the chaos. She looked over to the passenger seat, at the drowsy form of Chate. He was silent, sleepy and far less aggressive and charismatic than he had been when she had first met him.

A long line of cars coming in the opposite direction continued to make the pilgrimage towards the marquee, but the numbers of people were beginning to thin out now. Polly winced as pain shot through her chest. No, shot through the Selyoids inside her. They were lost, disorientated. They were dying. Driving became too painful, so she pulled the car into a slip road and parked it. She got out and ran over to open the passenger door. 'How are you?' Polly asked, helping Chate out of the car. He smiled at her. It was a drained, battered smile, but one that said he wasn't beaten.

'What do we do now?' he asked.

Polly tried to think of something comforting to say. Tried to think of something that would ease the poor man's suffering, but nothing came.

'You don't look well,' Chate rasped, clearly fighting his own pain. 'Perhaps you should sit down?'

Polly rubbed her stomach. 'These things... they're dying.'

Chate nodded. 'I know. What little was left in me... it's gone now. All their energy was exhausted healing me. They've been cut off from the others and couldn't take the shock. I felt them go, felt them say goodbye.'

'Something awful's happened to them,' Polly said. 'I hear them screaming inside me. I can hear all their screams.. They're lost, directionless. They can't survive.'

Chate and Polly walked to the edge of the main highway. The reaction was the same everywhere. People couldn't drive because of the Selyoid pain they were feeling so they had abandoned their cars and were wandering around, totally disorientated.

'They're not going to the hills,' Chate said. 'The film's not working.'

Polly looked up at the billboards, at the screens that should have been displaying Selyoid instructions to the eager masses, but saw nothing but a simple film poster.

'I can feel them dying,' she said as the realisation hit her. 'Didn't you hear them speak to you? Telling you that they've lost their leader. Without it... they're nothing. Locked in place they have no power.'

'And without that power no one will want to follow them. No one will want to share the dream.'

Polly felt the creatures' pain ripple inside her, felt them ebbing away as their life source diminished until she wasn't even aware of their existence. 'It's over,' she said grimly.

Chate put an arm around her waist, seeking comfort in his grief. 'Do you think things would have been better?' he asked. 'Do you think we would have been happy?'

'I don't know,' Polly said, watching people drift off and fall to the ground as the Selyoids inside them died. 'All I know is that this wasn't their time. Fame is fleeting, as they say.'

Fletcher's hands stayed clasped firmly to his mouth, no matter how hard De Sande tried to prise them away. By shoving his weight forward he managed to send his opponent flying to the ground.

De Sande felt a sickening feeling surge through his stomach. He felt the pain of the Selyoid inside him, felt its anger and frustration at the loss of its director.

Fletcher slowly removed his hands from his mouth and began

rubbing his stomach like a man finishing a particularly satisfying meal.

'You're giving in?' De Sande asked hopefully.

Fletcher stood up, then smiled and shook his head. 'Not really. It's just that... Well, it seems this Selyoid likes me.'

'Impossible,' De Sande said, shaking his head. 'It can't.'

'Seems it's been in a dead body for too long. For once it's getting some life. It's forgotten what it's like to share itself with another. It's lost, it's confused. It's too helpless to leave me unless I want it to. It's picking up on my emotions and can't help but be affected by what it's watching. Guess my life must be a real tear-jerker, huh?'

De Sande tried once more to attack Fletcher, but the pain all through his body was too great. He'd been joined with the Selyoid for too long. Its pain was his pain and he couldn't ignore it. The Selyoids in both men were refusing to attack each other.

'They're dying!' De Sande cried. 'The Selyoids are dying!'

'It's too late,' the Doctor said coldly. 'You underestimated your dependence on other people, on the other Selyoids. You thought you could create the ultimate society. But you failed. When stars fall they crush everything underneath them. Give up, De Sande. It's too late.'

De Sande's head pounded with tension. 'No!' he screamed, scrambling to his feet, 'We have to get it out of him. We have to get the Selyoid director back into one of the bodies!'

'It doesn't want to leave me,' Fletcher said smugly. 'If you try and force it out of me you'll kill it.'

De Sande struggled defiantly to ignore the pain inside him and pointed to Fletcher. 'What if we don't need that Selyoid to reassert control? If the director has betrayed us a new Selyoid must be found to take its place.' He smiled and rubbed his stomach gently. 'I'm stronger than everyone,' he said. 'I've been with the Selyoids the longest. I know them better than anyone. They're more a part of me than anyone. I've been the leader of the humans who helped the plan. What if the Selyoid in me could become the new director? Yes, it's certainly strong enough. I will be the new Selyoid director!' He looked at Fletcher and grinned. 'How does that make you feel, eh son?'

'That won't work,' the Doctor said. 'Any sentience, any free will, interferes too much in the Selyoid thought patterns, gets in the way. The director needs a brain it doesn't have to share with a human. There are just too many emotions in a living person. No Selyoid would be strong enough to suppress them.'

'But you don't understand,' De Sande said. 'If I block off my own thoughts, my own emotions. If I let it take me over, establish its control... It loves me, it needs me. It'll give me back my own free will once another suitable host for the new Selyoid director can be found... Yes, you know it might just work!'

'De Sande, you're crazy,' Fletcher said. 'You're too strong, the Selyoid will never break through your mental defences no matter how much you try and open up to it. You won't be able to hide your thoughts.'

De Sande shook his head and began to pace up and down the podium. 'What if there was a way to increase the strength of the Selyoid's control? What if there was a way to make it so powerful that it could drown out any interference from a human brain?'

He leapt down from the podium and went over to the table on which the vials of Selyoid essence stood. He quickly lifted each vial up and threw its contents down his throat.

'I will absorb as many of the Selyoids as I can,' he announced. 'Soon their influence will be so strong in me — will dominate every one of my thoughts, every one of my emotions — that there'll be no interference and through me they'll be able to control every Selyoid in the city.'

He raced up to the podium microphone and cleared his throat. 'Everyone,' he called to the groaning masses, all of whom were clutching their stomachs and sobbing with pain as life slowly ebbed from the Selyoids inside them. 'I can save you.' His amplified voice echoed around the marquee. 'I can save your new friends, but you'll have to make a sacrifice. You'll have to say goodbye to them, let them leave you.' The crowd gasped, and its wails got louder. 'It will only be for a short while,' De Sande reassured them. 'And all your friends will survive...' A pause for dramatic effect. '... In me! I will control you! The new world will go ahead as planned!'

He jumped down from the podium into the celebrity area and, one by one, began to kiss everyone he could see fully on the lips. As he did so, he felt the Selyoid essence inside each of them flood through his mouth and into his body. He felt the creatures surging desperately into him, knowing that this was their last chance at survival, their last chance at life in a form greater than a chemical stew.

He felt his stomach fill as he dragged more and more of the Selyoids from people's mouths. He knew that he'd never be able to get all the creatures inside him, knew that even if he could many of them would be dead by the time he reached the people they were living in, but he knew he had to try.

'Move and I'll shoot!' Fletcher said, raising a gun to the De Sande's chest.

De Sande laughed. 'And what if you do? The amount of Selyoids inside me now... They'll patch me up in no time.'

He saw Fletcher wince.

'See what you've done? The Selyoid inside you is dying. A piece of you is dying.'

Fletcher shook his head then staggered back and fell down, crashing into a row of chairs.

Most of the crowd were too weak to move but several people had managed to stagger over to De Sande and were hounding him, desperately trying to be the next ones to give him their Selyoids. He kissed one of them, but as soon as he had taken the Selyoid liquid into his mouth he retched it back up again. He couldn't ingest any more of the creatures, but as he felt his mind grow cloudy he knew it didn't matter. The plan was working. He felt the creatures take control and knew he had to get out of here. He had to get to safety, to a place where he could be worshipped, where the Selyoids could convert new people to their cause.

'The hangar,' De Sande said, shouting to a person he recognised as being one of the Star Light chauffeurs. 'Get me to the hangar, quickly!'

The chauffeur nodded and followed De Sande as he ran out of the marquee, ignoring the Doctor's shouts for him to stop.

'Come on,' the Doctor said, helping Ben to his feet. 'We must find this hangar. We must go after De Sande!'

Ben looked at the crowd of sobbing people, at the established celebrities and those who had only recently gained the Selyoid charm, all wounded and helpless as the creatures inside them died.

'But Doctor, what about this lot? We can't leave them.'

He sidled over to a middle-aged woman who was crying into her lap. 'Are you OK?' he asked.

The woman looked up at him, her face forlorn. 'There's something... missing,' she said. 'But I can't quite remember what.'

'You'll be fine,' the Doctor reassured her. He turned to Ben. 'They'll all be fine. Their memories will be cloudy, and in time all they'll recall about this is that they took a trip to the hills to see a motion picture. The casualties outside... I wouldn't be at all surprised if the police come up with some explanation for the media that will cover this up nice and neatly.'

Ben nodded and looked around at the bewildered masses. 'What about Polly?'

'She should be fine too,' the Doctor said. 'The Selyoid inside her will die and she'll remember very little.'

'That reminds me,' Ben said, turning to look back at the podium. 'Where's Fletcher?'

The cop was nowhere in sight.

'I don't know,' the Doctor said, 'but we don't have time to worry about him now. We must stop De Sande.'

Chapter Thirty-One

Having learned the location of the Star Light hangar from one of the crowd, it hadn't taken long for the Doctor to find an abandoned car, hot-wire it and drive it away. The place was buzzing with activity when he and Ben reached it. A large number of engineers and technicians bustled around its edges. Lit up, the building stood like a giant golden cube in the night.

The Doctor ran up to one of the technicians. 'Excuse me,' he said. 'You haven't seen Mr De Sande recently, have you?'

The technician looked up and pointed to the runway in front of the hangar where a row of sleek-looking planes were being prepared for take-off. 'Over there,' he said. 'But you'd better hurry, he'll be taking off in a minute.'

'Which plane?' Ben asked.

'The largest,' the man replied. 'The distribution plane.'

The Doctor nodded. 'De Sande probably wanted to make sure all the copies of his film were safe in case anything went wrong.'

He and Ben ran as fast as they could towards the plane. Before they could get there it had started to roll down the runway building up speed, its propellers creating cyclones of air that swirled around the area, blowing through everyone's hair and clothes, the deafening roar of its engines drowning out any conversation.

As the plane accelerated, the bright runway lights illuminated its clear glass cockpit and Ben saw De Sande sitting behind the pilot, looking back and grinning with satisfaction.

'There has to be a way to stop him,' the Doctor shouted. 'We have to force him down. If De Sande has his way he'll be able to get new hosts for the Selyoids that are currently inside him and all our efforts will be in vain.'

He looked around and ran over to the edge of the runway where a fleet of vehicles were parked. A young fair-haired engineer was washing dirt off the paintwork of a large pick-up truck. 'I need to borrow this!' he shouted, pointing to the truck.

The engineer looked puzzled. 'I'm sorry sir, you can't —'

The Doctor slipped past him and, as he did so, dipped his hands into the man's pockets and pulled out a bundle of keys. 'Hey!' the engineer shouted as the Doctor jumped into the vehicle and locked the driver's door. 'Get out of there!'

Ben opened the passenger door and jumped inside. The Doctor jammed the keys into the ignition and started the engine. 'I'm sorry!' he called out to the engineer who was frantically trying to open the locked door. 'I'll return it soon!'

The Doctor drove the truck away from the airport as fast as he could and, as he did so, Ben saw De Sande's plane finally lift off from the runway and fly into the night. 'It's too late, isn't it, Doctor?' Ben asked.

'Not yet, Ben,' the Doctor insisted. 'De Sande's plane is slow and heavy. We've still got time.'

Their journey back to Griffith Park took hardly any time at all — the roads were almost empty as everyone in the city was more concerned with seeing *Dying in the Sun* than with driving anywhere.

As they drove into the car park Ben saw that the projectors were still beaming a dazzling display of light into the air.

Around the projectors lay the robed corpses, completely inanimate. Now that their Selyoid inhabitants had died the bodies were decomposing rapidly, reverting back to their natural form.

The Doctor stopped the truck, then reversed it so that its rear was right next to one of the projectors. He jumped out of the vehicle and stepped over the corpses.

'We need to move the projector, Ben,' he shouted.

Ben hurried over to where he was standing and together they pushed the projector on to the back of the truck. It was heavy but their combined strength managed to move it in less than a minute, though by the end of the process Ben was exhausted. Lifting the generator connected to the projector was no easy task either.

Once the projector and its generator were safely loaded on the back of the truck the Doctor threw Ben the keys to the vehicle and jumped on the back with the projector. He opened a sliding window to the cabin so that Ben could hear what he was saying. 'Go on,' he called. 'I'll shout directions. Now drive!'

Ben sped away from the car park and the Doctor began to think out loud. 'Now these devices create monsters out of reality,' he murmured. 'If I can amplify the effects, make the light brighter, the Selyoids more powerful...'

Ben looked up into the sky and saw that the projections coming from the back of the truck were continuing to fight each other overhead, though they were getting weaker. The Roman armies had been reduced to barely a few men, the giant gorilla was becoming less giant with every moment. The Selyoids creating the images were dying, and as they did so the films died too. Frantically, the creatures continued to wage their battle. Until they received the order to stop they would form the images of warring cinematic icons, but the absence of the controlling Selyoid meant the order would never come and the battle would continue until the last of the creatures had died.

In the rear-view mirror Ben saw the Doctor reach into his pocket and take out the glass device he'd stolen at the FOCAL meeting. He turned it over in his hands, then looked back at the projector.

The Doctor placed his smaller device in front of the larger one that was already attached to the projector and angled it as far skywards as he could manage. He looked up and squinted as if aiming an archery bow, then gave the projector lens one final twist. A blinding spark of light shot out of the device, dazzling him enough to knock him off balance.

'Look,' he said, pointing up at the sky.

The giant monsters, demons, armies and fireballs raced upwards. The Doctor had changed their angle of projection and their strength was amplified by the device he'd placed in front of the projector.

In the rear-view mirror Ben saw a small awkward-looking shape appearing in the sky. It was De Sande's plane sweeping into view, straight into the heart of the projections.

'We can't let this go on too long,' the Doctor said. 'We'll just leave enough time to disorientate the pilot. Now keep driving! We've got to stay with De Sande!'

De Sande sat back in the plane and lit a cigar. He looked out over the sea of flickering lights from the city below and smiled. Soon he would be able to salvage his plan and the Selyoid control of Los Angeles could begin, despite the interference of the Doctor and his allies.

His concentration was shattered as the plane shook violently.

'What the hell?' he heard the pilot shout. De Sande peered forward to see if the pilot was OK and the view through the front of the cockpit was suddenly blocked by a gigantic winged demon with rows of teeth that dripped with blood.

'Get it off!' cried the pilot. 'What is it!'

De Sande looked out of the window and saw a sea of monsters rushing towards the plane. The sound of banging on the vehicle's hull began and the pilot's control of the vehicle became more erratic as he tried to shake off the creatures.

'You fool,' De Sande growled. 'They're only projections!'

But the pilot was too busy screaming to hear him.

As Ben drove he kept glancing in his mirror to see the dramatic spectacle unfolding above them. He saw the gorilla lash out at the plane, causing it to swerve slightly. Hundreds of soldiers scrambled across its surface, the Selyoids creating the illusion that they were picking pieces of metal off its side and throwing them to the ground. The plane's trajectory became erratic — the pilot clearly couldn't see where he was going. A hundred winged demons flew up to the aircraft, darting around it like flies and scaring the pilot enough to make the plane shake violently.

'Keep course with them, Ben,' the Doctor pleaded. 'Faster! Come on, I know you can do it!'

The plane was almost out of range, in the part of the sky where no projections roamed, so Ben swerved the truck and slammed his foot against the accelerator to make sure the aircraft continued to be surrounded by the nightmares.

De Sande tried to communicate with the Selyoids, tried to tell them to stop the attacks, but his control over them was too weak.

'They're just visions!' he screamed, feeling fear rush into him as a clawed hand burst through a window and gripped his neck. 'They're just visions, they can't hurt us!'

'But I can't see!' the pilot cried. 'I can't see anything!'

'Get off me!' De Sande shouted as he felt the demon ripping at his flesh. 'You're not real! You're playing with my mind! You're just in my imagination!'

The projections weren't listening. De Sande could feel the Selyoids inside him struggling to deal with the situation, unsure of how to proceed. He cried to them for help. Pleaded with them to stop the monsters.

You can't help feeling scared. You're only human.

'No,' De Sande sobbed. 'I'm not. I'm better than that!'

'Now stop the truck!' the Doctor insisted. 'That should be enough. They'll have to land now. The pilot won't have any choice.'

Ben looked up and saw the plane begin to spin as the projections continued to attack it, continued to block the pilot's line of sight. Once the truck had stopped following it the aircraft cleared the projections, but its flight path still looked troubled. The noise of its engines grew louder as it started to spin faster and faster, heading towards the ground at an alarming rate.

Suddenly the sky filled with light as a giant explosion smeared it with fire and a thunderous crash shook the hills.

De Sande's plane had just shattered into a million sparks of light that rained down on Los Angeles like fairy dust.

'What happened?' Ben wondered.

'Those projections shouldn't have been that powerful,' the Doctor said with dismay. 'They couldn't have done that kind of damage.'

'That plane was crammed full of prints of *Dying in the Sun*. They're highly flammable aren't they?'

'One spark, one overheating engine, one small fire. That's all it took.' The Doctor was clearly disturbed by what had happened. 'They should have tried to land. De Sande shouldn't have been so stubborn.' He paused and shook his head. 'Things shouldn't have gone this far.'

Polly and Chate had been comforting those who found themselves lost, who found themselves wandering along the road with no memory of how they'd got there or where they'd left their cars. Polly felt fragile, but knew that she was in a much better condition than most. At least she knew what had been going on. She felt guilty at the reassurance she was drawing from seeing others suffering as much as she was. She marvelled at the way many of the people she'd spoken to had quickly adjusted to what had happened. It was as if their minds weren't capable of comprehending what they'd been through and had instead chosen to shut the memories off and forget them, putting the whole Selyoid experience down to being nothing more than a particularly strange dream.

The scene had been peaceful, mournful. A world away from the rioting and selfishness that had consumed the city earlier that day. And then the peace had been shattered by the noise of the explosion overhead.

Everyone had looked up and seen the plane crashing to the ground, smoke and flames spewing out of its back.

As Polly watched she had hoped the Doctor was not involved in the crash, that he was safe. She had thought about going to look for him, but somehow she knew he would be OK.

So, together with Chate, she waited until the Doctor found her.

'How are you, Polly?' he asked. He had crept up on her while she was comforting a man in a battered tuxedo, a man who had been worshipped as a celebrity mere hours before.

She looked up and saw him and Ben smiling sympathetically at her.

'I'm sorry,' she said.

'It's OK,' the Doctor reassured her. 'Just let it all out.'

'I didn't mean it,' she cried. 'I just felt so good, so right. The Selyoids accepted me in a way that no one else ever has. I belonged with them.'

'No, Polly. You didn't. The only place you belong is with your real friends. With us.'

Polly smiled. 'I know,' she said eventually. She took a deep breath. 'I know that now. There is just one thing I was wondering, though.'

'Oh?' said the Doctor, clearly intrigued. 'And what might that be?'

'I was wondering... Would you like an autograph?'

The Doctor and Ben smiled. Polly felt a strong warmth from them that told her she had all the support she needed to get over her experience.

'Look,' Ben said, pointing to the sky. At first Polly was struck by how bright the stars were, but then she realised she wasn't looking at stars. From the point where the plane had exploded millions of tiny sparkling gold lights were swirling around in the air, a giant golden cloud that was gradually drifting down to Earth. She saw the ground start to glitter, and realised that the sparks were falling like rain. As she looked at them she felt grateful for her friends, for everyone she'd met. She felt wanted. She felt loved.

'What is it?' Ben asked, pointing to the rain.

The Doctor knelt down and tried to pick up one of the sparks, but it dissolved in his hand like a snowflake before he had a chance to study it.

'One final gift from the Selyoids,' he theorised. 'They're light beings so they'll live on, in some strange way, beyond death.' He pointed upwards to the golden cloud. 'That's their last remains. All the stored energy, all the feelings of harmony, of belonging... everything De Sande absorbed, raining down on Los Angeles.'

Everything positive about the Selyoids, all the hysteria and shared energy, all the ambition, all the selfishness, all the compassion, all of it was filtering down into the air, the water and into the ground. The people who lived in Los Angeles might forget the events of the last fortnight, but the city itself would remember for ever.

The Doctor stood up and looked around at the bewildered people helping each other to regain their bearings and deal with the loss they all felt. 'No,' he said. 'There won't be any more fighting today.'

Chapter Thirty-Two

'Are we all ready?' the Doctor asked, looking decidedly uncomfortable in his freshly hired tuxedo.

'Well I am,' said Ben.

'As ready as I'll ever be,' added Polly.

'In that case,' Chate said, grinning, 'let the show begin.'

He gestured through the high wooden archway that led to the makeshift screening theatre Harold Reitman had made out of one of his many living rooms.

When the clean-up operation around Griffith Park had turned up the body of Charles Wallis the policeman had been officially declared dead, and Chate had learned that his old man had been chosen by De Sande to be the heir to all FOCAL's assets, including the Reitman estate.

Wallis hadn't made any will as far as anyone knew, so under the law of the land all the assets automatically passed to his legal next of kin. To Chate. Revere was gone, De Sande was gone, Maria would fade back into obscurity... Chate's path was clear. He'd been given a chance. He'd been given a future. It had all happened so fast, and two days had now passed since the climactic events surrounding the release of *Dying in the Sun*.

To celebrate he'd held a party for everyone in FOCAL to explain what was going on, but very few had turned up. After the events of the last couple of days there weren't that many people who wanted to be reminded of what they'd been through.

The guests who did come were the few charitable people who had joined FOCAL because they genuinely wanted to help others, and a few of the monks who were extremely sheepish and embarrassed about having endorsed De Sande's plan so readily. Chate told them that no grudges would be held. That under his control FOCAL was no longer to be a secret society, but a charitable organisation in the genuine sense of the word. Its resources and funds would be put towards rebuilding and revitalising the city — to make a difference, to make an impact on the lives of ordinary people that was far more important than anything De Sande could have planned.

He had explained that he now knew he didn't need fame to be immortal. He had plenty of time, and plenty of money, to make amends for his past crimes. He wanted to work on revitalisation projects that would stand the test of time. He realised that he now had the resources to ensure his legacy would live for ever through the generations that would be helped by his charity.

When the guests had left Chate decided to hold a screening of the film that everyone was thinking about but which no one would talk about. With all known prints recalled from cinemas to be kept under lock and key, this could possibly be the last ever showing of *Dying in the Sun*.

Polly walked into the screening room first followed by Chate and the Doctor, with Ben bringing up the rear.

They took their seats. Chate asked one of the servants to dim the lights. The film began.

'Do you think this is wise?' Ben whispered to the Doctor.

'Very much so, Ben. I think we all need a bit of reassurance over this so-called masterpiece. I think this viewing should exorcise a few ghosts, if nothing else.'

Familiar images flickered in front of the nervous audience, but this time their impact was completely different. The three-dimensional monsters were unconvincing, clearly men in rubber suits. The amazing transformation of the city into a living hell consisted of some cardboard bits of scenery being taken down, even with the stagehands visible. In short, it was a very, very mediocre picture and by the time it finished everyone had tired of the experience.

The final reel was coming to an end, the lead character returning from hell to his home in Los Angeles refreshed, invigorated, renewed and reborn. As the character walked down the street Ben was sure he saw a couple of familiar faces in a crowd. 'Look Doctor,' Ben said. 'It's us!'

'So it is, Ben,' the Doctor said, clearly enjoying his cameo. 'Before they died the Selyoids must have taken that position in the crowd. We wouldn't join with them, but they liked us enough to create an image of us in their film, it seems. How nice.'

As the film ended and the lights went up Ben said, 'So they did manage to convert you to their cause, in a way. They made you a star after all, it seems. Lucky you.'

The Doctor grinned.

'It wasn't the same film, was it?' Ben said,

'It never was the same twice,' the Doctor reminded him.

'That's not what I meant though. I mean, it always looked good before, but now... Well, it's rubbish, isn't it?'

'That was the power of the Selyoids,' Polly said sombrely. 'They changed everything, made it look better, made you feel better. But underneath, once you strip them away...'

'You're still the same person you always were,' the Doctor said, finishing her sentence, 'and we wouldn't have it any other way.'

They made their way out of the screening room and Chate offered them a drink.

'Thank you,' the Doctor said, 'but I think we ought to be going now.' He checked his watch. 'It's almost four a.m. It will be getting light soon.'

'Will you be OK?' Polly asked Chate, giving him a goodbye kiss on the cheek.

Chate nodded. 'I'll be fine.' He opened his arms and lifted his palms slightly skyward. 'I've got all this now. It should keep me busy for a while.'

'Are you going to try to find Maria?'

Chate shook his head. 'I'll never forget her, you know. I assume she'll return to her life, as drained as the rest of us by everything that's been going on. One of the things I want FOCAL to do is to help out-of-work actors. That's what they always said it was meant for anyway. So you never know, I might bump into Maria again in the future, but I'm not going to look for her. I've learned that if you spend enough time reaching for the stars, you'll eventually touch one. But stars are damn hot. You touch one, you're probably going to get burned.'

After leaving the Reitman estate, the Doctor drove Ben and Polly downtown where, under a rippled orange and purple sky, the waking city was gradually depositing its early risers into the outside world. A cleaner swept the streets, a vehicle mechanic waxed a car outside his garage and an old lady walked her dog, completely unable to control the animal.

'Do you think these people will remember the Selyoids in years to come?' Polly asked the Doctor as they walked towards a café one of her friends had recommended to her.

'Extra! Extra!' a news vendor flogging gossip magazines shouted. 'Secrets of the stars revealed! New pictures and interviews inside!'

'There's your answer,' the Doctor said. 'People's attitude towards stars won't change for a while.'

A crowd of people began to buzz around the stand, eager to buy the magazines, eager to read the latest juicy gossip from Hollywood.

'Yes,' the Doctor said. 'I think it's safe to say that the influence of the Selyoids will be felt in this town for many years to come.'

On a rocky outcrop above the Hollywood Hills a man in a tattered trench coat sat cross-legged, watching the sunrise over the city below him. He'd watched the sunrise from here two days ago while he got to know his new companion, and had found the sight so moving he'd vowed never to miss another one. The creature inside him was content. Lonely, but content. Fletcher had found companionship at last. They were both survivors, he realised.

He'd spent two days wandering around, coming to terms with what had happened and trying to figure out where to go next.

For years the creature had been lonely, the top of the chain of command, having to devote its life to looking after and instructing others with no time to itself. Now the others were gone. It had found a new friend, and it was free. Fletcher was free.

He stood up and began to make his way down the hill.

As he walked he wondered whether he should return to the LAPD. He could do a lot of good, and the boost the creature would give him should guarantee a promotion, but somehow he felt that this was his chance to get away. This was the chance he'd been looking for. A chance to make a new start. Maybe he should move away from Los Angeles, move closer to his son. Whatever his future held, wherever it lay, it was an open book. A chance to start again.

Fletcher looked upwards and had to shield his eyes from the bright rays of the newly dawning sun as they burst through the orange clouds and slowly turned the sky blue. A new day was beginning.

THE END

(end credits roll)

Oscar Speech

I could never have written this book without the help of the following people.

Most of all, extra-special thanks must go to Mark Clapham, who not only has been unswerving in his proofreading, support and inspiration, but also suggested several key concepts, themes and ideas for the book.

Thanks to Justin Richards, Sarah Lavelle and Jac Rayner for numerous clever editorial things.

Thanks are also due to the following people who read through the initial proposal and gave invaluable feedback, then supported, suggested ideas and lent videos etc. along the way. I couldn't have done it without you guys:

James Griffin, Darren Gross, Simon Jerram, Shaun Lyon, Jonathan Morris, Lance Parkin, Henry Potts, Eddie Robson, Jim Smith, Keith Topping and David Whittam.

Thanks to David Wood. You're a rock, and you deserve a book acknowledgement. As do James Bland, Chrys Hudson, Johnathan Loggie and Tom Morley.

Finally, and most importantly of all, thanks to my family, for years of love, support, happiness and understanding.

Reach for the stars!

Jon de Burgh Miller, April 2001

About the Author

Jon de Burgh Miller's first novel was *Twilight of the Gods* which he co-wrote for Virgin Publishing's New Adventures series. He thus has the dubious honour of being the very last person to write for that range and hopes that *Dying in the Sun* won't have quite the same effect on the Doctor Who series.

Jon lives in London and when he's not writing spends his time creating web sites and listening to pop music.

ALSO AVAILABLE

DOCTOR WHO: THE NOVEL OF THE FILM by Gary Russell ISBN 0 563 38000 4
THE EIGHT DOCTORS by Terrance Dicks ISBN 0 563 40563 5
VAMPIRE SCIENCE by Jonathan Blum and Kate Orman ISBN 0 563 40566 X
THE BODYSNATCHERS by Mark Morris ISBN 0 563 40568 6
GENOCIDE by Paul Leonard ISBN 0 563 40572 4
WAR OF THE DALEKS by John Peel ISBN 0 563 40573 2
ALIEN BODIES by Lawrence Miles ISBN 0 563 40577 5
KURSAAL by Peter Anghelides ISBN 0 563 40578 3
OPTION LOCK by Justin Richards ISBN 0 563 40583 X
LONGEST DAY by Michael Collier ISBN 0 563 40581 3
LEGACY OF THE DALEKS by John Peel ISBN 0 563 40574 0
DREAMSTONE MOON by Paul Leonard ISBN 0 563 40585 6
SEEING I by Jonathan Blum and Kate Orman ISBN 0 563 40586 4
PLACEBO EFFECT by Gary Russell ISBN 0 563 40587 2
VANDERDEKEN'S CHILDREN by Christopher Bulis ISBN 0 563 40590 2
THE SCARLET EMPRESS by Paul Magrs ISBN 0 563 40595 3
THE JANUS CONJUNCTION by Trevor Baxendale ISBN 0 563 40599 6
BELTEMPEST by Jim Mortimore ISBN 0 563 40593 7
THE FACE EATER by Simon Messingham ISBN 0 563 55569 6
THE TAINT by Michael Collier ISBN 0 563 55568 8
DEMONTAGE by Justin Richards ISBN 0 563 55572 6
REVOLUTION MAN by Paul Leonard ISBN 0 563 55570 X
DOMINION by Nick Walters ISBN 0 563 55574 2
UNNATURAL HISTORY by Jonathan Blum and Kate Orman ISBN 0 563 55576 9
AUTUMN MIST by David A. McIntee ISBN 0 563 55583 1
INTERFERENCE: BOOK ONE by Lawrence Miles ISBN 0 563 55580 7
INTERFERENCE: BOOK TWO by Lawrence Miles ISBN 0 563 55582 3

THE BLUE ANGEL by Paul Magrs and Jeremy Hoad ISBN 0 563 55581 5
THE TAKING OF PLANET 5 by Simon Bucher-Jones and Mark Clapham ISBN 0 563 55585 8
FRONTIER WORLDS by Peter Anghelides ISBN 0 563 55589 0
PARALLEL 59 by Natalie Dallaire and Stephen Cole ISBN 0 563 555904
THE SHADOWS OF AVALON by Paul Cornell ISBN 0 563 55588 2
THE FALL OF YQUATINE by Nick Walters ISBN 0 563 55594 7
COLDHEART by Trevor Baxendale ISBN 0 563 55595 5
THE SPACE AGE by Steve Lyons ISBN 0 563 53800 7
THE BANQUO LEGACY by Andy Lane and Justin Richards ISBN 0 563 53808 2
THE ANCESTOR CELL by Peter Anghelides and Stephen Cole ISBN 0 563 53809 0
THE BURNING by Justin Richards ISBN 0 563 53812 0
CASUALTIES OF WAR by Steve Emmerson ISBN 0 563 53805 8
THE TURING TEST by Paul Leonard ISBN 0 563 53806 6
ENDGAME by Terrance Dicks ISBN 0 563 53802 3
FATHER TIME by Lance Parkin ISBN 0 563 53810 4
ESCAPE VELOCITY by Colin Brake ISBN 0 563 53825 2
EARTHWORLD by Jacqueline Rayner ISBN 0 563 53827 9
VANISHING POINT by Stephen Cole ISBN 0 563 53829 5
EATER OF WASPS by Trevor Baxendale ISBN 0 563 53832 5
THE YEAR OF INTELLIGENT TIGERS by Kate Orman ISBN 0 563 53831 7
THE SLOW EMPIRE by Dave Stone 0 563 53835 X
DARK PROGENY by Steve Emmerson 0 563 53837 6
THE CITY OF THE DEAD by Lloyd Rose ISBN 0 563 53839 2
GRIMM REALITY by Simon Bucher-Jones and Kelly Hale ISBN 0 563 53841 4
THE ADVENTURESS OF HENRIETTA STREET by Lawrence Miles ISBN 0 563 53842 2 (Nov '01)
MAD DOGS AND ENGLISHMEN by Paul Magrs ISBN 0 563 53845 7 (Jan '02)
THE DEVIL GOBLINS FROM NEPTUNE by Keith Topping and

Martin Day ISBN 0 563 40564 3
THE MURDER GAME by Steve Lyons ISBN 0 563 40565 1
THE ULTIMATE TREASURE by Christopher Bulis ISBN 0 563 40571 6
BUSINESS UNUSUAL by Gary Russell ISBN 0 563 40575 9
ILLEGAL ALIEN by Mike Tucker and Robert Perry ISBN 0 563 40570 8
THE ROUNDHEADS by Mark Gatiss ISBN 0 563 40576 7
THE FACE OF THE ENEMY by David McIntee ISBN 0 563 40580 5
EYE OF HEAVEN by Jim Mortimore ISBN 0 563 40567 8
THE WITCH HUNTERS by Steve Lyons ISBN 0 563 40579 1
THE HOLLOW MEN by Keith Topping and Martin Day ISBN 0 563 40582 1
CATASTROPHEA by Terrance Dicks ISBN 0 563 40584 8
MISSION: IMPRACTICAL by David A. McIntee ISBN 0 563 40592 9
ZETA MAJOR by Simon Messingham ISBN 0 563 40597 X
DREAMS OF EMPIRE by Justin Richards ISBN 0 563 40598 8
LAST MAN RUNNING by Chris Boucher ISBN 0 563 40594 5
MATRIX by Robert Perry and Mike Tucker ISBN 0 563 40596 1
THE INFINITY DOCTORS by Lance Parkin ISBN 0 563 40591 0
SALVATION by Steve Lyons ISBN 0 563 55566 1
THE WAGES OF SIN by David A. McIntee ISBN 0 563 55567 X
DEEP BLUE by Mark Morris ISBN 0 563 55571 8
PLAYERS by Terrance Dicks ISBN 0 563 55573 4
MILLENNIUM SHOCK by Justin Richards ISBN 0 563 55586 6
STORM HARVEST by Robert Perry and Mike Tucker ISBN 0 563 55577 7
THE FINAL SANCTION by Steve Lyons ISBN 0 563 55584 X
CITY AT WORLD'S END by Christopher Bulis ISBN 0 563 55579 3
DIVIDED LOYALTIES by Gary Russell ISBN 0 563 55578 5
CORPSE MARKER by Chris Boucher ISBN 0 563 55575 0
LAST OF THE GADERENE by Mark Gatiss ISBN 0 563 55587 4
TOMB OF VALDEMAR by Simon Messingham ISBN 0 563 55591 2
VERDIGRIS by Paul Magrs ISBN 0 563 55592 0
GRAVE MATTER by Justin Richards ISBN 0 563 55598 X
HEART OF TARDIS by Dave Stone ISBN 0 563 55596 3

PRIME TIME by Mike Tucker ISBN 0 563 55597 1
IMPERIAL MOON by Christopher Bulis ISBN 0 563 53801 5
FESTIVAL OF DEATH by Jonathan Morris ISBN 0 563 53803 1
INDEPENDENCE DAY by Peter Darvill-Evans ISBN 0 563 53804 X
THE KING OF TERROR by Keith Topping ISBN 0 563 53802 3
QUANTUM ARCHANGEL by Craig Hinton ISBN 0 563 53824 4
BUNKER SOLDIERS by Martin Day ISBN 0 563 53819 8
RAGS by Mick Lewis ISBN 0 563 53826 0
THE SHADOW IN THE GLASS by Justin Richards and Stephen Cole ISBN 0 563 53838 4
ASYLUM by Peter Darvill-Evans ISBN 0 563 53833 3
SUPERIOR BEINGS by Nick Walters ISBN 0 563 53830 9
BYZANTIUM! by Keith Topping ISBN 0 563 53836 8
BULLET TIME by David A. McIntee 0 563 53834 1
PSI-ENCE FICTION by Chris Boucher 0 563 53814 7
INSTRUMENTS OF DARKNESS by Gary Russell ISBN 0 563 53828 7 (Nov '01)
RELATIVE DEMENTIAS by Mark Michalowski ISBN 0 563 53844 9 (Jan '02)
DRIFT by Simon A. Forward ISBN 0 563 53843 0 (Feb '02)
SHORT TRIPS ed. Stephen Cole ISBN 0 563 40560 0
MORE SHORT TRIPS ed. Stephen Cole ISBN 0 563 55565 3
SHORT TRIPS AND SIDE STEPS ed. Stephen Cole and Jacqueline Rayner ISBN 0 563 55599 8